LUCINDA'S DEFENDER

SHENANDOAH BRIDES ~ BOOK 3

BLOSSOM TURNER

WILD HEART
BOOKS

ISBN-13: 978-1-942265-47-4

I would like to dedicate this book in loving memory of my grandmother Olga Kuerbis.

One of my most precious childhood memories is listening to my grandma pray upon her bed each night in her broken English. I would listen for my name spoken in German, and it would light up a tiny corner of my traumatized world. Her powerful prayers in the midst of chaos brought such peace to my soul and influenced me to walk toward God, not away.

She loved to read, and especially a good romance. I wish she was here to read this book, but I believe she is up there smiling down and cheering me on.

"For all have sinned and fall short of the glory of God."
Romans 3:23 (NKJV)

"But God demonstrates His own love toward us, in that while we were still sinners, Christ died for us."
Romans 5:8 (NKJV)

"For whoever calls on the name of the Lord will be saved."
Romans 10:13 (NKJV)

CHAPTER 1

"*P*lease, Jeanette, don't tell Ma and Pa. He's harmless."

Harmless and *hers*. The best-looking man in town was showing her attention and Lucinda Williams intended to be the woman who wore his ring. Her stomach twisted into a knot. She had to make her sister understand or her budding romance would be over before it began.

"After what I just witnessed..." Jeanette planted her hands firmly on her hips. "I would be doing you a great disservice to remain silent."

"Why do you have to be such a fuddy-duddy? You act like you're forty-one, not twenty-one."

Jeanette's chin lifted and set, not a good sign.

Lucinda put on her sweetest voice. "Come on, Jeanette. What's a little kissing? Besides, I'm sixteen now and perfectly capable of handling a little manly attention."

Jeanette's brows raised. "You two rolling around on the hay

1

did not look like a *little* manly attention to me. A whole lot more than any respectable girl would allow—"

"Nothing happened." Lucinda raked a hand through her long curly hair and pulled out a sprig of hay. She squared her shoulders.

"Don't lie to me. What you two were up to is not appropriate until one is married."

Lucinda laughed. "What would you know? Have you even been kissed yet?"

A blush washed across Jeanette's cheeks, and she pushed her horn-rimmed glasses further on her nose.

Oh dear, when would she tame her big mouth? Unkind things so often just spewed out.

"Ma and Pa have already told you Nathaniel is bad news, and I'm telling them what I saw for your own sake."

"I knew it." Lucinda could not stop a sarcastic laugh from slipping free. "You haven't even experienced the simple pleasure of a kiss. How can I begin to make you understand?" Tentacles of fury spread inside her. "Frankly, I don't care what Ma and Pa say. Go ahead and tattle, but I aim to marry Nat."

"Marry him? You're barely sixteen. Even the way you use his first name with such familiarity shows me this has progressed farther than it should have. You know nothing about the man, and besides, he's way too old for you."

"Oh, I get it. Don't think I haven't noticed your four eyes stuck on him. You're just jealous he picked me over you. In fact, he told me your owl-eyes—"

Jeanette's face crumbled, and a stab of guilt pricked at Lucinda's conscience.

"You're so cruel," Jeanette said. "You've had boys buzzing around you your whole life. You have no idea..." Her voice cracked. "No idea at all what it's like to be taller than most men and plainer than a barn door." Tears leaked free from behind her glasses.

"Jeanette, I'm sorry. I shouldn't have said—"

"You feel you're somehow superior to an ugly old-maid like me, don't you?" Jeanette clenched her teeth together in a tight grimace. Her hands formed fists at her side.

Lucinda's stomach clenched. "You know how my temper gets the best of me. I don't mean half of what just pops out." She hated that about herself. Her sharp tongue could cut and slice before her brain caught up.

"No. You're not blaming your red hair and the wild tempers of our ancestors. That's just a poor excuse for bad behavior. Ma has done you no favors over the years making light of your mean-spiritedness." She turned and ran out of the barn.

Lucinda flopped down on a stack of hay. Jeanette was right. Lucinda did have a spiteful edge to her, so opposite to her kind sister. Maybe that was why Jeanette got on her nerves. It was as if she inherited all the good, while Lucinda had only a bent for the daring, the bad.

The way Nat had touched her had sent a surprising desire racing up her spine. Surely this was how two people in love felt. If anyone could win the title Mrs. Nathaniel Weitzel, she could. Then her prude big sister could relax.

⁓

"I said no!" Ma put down the potato she was peeling and shook her finger.

Lucinda's eyes flicked to Jeanette, who stood in the background with an *I told you so* look on her face.

"You will not see that man again. Do I make myself clear?"

Lucinda's gaze swept around the kitchen, looking anywhere but at Ma. She had no intention of obeying, but she had learned that the best defense was to pretend acceptance until Ma's guard was once again down.

"Haven't you heard the rumors around town?" Ma pressed.

"He's kissing up a storm and doing a whole lot more with any girl who'll let him."

Lucinda's heart lurched. Could Nat really be playing a game? After all, he'd just told her he loved her.

"And he's a drifter." Ma added. "No one has seen him working since he came. That's sure not what your pa or I want for you."

What did he do for work? Lucinda had no idea. All she knew was that he was always flashing money around. He seemed to have plenty. He wore nice clothes and lived at the local hotel. Told her he'd made money in the railroad.

Ma stepped back, wiping her hands on her apron before picking up the knife to continue peeling her potatoes. "I'm sorry to be the one to have to tell you this truth." She pointed the knife in Lucinda's direction. "But you've set your attention on the wrong man. Now make yourself useful and help me with these potatoes. Jeanette, don't just stand there. See to setting the table."

Lucinda moved beside Ma and grabbed one.

"I know he's handsome," Ma said, "but you can do far better than that, my girl. What about Joseph? He's had his eye on you for years. A solid farmer who is able to provide—"

"Pff, Joseph. He's just a friend."

"I don't think he sees it that way. But never you mind, the right man will come along."

Ma prattled on, and Lucinda closed her ears to the nonsense. Nat loved her and no one else, of that she was sure. It wasn't his fault he was so handsome that girls fell all over him. All she had to do was get a ring on her finger, and the town gossip would stop. She'd take it nice and slow with him, giving no more liberties. Marriage was what she wanted, and she was prepared to reel him in with all the charm and propriety of a refined lady. Then, when he was crazy in love, she'd put on her Sunday best and accept that ride in the woods he kept going on about. He'd fall on his knees and beg for her hand in marriage—unable to live another day without her. Their wedding would be extravagant, and she'd be the envy of every girl in town.

"Did you hear me?" Ma's voice broke through her daydreams.

"Sure, Ma." She had no idea what Ma had gone on about, but she nodded in agreement.

A smile lit across Ma's face and she leaned in and gave a hug. "That's my girl."

Lucinda snatched up another potato to peel with a stab of anger shooting through her. Therein lay the problem—Ma still considered her a girl. She was a young woman now, and ready for all the world had to offer.

~

*J*oseph watched Nat slide into the pew as if he had every right to sit at Lucinda's side. He bent to whisper in her ear, and Nat's familiarity irked him something fierce. Not even a sacred place like church was honored by that reprobate.

Joseph was not wrong about Nat. After doing a little investigation, he found the rumors around town were true. Currently, Nat had two girls on the go and was still chasing after Lucinda. Why was she smiling up at him? Surely, she knew... Everyone else did.

Joseph had loved her for so long now that the ache inside his lonely heart felt as much a part of him as his skin and bone. Why did she seem oblivious to the obvious? Both Joseph's love and Nat's dark side. What hope did his average height and average face have against Nat's tall, dark, and handsome?

The sermon started, and Nat, the poser, fell instantly asleep. His head nodded down, occasionally jerking up, throughout the service. He awakened when the organ music started. He said something to Lucinda and left before the last song was even finished. What disrespect. An instant desire to slip out his cowboy boot and send the man sprawling came over Joseph as Nat smugly sauntered on by. His thinking was not too Christian, but sometimes a loving response was not what the moment needed.

A tightening pulled across Joseph's chest as he watched Lucinda hurry out after the rogue. Joseph swallowed hard against the bile rising in his throat. He slapped on his cowboy hat and headed out the church doors. Nat leaned against their oak tree, the one Joseph and Lucinda used to play under. The first buds of spring were unfurling, as if everything was as it should be.

Yet, there Nat stood, all confidence and swagger. He had Lucinda giggling at something. Joseph's fists clenched tight. There was no way a boring farmer like him could compete with that brand of dashing charm. He pulled off his cowboy hat and ran his hand along the back of his neck before slamming the hat back on his head.

He took the steps two at a time and crossed the church yard, not stopping until he stood in the shadows. He was not going to leave until that man was out of sight. Lucinda's Pa watched from a distance as well. Jeanette had her glasses pinned on Nat. At least Lucinda wasn't alone. She had people around her who cared. As a long-time friend he felt he had to warn her of Nat's lack of character before it was too late.

Joseph couldn't see Lucinda's face, but he could tell by the way she swayed her dress and tilted her head that she was smitten. Nat was laughing and running his hand down her arm. He leaned in real close—too close.

Joseph longed to rip that man's hands off his girl. Didn't Nat know? Didn't she? Lucinda was the only girl he had ever loved or would ever love.

When Nat turned away and Jeanette headed Lucinda's way,

Joseph breathed out a long breath. All was safe for another day, but he'd have to make time for that conversation with Lucinda, and soon.

∾

"*J*oseph, that's not very charitable at all." Lucinda did not like what she was hearing. She turned away to stare out the barn doors into the blue. A beautiful spring day ruined by yet another slice of gossip.

Joseph touched her arm, and she shook free. She stomped across the wooden planks of the dusty barn, kicking at a clump of hay that got in her way. The mother cat with her fresh batch of kittens let out a loud "meow" at the rain of hay sprinkled in their direction.

She needed a moment to settle the angst. Her insides churned at the thought. Nat with another woman? It was no different from what Ma had said, but, no, she would not listen. She whirled around to face Joseph. "You've never been the type to welcome idle gossip and pass it along. Why start now?"

"It's not idle gossip. I've done my own poking around, talked to a few of the girls he's been seen with, and they all believe they're his only girl, just like you."

"Why would you do that? I thought you were my friend."

"I am your friend."

"A friend wouldn't try to ruin my life." Lucinda wrung her hands. She wanted to marry Nat, not have yet another person, especially her best friend, tell her he was no good.

Joseph let out an exasperated puff of air. "How is telling you the truth ruining your life? If I didn't tell you and you married that rake, I could never live with myself. Nat is bad news."

"He's misunderstood. And he's changing, Joseph. Didn't you see him at church on Sunday?"

"Yeah, I saw him." Nat took off his cowboy hat and rubbed his brow. "He slept most of the service."

"Everyone deserves a little time in finding their way. I never thought you of all people would be so ungracious. Do you know he never had a Ma or Pa who cared? The least this town could do is show a little Christian love. But no, everyone is bent on nattering and gossiping."

Joseph grabbed the top of the wooden stall door until slivers bit into his flesh. "You just don't get it."

A spike of anger ran up her spine. Her feisty boldness couldn't hold back her frustration any longer. "What don't I get?" She stepped close, her hands fisted. "You're acting as if you have a right to be jealous, Joseph, when all we've ever been is friends. Go back to what you understand—your seeds and planting, instead of digging up dirt on poor Nat." She stomped her foot, and the dust billowed. "I don't need another sermon. Best you leave me alone."

His crestfallen expression spoke a thousand words. There she went again, using her sharp tongue to hurt someone she loved. She lifted her hand toward him. "I'm sorry. I didn't mean—"

"No. I think you meant every word and I won't bother you again. Our friendship is clearly one sided." He spun on the soles of his cowboy boots and walked out.

CHAPTER 2

Three weeks had passed since Lucinda's meeting with Joseph, and Nat had proved to be nothing but the gentleman she knew he was.

The late afternoon light dappled through the overhead trees as Lucinda's horse plodded over the new spring grass. Where was Nat leading her? Deeper into the forest they went. He was so dashing astride his black stallion, and every time he turned to smile at her, a delightful but dangerous spark of desire shot through her bones. Today was the day. She was certain of it.

"Here we are." The forest opened to a verdant meadow sprinkled with spring daisies. The babbling brook in the near distance sang a melody of joy. Her insides flipped in excitement. He'd found the most enchanting place to propose.

"Why, Nat, however did you find this place? It's absolutely magical." She slid from her horse and tethered the reins on a nearby tree branch. With both arms extended she twirled. "Oh, this is perfect. Our own secret hideaway..." She giggled. "We can kiss in private without any worry of being interrupted."

Nat's hands circled her waist and slammed her body up

against his. "I intend to do a whole lot more than kiss you, baby."

A shiver of fear skittered up her spine. What was that look she saw in his eyes?

His lips bore down, opening her mouth to the demand of his. His onslaught and intensity were shocking to her naivety, but she would never let him know. The last thing she wanted was for him to think she was not every bit a grown woman and ready for marriage.

Each time they'd had moments alone, his wandering hands had become more comfortable, but she'd been able to keep things respectable. Today, they roamed freely over her body. Only this time, with no threat of being interrupted, he was undoing buttons to ensure skin fell upon skin. She pulled back, and he dragged his mouth from hers. "Now, really Nat, we must keep this for after the wedding." She hoped her teasing sounded grown-up but firm.

"Keep that fire, Little Red. I'll be right back. He grabbed a rolled blanket attached to the saddle from the back of his tethered horse and spread it upon the lush green grass and plopped down. "Come." He held out his hand.

She tentatively placed her tiny hand in his. He gave a jerk and she fell on top of him. With a flip of their bodies, his six-foot six frame covered hers. When she was pinned beneath his hulk, he whispered. "Today, you're going to show me just how much you love me. You do love me, don't you?"

"Yes of course, you know I do. But—"

"No buts. You're a woman now, and it's time you start acting like one."

To control the involuntary widening of her eyes, she squeezed them tight. She didn't want to show her fright, but could not contain the quiver of panic climbing higher in her chest.

"Open your eyes, Little Red."

She obeyed. She'd hoped to find love in his gaze, but all tenderness was gone. "Your innocence excites me." His voice was gruff and unrecognizable. His lips crushed hers. Before she could think, he lifted her dress from the bottom, removing layers as if he were in a well-rehearsed play. He took his mouth off hers and lifted his head to stare down at her. His eyes were hollowed with darkness. He never took them off her as he ripped at the rounded neckline of her dress.

She squeezed her eyes closed. They'd all tried to warn her—Ma, Jeanette, even Joseph. But she'd been so certain of Nat... So wrong. She wouldn't allow this. She couldn't. "No, Nat. No!" She screamed, twisting and flailing beneath him. "Let me go."

He grabbed both her hands in one of his and held them over her head. "You can't lead a man on like you have been and not deliver."

"Please, please don't do this."

"I'll please you, all right."

She fought to free her hands, but she was no match for him. She struggled to thrash beneath his crushing weight enough to bring him to his senses, but it seemed to inflame him more. Her terror rose at the sound of a scream. It was silenced as he crushed his mouth against her and took all he wanted.

The minute the deed was done, he rolled off her and jumped to his feet.

She lay exposed and trembling. Her mind, her dreams, her imaginings had never taken her to this place. She pulled at her dress, covering her chilled body the best she could. Her hands shook as she smoothed them over the wrinkled mess. Painfully and slowly she stood. It took every bit of strength she had to stop her legs from buckling beneath her.

He turned his back and fiddled with the stirrups on his horse.

"We should go, dusk is setting in."

Go home, like this? How could he speak to her so casually

after what he'd done? But when he turned cold eyes on her, fear bristled up her spine. She clutched at her torn neckline. "How will I explain this?"

"Don't you have a shawl? And a little needle and thread when you get back will take care of it. It's all your fault, teasing me for weeks like you have." There wasn't an ounce of tenderness.

"Are we going to get married now?" Her voice quivered despite her best attempt to remain strong. They had to get married now, didn't they?

"Married?"

The way he spat out the word made Lucinda cringe. Her head swam with confusion. Her body felt numb.

"Don't you love me?" She turned toward him.

He sidestepped her and picked up the blanket and rolled it tight. He secured it to the back of the saddle in silence.

"After what you just did—"

"Of course, I love you." He didn't bother to look at her. "We can talk about that another time. We need to get moving before you're missed." He swung his lithe body into his saddle as if nothing more than a quaint picnic, like he promised, had taken place.

She turned toward her horse, grabbed the reins, and pulled her body up. The ache in her arms was nothing to the pain she felt as she settled in the saddle. Everything hurt.

With one more look back and a wink in her direction, he cantered off.

She followed at a much slower pace. What she had imagined would be a romantic proposal of marriage had been dreadful. Ma and Pa had been right. Nathaniel Weitzel was not the man for her. She would break off the relationship immediately. No one ever needed to know the horror that had just transpired.

He charged well ahead and tipped his hat to her at the junction where they'd met. Everything inside of her wanted to scream out her rage, but what good would that do now? He galloped off in the direction of town, and she turned toward the farm.

～

JULY 1874

*T*he church service was well underway when Nat slid into the pew beside her. "Hello baby," he whispered in her ear. "Do you miss me?"

Lucinda ignored him.

Ever since that fateful day in the forest back in May, she had kept her distance. She had begged God for forgiveness and promised she would obey her parents and stay clear of Nat, and she had done just that. Spring had turned into summer. The green grass turned gold, baby robins found their wings, the world went on as if nothing had happened. Yet, she knew. God knew. And Nat knew. The more she ignored him, the more aggressive his pursuit. She slid closer to Pa, who poked his head around Lucinda and gave Nat a stern look. Nat's hands went up, though he shook his head in disgust. For the rest of the service, he nodded off beside her.

Lucinda's love for socializing and shopping had been curbed by Nat's habit of popping up wherever she went. This was a new form of persistence, showing up in what he mocked as the most boring place on earth, church.

She shuddered. How would she get rid of him for good? He kept threatening to tell Ma and Pa and the rest of the town that he deflowered her, so she had to tread carefully. He could easily ruin her reputation. Then she would never find a respectable man to marry as her older sisters had. She wanted what Katherine and Amelia had—money, community standing, and a happy home with a man who loved her. Was that too much for her to ask?

She hoped he would tire of the game and move on to another. But her resistance seemed to have fueled the opposite reaction.

They stood for the last song and he leaned in. "Meet me outside, Little Red?"

She used to love that endearment, but now it made her insides roil.

"I've missed you so much."

She wanted to scream that she was not his Little Red. She wanted to demand he leave her alone. But here at church, she could pacify him, and so she nodded. He squeezed her arm and beelined out the door.

She waited until others were filing out before standing.

"Do you want me to talk to him?" Pa asked, leaning in close. "Seems the man has a hard time taking *no* for an answer."

Lucinda shuddered from tip to toe. Pa didn't know the half of it.

"I can manage. I'm sure you didn't have your parents poking in on your relationships at my age. Hadn't you already run off with Ma by sixteen?"

Pa's face fell.

Oh, why had she said that? Why could she not control her tongue?

"I told you the truth about my past to prevent you from making the same mistake. Not that marrying your ma was a mistake, but the lies, the cover up—that was wrong."

"I'm sorry, Pa."

"I was only trying to help. But mark my word, there's something wrong with that man. I can feel it in these old bones."

"Have I not done your bidding and stayed clear of him?"

"All right." Pa rubbed his hand through his thinning hair. "If you think you can handle this, fine. But by twenty-six a man should've learned a little more respect when a lady is not interested." He shook his head.

"I'm going to go talk to him, see if I can make him understand. But stay in view. I want him to get the message I'm not alone."

"Of that, you can be assured."

Lucinda made her way out of the church and across the yard. Nat looked so handsome leaning against the oak tree, that wide, lazy smile in place. The last thing she wanted was to fall under the spell of his attraction once again. She was well aware of her two warring sides, the one that gravitated toward him and the one that sent out warning bells, reminding her not to flirt, not to encourage a repeat of what had already happened.

As if on cue, the church bells rang at the top of the hour. She glanced behind her to the steeple and further into the heavens. She squinted into a shaft of sunlight that broke free of the clouds as if God were reminding her that He was watching. She both loved and hated the fact that she could never quite erase His presence.

She looked back at the smiling man. She had no one to blame but herself for the mess she was in and the power he had over her.

When she reached him, she stopped a few feet away. "What is it, Nat?" She clasped her hands together in front of her to hide their tremble.

"Baby, I miss you so much. And I've been thinking, we should get married." His words tumbled out as he moved in to take her hands in his.

She pulled them free and stepped back. "No."

His face was the picture of innocence when he asked, "Why not?"

"You took something from me I did not offer." She kept her voice low, but the words hissed out her anger.

"You look so amazing with that fire in your eyes." He lifted a

15

hand to her face and grazed his knuckles down one side of her cheek.

His touch brought both a spike of desire and a rush of shame.

"I'm so sorry, Lucinda. You've got to believe me. I've never done anything like that before. You overwhelmed me with your beauty."

"You did not look sorry after—"

"But I was. It was my shame at how I couldn't control myself. You can't begin to understand how a man given so much leeway can't just pull away the last minute."

Lucinda's cheeks flushed hot. She should not have snuck off alone with him. Was this truly the way it was for a man?

"I know it was wrong, but I was overtaken with your loveliness. Marry me, Little Red. Let me make this right. You're the only woman for me."

She looked into his soulful black eyes, and the pull of attraction drew her in.

"Lucinda, we're leaving." Pa's call shook her free of his spell.

"No." She stepped back and turned to go.

He grabbed her hand and yanked her back. Losing her balance, she stumbled and landed against his chest.

He leaned down and whispered, "You go on playing the good girl to your family and to this town, but we both know the truth. I quite like the bad girl, but chances are not too many other men will. So, go on, marry some dreary widower, because that's all *used goods* will get."

She gasped.

"And when you're dirt poor, pregnant with your fifth brat, and life is beyond boring, you'll remember this day and weep. Because no one will love you like I do."

She pushed off him. "You and I both know what happened that day."

"You were not so innocent willingly sneaking away unchaperoned into the forest and leading me on, now, were you?" His eyebrows rose. "I'll give you a few weeks to think about it, and then…"

He dropped her hand and tipped his hat. He strolled away—lean, tall, and handsome—with an arrogant saunter.

Had she made the right decision? What if he did tell the world? At least if she married him, she'd keep her good standing in the community, but if he told…she'd never find a respectable man who would want her. Fear lapped at the edges of her mind. *Used goods.* His threat rang through her head. Would he really feel so snubbed by her refusal he would soil her reputation? No. He'd be fine. She would have to pacify him until he grew bored of the chase, and moved on.

Jeanette's arm came around her shoulder and ushered her to the back of the buggy. "Good riddance to bad rubbish."

Lucinda's hands trembled as she climbed onto the back of the wagon. She hid them in the folds of her skirt. The thought of only being good enough for an old widower with a ready-made family, shook her to the core. No, she had to marry well, as her older sisters had, with maids and fine clothing and shopping to fill her days. And Nat seemed to have money aplenty.

A shudder worked its way through her body. She buried her head in her hands, glad her parents were facing forward and wouldn't see her tears.

"What's wrong?" twelve-year-old Gracie asked.

Jeanette hushed Gracie and slid in closer. Warm arms enveloped Lucinda and hung on tight. "Shh, everything will be all right," Jeanette whispered as she smoothed her hands down Lucinda's back. "Just you wait and see.

Guilt jabbed in so many places that Lucinda felt like a pin cushion. She had showed nothing but contempt to Jeanette the whole time she was sneaking away to see Nat and yet her sister went on loving her.

CHAPTER 3

*J*oseph had watched Lucinda's exchange with Nat. He had prayed things were cooling between those two. He hadn't seen them together in a few months and hope had begun to soar. But there Nat was again, his second visit to church. Seemed he only showed up when he wanted to latch onto Lucinda.

Joseph's only consolation was that Lucinda had not been pleased to see him. The look on her face when she'd walked away from their discussion was filled with sadness and worry. Joseph knew her too well. Her brow only furrowed like that when she was in distress. But why? What was Nat up to? If only he could step in and help her. But she had pulled away from him even more after he talked to her about Nat.

Joseph's brother Nigel sent out a shrill whistle from the wagon, and Joseph snapped out of his reverie. He pushed off the tree he'd been leaning against and crossed the church yard.

"Come on, Joseph," Pa yelled. "No time for your day-dreaming."

Joseph jumped up. "Shove on over." He nudged his younger

brother into the middle and took up the reins. With a snap, the buggy rattled into motion.

"I'm quite capable of handling the reins," Nigel said.

"So am I."

"Stop it, you two." Pa's voice brooked no argument. "You're too old for such squabbling."

"Why don't you tell him a couple years' difference in age doesn't give him the right to take the lead all the time," Nigel asked.

"I'd much rather tell him to get over that red head, Lulu—"

"It's Lucinda." Joseph hated it when his pa deliberately misspoke her name.

"Don't you see how Esther Dwyer is making eyes at you, boy?"

"I'd take that one for sure," Nigel said. "Pretty little blonde with curves in all the right places."

"It's Joseph Esther wants, and what a dandy choice she would be. Her parents and I go way back—a good respectable family. Much better than a girl who doesn't give you a second thought."

Joseph's hands tightened on the reins. "Why have you never liked Lucinda? Ma loved her."

"It's not that I dislike her. She's just flighty and uninterested in you. Anyone who thinks my son is not good enough for her is not good enough for me."

Joseph wanted to argue, but the words wouldn't come. They had all assumed through the growing years, him included, that he and Lucinda would share nuptials early in life. Instead, school days ended, ma died, and Joseph and his family had moved to a bigger spread much farther away. He could only see Lucinda on Sundays, and somehow their closeness faded. Their friendship had never blossomed into what he desired. Or had he been just too scared, too timid, too dang respectful?

"And then there's Lucinda's reputation," Nigel said.

An instant boil of anger pumped through his veins. "Careful, or I'll knock you into next week."

Nigel threw up his hand. "Don't blame me. I'm just telling you what's circulating. Apparently, Nat's been bragging that she's one of his conquests."

"That's not true." Joseph spat the words out, but a spike of fear shot up his spine. "If anything, she's been staying away from him."

"Seen them together in church today, and so did you," Pa said. "He's not exactly trying to hide his affection."

Those words ran over Joseph like boiling water over skin. He wanted to jump out of his flesh it hurt so bad.

"And what about the others he's had dangling on his arm?" Pa asked. "Why would she even want someone like that? Doesn't say much for her character."

"Leave it." Joseph spoke the words through clenched teeth.

"All right, all right, but it's time for both you boys to get married and give me some grandbabies. Pining your life away on a bad idea will never—"

"Pa." Joseph's voice boomed. "I've heard enough."

The sound of the buggy rolled along, wheel over gravel, was all that could be heard until Nigel started whistling a tune. Joseph gritted his teeth and stifled the urge to tell him to shut up. But just because he was tormented did not mean Nigel didn't have the right to be happy.

~

*L*ucinda pulled herself from bed and rushed for the privy. She had thrown up every day for the past week, and today was no different. She was barely sleeping after seeing Nat at church, carrying the worry into each new day, and it was giving her an upset stomach. Would he really speak of what happened that day in the forest and ruin her reputation?

After a swipe of her mouth with her handkerchief, she opened the door to find Ma waiting on the other side, her arms folded across her chest.

"Walk with me." She pointed to the path that meandered through the orchard toward Katherine's house.

"Ma, I'm not feeling so good today."

Ma handed her a dry biscuit. "I'm pretty sure this will help."

Lucinda nibbled at the biscuit, wishing Ma had buttered it. Somehow, the dry biscuit worked like magic, and the nausea diminished.

They walked in silence while the birds dipped and darted. The early morning summer sun was already beating down as they crossed the yard to the shade of the apple trees.

"That feels better." Lucinda wiped a few beads of sweat from her brow and took a sideways glance. "Out with it. I always know when you're bothered by something."

Ma stopped and reached out her hand to take Lucinda's arm. "Could there be any reason you've been sick most every day lately?"

"Must have some kind of flu. It seems to come and go." At least she hoped it was the flu.

"Is there any chance you could be pregnant?"

Lucinda's heart kicked up speed and beat wildly. Her monthlies were always so irregular, surely that was the case now. She did what she always did in a pinch. She lied. "How dare you accuse me of such—"

"Stop lying. I can see the truth in your face. You know exactly what I'm talking about."

"I...I don't know—"

"Yes, you do. You let that man have his way with you, didn't you? And now you're pregnant. You're sick every morning. And when is the last time you had your monthly flow?"

"Ma. Really must we?"

"Yes, we must."

Lucinda pulled her arm free and continued down the path, wiping a hand across her brow. She could not be pregnant. Her hand fluttered to her throat. *Please God, no.*

"You can't outrun the truth. If what I think is indeed happening, then the sooner we sort out your future the better—for your sake and for the sake of your child."

She blinked back a rush of tears and stopped. Panic edged up her throat. She had tried to lie to herself, thinking she could block everything that happened between her and Nat out of her head, but now she had to face the truth. It wasn't only her future she had to think of, but an innocent child as well.

A gentle arm came around her shoulders. "Tell me, girl, so I can help you."

Lucinda turned into her ma's arms and crumbled against her solid frame. She wanted to tell her ma everything but was so ashamed. If only she had not met Nat that day and caused him to...

"What's done, is done. And we need to figure out the future." Ma patted her on the back and pulled free. "Now out with it."

"It...it happened only once, and I didn't mean for things to get that carried away. I broke off everything after that, but Ma, he tells me he loves me. He tells me he wants to marry me. What should I do?"

"Considering the circumstances, a quick wedding would be the best."

Did she even want to marry Nat? Most times he was cordial, but then she had seen the other side too. He had not listened to her cries of no.

"But you and Pa don't like him."

"What we didn't like was him sneaking around rather than courting you like a lady deserves." Ma harrumphed. "At least he has enough decency to offer marriage. He must have some redeeming qualities."

"But..." Ma didn't understand, and how could she? Lucinda couldn't bear to tell her the whole truth.

"You got yourself into this. I begged you to stay away from him, but you wouldn't listen. Now the consequences of your actions require that you marry the father of your child. That poor child doesn't deserve to be born outside wedlock."

"This can't be happening." Lucinda's fingers pressed into her temples.

"Well, it is." Ma's voice was none too gentle. "There's no question in my mind that you're pregnant. Look at the way your tiny waist has thickened."

"I...I need to think. Please don't tell Pa. Give me some time."

"You have until breakfast tomorrow. I do not keep things from your father." Ma stomped off.

∽

*L*ucinda got no sleep that night. The next morning she rose with a plan. Maybe she could redeem her life after all. The circumstances pointed to one solution. Her reputation would be ruined unless she agreed to an immediate wedding, which Nat was pressing her for anyhow.

But should she tell him about the baby? The way he had referred to children as brats when he saw them playing in the street gave her pause. She would worry about that later. First things first.

She was down the stairs in the kitchen before Ma was even up, which never happened. She lit the fire and put a pot of coffee on to brew. The sound of her pa humming his way down the steps sent her scooting into the parlor to avoid him. She listened to his off-tune rendition of *Amazing Grace* as he poured himself a cup of coffee. The slam of the back door followed, signifying she was safe to return to the kitchen.

Not much later, Ma lumbered into the room and jumped at Lucinda's "good morning."

"Land sakes." Her pudgy hand went to her chest. "What are you doing up at this hour?"

"I need to talk to you alone."

Ma poured herself some of the strong brew, sat at the table, and nodded to the other chair.

"I've decided to talk to Nat and see if he is serious about marriage. But you have to promise me one thing. No one but you and Pa can know about the baby. I'm not even sure I'm going to tell Nat."

Ma's eyes widened. "That's not a good idea."

"You want me to give him a good excuse to go running?"

"Hmm." Her finger went to her mouth. "I see your point."

"I also want to move away so we'll have a chance at a normal life. If I stay, everyone will know... That piece of property in Rockingham County where we grew up—"

"Your Uncle John and Aunt May are farming that land, and it belongs to Katherine."

"Katherine said she was holding that for anyone in the family that may have a need for it. Aunt and Uncle can stay put, but I want to join them. Nat and I could build a small house and help farm the land."

"Nat is not a farmer. In fact, I don't know what he is." Ma threw her hands up. "He roams around town with way too much time on his hands. How does he have the money for that anyway?"

Lucinda had no idea. "You and Pa got a fresh start. You moved to this valley, a place where no one knew Katherine was not your baby, to get away from all the gossip. Now all I'm asking is for the same grace."

"But can't you stay close, where I can help and you'd be around your family? Wouldn't it make more sense for Nat to work on the ranch with your Pa?"

"You know what the rumor mill would do when I have this baby less than nine months after the wedding."

A sheen of tears filled her eyes. "Yes, I do."

"I need to go."

Ma moved forward and handed Lucinda a handkerchief. "Uncle John is finding the farm a little too much work, anyway, so maybe, if Nat turned out to be a good help—"

"Thanks, Ma." Lucinda threw her arms around her mother's neck. "I'm so ashamed—"

"There, there, child." She patted Lucinda's back and pulled out of the hug. "We'll make things work. Pa can talk to Katherine and Colby. I know they'll help out with the funds to build a small home. And I'll talk to your Uncle John and Aunt May. If Nat settles down and works hard, he'll be a good help to John, and you two can pay Katherine back for the house over time."

～

*L*ucinda was about to head down the stairs when she heard her name outside her parents' door. She stopped short.

"Lucinda will not marry that man. I don't like it," Pa said. He rarely raised his voice, but today it was a roar.

"She's pregnant. What choice do we have?"

"We thought the man was trouble before she got pregnant, it's now confirmed. Is this really the husband we want for our daughter?"

"Jeb, you of all people know what it's like to mess up and want to make it right."

"My past will forever haunt me. You'll make sure of that. At least I know the good Lord has forgiven me."

Lucinda's heart dropped to the souls of her feet. Her pa

sounded so dejected. She could hear the clip of her ma's shoes move across the hardwood floor. "I have left that in the past."

"Are you sure about that, Doris?" There was grit in his voice.

"Good heavens, Jeb. We have a pregnant daughter to think about, and an innocent child who'll be shunned by society if she doesn't marry the man. Is that what you want?"

Lucinda held her breath. The creak of the floorboards was the only reply.

"I don't feel good about this," Pa said.

"Neither do I, but it's the lesser of two evils."

"So, we resort to giving our precious daughter to the lesser of two evils."

"You know what I mean. Why do you always have to be so dramatic? Common sense is what we need here."

"This does not sound like common sense to me. You know the rumors. That man has bedded down far more women than just our daughter."

Lucinda pressed a hand to her mouth so she did not gasp out loud. Had he really?

"How about you stick to your farming, which I do not poke my nose into." Ma's voice was cold and measured. "I'll continue with wedding plans for my daughter, which is what any good mother in these circumstances would do."

"First, that is *our* daughter, not just your daughter, and let it be known that I feel God does not want this marriage to take place."

"Don't you be bringing God into this. If He cared a hoot about us, Lucinda would not be in this predicament."

"Don't you be blaming God. If Lucinda had not been rebellious and listened to our advice as well as what the Bible teaches—"

"Pff, the Bible. I do not care to get into a discussion about that."

"Fine then, Doris. Do what you want. But I do not agree!"

Lucinda heard his footsteps stomping toward the door. She ran back into her bedroom, barely disappearing inside before their door slammed shut, shaking the walls.

She had never known Pa to slam a door. This was all her fault.

CHAPTER 4

*J*oseph had to try. Seeing Nat show up at church brought a sense of urgency, a quickening in his spirit. Before Nat got his hooks into Lucinda once again, Joseph would act. He would finally tell Lucinda the truth. Bare his soul. Do whatever it took for her to know that he wanted far more than friendship. All this waiting, hoping, and praying had gotten him nowhere. For the first time, an urge to act overcame his fear. He would speak what he had felt and stifled for years—be honest with the only girl he would ever love. He could not let Nat win this battle without a fight. And while he felt strong, he would move in that strength. Why not right now?

Before he could talk himself out of it, he saddled his mount and rode out of the barn into the sunshine.

Pa came out on the porch. "Where you headed? Weren't we going to finish that back section today?"

"Got something urgent I need to attend to." He lifted his hat and galloped down the drive. The last thing he needed was to discuss his intentions with his father. When he and Lucinda were happily married and Pa had a passel of grandkids gathered around him, he would see Lucinda was the woman for him.

He arrived at the Williamses' farmhouse and skipped up the steps. A walk in the orchard would be the perfect setting for what he had planned.

He hammered on the door.

Mrs. Williams opened it wide, hand on her heart. "Goodness me, Joseph. You about sent me into next week. Come in. I'll get her." He didn't have to say a word, she knew who he was there to see, though it had been a long time.

"Lucinda, Joseph's here to see you," she yelled up the stairs.

He shuffled his feet as nervous tension flowed through him. And then Lucinda appeared in all her glory. She floated down the stairs in a pink dress with polka dots and lace trim. Her mouth smiled, but there was a sadness in her eyes he could not quite define.

She took the last step. "I haven't seen you in far too long."

"Do you have time for a walk?"

Her eyebrows bunched together.

"Come on, a little visit with your old friend?" He was not above using the advantage of their friendship to put her at ease.

She looked down the hall to where her ma stood.

Her ma nodded.

Odd. Why would she feel she needed permission?

"Well, all right then, I'll get my shawl. I don't think I'll need it on such a nice summer evening, but you never know."

The Lucinda he knew never asked permission. She did as she pleased.

She returned with a white shawl in hand. He held open the door. They walked in silence down the drive and into the orchard. She leaned her head against his shoulder for a brief second and then immediately removed it. "I've missed you, and I've felt terribly guilty about how our last conversation ended. I'm truly sorry."

He didn't care about their last conversation, nor did he want to waste one more moment not telling her how he felt. "That's in the past. I've come…I've come today…" Was he really going to stutter now, the most important moment of their relationship, possibly of his life?

She stopped him with some pressure on his arm. "What is it?" Her beautiful hazel green eyes looked deeply into his.

The words stuck in his throat. He lost his courage and said, "I've come to see how my best friend is doing." Why couldn't he just tell her? What a dolt he was using that dreaded word *friend* when what he wanted was to be her husband, her lover.

The evening light faded as the sun dropped below the tree line. She started chatting about which kind of fruit was on which tree. He cared not a whit.

Oh God, help me.

A surge of heaven-sent power gave him the courage to do what he had wanted to do for years. He hauled her up against him and lowered his mouth to hers. She sputtered and stopped moving, and he wasn't sure if the ecstasy racing through his veins was at all returned. He gentled his kiss, and she came alive. The tips of her fingers slid down his temples as she raised her delicate hands to cup his face. He enveloped her in his arms, and her hands circled his neck. Her sweet breath mingled with his. She pulled back, and he met her gaze. He wasn't sure what he'd expected to see there, but not agony on her features.

"Why have you never…?" Before he could answer, she pulled his head back down to meet hers. The kiss they shared held years of pent-up hunger and brought awareness to his whole body. With blazing passion, she returned kiss for kiss.

He must have misread her expression. She loved him too. Of course she did. He was such a fool for not having told her how he felt sooner.

And then he tasted a salty flow. She was crying.

He drew back. "What is it?"

She pulled out of his arms and gazed up at him. "Why?"

"Why what?"

Tears filled her eyes. "Why now? It's too late."

His heart went from bursting out of his chest to collapsing. "What do you mean, too late?"

"If you'd even once held me in your arms and did what you just did, I would've known we were far more than friends." She twisted knots into the folds of her dress. "I never would've looked twice at Nat."

Her words clamped down hard and squeezed the life out of his soul. "But you're not seeing him. Right?" His heartbeat hammered out of his chest.

Her troubled expression indicated an explanation lay on her lips, but all she whispered was, "It's too late." Then she turned and ran.

"Lucinda. I love you," his voice choked out, drowned by the cadence of a thousand crickets.

He would not lose hope. Her response to his kiss had been a good start, and there was no ring on her finger, so clearly it was not too late. He'd have to get his mother's ring from Pa, which would be no easy feat. But he'd finish what he started on Sunday. He'd put an engagement ring on her finger so the likes of Nat Weitzel could get the picture. No more wasting time.

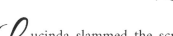

*L*ucinda slammed the screen door on her way in and took the steps to her bedroom two at a time. She flung her body on the bed and wept into her pillow. Joseph had always been close, and there was a time she had hoped for more. But they'd settled into friendship. He'd never encouraged more. But after that kiss...*oh dear Jesus, how wicked can I be?* She was supposed to marry Nat, yet she not only let Joseph kiss her, but she had kissed him back. What was wrong with her?

The very thought of marrying Nat after Joseph's tender yet passionate kiss brought sorrow and uneasiness into her soul. The comfort she innately felt with Joseph was not there with Nat. But what did she expect, Joseph had been her friend for years? She knew so little about Nat, other than he was fine to look at.

Joseph, though. She knew what made him happy or sad, his interests, his family, and how they'd shared a special bond going way back. What she hadn't known was how one kiss would affect her. How it would change everything. He'd been gentle, kissing her with a mixture of sweet and spicy, heart-stopping and respectful. There had been a time when she flirted shamelessly, but Joseph had never gone beyond the boundaries of friendship. She understood now, he was waiting for her to grow up. Then when his family moved, she'd seen far less of him, making it easy for Nat to waltz in and eclipse all others. What a fool she'd been. Tears fell afresh.

There was no point in even thinking about Joseph. If he knew she was pregnant with Nat's baby, he would've never come calling. A girl like Lucinda did not deserve an upright man like Joseph. It was as she had told him. Too late. The faster she got married, the better.

She pushed her head up from the drenched pillow and stood. Wiping the tears from her face, she looked in the mirror and lifted her chin. The day she had ridden into that forest with Nat, her destiny had been determined. *Used goods.* That's all she was. She would make the best of her life with the man who was the father to her growing child.

She rubbed her small bump and whispered, "Mama loves you, and I'll do whatever I need to ensure you do not pay for my sin."

～

*L*ucinda sat on a bench under a sprawling oak tree in downtown Lacey Spring, waiting for Nat to arrive. After Joseph's kiss, only a mild attraction remained for the father of her child. She would somehow have to find the strength to do what was right.

She had once longed for the day she would marry Nat. That all changed after that episode in the forest. She wished she could open up to someone about that day. Was that really the way of a man with a woman, that they couldn't control themselves? And did Nat's love run so deep that he would threaten to sully her name in order to avoid seeing her with another man?

She was haunted by the questions. Yet, who could she confide in? Certainly not Ma. And Jeanette was a bookworm with no experience whatsoever. Amelia was married and lived in Richmond, and Katherine was thirteen years her senior. It felt like she was married and gone before Lucinda got to know her. She'd have to figure this out on her own.

"Baby." Nat slid onto the bench beside her. "How's the most beautiful girl in town?"

Had he used that line on all the girls?

"I can't believe you actually agreed to see me," he said. "When I got that note at the hotel, I was shocked. You didn't seem interested that day at the church."

Lucinda swallowed a lump in her throat. "I've decided that I do want to marry you."

A Cheshire grin split across his face, accenting his startling good looks. He slapped his knee. "Well, I never saw that coming."

His laugher irritated her. "Would you really have ruined my reputation had I chosen otherwise?"

He reached out and placed a finger over her lips. "Shh. Of course not. I was talking through my pain. The thought of you marrying another had me tied in knots. Made me say crazy things I didn't mean."

The unrest gurgling in her stomach eased.

"I can't believe you've agreed to marry me. Am I dreaming?" He moved close. "May I kiss you?" Like a perfect gentleman, he waited for Lucinda to agree.

"No."

She thought she saw a flash of anger before his eyes softened.

"No?" He whispered. "Why not?"

"I wouldn't want to be responsible for leading you astray like I did the last time. Besides, we'll be married within the next couple weeks, and there'll be all the time in the world for kissing thereafter."

"What do you mean, married within the next couple weeks?" He pulled away leaning back on the bench. A hand raked through his black hair.

"If you want me, Nat, you can have me. But I don't want to wait. I've already talked to my parents and have their blessing. We'll be moving to Rockingham County—"

"Whoa... You're moving way too fast for me. Rockingham County. Why?"

"I'd like to get away from this old town, where you and I can have a fresh start." She wouldn't admit that she wanted to be around some family, or the reason a fresh start was necessary. Tongues in this little town would soon be wagging. "My aunt and uncle live there, and we'll have an opportunity to build our own home and help farm the land."

Nat laughed. "Me, a farmer? What gave you the idea I know anything about farming?"

"If you don't want to farm then we can live off all the money you have—"

"I have a lot of money?" He laughed.

"Don't you? You live at the hotel, dress nice, flash bills around like nobody I know."

He looked off into the distance. "Truth is, I'm running low these days..."

Oh great, she was destined to be poor on top of everything else. How many ways would she pay for her stupidity? "Well then, all the more reason this is a good idea. Uncle John's a nice man, he'll teach you all you need to know. And it'll be a place to call our home. You told me your parents never stayed anywhere for long."

"You remembered that?" He ran the back of his knuckles gently down the side of her cheek.

"Of course, I remembered. And I want to give you a home, a family—"

"I'd do most anything for you, Little Red, but a farmer?"

She held her breath. Her insides churned. Something deep inside felt wrong about this union, but what choice did she have? Their baby deserved the chance of a family.

"Don't you want a frilly wedding dress and a day with all the trimmings? A couple weeks seems mighty fast to pull that off. Why the mad rush?"

"I'm going to wear Ma's wedding dress. Katherine has offered her big house and all her staff for the reception, and Jeanette's going to decorate. The minister said he can marry us directly after church in two weeks' time, and whoever wants to come is invited."

"Looks like you've thought of everything, but..." His eyes narrowed. "Why the sudden change of heart? One day you tell me no, and the next you have our whole wedding arranged. And how did you convince your folks? Your ma has sent nothing but daggers my way every time she looks at me."

Lucinda almost told him the whole story, but just the way his eyes held a steely glint made her hold the news back.

"I couldn't get your words out of my head…that I'd never find anyone who loved me like you do."

He pulled her in close to his side and lifted her hand to his lips. Slowly, he kissed each finger.

"That is true, Little Red. I need you more than words can say."

She looked deep into his dark eyes and handsome face. Maybe they would be all right after all, and their child would have a family. That thought alone made it all worthwhile.

He sent her a crooked charming smile. "You have a knack for getting your own way, don't you?

"Is that a yes?" She gave him a sassy grin.

"Your power of persuasion is truly impressive. Heck. A home. A job. And a beautiful girl. Who in their right mind would say no?"

∽

"*D*id you hear the latest?" Nigel strode into the kitchen and plopped the sack of flour and spuds on the table.

Joseph slid the ring and chamois into his pocket. Pa had not been happy to hand it over but conceded when Joseph reminded him about his desire for grandchildren. Nigel knew nothing of the plan to propose to Lucinda tomorrow after church, and Joseph wanted to keep it that way until it was official. His mind was on little else…how he would get down on one knee—"

"Well, aren't you even going to bite? I go to town and learn a few juicy morsels, and you're not interested? It concerns Lucinda."

Joseph's head snapped in Nigel's direction. He was listening now. His heart rate kicked up a beat. Would Lacey Spring ever tire of the gossip?

"What about Lucinda?" Pa entered the room and sat at the

table. He pushed all the clutter out of his way and pointed to the stove. "Bring me some of that coffee you're brewing. It smells good."

Joseph hefted the pot in hand. Pa found his cup in the clutter and held it out.

"Word is that Lucinda's engaged to Nat. They're having a wedding in a few weeks. It's all a rush, rush and hush, hush. Harriet thinks she's pregnant."

The pot in Joseph's hand trembled. He turned back toward the stove and slammed it down. "That can't be, I was just talking to her. And that loudmouth Harriet has got to stop gossiping."

"Face it, son," Pa said. "You dodged a bullet."

"Have I missed something?" Nigel asked.

Joseph whirled around. "Nigel, are you sure?"

"I ran into Lucinda's mama at the store buying some lace and flowers, she said it was for a bouquet, and then Harriet filled me on the possible reason for the hasty wedding."

Joseph may as well have had his skin turned inside out. He slipped his hand in his pocket and fingered the ring. That's what she meant by too late.

"Your brother was thinking of proposing to her tomorrow," Pa said. "I guess he's a little late."

Joseph's hands fisted to white knuckles. "Don't sound so overjoyed, Pa."

"I know you love her, but she doesn't love you. Never has. It's time to let her go. Move on to greener—"

"I don't want to move on. I'm going to go see her. Sort this out. If Harriet's guess is right, then she must feel trapped into marrying Nat."

"To what end?"

Joseph turned away, bracing both hands on the counter to hold him up. That was a question he needed to answer. His beautiful lady had been with someone else…and if she truly was pregnant, could he take on another man's child? The thought of it brought a bitter taste to his mouth. But this much he knew—he still loved her, crazy as that was.

"I'll marry her, Pa, baby or not."

Pa stood. "You will not disgrace this family in such a way." His voice rose to a near roar. "Your mother would turn in her grave if she could hear you now." He took a breath and settled back into his seat. "Lucinda's set to marry the father of her child, as it should be. To meddle now would be wrong. Please, son, let her go."

Joseph dropped into a chair. His head fell into both hands. The last thing he wanted to do was cry in front of them—or admit that Pa was right. He needed to let it go. Just because she'd responded to his kiss didn't mean she loved him. If what Harriet thought was true, then she could obviously respond to any man's kiss.

Nigel clapped him on the shoulder. "I'm sorry. I had no idea. If I had, I wouldn't have been such a blockhead in the telling."

"We'll leave you some time alone." The scrape of Pa's chair and receding footsteps indicated they were both gone. Joseph put the back of his hand to his mouth to curb the groan that rose from the pit of his gut. Nothing but pain and loneliness lay ahead.

CHAPTER 5

Late August 1874

Joseph forced himself to attend church that Sunday, but it took every bit of strength he had. He stayed for the wedding despite the aching desire to scream. When the pastor asked if anyone had a reason to object to the union, he almost jumped out of his skin.

The dialogue chanted in his brain, but his lips remained quiet. *I object. That reprobate has been dallying with every available skirt in town, and now he wins the hand of the only woman I will ever love. She's headed for a heartache and yes, yes, yes, I object.*

But what good would it do him? Lucinda had made up her mind, and that was that. Even their best friend status had slipped into the background. It was as if she'd forgotten their history, that one-room schoolhouse where they'd met and formed a fast friendship. They'd played, laughed, fished, and even cried together when he lost his Ma. Time constraints and distance after his family moved away proved challenging, though his heart had never swayed. He had thought to wait until she was old enough to court and had worked hard to prepare a future befitting her. But all he'd done was give her opportunity to find another—the tall, dark, good-looking devil now at her side.

Joseph's stocky build and average height could never rival the likes of the six-foot-six Nathaniel. But he knew trouble when he saw it, and Lucinda was headed for a wagon full.

Why God? I've prayed for your wisdom and served you with my life. I've remained pure in your sight and worked hard so that I could provide for her, and yet that immoral womanizer wins my girl. How does this work? Where did my prayers go?

Joseph sat in the pew fuming. Angry at Lucinda for being so foolish. Angry at her parents for not stopping her. And angry at God for not answering his prayers. Angry. He crushed his cowboy hat back on his head and stomped out just as the minister said, "You may kiss the bride."

He stood in the church yard gazing over the hay field beyond the fence, his brain assessing how many more days until harvest, what type of grass it was, and how many head of cattle it would feed over winter. He was the farmer. Not the pinhead in that building who Joseph had heard was being given a parcel of land and a home, without a lick of good sense with which to run or maintain them.

"I couldn't stand one more minute either."

Startled by a voice, he turned as Lucinda's sister approached.

"Hi, Jeanette." He tipped his hat, not much in the mood for small talk but not wanting to be rude.

"I hope I'm not overstepping propriety in speaking."

"Go ahead."

"I know you love her, Joseph, and have loved her from the time we were kids. I'm sorry."

"Am I so obvious?"

"I notice more than most. Hiding in the background does that." She touched his arm and squeezed lightly.

He turned toward her. "So, you know why I'm out here, but what about you?"

"I've had an uneasy feeling about Nat from the get-go. He swooped into town, and before you knew it, he had most every eligible young woman eating out of his hand."

"The guy's trouble. Why can't Lucinda see that?" He pulled off his cowboy hat and raked a hand through his hair before flipping it back on his head.

"With her predicament—" She said no more but the message was clear.

"So, the rumors are true?" Why did his heart slip into his boots? She had obviously made her choice for Nat months prior.

"She feels trapped. I know she does."

"Nothing to be done now. The deed is done." Fresh pain clawed at his gut.

She adjusted her glasses on her nose, peering over the top. Pity laced her eyes.

How he hated that.

"You would've made the most wonderful husband for her." She moved forward. "This is not like me, but God says you need this right now." She pulled him into a quick hug. Her cheeks blushed red as she stepped back. "Keep the faith, Joseph. I have a feeling only someone with your strength of character will be able to pick up the pieces when this is done. And mark my word, there will be pieces."

Joseph watched her walk away with her head down as the happy couple exited the double doors, the congregation close behind. They made a striking pair. Lucinda, the petite one with her long hair in every shade from cinnamon to russet shimmering in the sunlight, and the devil, tall and dark in contrast.

Joseph decided to stick around just long enough to get one more moment alone with his best friend, and then he would turn the page and beg God for a new story.

He waited for the perfect opening. The crowd was milling about, waiting for the food to be served. Nat was preoccupied talking to widow Nellie.

Joseph approached her. "Lucinda." He caught her attention.

"Joseph." She ran over. "I'm so glad you came." She pulled at his hand. "I want to introduce you to my new husband."

He resisted, and she stopped short.

"We've met. I just want one moment alone with you."

"What is it?" Her brows knit together.

In the past he would've make some remark about the cute freckles sprinkled across her nose just to get a rise out of her, but today he had only one message in mind.

"If you ever need a friend, anytime, anywhere, for any reason, I'll be there for you."

"Thank you, Joseph." Her eyes grew misty. "You're the best friend any girl could ever have." She pulled him into a quick hug. "Your words mean the world to me."

He breathed in the smell of rain-washed lavender and almost lost his bearing. Stepping back, he said it again. "Promise me you'll remember what I'm telling you today."

She lifted her wide eyes…so green today. He took it all in—the cinnamon-toned freckles that kissed her pert nose, the little bow mouth, the cameo-like profile, the spicy, impulsive wild child who lived behind that beautiful face. She was a married woman now, he had no right thinking how much he wanted to kiss her lips.

A rip of anger screamed through his veins. He should've been the groom. He had to get out of there.

"Promise me," he insisted.

"I promise."

"All right. Go. Your man is walking this way, and he looks none too pleased."

"Oh heavens. Surely, he's not going to fret about me hugging my best friend."

"Lucinda." There was a bite to Nat's voice, though he'd pasted a fake smile on. "We're not married five minutes, and I catch you in the arms of another man."

"Nat, this is my good friend, Joseph. We've known each other since we were kids." Her words came out fast and nervous. "He was the first person who talked to me on the playground at school when I moved to the valley."

Joseph was surprised she remembered that small detail. He remembered that day well. It was the day he fell in love with her.

Nat grabbed her arm none too gently and propelled her away without a glance in Joseph's direction.

Joseph paid close attention. They turned so he could catch the side view. The shake of her head. The dark frown on his face. The way his large hand dug into the delicate flesh of her arm. The fake smile they both pasted on as her parents walked over.

A surge of fury rippled down his spine. He wanted to bust the guy into a thousand tiny pieces, and the marriage wasn't even an hour old.

∼

"*D*o you really need that?" Nat lifted his face with a scowl from his stack of maple syrup smothered flapjacks.

Lucinda stood above her plate holding the hot skillet and a fresh flapjack on the edge of a flipper.

He lifted his fork and pointed it her way. "You're getting fat, and I don't much like fat women."

Lucinda slapped the flapjack on her plate and turned from his glare. It was the first day in their new home, and she had thought to please him with one of his favorite breakfasts.

Seemed in the first month of marriage, she had done little to achieve that.

"It's not fat. It's...it's..." But she was afraid to tell him.

"It's what?" His voice sounded harsh. Hardly the opportune time, but she couldn't leave it any longer. She'd been waiting for an agreeable temperament, but he saved agreeable for when they were in public. In private, he was always touchy and temperamental. The truth spilled out. "I'm pregnant."

He scoffed. "You can't know you're pregnant that fast. We've only been married a month."

She slid the skillet back onto the wood stove. "This baby goes back further than a month."

His hands slammed down on the table and his plate flew up and crashed to the floor. He rose in one swift movement and crossed the room, towering over her.

"You mean you were pregnant before we married, and you didn't tell me?"

His large hand grabbed her wrist and twisted.

"You're hurting me," she screamed.

"Whose brat is it? Your best friend's?" A glint in his dark eyes flashed. His lips curled into a snarl, and he twisted more.

"Please stop, Nat. You know I've never been with anyone but you. I love you."

Her words seemed to snap him out of his anger, and the grip on her wrist lessened. "If it's mine, why didn't you tell me?"

"I've tried, honestly I have. But you don't seem to like kids. And with everything that's been going on getting settled..."

He let her go and rubbed the back of his neck. "A kid? What are we going to do with a kid?"

"Please don't be angry with me."

He fixed her with a black glare. "I can't do this right now." His jawline clenched. "Get this mess cleaned up, I've lost my appetite." He stomped across the main room of their two-room cabin to the bedroom and grabbed his pocketbook from the top of the dresser. Marching to the door he yanked it open. It slammed so hard behind him that the few dishes on the open shelf clattered together. Lucinda shuddered from tip to toe. Who had she married?

She gazed out the window at the new barn her Uncle John and the community had raised a week earlier. The two front doors hung wide open. Should she go talk to him? She stood there until Nat flew out on the back of his horse in a full gallop. She watched the plume of dust disappear into the distance and moved from the window.

Her hands trembled uncontrollably, and she rubbed the fresh pain in her wrist. She would be no match for the likes of Nathaniel if he decided to use greater strength against her.

She'd best get busy with something, anything, to get her mind off the what-ifs. The short rap on the door made her jump.

Aunt May's singsong voice called out. "Just me."

Lucinda snatched the flapjacks from the floor and threw them into the basin. "Come in. Come in. But watch out for the glass." She worked hard to make her voice sound normal as she grabbed the broom.

"Whatever happened in here?" Aunt May stood in the open doorway with a basket full of preserves swinging from one arm.

"I was cleaning up and a plate slipped right out of my hand. Can you believe it? I've already broken one of my new dishes." She clutched the broom handle tightly with both hands to still her shaking and busied herself with the cleanup, avoiding her aunt's gaze.

Aunt May laughed. "Goodness me, but that does remind me of my pregnant days. I was clumsier than an ox in a china shop. Not sure why that is, but it's quite normal."

"So, you know?"

"Not much in that way escapes my eagle eye. Good thing folks around here don't know how long you've been married.

Don't you worry, your secret is safe with me." She picked her way across to the counter and set down the basket. "Brought you some jam and canned veggies to get you started." Her eyes moved to the basin, and her eyebrows lifted at the flapjacks thrown in.

"Not a great batch. I think I overdid the salt." Lucinda hated how one lie bled so easily into another. "Nat pretended to like them, but when I pressed... Well I put him out of his misery." She forced a laugh.

"So much to learn in the beginning, but don't you worry, you'll do just fine. I stopped over to see if you and Nat would like to come for dinner tonight. With all the activity of moving in and being pregnant and all, I thought you'd be tired."

Lucinda swept the broken china into a pile. She would love nothing more than not to have to cook that evening, but she had no idea where Nat had gone or when he would return.

"I was looking forward to cooking in my own home for the first time. Besides we've been eating your meals since we came, it's time I do something."

"Oh, you are a plucky one, aren't you?" Aunt May kissed her cheek. "Very well then, I shall be off. Those four boys of mine are constantly hungry, not to mention your Uncle John. Seems they all have hollow legs." She laughed. "Good thing I have Sarah to help in the kitchen."

Lucinda let out a sigh of relief as her aunt turned to go.

With her hand on the doorknob she twisted back. "I assume Nat was headed our way to meet John for farm training. Tell him he doesn't need to race. John will not fire him if he's a bit late. We do remember all too well the way of young love." She winked. Her laugh tinkled like joyful bells as she closed the door behind her.

Lucinda sunk into the nearest chair. If only Aunt May knew. From the moment that ring had been put on her finger, Nat had been distant and disinterested.

Lucinda rested for a bit and then pulled her tired body from the chair. She hoped Nat had gone next door to work, but she had her doubts. The last thing she wanted was another fight, so she'd best have supper made, especially on the off chance he worked all day.

Never much for the kitchen, she was glad Ma had insisted she learn to cook. Her life was not going to have the luxury of maids, cooks, and the finer things. She looked around her small cabin. This was the best life was going to offer her. If only Nat went back to the way he'd been in the courting days—attentive, charming, loving—she could handle almost anything.

She just had to try harder to be the wife he wanted.

She spent the day washing the laundry and hanging it to dry, then began making supper.

The table was set. The candles lit. The savory smell of brisket simmering on the stove. Aunt May's vegetables added color to the potatoes on the plate. Where was Nat?

After hours of waiting, she ate, cleaned up the dishes, and slipped into their bed alone.

In the wee hours of the morning, she heard him stumble in and turned toward the wall. The crash of his body upon their bed would have woken an elephant, but she remained quiet and still.

"I'm sorry, Little Red. Come to me." He hauled her body against his.

The smell of tobacco and alcohol assaulted her senses. He must've visited the local saloon. She shivered as his hands roamed freely over her body. "Wake up, baby. I'll make it up to you."

Tentacles of fury spread inside her. How dare he be gone all day and most of the night and expect her to fall into his arms. She lay very still.

He nuzzled into the back of her neck and his hands calmed.

She waited afraid to breath normally.

The snort of a snore brought a smile to her lips and then tears to her eyes. How was it that, after only a month of marriage, she was glad her drunk husband slept?

~

*S*he waited until noon. By the time the sun was high in the sky, she was hotter than its steaming rays. She banged every pot she had as she prepared lunch.

"What's all the racket?" Nat came from the bedroom scratching his head. His black hair stuck up in every direction, and his body reeked of stale tobacco. He dropped a kiss on her cheek, and the stench of fermentation like a bad batch of sauerkraut assailed her senses.

"Where were you yesterday? You stink."

He grabbed her close and held tight. "I love it when my Little Red gets fiery."

She swiveled out of his arms. "Well, I don't love that stench. I'm serious, Nat. Where were you? Uncle John came over around supper to see where you were. I lied and told him you were in bed and not feeling well. I had to do the same this morning."

"Nothing I love more than a girl who will lie for me." He grabbed at her. She did her best to avoid him until he pinned her up against the wall. "Come on, baby. You can't stay mad at me forever. I just went to Dayton for a drink. This whole having a kid thing has got me scared. My dad was meaner than a rabid dog. What do I know about fatherhood?"

Her anger fizzled at his honesty. How could she fault him after springing her pregnancy on him the way she did? Of course, he was afraid of being a daddy after all he had gone through in his childhood. She should've been more sensitive. Her fingers gently touched the side of his face and he leaned into her cupped hand.

"Am I forgiven?"

"I don't recall you asking," she teased.

"Lucinda Marie, I'm sorry about yesterday. All of it."

He lifted the wrist he had twisted the day before and bent his head to place a feather light kiss on the faint bruise.

Her heart melted.

"Well, just don't let it happen again." She ducked out of his reach. "And get yourself into the tub sooner than later." She pinched her nostrils together, and he laughed.

With a salute to his forehead, he said, "Yes, ma'am. Then expect your sweet-smelling good-looking husband to come find you for some afternoon pleasure." His eyebrows danced up and down.

She giggled and her heart soared. They were going to be all right.

CHAPTER 6

"We've been invited to the Dwyers' for lunch after church on Sunday," Pa said.

Joseph turned his back, lifting the blackened coffee pot from the kitchen wood stove. "Count me out." He poured the thick brew into his tin cup.

"Why?"

"You'll all be trying to thrust Esther on me, and I'm not interested."

"What's your problem?" Nigel said, slopping a spoonful of oatmeal into his mouth. "A fine-looking filly like Esther. Why, if she was interested in me, I'd—"

"You can have her." Joseph slumped into his chair.

"You're going and that's that." Pa's brow furrowed into an angry knot. "There's no way I'm insulting a good family friend with your dismissal of their invitation. Since your mother died, they're one of the few families that have consistently cared about us."

"In case you haven't noticed, Pa, I can make my own decisions. I'm a grown man."

"Then act like it. At the very least you can attend and be polite."

How could he make Pa understand? If he went, a refusal to show interest in Esther would result in more disrespect. "I have no intention of leading Esther on."

"Then don't. Take her up on her clear invitation to court and start living again. You've been moping around here long enough."

"I can't make my heart feel something it doesn't. Lucinda was—"

"Lucinda. Lucinda. That's all I hear. When are you going to get it in your head, she's a married woman—and by everything that is good and right, that means she's no longer yours? Do you intend to pine away the rest of your life?"

"Enough already. I'll go." Pa was right. He had been brooding and he needed to move on. There was no better match for him than Esther. She was bright and beautiful, and she loved the countryside and farming as much as he did. Unfortunately, she wasn't Lucinda.

Pa smiled. "That's the spirit."

❧

Sunday rolled around too soon. The church service flew by. Dread settled in Joseph's gut as they bounced their way down the rutted Dwyer farm driveway. The day was as gray as his mood. How would he let Lucinda go? He had to. It was wrong of him to harbor a married woman in his heart.

He looked into the heavens. *God, please deliver me from this heartache. If Esther is the woman you've chosen for me, then help me move forward. Give me wisdom. Please.* His heart whispered the prayer in surrender. He was beyond tired of feeling so sad.

Esther opened the door. Her eyes were pinned on him. "Come in," she said with a welcoming wave of her dainty hand.

As Joseph passed, she slipped her hand into the crook of his elbow.

"Ma and I worked all day yesterday and today preparing." She looked up at him and fluttered her eyelashes. Oh, how he hated that.

"Fresh apple pie for dessert. You do like apple pie, don't you?"

He forced a smile through clenched teeth. "Absolutely."

She squeezed his arm and pressed closer. As he, Pa, and Nigel gathered with Esther and her parents around the kitchen table, Esther sat in the chair next to him and moved it as close as possible.

Pa smiled in approval. It felt right to make his pa happy, but aside from that, Joseph felt nothing for the beautiful blonde beside him. He worked hard at being polite, engaging with her in small talk, but he was so thankful when the conversation took off in the direction of farming. He joined in wholeheartedly.

"Which one of us is going to get Joseph's farming genius once these two tie the knot?" Esther's father, Eli, asked.

His wife gave him a pointed look. "Now Eli, give the courtship a chance to blossom before you go bringing up something so forward."

Pa slapped his knee. "Now wouldn't that be a nice problem to have? As my oldest boy, Joseph here is set to inherit the running of the whole spread, and I'd like him taking over sooner than later. I'm ready to slow down a bit, rock some grandbabies on my knee."

Joseph could feel his neck and face warming. Really? The first invitation he accepts and already the fathers were cooking this up? The perfectly tame conversation about farming, ruined in a split second.

Esther slid her hand under the table onto his knee and squeezed. When he ignored her, she removed her hand.

"Why don't you two young ones go for a walk? We'll have the apple pie when you return." Flo smiled at her daughter.

"Make it snappy," Nigel said. "I've been eyeing those pies all through meal." All three adults gave Nigel a not-so-subtle look of displeasure.

Esther was already on her feet. "I'll get my shawl. I want to show you the new batch of kittens in the barn."

Mother and daughter looked at each other as if they were playing out a well-rehearsed production. Joseph let out a deep breath of air before he stood.

"Lucky man." Nigel teased. Esther looked over her shoulder and gave Nigel a big smile.

Why couldn't those two hit it off? If only Nigel didn't make his distaste for farming and his love for inventing so obvious. He didn't endear himself as a prospective husband to the parents of eligible daughters when anything and everyone took second place to the hours he spent holed up in the barn.

"All ready." She skipped down the hall to the door where he was waiting. From her new dress and shawl to her hair done in perfect golden ringlets to the pungent smell of too much perfume, she couldn't be more obvious.

He held open the door, and they stepped out into the crisp October air. Leaves from the red maple sifted to the ground, signifying the death of summer…and of his love for a specific redhead. Dark clouds hung low and depressing. The threat of rain was in the air.

Walking across the yard with her hand snuggly tucked in his arm, he prayed. *God, please help me let Lucinda go. Help me feel something, anything...*

They were not in the privacy of the barn more than a split second before she turned into his arms and pressed her body against his. "Kiss me, Joseph." She closed her eyes and lifted her lips towards him.

He bent his head and placed his mouth on hers and felt...
Nothing.

He pulled out of her embrace. A stab of guilt pricked his consciousness. Why did he feel like he was cheating on the woman he loved?

"I'm sorry, Esther. You're a beautiful woman. Truly you are."

She held up her hand. "The ghost of Lucinda haunts you, even when she's married and moved away."

He nodded. "Wish I could turn it off."

"What would it be like to have someone love me like that."

What could he say to that? He took off his cowboy hat and raked a hand through his sandy brown hair.

She chuckled. "No offense, but I think I liked the idea of you more than the real you. I'm not sure I actually feel anything either."

He let out a long breath of air with a whistle. "Whoa, that's a relief. I didn't want to hurt you."

"Not devastated one bit. But our parents, they'll be disappointed."

"I know. I pray that in time I'll get over her. Over this nonsense—"

"It's not nonsense to love someone so fiercely. I hope someday someone loves me like that." She smiled up at him. "Guess I don't need to flutter my eyelashes and work so hard to get your attention. Maybe we can just be friends."

"Friendship I can do, but anything more—"

"Thanks for being honest. You're a good man. No wonder my parents have been pushing me."

"You mean it wasn't my good looks and exceptional charm?"

Amusement filled her features and made her pretty face radiant. "You're a good-looking man, just not *my* man. Come on, we have some kittens to see so we have something to talk about when we get back, and I have an outstanding apple pie waiting for your consumption. One bite and you just might change your mind."

He raised his eyebrows.

"Oh, stop," she said, slapping his arm. "I'm already over you."

"There's always Nigel."

"Hmm. Don't think I haven't noticed him."

He laughed. "Interesting turn of events, indeed."

"Pa is all about how great a farmer you are. Quite frankly, I like Nigel's creativity, and that he's not afraid to reach for his dreams even if they're different than the norm."

That pierced his heart. Had he been more forward and not wasted so much time, Lucinda might be his now.

"Enough about all of that." She pulled his hand to the back of the barn and into a stall. The tabby cat had a swarm of kittens surrounding where she lay on the hay. "Do you need a mouser? You can have your pick of the litter."

He picked up an orange one and held it close. Lucinda's shimmering russet hair came to mind.

One eyebrow lifted. "Not surprised you chose that one."

"I just grabbed one. It's not—"

"Nothing to do with a certain red head?"

He shrugged, refusing to lie and unwilling to tell the truth.

"May I ask you something personal?" She bent to lift a kitten and snuggled it in her arms.

"Shoot."

"Rumors circulated that Lucinda was pregnant. I know you heard them too."

Again, he opted for silence.

"Weren't you angry? Hasn't that helped turn off some of the feelings?"

Joseph didn't know how to answer her. He had not properly worked through the myriad of emotions—disappointment in Lucinda's fall from grace, disillusionment in who he thought she was as a woman, anger even. Despite all of that, he still loved her.

"I shouldn't have asked," Esther said.

"I'm not sure what to say. I was disappointed—"

"It's none of my business." Her face flushed red. "Ma says I'm too nosy at times." She gave the kitten back to its mother and he handed her the one he held. "Come on. Let's get some pie."

CHAPTER 7

January 1875

oseph took the church steps two at a time. He had to get out of there. Ever since Lucinda was out of the picture, he had half the eligible women batting their eyes, turning around to stare at him, or beelining after each service to be the first to make contact. He was exhausted. All the attention made him want to avoid church altogether.

He cut across the yard toward his wagon. His boots slipped on a patch of ice. He'd better slow down. The last thing he needed was to hurt himself and have no ability to run. If only he could roll out, but he had to wait for Nigel and Pa.

"Thought if I snuck out early, I could catch you here before anyone else."

He turned and blew out a relieved breath when he saw Jeanette. "So glad it's you. Stay until Pa and Nigel get here, and I'll owe you a big one."

"Running from the eligible ladies, are you?"

"Am I that obvious?"

"No, but they are."

"If you're with me, I think they'll stay back. By the way, why are you here? It's not your thing to chase me." The brisk cold of January had already turned the tip of her nose red. Her cheeks brightened to match it.

"I have something I need to share with you." She pulled a letter from her satchel and handed it to him. "It's from my Aunt May."

He opened it and began reading.

Dear Doris and Jeb,

I've kept at Lucinda to write, but she doesn't yet understand a mother's worry. Soon, she shall know what it means to be a mother. Her pregnancy has progressed nicely, and she is due the first week of February by our best calculations. (She has confided in me, so that we can prepare accordingly.)
I don't want to worry you unnecessarily, for she is healthy and strong and a very hard worker. She has made a far better farmer's wife than Nat has made a farmer.
Things started out well. Nat worked hard in the fall helping John bring in the crops. Since then, the town (if I'm being honest, the saloon) has seen more of him than John and Lucinda.
She's a plucky girl, that one. I love her to bits, and she's surviving. We'll take good care of her. John and I have suggested she come stay with us as her due date draws nigh, but she is insistent that she needs to be at the house when Nat does come home. The poor girl is desperate to please him. Seems like he has little inclination to return that sentiment.

Joseph had to work to keep the tremble from his hands. The urge to hit something, anything, was screaming through his veins. Didn't that man have a clue the treasure he held in his hands? He took a deep breath slowly in and out and kept reading.

I'll be checking on her daily no matter what the weather. We have a well beaten path to her door, and Doc Abrams lives only a hop, skip, and a jump from us. Our Jacob has a well-worn path to his door as he is in love with Doc Abrams's daughter Victoria.

Sorry to give you the news on Nat, but I thought it best you know why your daughter has not written. I'm sure she doesn't know how to put into words the state of her predicament. John is not at all confident that Nat will succeed at farming, but rest assured we have your dear daughter in our good care. And let's not forget how much our dear Jesus loves her too. Doris, give that brother of mine a big hug from me.

Lovingly,

May and John

Joseph looked up at Jeanette, whose glasses had slipped to the tip of her nose. "Why are you showing this to me?"

"Because we were right. That guy is nothing but trouble."

"There's nothing I can do about it."

"I was thinking. Maybe you could write Lucinda at my aunt May's address so Nat doesn't find out and—"

"And what? She's a married woman, and it's not right for another man to be sending her private letters."

"But you're her best friend. She'll talk to you. There's nothing immoral about a letter from a friend."

He shook his head. "You and I both know it would be more than that. I need to forget about her, not embroil myself in her business. I told her if she ever needs me, all she has to do is reach out. There's nothing more I can do." He handed the letter back.

"I'm scared for her. I just want to know if she's all right."

"You write her."

"I have. Every month, but she hasn't written any of us back. I'm worried sick. So are Ma and Pa, but it's the middle of winter and travel is impossible."

"I'd like to help. But even something as simple as writing to Lucinda would stir up the past. I need to move forward with my life." Joseph pointed to a couple of the eligible ladies hovering in the background. Waiting.

"We both know, if you were interested in any of them, you would've acted by now."

Joseph could see Pa and Nigel coming up behind Jeanette and relished the intrusion. He would never be over Lucinda. His hands fisted into balls at the thought of what he would like to do to Nat.

There was no way he could get involved.

"Oh, it's only you." Pa looked at Jeanette with such disappointment, Joseph nearly rose to her defense. "I thought Joseph was finally engaging one of the eligible ladies—"

"I am," Joseph answered quickly. Couldn't Pa see how cruel his words were? Jeanette was as much an eligible lady as anyone was, but the town had long since coined her a spinster.

After a polite nod, she turned and walked away, but not before Joseph saw the tears gather in her eyes.

～

W ith her large girth, Lucinda struggled to bend at the fireplace, place the logs, and light the fire. Cold bit at her fingers and toes, and she would have much preferred to crawl back in bed, but Nat had come home last night for the first time in days, and he didn't much like getting up to a cold house. Once she got the kindling flickering with flame, she stood and smoothed her hand over the large mound in front of her. The baby kicked, and she smiled. Her one joy left—the thought of holding a beautiful baby in her arms. Yesterday, the twinges of cramping started and stopped numerous times during the day. Aunt May said it would not be long.

She filled the kettle with water from the bucket she'd hauled in from the outside pump and lumbered to the wood stove, which also needed to be lit. She was thankful her cousin Jacob had popped in the day before, chopped her wood, and filled up her woodbox. She shuddered to think what she would do without her aunt and uncle living so close.

The dark bruise on her forearm was finally fading. It'd been a week since she'd gotten that one. She would do well to remember and keep her fiery temper in check. Apparently, she had no right to question Nat's coming or going, or her need for essentials such as chopped wood, water, and money to buy the basics. She had learned that one the hard way.

It would be hours before he surfaced, and when he did, God only knew which Nat would emerge. He either woke up contrite and next to tears or still half drunk and meaner than her pride would allow her to share with any living soul.

She took the morning to scrub the laundry on the wash board and hang it out on the line. She marveled at how the bitter cold actually took the moisture out of the fabric. After a couple hours in the cold she would bring them in frozen, let them thaw, and hang them on her makeshift line in the house. This process took less time to get dry clothes than if she hung them up wet inside to begin with.

She looked down at her red workworn hands and wondered where the life of love and excitement that Nat had promised her was. She would've done far better to marry a widower with a houseful of children. At least she would have had a partner, a helpmate and some children to distract from the gripping loneliness.

Joseph came to mind. Their easy friendship, his kind heart, the way he laughed at most everything she said. The promise he made her agree to on her wedding day—that all she had to do was ask and he would be there—was never far from her mind. Had he known? He'd never trusted Nat. Maybe he'd seen something she'd missed.

As near as those words he'd uttered to her on her wedding day was the kiss they'd shared just a couple of weeks before that. If only…

She shook her head. She had to get Joseph out of her mind. She had done a lot of things wrong in her life. She didn't want to add wanting another man when she was married to her list.

Who was she kidding? She wanted him.

The urge to write him and be honest had surfaced many times, but what would that serve? He was probably married to a nice girl, one who wasn't used goods like she was. She wiped away a lone tear.

What would Joseph do if he knew just how badly she needed his help?

A sharp pain shot through her abdomen, and she gasped.

Could labor be starting? She placed her hands on the small of her back and stretched out the heaviness.

"Oh, that's attractive."

She jumped at the sound of Nat's voice.

"You look bigger than a pregnant cow. When are you going to pop that thing already, so I can get a glimpse of the girl I married?"

She knew better than to respond. She had learned quickly that she was no match for Nat's strength.

"Answer me when I talk to you, woman."

A shiver ran up her spine, and she weighed her words carefully. "I'm due any day." She tried to keep an upbeat tone to her voice. "Can I get you a fresh cup of coffee? I just brewed some." She pointed to the black pot on the wood stove.

"I don't want coffee." He spat on her clean plank floors, leaving a big gob of saliva for her to clean up. "Bring me the bottle from underneath the wash basin." A loud belch followed his demand.

"But Nat…" She turned toward the counter, frantic to get some food down him before he started drinking again. "How about some breakfast?" She was afraid to bring up the fact it was well past lunch. "I could make your favorites, eggs and bacon, with—"

A whack at the back of her head sent her skull snapping forward. She hadn't heard him coming.

"Did I say I wanted eggs?" He grabbed her hair in both his hands and slammed her body against the counter.

She crumbled to the floor in a heap.

"Get up."

She knew from experience she had to make every effort to comply. When she looked up, she saw a feral glint light his eyes. That meant only one thing—he was in the mood to inflict pain. She clawed at the cupboard door for support, dizzy and straining under the weight of the baby. Wavering back and forth, she held onto the counter.

"Now, get me the bottle like I asked you to." His sneer crawled over her like a slimy snake.

She moved along the counter using both hands to steady her progress and bent slowly in hopes of not passing out. Her head swam and the pain in her abdomen sliced through. She clutched at her stomach. "The baby—"

He shoved her aside so hard she sprawled on the floor. A string of vile words ripped from his mouth as he reached past her and grabbed the bottle. In one easy movement he rose, kicked her in the back, and swigged half the bottle.

She screamed in agony, writhing.

A gush of liquid drained from her body.

"You're such a bore, wench. I only married you because you broke off with me. I had something to prove. I wish I'd never saddled myself with the likes of—"

"Lucinda, it's just me." The door swung open, and Aunt May and Uncle John waltzed in. "We thought we'd bring you…"

Lucinda struggled to lift her body from the floor, but it was too late.

She watched as horror filled her aunt's eyes.

Her uncle rose to his full height. He squared his shoulders and bit out his words. "May, attend to Lucinda. Nat, sit down and don't move."

"She just fell. I was trying to help her—"

"Not one word." John pushed the half-drunk man into the nearest chair then helped May get Lucinda to her feet and seated on a chair.

"She's coming to our house and that's that." Aunt May said.

Nat stood on wavering legs. "Now you wait a minute. My wife is my business."

John pushed him back into the chair. "You're disgraceful. Your poor wife has gone into labor, and you're too drunk to get her the help she needs." He grabbed the bottle from Nat's hand, opened the door, and threw it crashing to the icy ground outside.

"But—"

"You had your chance to be the husband she needed. We're taking over." John shook his head.

What would Nat do, if she left him to fare on his own? He demanded his every need be met. She did not dare look in his direction. She figured she would pay for leaving in the weeks to come, but today she had something bigger to do. She needed somewhere safe to have her baby. The way Nat had just thrown her to the floor and kicked her, would the baby even be all right?

Pain ripped through and she buckled in the chair, a scream split the air.

"John, we need to hurry."

John grabbed her elbow and together they helped her stand.

"Thank God we brought the wagon," Aunt May said.

Lucinda leaned into her aunt's body, soaking up the kindness.

Aunt May sent a pointed look Nat's direction. "And don't let that drunk in my house until he's sobered up."

CHAPTER 8

January 23, 1875

Sweat dripped from Lucinda's matted hair. Her body screamed in agony, but there was no sweeter moment in her life thus far than when she pushed her baby into the world.

Doc Abrams held up the wailing child, so perfect in every way. She had been so afraid that kick to her back would injure the baby.

"You have a healthy baby boy."

Lucinda held out her shaking arms and gathered the warm, wet bundle close. She stroked the fine red hair that crowned his small, sweet head and relaxed back into the comfort of the bed.

Doc Abrams touched the bruise on her arm, and her body tensed. His bushy brows knit together. "What happened here?"

She swallowed a knot and cleared her throat. "I fell last week. Slipped on some ice."

"Seems this girl has been doing more than her fair share of falling, bumping, and gathering bruises." Aunt May's voice held an undertone of meaning.

His eyes widened. "If it's okay with you, May, it might be good to keep her here under your watchful eye for a few weeks, just to make sure I'm not missing something. Easier for me to pop over and check on her too."

"No, I can't," Lucinda said. "Nat needs—"

"My dear girl." His bushy eyebrows lowered over aged eyes. "At this point it's not what your husband needs, but what you need. Is your husband around during the day to help?"

Lucinda felt heat flood her cheeks. "Well, he can be rather—"

"The answer to that is *no*." Aunt May cut in. "Sorry, Lucinda, but I promised your parents I'd look out for you. Every woman needs a little help after her first child is born. Besides, you have a baby now to think of." Aunt May patted her arm and fluffed the pillows behind her head.

"I don't want to be an imposition, you have enough—"

"Nonsense. You could never be an imposition. Sarah and I will be fighting over who gets to hold that beautiful baby of yours, and you're going to have a much-needed rest." She nodded at Doc Abrams, leaving no room for further discussion, then turned her attention to the infant. "Now that that's been decided, on to more important things. What will you name him?"

"I like Samuel, Pa's middle name. But I haven't had a chance to ask Nat."

"Samuel it is," Aunt May said. "That's a fine, strong name."

~

"*P*lease come home." Nat leaned over the rocker where Lucinda sat holding the baby and planted a soft kiss on her cheek.

She flinched at his nearness, but knowing her aunt and uncle were in the next room gave her courage. "I'm not sure I ever want to come back," she whispered. "You've been so cruel."

He let out a sharp breath, but his voice remained pleading. "Please, baby, I miss you so much. You're the only one who has ever shown me true love. I need you."

"Shut the door." She nodded to the hallway. "There are ears that might hear what I need to say."

He narrowed his eyes but moved across the room to do her bidding.

When he returned, she took a deep breath and expelled the words she'd been pondering for days. "You hurt me, Nat." Her whisper hissed out the pain. "I had some fancy explaining to do to Doc Abrams at the bruises I had on my body, especially where you kicked me in the back. You should've seen what that looked like a few days later, and quite frankly these past few weeks have been so peaceful." She pulled baby Samuel closer and shifted away from where Nat stood. "I have bigger things to worry about than catering to your mood swings and drunken episodes." She looked down at the sleeping child. A tear slid down her cheek.

"I promise, it won't happen again."

"You say that every time."

"I've stopped drinking, and I haven't been back to town at all. Ask your Uncle John, I've helped him every day."

"Everyone is on to you. Funny how I've had no mysterious falls, bumps, or bruises since I've been here. The Doc told me yesterday that I'm healthy enough to go home if I can avoid the accidents that seem to keep happening when you're around me."

"Why, that meddling old—"

"He was letting me know that he wasn't fooled by all my stories. Uncle John and Aunt May know too."

Nat's dark eyes turned soft and pleading. "Give me one more chance. We have a baby now. Our marriage is worth one more try, for his sake."

Lucinda gazed at the sleeping child and lifted his tiny hand in hers. "He is pretty amazing, isn't he?"

Nat dropped to his knees beside the chair. "He sure is." He ran a finger softly across the baby's brow. "He has your hair, Little Red."

"And he has your long, lanky body. Aunt May says she's never seen a baby with such a long torso and legs. He's going to be tall."

"Don't you wonder what he'll be like, what kind of man he'll become? I sure hope he grows up to be a way better man than his daddy."

Lucinda prayed he would.

Nat brushed a tear from his cheek. "I'm so sorry. I don't know how I could've hurt the person I love the most. Please believe me. I promise…" Deep heart-wrenching sobs poured from the big man. "I'll make it up to you."

"I could love you all day long and into eternity Nathaniel Weitzel if you remained like you are in this moment." She held her baby in one arm and smoothed a hand through the thick black hair of the broken man who laid his head on her lap and wept.

~

"*Y*ou look so fine, Little Red."

He smoothed his hand over her naked body, and she shivered. Would he be gentle?

"Now, this is what I've missed, some afternoon action." He lowered his lips to hers and quickly partook. She wondered why the act seemed so satisfying to him and so pointless to her.

He rolled to the other side of the bed and stood. "Sorry to say, but your body during pregnancy just did me in." He pulled his pants on and worked the buckle. "Hope you agree one kid is enough." He looked her way.

She didn't want to disturb the peace, so she didn't argue. But how did he think she was going to avoid a second pregnancy?

More than a month without one misstep on his part was beyond belief. She'd do most anything to keep him happy.

∾

April 1875

"*Y*ou can't be serious. The kid is only three months old and you think there's another one on the way."

"I've been sick in the mornings like I was with Samuel, as well as—"

He held up his hand. "I don't need the gory details. We agreed. No more kids." His jaw clenched and unclenched.

"Do you really not know how this happens?" Hot fingers climbed up her spine as her temper flared. "Should I tell you to stay away? I wouldn't mind. I barely get any sleep between you and the baby. I'm the one who's up all night."

"There's a way to remedy that, now isn't there?"

"What do you mean by that?"

"I don't exactly go into town and not get my fair share of attention from the ladies."

"Why, you cheating… I knew it." She raised a hand to slap the smirk off his face and he grabbed her wrist in a tight squeeze.

"I thought you didn't like the use of violence to solve a problem. Don't be whining when your sassy mouth and flying hands start something you can't finish." He flung her hand away and rubbed a hand around the back of his neck. "See, you push me to the brink then blame me when I can't stand being here another minute or lose my temper. If I land up going back into town, it'll be your fault, not mine."

"Nat, I'm sorry. I just don't know what you expect from me." Tears spilled down her cheeks. She wanted peace in her marriage so badly, yet keeping it was like tightrope walking.

"Things have been going so well, and I wanted to be honest with you, not wait until you notice my body changing into what you clearly don't like." She remembered the way he looked with disgust at her thickening body on their wedding night and had told her how he hated fat women. And all the nasty things he had said during the last pregnancy. A wave of hopelessness threatened to overwhelm her. What was she to do?

"There's a way out of this, but you'll have to trust me." He held his arms out to her. "Come here, Little Red. I have no desire to fight with you."

She walked into his open arms. What did he mean by a way out? A way out of what?

He smoothed his hands down her back and held her for a moment. It felt so good. He rarely ever touched her unless it was for his pleasure, or for violence. In all honesty, he seemed to get equal pleasure from both. The thought sent a shudder up her spine.

"Tomorrow, ask Aunt May if she can look after the baby this weekend, and we'll go to town. Tell her we need a break and want to pick up some supplies. It'll get you out of the house for a change. Would you like that?"

She gazed into his shining black eyes. "Why, that would be wonderful. I haven't been off this farm since we came."

"We'll even buy you some fancy new material for that dress you've been going on about wanting to sew. How does that sound?" She stayed in his arms but leaned back so she could read his expression.

"No point in sewing a new dress when I won't be able to wear it for months."

"You leave all the details to me. You'll see that your husband knows a thing or two about problem solving. Oh, and don't mention to anyone that you're pregnant."

"Too late. Aunt May came over yesterday morning when I was sick. She guessed."

His expression darkened and he pulled apart. "Must you discuss everything with that woman?"

"No. But I was complaining about being sick and she recalled her situation between the two oldest boys. She had both of them within the span of a year."

A foul word slipped from his mouth as he raked a hand through his hair. Suddenly he brightened. "I'll have to ride into Dayton tomorrow."

"Why? You know the saloon is a temptation, and... other things."

"I was only messing with you, my wild one. You're the only woman for me." He pulled her close. "I'll be back by noon, and no saloon visit. I promise."

She allowed a shaky smile to peek through, but a knot of tension filled her stomach.

CHAPTER 9

The minute Lucinda and Nat started toward Dayton, the sun peeked from behind a billowing cloud, warming her skin. Hope bloomed fresh and intoxicating. If she could just be cooperative and not irritate Nat in any way, they would have a good time.

"You're excited, aren't you?" Nat squeezed her hand, as the buckboard rattled down the rut strewn path.

"Of course. I haven't been to the shops since before we were married. Now, you're not going to rush me, are you? I'll need plenty of time to pick out that material you promised." She threw him a saucy grin, but a shadow flit across her soul. Why couldn't she relax?

"You shall have all the time in the world, Little Red. You shall indeed." He sent a ready smile her way, and her heart lurched. No wonder she had fallen for him. He was absolutely gorgeous.

"What a glorious day." She spread her hands to the surrounding hillsides as the horse plodded along. "And what a great idea to suggest we do something fun together." Both hands squeezed his arm as she gave him a loving look. "Thank you. This means a lot."

He grinned down at her. "You're like a kid eyeing up the candy at the local mercantile."

"Well, I've been cooped up all winter, and this little chick is ready to fly."

He laughed.

Lucinda gazed around at the verdant hillsides decorated with a sprinkle of wildflowers. She took a deep breath of fresh air in and exhaled slowly. The Allegheny Mountains on one side and the Massanutten on the other gave the calming assurance of all that was steady, true, and unchanging. How little she lifted her head from the everyday grind to appreciate the beauty of nature around her.

She leaned into his shoulder, and he wrapped his arm around her. "You're going to trust me, right?" He kissed the top of her head.

She pulled back. A thread of uneasiness stitched its way through her heart. "What do you mean?"

"Well, you know…concerning your predicament."

"You mean my pregnancy?"

"Yeah, that."

"I thought we were going to have one weekend away and not concern ourselves with everyday life. You promised me a break. Isn't that what this is about?" She hated the way her voice wavered.

"Of course, that's the main reason." He threw his arm around her shoulders and hauled her close against him. "A man can have more than one wonderful surprise planned for his beautiful wife, can't he?"

She nodded into his shoulder, but much like an approaching lightning storm, a strained, charged emotion flashed between them. Silence brewed. She wanted to ask him what he had planned but didn't dare.

The first smattering of homes came into view, and the parcels of land grew smaller as the edge of town approached.

Excitement and tension contended for supremacy. Why didn't she trust that her husband's intentions were good? He'd been trying so hard lately, and yet his words made her body break out in a cold sweat. Something was off.

"It's a fairly small town." He waved his hand from side to side. "But it has the essentials."

Her thoughts went to the saloon and what Nat would call an essential. She pushed her uncharitable thinking aside and tried to concentrate on the surroundings.

"I asked Madame Dovel where the best place might be to get the material you wanted, and she suggested—"

"Who is Madame Dovel?" Lucinda's thoughts swirled.

"Oh, just a friend. I'll take you to meet her later."

Bristles stood up on the back of her neck. "You've made women friends?"

"Stop trying to ruin a perfect day. She's married," Nat said. He pulled up in front of the General Mercantile and jumped down. "I'll drop you off here and be back after I take the horse and buggy to the livery." He held out his arms and swung her down. "Can you be happy, please?"

A barb of guilt pierced her heart. She was too suspicious to be happy, but she offered a half smile and pulled on her gloves to cover her work-worn hands.

"Green looks good in your eyes, baby, but not at the mention of every woman's name." He laughed.

"Go." She swatted his arm. "I'll await your return with bated breath."

"Now that's more like it." He dropped a kiss on her pouting lips.

A bell above the door tinkled as she entered. She stopped to take in the collection of items, breathe in the smell of goods from leather to spices, and feast her eyes on the bolts of colorful material and lace.

"May I help you?" A dark-eyed beauty stepped from behind

the counter. Her long flowing chestnut hair pinned back at the sides accented her sculptured cheeks. Her blue dress, clearly the latest in fashion, hugged her tiny waist and emphasized the size of her voluptuous chest. Lucinda blinked twice, suddenly feeling frumpy and unfashionable in her homespun farm dress.

"I'm just going to look at the fabrics." She beelined across the store to the far corner, where the bolts of material sat.

"You let me know if there's any way I can help." Her singsong voice irritated Lucinda.

Soon lost in the world of color, texture, and calculations of what their meager income could afford, she did not see Nat come in. She did hear the commotion. Her head snapped up.

"Nat." The shopgirl squealed and flew from behind the counter towards him. "Where have you been? I haven't seen you for weeks."

The woman would have run straight into his arms had Nat not looked Lucinda's way and pointed. "Rebecca. Meet my wife. We're here to buy some fabric for a new dress."

"Wife?"

The surprise in the girl's single word told Lucinda that Nat had never mentioned her before. A thorn of displeasure pierced. She stepped out from behind the bolts. "Yes, wife."

"Rebecca, my wife, Lucinda. Lucinda, meet the store owner's daughter, Rebecca. I've told you about Jack Witts before. He's the man who's been kind enough to extend credit until we get on our feet."

Lucinda gritted her teeth. He had told her about Jack Witts, but certainly nothing about his beautiful daughter. She nodded politely, not missing the glare Rebecca sent Nat's way.

"Did you find anything you like?" He steered Lucinda away from Rebecca by putting pressure on the small of her back.

"This green would be dazzling with your eyes." He held up an impractical silk, a material she would love if she weren't desperately in need of material for everyday clothing.

"I'd love that," she whispered, "but the baby needs new clothes, and I need a new day dress—"

"I'm trying to buy something to pretty you up, get you out of the drab." He pointed at her dress.

"But how will we pay for this?"

He waved his hand. "That'll take care of itself. Haven't I been working hard at the farm?"

"Yes, but—"

"John thinks we're going to have a bumper crop this year and I'll be able to pay off my debt here. Are you going to deny me the pleasure of pleasing my wife?" He tilted his head to the side and gave her a winsome smile.

She pressed her finger to her mouth. "Oh, all right, how can I say no to such a lovely gesture?"

He snapped his fingers. "Rebecca, wrap up whatever is needed for my wife to make a gorgeous dress for herself in this." He held up the green bolt of silk. He turned to Lucinda again. "And add whatever you need for another day dress and clothing for the baby."

Rebecca stepped forward, eyes wide. "You have a baby?"

"Yes, in January, that's why I haven't been to town. A father has to take care of his kin, does he not?"

The young woman shot him another poisonous look. Her lips formed a tight, ashen line. When her eyes came around to Lucinda's, though, they filled with pity.

Lucinda wasn't sure which look she despised more. Rebecca clearly had a reason to be upset. What kind of encouragement had Nat given her? How had she not noticed his ring? Had he taken it off?

Nat rattled on, but neither Lucinda nor Rebecca said a word other than to discuss the order.

"There now, are you happy?" Nat asked, as he balanced the package in one arm and held the store door open with the other. He didn't wait for an answer but started down the street.

"What just happened in there?"

"You know what? I'm finding your questioning real tiresome. I've tried my hardest to give you a wonderful time away from the farm, and all you do is gripe."

"But Nat—"

"If you want to know the truth, I was glad you were there today. I can't help that women find me attractive, and Rebecca was not taking no for an answer. She has repeatedly thrown herself at me. Maybe now that she's seen my beautiful wife, she'll leave me alone." He threw an arm around Lucinda's shoulders. "Now, stop grumping and give me a kiss." He dropped his lips to hers, apparently not noticing when she didn't return his gesture. "We're going to head to Madame Dovel's place. She has a room for us for the night."

"Does she run a hotel?"

"More a boarding house than a hotel. That's why I came to Dayton a couple days back. I wanted to ensure she had room."

A niggling uncertainty scratched its way to the surface. "I thought boarding houses were for more permanent stays than a night or two?"

"As I said, she's a friend, and we don't exactly have a lot of extra money right now. She's giving us a free room, and I'd far rather our money go to this silk for my beautiful wife." He held up the package, and she zipped her mouth shut.

～

*L*ucinda recoiled at the sight of Madame Dovel. It was not her thin heron-like features, or the peppered-gray frizzy bird's nest piled high on the top of her head, or even her overly painted eyelids and cheeks that made her want to run. It was the dark aura that flowed from empty gray eyes.

Lucinda's first instinct was to turn away, but Nat had his hand on the small of her back, nudging her inside and past the fearsome woman. Lucinda stepped into the parlor while a knot of nerves twisted in her stomach.

"Come in. Come in." Madame Dovel waved them forward with the crook of her finger. "I have everything ready." She kissed both of Nat's cheeks and lifted a cold hand to Lucinda's face. "She is a pretty one, Nat."

"Yes, she is."

"And we want to keep her that way." She laughed in a way that gave Lucinda the goosebumps.

"What...what is it you have ready?" Lucinda moved out of the range of her touch.

"Your room and teatime, of course. Nothing like a hot cup of tea and fresh biscuits to set a late afternoon to bed." She winked at Nat. "Go take your wife up and show her the lovely room and drop off those packages." She pointed to the stack Nat had in one arm. "Meet me back here in fifteen minutes."

Lucinda climbed the stairs. Nothing about this place resembled a boarding house, but what did she know? Best not to bother Nat with yet another question.

Nat swung the door wide.

"You've already been here?" Lucinda worked hard not to stitch her brows together at the sight of her carpet bag in the room.

"I stopped by on the way through before I dropped off the horse and buggy. Do you like it?"

Lucinda took in the flowery wallpaper, the matching basin and pitcher on the washstand, and the stack of fresh towels. There was even a pretty Japanese divider to change behind. There was nothing not to like, and yet she felt an eeriness in the room she could not define.

"It's lovely. Thanks for all your effort." She rose up on her tippy toes and planted a kiss on his mouth.

"Ahh, that's my girl." He melted into her embrace. "You little vixen." He pulled reluctantly away. "Don't get me sidetracked when we have to head back down."

Uneasiness sliced through her. "We have such precious little time to ourselves, and I for one don't want to share it with Madame Dovel." She touched him in a way that usually drove him wild, yet he groaned and stepped back. Never had he shown any kind of restraint when it came to that part of their life. With a grab to her hand, he pulled her out the door and down the stairs.

Madame Dovel had a beautiful teapot and matching teacups with a plate of cookies, a jar of jam, and a pitcher of rich cream waiting on the sideboard. She handed Lucinda a steaming cup and proceeded to pour two more from the teapot.

"Help yourself to whatever you like." She pointed to the rest of the goodies, but Lucinda declined. The sooner they could get out of that woman's company the better she would feel.

Cup in hand, Nat led her to the settee. Madame Dovel followed and sat across from them.

She took one sip and almost gagged. A harsh, bitter mint taste burned down her throat. Rather than make a fuss, she set it on the table in front of her. She'd skip the tea.

"Oh my, I forgot the biscuits." Madame Dovel rose from her chair, sent a very pointed look Nat's way, and headed out of the room.

"Drink up." Nat whispered. "I know her tea is terrible, but we mustn't insult her hospitality."

He picked up his cup, crossed his eyes, and gulped it down. "Do it fast so you'll barely taste it."

A warning lurked in the shadows of her mind, but she didn't want another fight. She gulped the liquid. It stung all the way down to her stomach, making her reflexes lurch in protest. It took everything she had not to let the liquid come back up.

Nat passed her his handkerchief as she coughed, and he winked at her.

Madame Dovel returned to the room with a plate of biscuits, which she placed on the sideboard. "Do help yourself," she said, as she took one and smothered on a generous dollop of jam. She slid back into the chair across from them and nibbled the corner.

Lucinda let Nat carry the conversation. Her head began to swim and swirl. "Nat…I…I…" Her words came out slurred.

Lucinda pressed her hands to her temples. Why did she feel so ill? "I don't f-feel so good."

Madame Dovel stood and raised her eyebrows at Nat. "There's been a nasty case of influenza going around. I do hope you haven't caught it. But let's get you into bed."

He helped Lucinda stand. Her body swayed, and she leaned into him as he propelled her up the steps and into their bedroom.

"Are we going home?"

"After a good night's sleep. Now, let's get you undressed and into bed."

"I like it when you're so…tender with me. You've never helped me into my chemise before, only out." She giggled, feeling much more relaxed as she laid back on her pillow. But so dizzy that she couldn't string a sentence together. She had almost fallen asleep when the door opened and Madame Dovel waltzed in.

Lucinda couldn't understand why she would walk in on her guests, but when she tried to ask the question, her words came out garbled. She could hear their conversation but could not understand what they were saying. Lucinda thought she was dreaming as their voices floated in and out.

And then, acute pain hit her abdomen.

"Take a swig of this." Nat held a foul-smelling bottle to her mouth.

She shook her head. "No, I don't want…" He poured it down

her throat, and she spit it out and coughed. A scream split the night air as pain ripped through her body.

"She's hemorrhaging." Madame Dovel's voice was shrill and panicked.

Everything went black.

CHAPTER 10

*I*t had been the longest eight months of his life. Joseph could not get Lucinda out of his head. His focus had to be on his farm, not a married woman who was now a mother. Jeanette had confirmed a baby boy had been born in late January. Yet Lucinda haunted his memories. If only he had never kissed her.

He felt around in the pitch black for a match on the bedside table and lit the candle. What time was it anyway? He flipped open his pocket watch. It was only 4:00 AM. With a sigh, he sank back onto the bed flipped his body over and punched his pillow, begging God for sleep and for a way to purge her from his mind.

"Missed me. Missed me. Now you have to kiss me." Eleven-year-old Lucinda dodged him again in their game of tag. Her two red pigtails flew behind her as she looked back for a split second and gave him a saucy grin. Little did she know he'd deliberately missed her so she would invite him to do what he most longed to do.

"One of these days, Lucinda Marie, I'm going to catch you and do just that—kiss you."

She stopped dead and swung around.

He almost smacked right into her.

"You wouldn't know what to do with me even if you did catch me," she said.

"Oh yeah?" He reached out and pulled her close so she couldn't take off running again.

"Whatcha gonna do now?" Her laughing green eyes taunted him.

"This." He pulled both her pigtails and took off running.

She screamed and chased. "Joseph Daniel Manning, I'm gonna hurt you."

It was his turn to run and laugh. She would never catch him unless he wanted her to, and oh, how he wanted her to.

His mind snapped awake, and he took a deep breath. Even his dreams would not free him.

Please God, please set me free.

He rolled over, kicked off his blanket. The vision of her loveliness, even back when she was a young teen, set his heart to racing and his blood running hot.

"Oh God. Why?"

You need to pray and prepare.

Prepare for what? Where did that thought come from? What was God saying? Or had he finally gone over the edge?

Pray for her. The words filled his mind. Concise. Clear. Critical.

He rolled from the bed and dropped to his knees. If there was one thing he knew, it was when the Lord wanted him to pray. Then he might as well get on with his day. If he wasn't going to sleep, there was no point in rolling around in bed. The farm work was never done and with spring planting, the sooner he got the cows milked and chickens fed, the sooner he could get out in the fields.

~

"*T*hat was not a miscarriage, Nat, and you know it." Lucinda turned her back to him, looking out over the landscape. The buggy rumbled down the dirt path toward the farm. "The minute I drank that so-called tea, I began to feel nauseous."

"Shut up already." He ripped at his hair with one hand. "Quit your whining. You agreed. No more children."

"I didn't think even you'd stoop so low."

"Give it a week. You'll be happy. We'll go back to our life, and you can make that nice green dress and actually look good in it."

"You killed our baby and I almost died. I will never forgive you, Nat Weitzel. Never. And just how are you going to explain to Aunt May my absence of over a week instead of two days?"

"I went home while you were sick and explained you were with friends and came down with a nasty flu and had a miscarriage."

"Ha." She spat the words into the air. "Is that what you call what you and that witch did to me?" Her body shuddered at the memory. All she wanted to do was curl up and die, but she had a son who needed her.

"Whoa." He pulled on the reins and stopped the buggy. He grabbed her arm and jerked her to face him. "Speak one word of this to anyone, and I'll take Samuel, and you'll never see either of us again."

"You would not."

A wicked grin crossed his face. "I see by the fright in your eyes that I have your attention."

Fear bristled up her spine. "You don't even like your child."

"Yeah, but you do." His laugher split the late afternoon air.

Her hands shook as she laced them together. She swallowed hard against the fear.

"Do you understand what I'm saying to you?"

She stared into the menacing eyes of the man she had once thought she loved.

"Answer me." He pinched her arm so tightly she knew she would have another handprint bruise.

"I understand."

"Glad we got that out of the way. Now let's concentrate on leaving the past in the past and enjoy the fact there's not going to be another wailing brat to look after. One is bad enough."

Well, there was only one way she knew to ensure there would be no more children, and she'd gladly oblige. Besides the thought of him near her made her stomach pitch and roil.

With a snap of the reins and a crack of his whip, they were back on their way to a place that felt anything but home. She had only herself to blame. If only she had listened to her parents and not been so rebellious. If only she had heeded Jeanette's warning. If only she had taken Joseph up on his offer the day he'd kissed her so passionately. Too many *if onlys* to live with.

LATE MAY 1875

"Can you meet me outside after church?" Jeanette leaned in and whispered her question to Joseph as they climbed the church steps together. "It's important."

"All right. I'll wait under the oak tree." He pulled his cowboy hat from his head as they entered.

"Thanks." She offered a weak smile.

He could barely concentrate on the service and fidgeted in his seat as the minister droned on. What could Jeanette want? Was it about Lucinda again, when he was trying his darnedest to forget her? The last amen could not come quickly enough. He was up and out of his seat and down the steps before most had even registered that the service was over.

He fiddled with the rim of his hat, twirling it round and round as he gazed out over the field. He hoped it wasn't bad news about Lucinda. For days now, God had him up in the night praying for her.

"Thanks for meeting me."

He swiveled around at the sound of Jeanette's voice.

"I'll get right to the point, as we don't have much time."

"What is it?"

"The school year is almost done, as is my commitment to helping Mrs. Beasley with the children. I've decided I must go visit Lucinda. I know I shouldn't put this on you, but I need you to come with me."

"What?" His heart galloped at the thought of seeing her.

"I know this is a highly unusual request but hear me out." Her hand fluttered to her throat and trembled in nervousness.

"I don't want Ma and Pa to worry, but I fear the worst. Aunt May's letters have been getting increasingly worrisome. They speak without really saying what is going on."

"Why concern me?"

"Because I know you still love her—"

"I don't..." But he could not finish the sentence, though he knew he should be able to.

"You'd be dating others if you were free of her. Lord knows you've had enough attention buzzing around you all winter."

"Just haven't found the right one," he argued, angry that she was right.

"Pff." She waved her hand at him. "Tell that to someone who believes you. All I'm asking is for you to care about your friend's safety."

A tremor tripped up his spine. What he sensed in his spirit now collided with his heart. "You believe she's not safe?"

"Yes."

"So do I."

She touched his arm. "I knew I could count on you to hear

the same thing the Spirit is speaking to me. Please come," she pleaded. "Nat has never liked me. I'm much too ugly for the likes of him."

"You shouldn't say things like that about yourself."

"What's true is true. He said as much to Lucinda. Anyway, I don't feel safe around him, especially if I uncover what I think I'm going to. I have to know if she's all right. If she's not, I want to bring her home."

"Where would I stay?"

"Aunt May and Uncle John can put you up. They live just across the field from Lucinda's."

"How will you explain my presence to Lucinda?"

"You'll have to be my suitor, if it comes to that." She blushed a crimson red. "Of course, you won't be, but it will allow us freedom to poke around so that neither Nat nor Lucinda will be suspicious."

"What about your parents?"

"They've already agreed to my visiting her when I begged for some sister time." She pushed her glasses further up her nose and looked at him through the spectacles. "We all just dance around the subject, hoping she's all right, but I need to see for myself. And I don't want to admit to my parents that I'm too scared to go alone or they won't let me go at all." She placed a hand on his arm. Tears filled her magnified eyes. "Please, Joseph."

"Well, I do have some supplies I could get in Harrisonburg."

"Then how about coming a bit farther and staying for free at Auntie and Uncle's."

"That won't look planned?"

"Ma and Pa understand how farmers pinch pennies, and they trust you, Joseph. You were a fixture around our home for years. Plus, they'd be thrilled that I don't have to take the coach alone, and I know Auntie and Uncle won't mind putting you up."

He couldn't refuse Lucinda's sister. He couldn't refuse his own heart. Even if Lucinda could never be his, he could help her... But, oh how it would cost his lonely soul. "Give me a few days to work out the details. Pa won't be happy, but Nigel can step it up for a few days. It won't hurt him to put aside his inventions and pitch in a bit more."

She gave him a rare full smile, and he was surprised at how it lit up her usually dour face. "Thank you. Thank you. I must run. If you're at all interested in affirming that the ladies around here think you're the catch of the valley, take a look across the church yard and notice Diana Redburg giving me the evil eye for talking to you." She laughed as she walked away.

He lifted his eyes to the beautiful brunette with long flowing hair cascading from underneath her bonnet. Her eyes were pinned on the receding Jeanette with a grim look to her face, then flicked back to him. Their gazes met, and her generous lips curved into a wide charming smile. She batted her eyelashes above the fan she snapped open and waved.

He smiled back but felt nothing. As she hurried toward him, he turned and headed for the hitching post where his steed was tethered. He had zero patience for idle chatter at the moment.

CHAPTER 11

June 1875

"How stupid can I be? Stupid. Stupid. Stupid." Lucinda stomped back and forth in her small two-room cabin. She twisted her hands in the folds of her apron and then ripped them free. "I should not have refused him." But the thought of getting pregnant again made her shudder.

Baby Samuel whimpered, and she silenced her rant. She paused before the only mirror in her tiny home. This time, her face showed the carnage. A split lip, a black eye, and a gash across her forehead where her head had caught the edge of the stove. Good thing it had been cold.

Even if she could avoid Aunt May and Uncle John for enough time to let the wounds heal, Jeanette was due to arrive any day. News was sure to get back to Ma and Pa of the monster she'd married.

Nat's anger had escalated over the past month. When he was home, he expected her undivided attention. He hated the noise of a crying baby, and when she attended to Samuel, he was jealous of the time.

No matter what she did to appease him, she failed. Her life felt squeezed into a very thin place. She was exhausted, beaten, worn. All she wanted to do was go home and have Ma and Pa cradle her in their arms of love, but Nat's threats had gotten dark.

Her reflection in the mirror blurred as tears poured down her face. There was no way out. She fingered the bruise underneath her eye, reminded of his parting words as he stood over her crumbled body on the floor.

"And don't even think of running while I'm gone. I promise I'll hunt you down and find you wherever you go. But before I do that, I'll burn down your Aunt and Uncle's home in the dead of night with all of them in it."

She tasted the terror as bile rose in her throat.

"Nat, please—"

"Yeah, you better learn to please me, or you'll find yourself in the same predicament that my previous wife found herself."

She gasped. "Wife?"

He leaned in real close. The putrid smell of fermented alcohol spewed from his mouth with each clipped word.

"She's six feet under. Terrible, terrible accident." He stood, laughing. "Yup, her and the brat. But the hefty little inheritance she left me sure did come in handy."

It took all Lucinda had not to react.

"How do you think I had money to live on when I arrived in Lacey Spring? Too bad I blew through it too fast. Had to marry you for a roof over my head."

She kept her eyes from widening and her fists from clenching. She turned to face the floorboards, choking back the vomit heaving in her gut.

"You are mine. Do you understand?"

She could not answer through the pain and tears, but she nodded.

"Look at me when I speak to you."

She turned her face up to him.

"Say 'yes, my darling, Nat.'"

Fire surged through her veins, and she clenched her teeth to keep what she really wanted to say from coming out.

He walked with staggered steps to the bassinet in the corner of the room where Samuel lay sleeping and looked down. "Just how much do you love this kid?"

He reached for the child, and Lucinda yelled. "Yes, my darling Nat. Yes, my darling..." her words were lost in the sobs.

He walked back, towering over her again.

She had learned never to get up until he told her to, or he would knock her down again.

"That's better. I think I've finally broken my little redheaded filly. Get up and make yourself presentable. Make sure you find a way to hide those bruises. Maybe next time you'll come when I call."

"I told you that my sister is due any day."

"She had better not be planning to stay in this house. Can't stand her creepy eyes peering through those glasses at me. Ugly is not what I like to look at."

"If I say she has to stay at Auntie and Uncle's, she'll suspect the worst. And the others already do not believe my excuses."

"Then you'd better learn how to lie a whole lot better. Tell her the kid is too fussy and keeps up the household all night."

"But he's such a good baby."

"I don't care what you say. I don't want your sister here, and you'll pay if I have to look at her ugly face." He stomped out, slamming the door behind him.

She rose from the floor, her body aching in too many places to count. She limped to the window and breathed a sigh of relief when Nat galloped away on his horse.

Her reflection came clear in the mirror. There was no way to hide the damage. Over the past few days the black eye had deepened, and the bruises had purpled. She had rushed into the bedroom when her aunt came calling the day before and lied that she was having a bath. Thankfully, Aunt May had left the fresh garden lettuce on the counter and had not returned.

Lucinda rarely prayed, but today she whispered her request to the Lord. "God, please don't let Jeanette arrive soon." She needed at least a week for the wounds to heal enough to disguise.

A knock on the door sounded.

Lucinda was glad the baby was with her in the bedroom. She raced to shut the bedroom door.

After a moment, the creak of the main door gave way to her sister's voice. "Lucinda, it's Jeanette. I'm a couple days early. Hope that's all right."

~

*J*oseph had wanted to run to Lucinda's home the night before when they arrived at May and John's. But with it being almost dark and the horses needing attention, that behavior would've looked strange.

He stood in the background as Jeanette poked her head into the house and called out. She stepped back out onto the small porch. "Maybe she's in the barn. I don't see her or the baby."

"I'll go check." Joseph had turned toward the barn when he heard a whimpering child and the sound of Lucinda's voice.

"Jeanette. Come in."

Jeanette motioned Joseph over. They both stepped into the small cabin.

He took one look at the beaten waif and the child in her arms and wanted to punch something real hard. Where was that sorry excuse for a man?

"Oh, my good Lord, Lucinda. What happened?" Jeanette ran and gathered her and the child close.

Lucinda pulled free. "Clumsy me. I tripped on the way to the barn and went for a good spill." She turned toward Joseph with a flash of joy, but she hid it quickly. "Joseph, what a surprise to see your smiling face."

He was not smiling, nor was he fooled.

"That looks more like a fist plant to me." He crossed to her and stared into her beautiful golden-green eyes.

A rush of red flooded her cheeks, and she shifted from foot to foot, a tell tale sign when she wasn't being honest.

"Where is he?" Joseph gritted his teeth. His fists clenched tight. "I'm going to show him what it feels like when I bust him wide open."

"He's...he's gone to town. I don't know when he'll be back."

"Well, that's it." Jeanette paced the floorboards. "We're getting you out of here and taking you home."

"No." Lucinda's voice screeched out the word.

Joseph heard the fear in her voice. Anger and irritation had him crossing his arms. Surely, she didn't still want to be with Nat, not after what he'd done to her. "Why not?"

"It's complicated."

"I don't care what it is," Joseph said. "We're not leaving you here to be his punching bag whenever he feels the urge."

Jeanette's head bobbed in agreement. "We're here to help."

"I don't need your help." Lucinda turned from them and rocked Sammy in her arms.

"Yes, you do." Jeanette straightened her back standing tall. "We'll pack up right here, right now, and be miles away before he knows it."

"No!" She spun, her eyes blazing with fire.

"Give me one good reason," Joseph demanded, his insides churning. Why would she not let them help her?

"The man beats you," Jeanette said, "splits your lip, gives you a black eye, and bruises on your arms, and that's just what I can see. Why do you want to stay?"

Lucinda looked down at her child. Her shoulders heaved,

and she snuggled him into her chest. "Because I love him with all my heart."

A dormant ache welled up and became fresh again. Of course, she did. That was what a wife is supposed to do, love her husband. If only she had felt that intensely for him. Why was he there? *Oh God, why did you send me, of all people?*

Jeanette shook her head. "You love him, after all that?" She reached out to touch Lucinda's arm, but she shrugged it off. "You can't mean that."

"I'm not going anywhere." Lucinda's eyes turned stormy, daring them to argue the point. When they remained quiet, she turned toward the window and stared out blankly.

"Jeanette, you're welcome to visit, but you cannot stay in this house. Nat has picked up on the way you dislike him and has asked me to respect his wishes and have you stay at Aunt May and Uncle John's. As you can see, this house is way too small anyway, and Nat likes his privacy."

"I've never said I don't like him," Jeanette said.

She spun toward them. "Well, do you?"

Jeanette looked down at the floorboards. "After what I see today, I do not."

"Then best if you remain at the big house, and I'll visit you there when I can. There's a lot of work to being a mother and looking after the animals, planting a garden, washing the clothes and all the other chores in a day. So, visitations will be minimal." She turned to Joseph. "Why are you here, Joseph?"

"We were worried about you."

She carried the baby to the bassinet in the corner and laid him down. "I find it rather unnerving that you would come and offer to take part in stealing me away from my husband," she said without turning around. "If you're hoping—"

"You have nothing to worry about." Joseph kept his words measured and emotionless, the opposite of how he felt on the inside. "Since that day when you made it clear we were no more than friends, I've moved on. In fact, Jeanette and I are courting. It was at her insistence I came."

Lucinda spun.

To press the point, Joseph put his arm around Jeanette's shoulder and pulled her close. He caught a flash of something he couldn't quite decipher in Lucinda's eyes.

Jeanette beamed up at him, playing along beautifully.

The leaden stone in his stomach dropped deeper. If only he had fallen for Jeanette instead of Lucinda, how much simpler life would be. The two of them had discussed using this excuse only if they had to. He had to, or Lucinda would know her words of accusation were dead on. There was nothing he longed for more than to break up her destructive marriage and gather his poor beaten Lucinda in his arms and never let go. Instead, he had his arm curled around Jeanette's shoulder. Things could not get worse.

"I see." Lucinda walked toward them. "I…I'm happy for you both."

She placed a hand on Jeanette's cheek and ran it lightly down. "You could not find a better man than Joseph to share your life with. I pray things will work out you."

Joseph was so close he could smell the lavender waft from Lucinda's skin, and the reminder of their kiss assaulted his senses. He didn't move. His arm remained firmly around Jeanette's shoulder. He needed her support just to stand.

Lucinda glanced at Joseph. "Love and cherish her. She'll make you the happiest man alive."

The anguish in Lucinda's eyes was bottomless.

A wall of sorrow took his breath away. He turned from her tortured gaze.

"I must get on with my daily chores while Samuel sleeps. But tell Aunt May I'll come for supper tonight, as long as Nat doesn't get home this afternoon."

She turned from them and picked up a basket of laundry.

"Come, Jeanette." He placed his hand in the small of her stiff back and propelled her out the door. When they were far beyond hearing range, she let him have it.

"Why did you give in so easily? She is lying through her teeth. Did you see the way she looked at you when you put your arm around me? My sister is not in love with her good-for-nothing husband. She almost started crying when she acknowledged what a great husband you would make. I bet if she could reverse her steps, knowing what she knows now—"

"She can't. And she said she loves him with all her heart."

"You numbskull. She was looking down at her child when she said that. Are you really that blind?"

"Then why did you join in so convincingly?"

"Because until we can regroup, that smokescreen works. And I have a few secrets of my own. It wasn't you I was thinking about when your arm went around me."

He nodded. "You're a plucky girl."

"We have work to do, and I have a plan."

"What plan?"

"It starts with talking to Auntie and Uncle."

CHAPTER 12

*L*ucinda was annoyed when Jeanette and Joseph would not keep their distance. Every morning they showed up with a smile and a purpose. Joseph headed to the barn to milk the cow and feed the chickens, then spent time in the garden. Jeanette was either helping with Samuel or preparing for the evening meal. This morning she had a pot of stew on the wood stove already simmering. Without words, they showed their love.

"It's been two weeks since we arrived, and Nat has not come home. Does he disappear like this often?" Jeanette voiced her question as if she were asking about the weather.

"I...well, that is a rather personal question."

"Not really. Most married couples who love each other as much as you claim to love him can't bear to be apart for one night, let alone many. And shouldn't Nat be helping Uncle John with the farming? Isn't that his job?"

Her questions hit a nerve. Lucinda was living off the kindness of her aunt and uncle. He was sharing the proceeds from last year's hay crop, even though Nat had done little to help. She couldn't give a satisfactory answer to any of Jeanette's questions. Instead, she said, "Isn't it time for you and your man to head home?"

Jeanette had the nerve to laugh. "Not just yet. Even if you don't like our help, don't you enjoy the company?"

Lucinda regretted her sharp tongue. She hated Nat for his sarcastic ways, but sometimes she was no better. When would she learn? Jeanette was nothing but kindness, and Joseph... She dare not let her mind think about what he was. If she were honest with herself, she'd admit that she envied Jeanette straight through to the core. How had Lucinda gone so wrong in her decision-making to give up on the best friend she ever had, the friend Jeanette had so wisely gained?

She walked across the small cabin room and put her arm around Jeanette's tall willowy frame. "I do love you here. Thanks for all your help."

Jeanette stopped stirring the stew and pulled the wooden spoon out. She pushed the pot to the coolest edge of the stove and plunked on the lid. "Well, that's good to hear." She leaned her head down to touch the top of Lucinda's curly hair.

"And Joseph's not my man, and you're not all right."

"What?" Lucinda could not help the smile that spread across her lips. "You and Joseph aren't courting?"

"Let's sit. I'll tell you my story if you tell me the truth about Nat. Deal?"

Crazy as it was, relief spread through her body at the thought of being honest and finding out whatever possessed the two of them to pretend they were courting.

"You first," Lucinda said as she picked up Samuel from a blanket on the floor and slid into the nearby rocker.

"Not a chance." Jeanette laughed. Her large eyes looked down at Lucinda, and her glasses slid to the tip of her nose. She pushed them back into place as she sat on the wooden bench across from her. "One too many times of being outsmarted by my conniving younger sister and I've learned. I get what I want first."

Lucinda smiled at the good memories, but the smile quickly faded.

"How about I tell you what I think I know," said Jeanette, "and you can correct me if I'm wrong."

Lucinda lifted her chin. She met Jeanette's gaze full on.

"Do you know where Joseph has disappeared to each afternoon?" Jeanette asked.

"I haven't been keeping tabs on his coming and goings."

"Oh, but you have." Jeanette gave a knowing nod. "But never mind that. Joseph's been riding into town to spy on your husband. And what a—oh, don't even get me going, or I'll spew words no good Christian woman should ever speak. Sorry to be the one to tell you, but your husband is a two-timing, or should I say three-timing—rat. He has a thing going on with a young girl named Bella Latchum. Do you know the family?"

"I've only ever been to town once."

"He's playing with fire because Bella is the daughter of Marcellus Latchum, the cattle baron in these parts, and he has more money and power than you can imagine. If Bella's daddy catches wind, there'll be nowhere your Nat can go to outrun him. And he's known for his hard hand. Men who have crossed him have been known to mysteriously vanish."

"You know for a fact that Nat's cheating on me?"

"I think you know that, too." Jeanette's voice softened. "Correct?"

Lucinda lowered her eyes to her child. "I've suspected." She rose from the chair and placed Samuel in his bassinet. It took every bit of courage she had to return to her chair and the conversation. "Go on." She flicked her hand as if the news didn't faze her.

"Then there's an older woman. Widow Nita LaSalle. She is loaded and is keeping him comfortable most nights. And rumors circulate that he's also been with the store owner's daughter, Rebecca Witts, and the young Louisa Hess, who was decidedly pregnant out of wedlock one minute and mysteriously miscarried the next…after a visit to a woman named Madame Dovel. She's apparently a good friend of Nat's and gets rid of—oh, it's all too despicable to say, but the townsfolk are only too happy to talk. Instead of Nat Weitzel, they call him Nat the weasel."

"Enough." Lucinda's hand shot up. Her heart palpitated like a jack rabbit inside her chest. She was sure Jeanette could hear it.

"I made the biggest mistake of my life marrying that man." She stood and paced the floor, her fists clenching tight. "I hate him, Jeanette." She gritted her teeth. "I hate him with everything that is within me."

"So why won't you come home with us?"

"He's threatened to hunt me down and kill both me and the baby. But first, he said he'll light a match to Auntie and Uncle's house in the dead of night if he ever comes home and I'm not here. He said he had a wife and child before and they're dead. And I believe him."

Jeanette gasped. She popped up from the bench and threw her arms around Lucinda.

Lucinda rose and tears poured from her eyes. Guttural sobs worked their way up from deep within. She couldn't stop. All the sorrow she had bottled up for months now poured out. Freely. Frighteningly. Furiously.

"I'm so sorry." Jeanette stroked her hair and hugged her close until she quieted.

"I have to stay. How can I risk—?"

"Shh. It'll be all right. We figured he'd threatened you, and we have a plan."

"We?"

"Joseph, Uncle John, Aunt May, and I. We have a plan."

"All of you are in on this?"

"The day we arrived and saw the carnage, God birthed a plan. We're not going to tell you any details, just in case Nat comes home before we're ready to implement. Or if he catches on that we're gathering information. This way you know nothing. Also, Joseph has been sleeping outside your door every night just in case he returns. Nat will never have the opportunity to hurt you again."

Lucinda could not hold back the tears of relief that spilled in rivulets down her cheeks.

"And you and Joseph?"

"Have never been more than friends and two people who love you with all our hearts."

Lucinda looked up at Jeanette, who wore a smile and had never looked more beautiful. "You're kindness to the core."

"And so is Joseph. I couldn't have done this without him."

"I sure messed that one up, didn't I?"

"He loves you, Lucinda. I know he does. He hasn't had eyes for anyone, though many a girl has tried."

"Then why the ruse between the two of you?"

"We talked about the possibility of having to pretend we were a couple so that Nat would not suspect anything while Joseph poked around. But when Joseph grabbed me that first day without Nat around, I was most curious. It was his defense against the fact you said you loved *him* with all your heart. I suspected you were talking about your baby. He thought you meant Nat."

"You've always been the perceptive one."

"Joseph is focussing on your safety and Sammy's, but truthfully, I believe he still loves you."

"It's too late. I've ruined everything." Lucinda shook her head. She was responsible. She'd made bad choices from the beginning. Maybe if she had tried harder like Nat kept telling her, been a better wife...

No, she was not fit for anyone, especially not one as kind and respectable as Joseph.

~

*J*oseph found the pain of being in Lucinda's presence everyday excruciating, but he wasn't going to leave the farm animals to her care on top of all the other work she had to do. He kept reminding himself that the goal of getting her and the baby to safety was worth every moment of torture. All was falling smoothly into place. God was with them.

He stabbed at the haystack with the pitchfork and imagined using it on Nat. A smile split free as he lifted a large bundle of hay into the cow's feeding trough.

"What are you smiling about, Joseph Daniel Manning?"

He jumped at the sound of Lucinda's voice, and she laughed. "Got you."

The old game they used to play, seeing who could startle the other, came flooding back. "You really want to start that? I always got you at least two to one." He lifted another stack of hay, unable to look at her without thinking thoughts one should not have about a married woman. Even the marriage she currently had.

"Jeanette told me you've been following Nat and...what you learned. I guess I knew in my heart, just didn't want to believe it."

He turned toward her and leaned the pitchfork against the barn wall. "If I could arrange a clean break where everyone is safe, a break that includes a divorce, would you want that?"

She did not hesitate. "Absolutely. I won't marry again, but to be free of him would be heaven."

His heart dropped.

"I take responsibility. You all tried to warn me." Her eyes were pinned to the knotty floorboards.

He took a step closer.

"But if I could do it all over again—"

He was now within reach. He could haul her into his arms and do what he'd been dreaming of, but she was married, and God had not sent him here to confuse an already tortured soul.

"It's not your fault," he said.

She looked up at him with her wide hazel eyes. A shaft of sunlight poured through a knothole, haloing her copper curls. He almost forgot himself.

"Oh, but it is. I was headstrong and—"

"Shh." He lifted a hand to touch her face but then dropped it. "No one deserves abuse."

She touched his arm, and a jolt of heat shot through his body. Everything within him longed to give in to the temptation. His body objected with vigor when he stepped back.

"I better go," he said, turning swiftly. "All the animals have been taken care of, and I have to ride into town." He walked out of the barn without looking back.

Marching across the field to May and John's, he berated himself. What was wrong with him. She was a married woman, and a damaged one at that. Had he no sense? His temptation was so inappropriate.

But you resisted. You fled. I am pleased.

Oh God, she couldn't begin to understand what even a touch does. She's never felt for me what I have for her.

He raced into John's barn, saddled his horse, and lit out. Miles down the road after a good gallop, he slowed his steed. With the gentle sway of horse and saddle, his mind wandered back to that day in the orchard...

She had raised tear-drenched eyes to meet his. "It's too late— too late."

He had not understood what she meant by it being too late...

pregnant and trapped into marriage, but when he did, oh how he wished he had followed his intuition and did what the Spirit of God nudged. He should've gone after her and begged her to marry him and told her he would love any child of hers. He should've fought for her. Instead, he had listened to his pa and if he was truly honest, he'd let his disappointment in her and the anger he felt fuel the day.

The jostle of his saddle and the thickening of houses reminded him of what lay ahead. He best keep his mind focused on the present, not off in what could've been.

CHAPTER 13

*J*oseph sat across the room in the personal library of one of the most influential men in the area, feeling nothing but complete calm. God was with him. He could feel the presence of peace.

Marcellus Latchum, a hulk of a man, stretched out his long legs and shifted in his oversized chair. He took a long pull on his pipe and slowly pushed out tendrils of smoke that curled into the room. The acrid smell permeated the fibers of the cotton covering the chair Joseph sat in, and probably even the paper of each book on the shelves.

Marcellus set the pipe on the stand beside him and fingered his dark walrus mustache. "So, you're telling me a married man has been seen with my daughter."

"Yes, sir."

"Do you have any idea what I could do to you for sullying my daughter's reputation?"

"Yes, sir, I do. But I tell no lie, nor has this information been passed on to others."

"Why are you here? What do you want?"

"I want you to know so that you can protect your daughter

from further harm. The woman Nat is married to is an old childhood friend of mine, and she's suffered great abuse at his hand."

"Abuse?"

"You should see her bruises and scars. He's made all kinds of threats to keep her silent."

"Why should I believe you?" The big man lurched to his feet. Joseph swallowed hard against the knot in his throat. But Marcellus walked past him to the door of his study and swung it wide open.

"Tom, find my daughter and bring her to me directly."

"Yes, sir."

Marcellus slammed the door and walked back to his desk. He stood with his back to Joseph and stared into the bookcase.

"Sir…"

He whirled around. "Not one more word until I talk to my daughter."

Joseph bit back his words. What if his daughter lied? She was bound to. Who would Marcellus believe?

A quick rap on the door warned a moment before it opened, and a petite brunette waltzed in with a pretty smile on her face.

"Sit." Her father barked out the order. Her eyes traveled quickly between the two men as she dropped into the chair beside Joseph.

"This man has made some heavy allegations concerning your behavior. For verification, he's going to tell you about a time, a place, a moment you think no one else knows anything about."

Joseph had no idea this would be sprung on him. He cleared his throat. "You went on a horse ride with a man named Nat to a glen in the woods on your father's property, the one with the little brook running through. You were wearing a blue dress that day. He laid a blanket down, and you joined him. That's when I left. That man is married to my best friend. He has a baby at home."

Joseph watched her face whiten with each word as he spoke. She popped up from the chair. "Daddy, I didn't mean for it to go that far. I thought we'd just kiss, but...but..." Tears filled her eyes. "I told him to stop, but he..." She turned toward Joseph. "Didn't you hear my screams? Why didn't you help me?"

Joseph lifted his hands in surrender. "I swear, miss, I didn't hear anything. I rode away. But are you saying he... he raped—?"

"Enough," Marcellus thundered. He slammed his hands on his desk and stood, his body almost coming over the desk.

Joseph's head was reeling. Had Nat done the same to Lucinda?

"Daddy, I swear I didn't know Nat was married or I wouldn't have gone with him. I wish... I haven't seen him since that horrible day." She crumbled in her chair, her head forward, sobbing into her hands. "I'm so ashamed. He said if I say anything, he'll burn our house down with all of us in it."

Marcellus' hands clenched and unclenched. His face radiated rage.

"Bella, go to your room and stay there until I come for you." She took one glance at his menacing look and ran out of the room, slamming the door behind her.

"That...that swine raped her. I want to break every bone in his body." Marcellus slammed his fist so hard on his desk, he split his knuckles and blood oozed out. "You'll not repeat this to anyone. Do I have your word?" He pulled out his handkerchief from his pocket and swiped at the oozing flow on his hand.

The thrum of blood in Joseph's ears kept in beat with his racing heart, but he couldn't stop now.

"I have one more visit to make. It's necessary your daughter's name be brought into that conversation."

"What?" Marcellus came out from behind his desk. "You dare to defy me?"

"I need him stopped, sir." Joseph kept his voice steady and

strong.

Marcellus leaned his large frame against his desk. "I admire your guts, but you're not speaking a word of this to anyone. Tell me how I can help. I owe you at least that much."

Joseph let out the breath he had been holding. "Do you know the widow Nita LaSalle?"

"Her late husband and I used to be good friends. She's still friends with my wife."

"Nita LaSalle is another woman Nat is involved with. In fact, she's housed him for the past month and pays for his drinking habit as well as many other conveniences. I want her to know that Nat is married and that he's having a relationship with your daughter so she no longer helps him."

"My daughter's name will not be brought into this. I'll speak to Nita myself, and I'll let her know Nat is married and has been seen with other women. She'll trust my word. This Nat character is about to become a very unlucky man."

"As much as I hate what he has done, I won't be an accomplice to murder."

Marcellus was silent for one long moment, running his fingers over his mustache.

"I admit, it will take everything I have not to send out my men to crush his skull, but I can compromise and find my revenge in more creative ways—where the torture lives on. Besides, I stay out of jail that way."

"I don't want to know the details," Joseph said. "But if I could ask one favor?"

"You can ask."

"His wife needs a clean break. Divorce papers signed. He's threatened to hunt her down and harm her and their baby as well as other family members if she leaves. I need to be sure Nat is never in this valley again and I think you're just the man who can ensure that."

Marcellus leaned forward and extended his hand. "I'll

personally get those papers to you. And I'll run that scoundrel clear out of Virginia."

Joseph stood and shook the man's hand. "I intend to take my friend back to her home in Lacey Spring, and the last thing she needs is the trauma of him showing up there or hurting any of her kin."

"I'll personally arrange Nat's escort and make sure he understands he's a dead man if he returns to this state. My trusty hunting knife will make certain that no woman will look twice at him from now on."

Joseph held up his hand. "Sir, I don't want to know—"

"I'm a man of my word. And I thank you for protecting my daughter's honor the way you have." Marcellus walked beside him as Joseph headed for the door. He slapped him on the back. "You let me know if there's ever anything else you need. You hear?"

Joseph nodded. "Thank you, sir."

"What?" Lucinda asked.

Joseph stood in front of her with an envelope in his hand. Jeanette stood behind him smiling. She rarely smiled. Something was up. Lucinda took the envelope from Joseph's hand and pulled out a document. Could this be true?

"You're free to go, live, love whoever you want," Jeanette said. "You're free of him."

Lucinda's hands shook as she looked at Nat's scrawling signature at the bottom. She never dreamed that this day would ever be possible. How could it be? Where was Nat? How was she safe from him? But they were both smiling at her, so it must be so.

"Am I truly safe to take Sammy home to Ma and Pa?"

"Yes, Lucinda." Joseph's crooked smile was like an embrace,

warmth flowing to her, over her, through her. "You're safe now. Nat's been taken care of, and we have time on the journey home to explain how God worked out every detail, including an anonymous gift to pay off all the bills Nat racked up at the General Mercantile."

Jeanette hooked her arm around Lucinda's shoulders. "Come. Aunt May has a celebration farewell supper planned for you tonight."

Joseph stepped in front of Lucinda. "You do want to go back to Lacey Spring, don't you?"

She looked into his soft blue eyes, so full of hope, and gulped back the knot of emotion in her throat. She wanted to hug him but dared not. "This place has far too many bad memories."

"Good memories are all the future holds." Joseph's eyes locked with hers. He said the words as if he were personally going to ensure their truth.

"Good," Jeanette said, "because Uncle John knows a family that needs a home, and this time the man knows how to farm. He's willing to pay off what you owe Katherine for the build too."

Lucinda had to drag herself away from the intensity of Joseph's blue eyes in order to concentrate on what Jeanette was saying. "They've been so good to me when all I've been is a drain."

"Don't you worry about that. They love you. Now let's go celebrate."

Lucinda lifted Sammy from a blanket on the floor, where he kicked his chubby legs and chewed on a wooden rattle. She whirled him around in circles, and laughter spilled out for the first time in months. "We're going home, Pumpkin. We're going home. To a lovely place where there is safety and warmth and oh, so much love."

She blew bubbles on his tummy, and Samuel giggled. Jeanette and Joseph were smiling at her. She held out her free arm, and they closed in. The three of them hugged, but all she could concentrate on was the feel of one man's strong, kind arms wrapped around her and the smell of his familiar woodsy scent.

"How will I ever thank you?" She meant the words for both of them, but somewhere in the hug, Jeanette had pulled away.

"By being happy." He stared down into her eyes.

Jeanette cleared her throat. "Hate to interrupt, but Aunt May is going to kill me if I don't get you over there soon."

"Give me five minutes to change out of this old rag." Lucinda pointed to her worn day dress. "I think I have something a little better for a celebration supper."

Joseph took Samuel and lifted him in the air.

Samuel clapped his pudgy, dimpled hands each time he was brought down.

Jeanette raised her eyebrows, and Lucinda smiled. She could have stood there watching them all day. Instead, she went into her bedroom and closed the door. Nat had rarely held his child, and never had he stopped to play. A sadness, a sorrow, a deep regret at who Samuel had for a father welled up. She tried to push back the darkness, but it crept in. She was responsible. She had married the wrong man, a man incapable of love. A man far darker and colder on the inside than she could have ever imagined.

～

A warm breeze carried the fragrance of wild roses, and the sky above arched brilliant blue as the first hint of summer graced the valley. Yet, Joseph had to work hard at keeping the buggy on the road ahead and not feast his eyes on Lucinda. His beautiful friend with copper curls, wide autumn eyes, and cinnamon-toned freckles that kissed the tip of her nose was coming home, and he could not be happier.

He didn't care that some would see her history as tainted. He loved her. But he was not fool enough to jump in yet. She needed time to heal. The only thing he would not do was repeat the mistake of his past. He would make his intentions clear that, down the road when she was ready, he wanted to marry her.

Pa would be sure to balk. He still went on about Esther and what a fine bride she would make. But Joseph was prepared to fight for Lucinda. It made sense to him why he had never lost his feelings for her, and he wasn't going to waste this second chance at happiness.

Jeanette jumped from the back of the wagon the minute they pulled to a stop at the farmhouse. "Give me Samuel and I'll go introduce him to his grandparents." She held out her hands, and Lucinda handed him down. "You two need a few minutes to talk before Joseph heads home. The barn will afford a little privacy." Her eyebrows danced up and down. "Thanks again, Joseph, for all you did in helping to bring my sister home. I shall forever be grateful."

Joseph could feel the heat creep up his neck. Why had he confided in Jeanette? She was far too obvious.

He rolled the wagon into the barn. Going from the sunlight into the shaded dark felt intimate.

"What was that all about? Ma is going to come apart at the seams if I don't get in there fast." She turned to hop down, and he touched her arm.

"Give me one moment."

She turned wide eyes his way.

"I've erred in the past by not making my intentions clear. I intend to court you, Lucinda."

"I can't even think of that right now, if ever."

"I don't expect anything from you. I want to respect whatever time it takes for you to heal, but I just want you to know my heart and my intentions. I've been quiet for far too long."

Her beautiful hazel eyes filled with tears.

He squeezed her hand. "What is it?"

"I'm broken so much more than you know. I'm not the woman for you. I ruined everything the day I took up with Nat."

"No, don't—"

"Please, don't make this harder than it need be. I shall always be grateful to you for rescuing me, and I shall treasure your friendship."

He raised his arm to put it around her shoulders, and she flinched.

"Whoa." He held up both his hands. "I was only trying to comfort you."

"I'm sorry. It's not you."

His hand ran behind the back of his neck and he ground his teeth. What had that animal done to her to make her flinch at a simple hug? "If I weren't a Christian, I swear I'd—"

"Now you understand."

"I understand only one thing." He looked deep into her eyes and brushed a whisper of a kiss on her brow. "It is far more than friendship I desire," he said with all the tenderness he could muster. "I never again want you to mistake my patience for friendship. I'll wait as long as it takes, but I want to marry you." He placed a chaste kiss on her cheek.

"No." She shook her head.

"Lucinda, I can't help loving—"

She stifled his words with her lips and kissed him with an intensity that made every nerve in his body tingle with aware-ness. Then she ripped away and jumped from the wagon. "That was a good-bye kiss. You deserve someone far better than me." She had let her hair down during the ride and her auburn curls flowed behind her as she ran out of the barn.

A groan of despair slipped out. To wait patiently was his only option. Despite her words, that kiss held a whole lot of fire and a whole lot of hope.

CHAPTER 14

July 1875

*T*he soft mews of Samuel sucking his thumb slowly awakened Lucinda to another day. She stretched upon her bed and looked over to his crib and smiled. How good it felt to be safe. To not dread that she would do something or say something that would ignite into an explosion of horror. To know that Nat would never again stand over Samuel's bassinet and make threats filled her with a peace she had not experienced in a long time.

I do not feel worthy, God, but I'm so thankful. She whispered the words into the heavens, pulled her body from the bed, and padded to the window. From her upstairs perch, she could see her sister Katherine and Colby's large house in the distance. The fingers of dawn fanned out, draping the valley in a mysterious glow of mist and dancing sunbeams. She was content to watch the liquid gold scatter the darkness, much like Jeanette and Joseph had done for her.

It had been three weeks since she'd said good-bye to Joseph in the barn. She had purposely avoided church for fear she would run into him and feel way too much. She didn't deserve the goodness of Joseph, nor God for that matter. Best not to get too close to either of them.

Nat's words crowded in. *This is your fault. Your sass drove me to shutting you up.* She did have a sharp tongue. How many times had she hurt Jeanette and others with her sarcastic attitude and hurtful words?

At Samuel's soft cry, she turned from the window. Her only purpose left in life was to be the best mother to her little baby as she could possibly be. Lord knew, with whatever they did to her when she had blacked out and all that bleeding, the chances of her having another child were surely next to impossible. Her cycles had become increasingly scarce. She was washed up, used up, and damaged beyond repair.

She nuzzled her son close. After changing his diaper, she laid back down on her bed and pulled him close to nurse. He was a good feeder and such a happy baby. How could Nat have turned his back on such a beautiful gift? She listened to the soft sucking sounds of her content child. "Mama loves you more than life itself." She kissed the baby's feather soft curls on top of his head.

If only she had chosen well, how different her life would be today. But it was all too late—the damage done to her body, to her mind, and the fact she had another man's child. No. Joseph deserved a whole lot better than a divorcee. It didn't matter what his intentions were. She was going to keep her distance. And since he worked his father's farm many miles away, all she had to do was make sure she didn't show up at church on Sunday, and she would successfully avoid him.

"It's your fault kissing me like you did…no man could withstand…"

When would Nat's voice disappear for good? But he was right. Hadn't she kissed Joseph in the barn the same way, ever the terrible temptress? She was the one with the problem. Joseph needed to stay away from her.

But oh, Joseph's kiss, each one she should not have indulged in. He made her heartbeat skip and bubble, like water in a swift-running brook, rippling and flowing in directions she never thought possible. Directions she had to control in order to learn from her mistakes, in order to make sure a good man like Joseph got the kind of woman he deserved.

∾

"*B*ut, Ma, I need to make a living," Lucinda insisted. She punched down the dough ball with added energy and refloured the counter surface. She had to make her mother understand. This past year had changed her. She was no longer a spoiled child, and she needed to prove she was capable of caring for Sammy.

Ma was having none of it. "Come September Jeanette will be doing a year of schooling in Richmond before she takes over teaching for Mrs. Beasley, and I'll need extra hands around here. You'll be a welcome addition."

Lucinda looked up from her work around the comfy farmhouse kitchen. It would be so easy to fall into the routine of letting others care for her. "I can't lean on you and Pa forever—"

"How are you going to work with a baby to care for? Your place is with your child, at least until he's older."

Lucinda's spirits sagged. "I don't want to be a burden." As if she weren't. Back home at seventeen with another mouth for her parents to feed.

Ma crossed the kitchen and placed an arm around her shoulder. "Pa and I are so thrilled to have you and Samuel safe in our home. You're not a burden, you're a joy. All that sass you used to have is plum gone." Ma chuckled as she gave one last squeeze.

"It was beaten out of me." The words were out before she could think. She slapped her hand over her mouth.

Ma's chuckle died on her lips. "I knew it. Neither Jeanette

nor Joseph would give much information, but I had a bad feeling."

"I'd rather not talk about it."

Ma's shoulders dropped, and she shook her head. "It's my fault. Pa didn't want you to marry that man, but I insisted. I thought..." She walked to the nearest chair and plopped her large frame down. Her hands tented over her protruding tummy as tears filled her eyes.

"It was my decision. I thought Nat loved me."

Lucinda went back to punching down the bread with more vigor than ever. Turned out she was unlovable, boring and useless, according to him. But she had gotten really good at making bread. She hadn't been able to voice her feelings, and she'd dared not cry and incite Nat's anger, but she could knead the bread dough.

"How about we change the subject?" Lucinda forced a smile. "I have an idea that could bring a bit of money in, but you'd have to share your kitchen."

Ma stood. "Anything that would make you happy."

"Everyone raves about my bread."

"Don't I know it. I swear I'm carting around another five pounds since you've been home." Ma jiggled her belly with both hands.

Lucinda laughed at Ma's rare antics. "I was thinking of making extra and taking it into the market once a week to sell."

"You're not only good at making bread, you're a real good cook. I heard Katherine is having a hard time finding help to replace Delilah. She's getting too old to go at the pace she's going, but the men working on the ranch need good hearty meals. You could go over in the afternoons and give help with supper in exchange for using that fine outdoor oven they have. Gracie and I will fight over who gets Samuel."

Lucinda smiled a real smile for the first time in weeks. "Ma, you're a genius. I'll head over directly and talk to Katherine before the opportunity is gone. Can I leave Sammy? He's having his afternoon nap."

"Of course." She moved close and bumped Lucinda with her generous hip. "Scat. I'll shape this dough into balls and get the buns in the oven when its time."

Lucinda dusted the flour off her hands and headed to the nearby basin to wash. She was out the door and down the well-beaten path to Katherine's house without another moment wasted. A surge of hope skipped through her heart. Who would've thought a year ago that she would be happy to get a job at her sister's house? Back then she'd dreamed of marrying well. She'd anticipated dinner parties, fancy dresses, and frivolous moments to wile away the days. She thought she'd have maids to cook the meals, not be begging for work to cook for others. How things had changed. Now, life without fear was a gift. Being able to watch her baby boy grow in a happy home brought a humble thankfulness. And the meaningful practice of hard work without the possibility of terror busting through her door was beyond peaceful.

She rapped on Katherine's door lightly, and it swung wide. Her sister waved her in. "Goodness, Lucinda. You don't have to knock. You're welcome to make yourself at home any old time. Come, we'll have a cup of tea." She swung her thick mane of black hair over her shoulder and headed down the hall toward the kitchen. Lucinda followed. A pang hit her heart when she looked at the sweeping staircase up to the many bedrooms and passed the opulent ballroom to the left where their wedding reception had been held. What a difference in lifestyle between them. She got the two-room farm cabin and the wife-beater husband, and Katherine—no, she would not feel sorry for herself. She only had herself to blame.

"I can't stay long," Lucinda said. "So, don't worry about the tea. Samuel is sleeping, but when he wakes up, he'll be hungry."

"I remember those days. Just before they get on solids, the feeding is constant."

"And he's going through a growing spurt right now." Lucinda rolled her eyes. "Don't want to leave Ma with a problem she can't solve."

They both laughed.

"It'll get easier, I promise. Jillian is a year old and eating most anything I mush up for her. And Sammy's what?"

"He'll be six months next week."

"Time to start him on solids any day now. Sit. The kettle is hot and tea will take but a moment." She poured steaming water into the teapot. "I need time to catch up with my sister, and Ma knows how to soothe even a hungry child."

"I've actually come to ask a favor."

"Ask away." Katherine set the honey, teapot, and a plate of sweets on the well-worn kitchen table. She poured them each a cup.

Lucinda slid onto a chair. The kitchen was large but homey. She looked around the room through the eyes of a potential cook.

"Still my favorite room," Katherine said. "No opulence here."

Lucinda nodded. "I was imagining working here."

Katherine's bright blue eyes popped wide, and Lucinda rushed on. "I need some way to provide for Samuel. Ma seemed to think maybe you need help in the kitchen. Much to my surprise, cooking is the one thing that comes naturally to me."

Katherine shook her head. "I can't have my sister working for me. That would not feel right."

"Would you rather I starve?"

"Ma and Pa would never let that happen."

"I'm responsible for the mess I'm in. Why should Ma and Pa be stuck—"

"How much do you need? I can give you whatever—"

"That's my point. I don't want a handout. I want to work.

And with Sammy so young, my options are slim. I was thinking I could work afternoons in trade for your outdoor oven. I want to make my sourdough bread to sell at the market on Saturdays."

"Oh heavens, Lucinda. You wouldn't have to double up the work selling bread. There's more than enough work here, but—"

"Please, Katherine."

Katherine took a tea biscuit and pushed the plate across the table to Lucinda. "I get that it's important to work and take care of yourself."

"Well then, do you have work for me or not?" Lucinda ignored the food. Her insides churned. She had to make Katherine understand. She needed to work. To stay busy. To earn her keep.

"If the truth be told, I need you more than you need me." Katherine looked to the back porch through the kitchen and lowered her voice. "Delilah's struggling to keep up these days, but she doesn't want to admit it. Every woman I hire to take over the lead role, Delilah inadvertently makes things so difficult they look for employment elsewhere." Katherine's eyes kept darting to the back door. "The ranch has grown so much, and we have more men than ever to feed. But, honestly, it's too much for her to handle. She's forgetting some of the essentials. And frankly, there's no such thing as two head cooks in one kitchen."

"I don't have to be the head anything, and I can work alongside Delilah. I'd find it an honor to learn from her, and I can pick up the loose ends without demeaning her role." The plan sparked a flicker of hope inside Lucinda. She would not have to rely on Ma and Pa for everything. She would be able to provide for her son.

"Would you consider working a full day?"

"That would be hard with Sammy and breast feeding—"

"Oh, but of course I assumed you would bring him. The nanny who helps with Seth and Jillian can attend to him as well."

"Really?" Lucinda couldn't believe the good that was coming into her life. She didn't feel worthy, so accustomed to waiting for the next thing to go wrong, not right.

"It would be fun for the cousins to grow up together. And you'll be right at hand when Sammy needs you."

"Oh my, yes," Lucinda said.

Katherine mentioned a weekly sum that made Lucinda's head swim. "I couldn't take that much."

Katherine laughed. "Trust me when I say, you'll earn every penny. Besides, this horse ranch is making far more money than we ever imagined."

Lucinda looked away from her sister's dancing blue eyes to mask the tears that sprang into hers. Their lives could not be more opposite. She jumped to her feet. "I best get back. But I'll be here first thing tomorrow."

CHAPTER 15

*J*oseph gazed from his perch upon his horse over the
rolling hills of wheat. Even in the pearl-gray light
of early morning he could see it would be a bumper
crop. His heart swelled with pride. Most of what he could see
was from the labour of his own back, his careful attention to
detail—the tilling of land, the sowing of the best seeds, the
hiring of just the right workers to help in the care of the crop.
How could God possibly be asking him to leave all this? Was
this unrest and conflict inside his head just another sad display
of his inability to let go of Lucinda, or was God truly speaking?

If she wanted even his friendship, she would've shown up at
church. But she was not there, clearly making a statement.
When she said good-bye after he'd bared his soul, she'd
meant it.

He spurred the horse's flanks and lit out across the pasture
to the hills in the distance. He needed a little speed to purge his
troubled mind and cool the heat at the thought of her. A rare
August morning free of the suffocating humidity and the wind
in his hair refreshed his body but did nothing for his tortured
soul. He reined in his steed and, with one lithe swing of his leg,

his boots hit the ground. The reins dropped, and his horse, as trained, lowered his head to munch on the grass.

Joseph found the nearest rock and sat overlooking the valley. He heard from God best out in nature and often as he worked the fields, but today his soul needed no distractions. The first touch of sunlight blushed gold on the eastern ridge of the Massanutten, and a Bible verse came to mind. *I will lift up my eyes unto the hills from whence cometh my help.*

"You know what I've been wrestling with, God, for weeks now. I need your wisdom to decipher clear direction." He spoke with his head lifted to the heavens above the ridge. "I want to be still and know that whatever decision I make is from You, not birthed out of my own desire."

He pulled off his cowboy hat. A slight breeze kicked up wisps of flattened hair. He ran his hand through the locks and waited. He was prepared to stay all day if he had to. He wanted God's peace in whatever direction he decided to go. The sun strengthened and his stomach growled for breakfast.

Go where I lead.

The word go clutched at his heart and squeezed. That meant leaving the land, his pa, and his brother.

You still love her.

"You know I do."

Go to her.

"Father, am I hearing right or is this just my yearning? And what about Pa? He needs—"

She needs you more.

He waited in stillness and praised the name of God. A peace washed over him. Then an urge to speak to the one person who could help make this possible.

He rose and ran to his horse. With a swing into the saddle and a flick of the reins, the hoofs of his horse were pounding up a trail of dust back to the farm.

He dismounted, knowing just where to find his brother. The

barn doors swung wide. Sure enough, there he was bent over his latest contraption.

"Nigel, I need to talk to you."

Nigel looked up. "Where have you been this morning? Pa was looking for you. And don't worry I'll get to my chores, I promise." His head went back down to his work.

"It's not about your chores. Besides I'm not your keeper."

"Since when? You're more task driven than Pa."

"Never mind that. I have the biggest ask of my life, and I need your help and your word that you will follow through."

Nigel stopped his tinkering and looked up, his brows knit together. "Why do I get the distinct feeling I'm not going to like what you're about to ask me?"

~

AUGUST 1875

"*I*f you leave, Joseph, I'll be forced to give the lead position and farm to your younger brother. I can't have him taking over your tasks and not give him his fair due."

"I've talked to Nigel, and he's willing to step up."

Pa's hand waved the words away. "Nigel. You know how that goes. He'll only be of help until the next hair-brained idea of his has him off on another tangent."

"All I need is a little time." Joseph looked over the top of his pa's head at the dust mites dancing in the sunlight pouring through the barn door. If dust could be made into a thing of beauty, surely a broken waif of a woman could be too.

"Planting and sowing don't allow time. And I'm tired. You know that. I just gave you the full reins, and this is what I get in return? You want to leave this farm to an old man and your brother with his head in the clouds?"

The two needs warred inside Joseph's head. Help his pa or

follow where he felt the Lord was leading. Both were honorable. But he couldn't be in two places at one time. He'd just have to trust that Nigel would step up as he promised. He was quite capable, though not enthusiastic about the task.

"How long are you thinking?" Pa scratched at his head as if he were contemplating the possibility.

"A year, maybe more."

"Do you have rocks in your head, boy?"

"I love her, and this won't be a quick heal. What Nat did to her is unspeakable. I have to woo her slowly."

"She's a divorced woman." Pa spat out the words. "That fact alone brings shame to our good family name, not to mention that she obviously can't keep a man happy."

"You know nothing of the circumstances. I've kept them private because they're none of your business, but there's good cause for—"

"For what? Running out on her man like my ma did? Leaving Pa and I to fend for ourselves when I was only seven."

The revelation gave him pause. Pa almost never mentioned his childhood. "I had no idea. You've never spoke of your ma."

He spat on the ground. "Because she's not worth my breath. That's why. Any woman who runs out on a marriage and hitches up with another is not worth the ground they walk on."

"Not all circumstances are the same."

"When Lucinda spurned you and married that reprobate who the whole valley knew was sleeping around, I knew what kind of woman she was."

"I've made mistakes. You've made mistakes."

"What she did is far more than a mistake. She was rebellious and immoral. Do you forget that she was pregnant before marrying the man?"

"Should that blunder define the rest of her life? And she's different than your ma. She did not leave her child. In fact, she was staying to protect him."

"What is wrong with you? Don't you have any pride? Do you really want to be father to someone else's kid? Not to mention what she put her parents through. It's downright disgraceful. Not the kind of woman I want for you." He shook his head.

"I feel God is telling me to do this."

"Oh, using God as an excuse. That's convenient. Your Ma would turn in her grave if she knew. Had I any inkling that giving you those weeks off would result in you bringing back the damaged goods and thinking—"

"Pa, stop." Joseph shook his head. He had never been more disappointed in his pa than he was in that minute. Pa's rant ripped his heart open, for he was not the only one who would think that way. "I've never heard you speak so unkindly. You've taught me to love God and to love and forgive people."

"Forgive, yes. But pick up the leftovers where some other man has left off, now that's a whole different story. No. I won't make this easy. If you go, you forfeit your inheritance as the eldest of this farm. Your brother will have the opportunity to take over."

Joseph's gut lurched and fell. He loved working the land, and he was a darn good farmer. He was in line to inherit one of the richest and most fertile pieces of land in the valley. He had once had such wonderful dreams of marrying Lucinda and bringing her here. Building their own home. Raising their kids. Doing what he was born to do, farm the land and give the love of his life everything her heart desired. But then Nat had come along.

"You're saying that, if I leave now, you won't take me back onto this farm?"

"You've always been a good son." Pa took off his hat and ran a hand through his thick bushy hair. "And I'll always take you back. But the farm will no longer be yours. You'll work for your brother under his lead for the rest of your life. He'll inherit what was meant to be yours."

Joseph dropped his head and kicked the dust at his feet. The farm was a huge price to pay, and giving it up a leap of faith. He didn't even know if he could win Lucinda's heart. And would he find work somewhere close enough to interact with her and have a chance?

If he did win her over, it sounded like his pa would never accept her, and he wouldn't have a home to bring her to. Why couldn't his sorry heart move on? There were plenty of pretty girls vying for his attention. Why did he feel God nudging him to go, to leave everything and step out in faith?

Joseph lifted his head and squared his shoulders. "I'm sorry to hear that, Pa. I love and respect you more than I can say. I love this land, and I was born to farm, but I have to obey what God calls me to do first and foremost. I'm leaving."

~

*L*ucinda laughed at Delilah. "See, I told you I could master your sour dough recipe." She slid in close to the old woman and gave her a nudge with her hip. Her flour-covered hands prevented her from hugging.

"You did. You did. Why, I be thinking you can learn most anything in the kitchen. Not like Katherine. Nope, she's hopeless." Delilah's cheeks jiggled while she laughed. "But don't tell her I said that."

Lucinda wiped the flour onto her apron. "I love working with you. In the past few weeks, you've taught me so much."

"And you, girl, are a natural. I don't pass down my secrets to just anyone, but I have a feeling you're going to get every last one."

Lucinda stopped working the dough and looked into Delilah's rich black eyes. Her brightly colored checkered turban highlighted her round dark cheeks. A surge of gratitude welled up. "I'm honored you've allowed me to work alongside you. I need to make a living, and cooking doesn't even feel like work to me."

"You've been nothing but a joy. Not like those silly town girls who came in here thinking they had nothing to learn." Delilah harrumphed. "I can't abide such pride. Had to take them down a button-hole or two, and then they up and left."

Lucinda smiled. "I'm quite glad they didn't work out. Their loss is my gain. Thank you for this opportunity."

"No need to thank me. I'm tickled pink to have someone who knows how to work by my side. These rickety old bones are not what they used to be."

"I've made so many mistakes in this past year, but this is not one of them." Lucinda worked the dough into nice sized loaves.

"Don't you be looking back, girl. The good Lord forgives all and gives us the gift of each new day to live better than the one before."

Lucinda buttoned her lip. If Delilah knew her shame, she wouldn't be so generous in her assumptions. Attracted to a man as dark as the devil himself and blind to the kindest man alive, Lucinda did not qualify for a fresh start. Rebellion and head-strong reaped its own reward, and she couldn't shake the feeling she deserved every terrible thing that happened.

"I know I'm preachin' what I didn't do so well these past months." Delilah laughed. "I've been sorely tested with the useless help I've had to put up with. Had to get down on these old knees a time or two and repent of my harsh tongue." She nodded her head. "Yes'um, I did."

"I used to be that way, speaking before I gave thought—"

"You sure don't do that anymore. Why, you've been nothing but a pleasure."

Lucinda dared not admit how she came to the discipline of watching every word that came out of her mouth.

CHAPTER 16

"*J*'d be honored, Jeb." Joseph reached out to Lucinda's Pa and gave a hearty handshake. Corn stalks as high as they were swayed in the late afternoon breeze as if they were dancing in agreement. "Looks like a bumper crop. Glad I'll be around for the harvest."

"The Lord has indeed blessed us."

"You must be proud of the fruit from your labor."

"Katherine and Colby have a very successful ranch here, and the farm, which I look after, is but a drop in the bucket. Keeps my head from getting too big."

Joshua thought of the fields ripe for harvest that he had left behind. It had taken every bit of obedience he possessed to do as he felt God was leading. Bringing in the crop was the most rewarding part, not to mention the guilt he felt at seeing Pa's long face. Before he left, he spent hours arranging every detail, right down to notes for Pa and Nigel to follow. He prayed God would bless them and things would run smoothly.

Jeb slapped him on the back. "I've always liked you, son. I

think we'll work just dandy together. But how does your pa feel losing his hardest worker and lead man?"

No one knew the half of it. Joseph had just walked away from his life dream, and his pa was sour to say the least.

"Nigel will step into the lead role."

"Would've been easier with the farming if I'd had a quiver of boys instead of girls." Jeb chuckled. "But I wouldn't trade a one. They've been my joy. But I've always wondered…" A faraway look crossed over his face. "What it would've been like to have my twin sons working alongside me." His eyes darkened with pain. "The loss from that blasted war will always leave a hole." He put a hand to his heart.

"I'm so sorry." Even without death, circumstances could kick the life out of people. Lucinda and all she had suffered came to mind. He had to stop second guessing his decision and lamenting his loss. She was worth more than a thousand acres of land.

Sadness simmered around the edges of Jeb's mouth, stealing his usual smile. "Never mind that." He dug his shovel into the rich black earth. "God is good. I was just praying for a good lead, and along you come with all the work of training done. I know your pa and his fine reputation as a farmer. He's going to miss you."

"He will."

"I was going to ask why, but I'm guessing this has something to do with my redhaired daughter."

"It does." Joseph's heartbeat sped into a gallop at the mention of Lucinda. "I won't lie to you. I've loved that girl from the moment I met her, and I thought I lost her for good when Nat came on the scene. But I have a second chance—"

"She's not herself, son."

"I know."

"It's like he kicked the spark and spice right out of my little girl." Jeb's hands fisted. "I never wanted them to get married, but when…"

"She was pregnant. I know."

"You knew?"

"Not much concerning her escapes me."

"Other's will think you a fool."

"I'm not bothered by what others think. I care only what my good Lord thinks, and He sent me."

Jeb dropped the shovel and threw his arms around Joseph. "That's all I need to hear. You have no idea the hours I've prayed for that girl." He pulled back. "Only God truly knows what she's been through. You'll have to be patient with her."

"I intend to."

"I don't much like divorce, but sometimes it's a welcome necessity. Especially seeing how she came back, so sad, so broken. I shall regret…"

Joseph laid his hand on Jeb's arm. "Sir. We have to believe that God can heal and restore."

Jeb looked into Joseph's eyes. "I shall indeed enjoy working with you. Now, come in for the evening meal." He clapped him on the back, and the two of them walked between the corn rows toward the house. "I'll set up your lodging with the rest of Colby's crew. The ranch and farm hands bunk and eat together. We're all one big happy family. And guess who just happens to be the cook and serves the meals?"

Joseph looked at the back of the wiry man ahead of him. A grin pulled at his lips at the thought of seeing Lucinda every day.

"Yup. You'll have a lot of access to my fine little girl. As do the other cowboys. I've already heard their comments. Don't be as slow at the game as you've been in the past." Jeb chuckled.

Joseph was glad Jeb wasn't looking at him. The sheer heat blazing across his face proved that the comment stung. He had just boldly declared he didn't care what others thought, but down deep there was a stab of guilt. Maybe if he hadn't been so slow, he could have saved her.

"She's home tonight. Saturday and Sundays are her days off. I'd suggest you use those days to your advantage as well."

Joseph's hands turned clammy, and he wiped them on his pants. He hadn't been prepared to both get a job on the farm and a chance to see Lucinda. Everything was falling into place. Why had he wrestled with God for so many weeks?

He rubbed the dust from his boots on the porch rug and entered the house he had visited many times over the years. Today, it felt different. Like God Himself was smiling. He hung his cowboy hat on the hook and lifted his flattened hair with his fingers. With squared shoulders, he brought his stocky frame to full height. Few were as handsome as Nat, but now that he was aware of the attention he received from the women at church, his confidence was boosted.

Jeb held his finger to his mouth to Doris and Jeanette as they entered the kitchen and cocked his head in Joseph's direction. The game was on. Doris smiled at Joseph and pointed to the chair at the end of the table.

Lucinda had her back to them, cutting a fresh loaf of bread. She picked up a spoon and stirred the pot that bubbled.

Joseph slid onto the chair Jeb had indicated, and Doris winked at him as she set the table.

"Looks like we're ready," Lucinda said. "Ma, can you bring the plates over, and I'll serve up. And Jeanette, can you yell up the stairs to Gracie."

Joseph could not contain his smile. How many times had they played this game over the years? He would sit in the parlor or at the kitchen table or lounge against the hall wall outside her bedroom until she flounced in, giving him the opportunity to surprise her. He could not even remember when this game started, but her Pa had been the instigator years earlier. Both father and daughter shared a penchant for playing pranks on the other.

Gracie bounded in with a smirk on her face. Jeanette must have filled her in.

"Ma, where are those plates?" Lucinda turned around with the wooden spoon in her hand. When she saw Joseph she jumped and dropped the spoon. Without saying a word, she burst into tears and ran out.

The screen door slammed.

Joseph and Jeb stood. Deep crevices furrowed Jeb's brow. He held out his hands and shook his head. "I don't understand. We've played this game a hundred times."

"I'll get her," Joseph said. "I bet we triggered something…" He held off from finishing his sentence because Gracie's eyes were as big as a full moon in an October sky.

Joseph found her at the edge of the orchard weeping. He called out her name so she was sure to hear his approach. "Lucinda, I'm sorry." He stood right behind her but dared not wrap his arms around her, though every part of him craved to do so.

"Can you tell me what happened back there? Your pa was just playing that silly game we've played for years."

"I know." The words came out in a strangled whisper. "He… Nat would creep around. I'd think he was in town and suddenly he'd be right behind me. After dark was his favorite."

How dare he? Just one moment alone, man to man, was all Joseph needed. He'd show that guy what fear looked like.

"The bigger my fright, the better he liked it. Fear…he loved my fear… He did things to keep it going." Sobs wrenched out of her petite body, and she turned away. "Go. Please go," she said between sobs.

Joseph turned away but heard the Spirit whisper into his soul, prompting him to stay.

He stepped alongside her, pulled out his handkerchief, and

handed it to her. She took it and blew her nose and wiped her tears.

With one hand he gently touched her arm, so afraid to misstep. She didn't pull away but sank against his solid frame. He gathered her into his arms.

"What he did... I can't even speak of it." She hiccuped against his shoulders.

"Shh, you're safe now." He soothed a gentle hand up and down her back while his gut twisted in rage. Why did the thought of an eye for an eye sound like the only justice that made sense?

They stood that way for a long time. Her weeping subsided. The Spirit cradled them in peace.

You must forgive or you will not be able to help her.

Really, God? Right now, that's what you speak? How about I...I...

She pulled apart. "What will my family think? How can I explain?"

"You don't need to worry. They love you."

Her tear-washed green eyes looked up at him, and it took all he had not to tell her that he loved her too. But it was far too soon, and she was far too damaged, more than he'd imagined.

"Let's go eat that lovely meal you made. Your pa said you've become quite the cook. Helping out at the big house, are you?"

He offered his arm, and she placed her small hand in the crook. He noticed how petite her fingers were. How could any man hurt such a delicate flower? When they reached the porch, he turned her to face him. "Whatever you share with me, I won't tell a soul. You have my word."

She kept her eyes down.

With one finger, he gently lifted her chin. "You can trust me, and everyone needs someone to talk to."

She wouldn't meet his eyes. She stared at the stubble on his chin. "Good thing you're not around much. You have a way of making me tell things I never..." Her face turned a deep red.

He wrestled with sharing the truth after such an emotional bout, but he had to establish absolute trust. "I'll be working the fields alongside your pa starting first thing tomorrow."

"You'll be what?" Now her flashing green eyes met his with a combination of anger and what looked like apprehension.

"I'll be helping your Pa—"

"No!" She spat out the word.

"Yes." He kept his voice soft and level. He fought a grin at the way she stood, hands fisted, stubborn jaw raised, and fire dancing in her eyes. Now, that was the Lucinda he remembered.

When he matched her glare, she turned in a huff, ran up the steps, and slammed the door in his face. He stood on the porch scratching his head until Jeb came out and held open the door.

"Quite frankly, I'm glad to see some of her spunk back. That flat personality is not my girl." He waved Joseph in. "Come on. This is still my home, and I can invite who ever I like for a meal."

"I best be going."

"No, you best come in. The sooner she comes to terms with the fact you're going to be around, the better."

Joseph shifted on his feet.

"Come on, son. Seems the thought of having you around has got her into quite the dither. And in my books, that's a good thing. You're making my little girl feel again." He squeezed Joseph's shoulder as he stepped into the house.

"*P*a, what were you thinking hiring Joseph?" Lucinda paced back and forth in the parlor.

"He knows farming inside out, and he's one of the hardest workers I know. Why shouldn't I have hired him?"

"Because he…well he was…used to be a close friend, and I don't want him to get the wrong idea."

Lucinda looked over at her ma, sitting quietly on a chair. "Ma explain it to him. You understand how awkward this will be."

"Actually, I don't understand. Joseph will get no wrong idea if you make your wishes clear. He is a very respectful man." A slow smile of agreement passed between her parents. "Besides, your pa needs some good help out in the fields. Would you deny him that because you feel uncomfortable?"

Lucinda couldn't believe her ears. She hadn't slept all night and was hoping to make her parents understand. It was not going as planned.

"What are your wishes, dear? Maybe that's where the confusion lies." Ma said the words like she was looking right into Lucinda's soul.

"I'm not available to him or anyone else—ever."

"Well then, that's settled. You communicate that to Joseph, and the problem is solved." Ma slapped her hands on her legs and stood. "I've got chores aplenty and the day's a-wasting."

"Me too," echoed Pa.

"But…but…"

They turned and walked out of the room.

Lucinda nibbled at her baby finger's nail until it was a jagged mess. She could no longer avoid church and avoid Joseph. And he could not be closer, working the land with Pa and showing up at every meal. Life was complicated enough. She didn't need to see the man she should've married every day and be reminded of her foolishness.

Well, she would just have to put some starch in her spine and make her wishes crystal clear. She could see she was not going to get any help from her parents. Friends she and Joseph had always been, and friends they would stay. All this hugging and kissing and longing for more had to stop. His moving closer changed nothing. She was incapable of ever having a normal relationship again. If her outburst had not been a clear indication, then she didn't know what would be.

And why would he want her anyway? She'd seen the looks and the wide berth people took to avoid her when she went to town for supplies. Even the cowboys treated her differently, making advances they would not to a lady. There was no way she was subjecting Joseph to that and damaging his reputation.

CHAPTER 17

*L*ucinda knocked on Jeanette's bedroom door.

"Yes."

She poked her head in to see her sister in her traveling dress, straightening her hat. "Can I come in?"

Jeanette waved her in with one hand and fussed with the other. Hat pins dangled from her mouth as she worked to fix them in place.

"I wanted one last moment with you. I shall miss you more than I can say." Lucinda crossed the room and draped an arm around her sister's thin shoulders.

Jeanette took the pins out of her mouth and turned into the hug. "And I you." She pulled back and straightened her glasses, which had twisted on her nose.

"Seems so unfair. I finally appreciate you as the amazing person you are, and you're leaving me."

"I won't be gone forever. And having the opportunity to attend Richmond's finest academy for teachers, thanks to Grandma and Grandpa, is not something I can pass up. Lord knows, I'll never marry. If I can't have children..." Her voice softened, and her eyes misted. "I might as well teach them." She thumbed a tear from underneath her glasses.

Lucinda moved in for another hug, and Jeanette shook her head. "No, I said I wouldn't cry and you're not helping."

"All right. The faster you go, the faster you shall return. And who knows, maybe you'll find your prince charming in the big city."

Jeanette harrumphed. "Not likely. Look at me. But for these"—she pointed to her well-endowed bosom—"you'd never know I was a woman. I'm straight as a railroad beam. Pale as milkweed and taller than most men.

"More intelligent than most of them too," Lucinda said. "You need to stop pointing out things you find negative and accentuate the positive. You're the kindest, most caring individual I know."

"Intelligence and kindness are not what a man looks for to warm his bed. You and I both know that. Look at what Nat said about me. 'Ugly as a mud hole,' was one of his favorites."

"Are you really going to listen to anything that man said?"

"Are you?"

"What do you mean?"

"He changed you, Lucinda. You used to be confident, sassy and fun. Now you're…"

"I'm what?" Lucinda felt her chest tighten and a tremble take to her limbs. Just hearing Nat's name sent her back there.

"You're quiet, subdued…lost."

Lucinda dropped her gaze. She couldn't argue.

"How about we make a promise to each other?" Jeanette said. "I'll try to believe there's someone out there for me—most likely a blind man." She laughed at her own humor, but the smile did not reach her eyes. "And you promise that you'll find the old you and open your heart once again."

Lucinda creased the folds of her dress in her hands, then

smoothed out the crumpled mess. It was so much more than opening up her heart again, and that old innocent girl with stars in her eyes was lost forever. She no longer trusted herself, her decision-making processes, or her lovability. So much was in question. "I don't think I can make that promise."

"Then we understand each other. I know how hard it is to think differently of myself. Pain and suffering are cruel teachers, but teach us they do."

"I don't want you to give up hope." Lucinda took her hand. "You've lived a life that deserves nothing but blessing from God. I, on the other hand—"

"No one deserves to be abused." Jeanette got a fierce look in her eyes. "You set out to love him, did you not?"

"I chose wrong."

"We all make mistakes. Will you please try to understand what God's grace means?"

"If you'll try to understand that you're one of God's most beautiful creations, far more beautiful than I."

Jeanette gave a wobbly smile. "I'll work on that."

"All right then, I'll explore the meaning of grace."

What did grace mean anyway? If Jeanette knew the half, she wouldn't be throwing that word around as if it applied to her.

"Promise?" Jeanette's brown eyes peered over her glasses.

Lucinda looked square into her eyes. Anything to make her happy. "I promise." The minute those words were out of her mouth, she felt every bit the deceiver she had always been. She had lied to get alone with Nat. She had hidden her pregnancy until after they were married. She had lied a thousand times to her aunt and uncle to cover up the truth. And she was lying now. What a wicked woman. Would she ever change?

"And while you're at it, delve into what mercy means as well. They are quite different, you know, and thankfully, we receive both from our Heavenly Father.

Lucinda was really confused now. Weren't they the same thing? But what did it matter? They didn't apply to the likes of her. "Having faith in God has always been so much simpler for you than me."

"So says the woman who doesn't look like an unpainted barn door." Jeanette took one last look into the mirror, crinkled her nose at her reflection, and picked up her carpet bag. "Off to the big city I go. It scares the wits out of me."

They linked arms and headed down the hall. "You'll have Grandmother and Grandfather, and Amelia's family. And like you said, the school year will go fast."

"That's if I pass the Academy's rigorous exams."

Lucinda laughed. "There is little doubt. You could have just written the exam for the state certificate, but no, you chose the hardest route to becoming a teacher. When you were telling me they teach Latin, Greek, chemistry, and astronomy, your eyes lit up. Not my idea of a pleasant pastime."

~

*J*oseph hurried to the cook hall beside the outdoor kitchen. Jeb had told him that the ranch had gotten so big, they had to build a separate area to feed the gang. He slid onto a chair at the long table. The midday meal would be served shortly. He had learned to arrive a few minutes early so he could position himself where he could watch Lucinda coming and going.

He had been at the ranch for a month now and September was upon them. Still, she ignored his every attempt at conversation, and if he arrived at her house on the weekends, she disappeared up to her bedroom. Not exactly the close proximity he was hoping for. The ranch hands called her the ice maiden and had given up on the flirting he'd noticed in the beginning.

However, much to his irritation, they all liked to watch her serve. Who was he to talk? He was spellbound.

She entered from the side room off the long main hall, and most every eye turned in her direction. She didn't look up but carried a large salad their way. The canted sunlight streaming in from the window caught the swirls of auburn silk piled high. Every shade from cinnamon to copper danced upon her head. He had to inhale deeply to catch his breath.

"Why always the vegetables first, pretty lady," one cowhand teased. She placed the large salad on the table and exited without a word. "Seems that one is a might bit pricklier than she looks."

"Heard she was married but flew the coop. And she's got a kid, you know."

"That young thing, a mother already? What a shame," another said. "I'll keep my distance. My folks would be none too pleased at me bringing home a woman with another man's child."

It took all Joseph had to button his lip and not tell them to mind their own business.

They quieted as she brought in a couple baskets of her homemade buns and butter. The men dug in. "Best buns this side of the Alleghenies," one yelled. They laughed as they watched her retreating backside.

Joseph's fists clenched tight. Their teasing was harmless, and Lucinda would hate it if he interfered.

"One day I may have to melt that ice maiden behind the barn with one of my hot kisses."

Joseph was instantly on his feet. He lifted the cowboy from his chair by the scruff of his neck. "Show some respect." He plopped him back down real hard.

The room went quiet.

"I was only teasing, farmer."

"Keep that kind of teasing to yourself."

"What are you, her guardian?" another asked from across the table.

"I'm her friend and have been for many years."

"Friend, ha. I'd say you're sweet on the girl," said an older man. Heads all around the room bobbed.

"Got me there." As Joseph returned to his seat, everyone laughed but the young cowboy he had just manhandled. He leaned back on the bench with his arms folded on his chest. If a glare could kill, Joseph would be a goner.

Lucinda would not be pleased if she knew what had just transpired. Though glad she had not caught the exchange, he was not a bit sorry. He had drawn his line in the Shenandoah dirt. Every man working the ranch now knew his mind on the matter.

Her tiny arms weighted down with two large plates of roast beef, she hurried to the tables. He wanted to jump to her aid but balled his hands in his lap instead.

Then she brought a pot of steaming gravy.

"My new creation," she said. They all stopped their chatter and looked to the end of the table where she stood. "This is how you put it together." She opened the sliced bun and spread it on the plate. Next, came a generous amount of beef. Lastly, she ladled a scoop of gravy on top and held it up. "Beef on a bun."

"No spuds coming?" one said.

"We've practically ate all the buns already," another whined.

"There's plenty more buns. Now who wants to be the first to try?"

Joseph stood and sauntered on over. He held out his hand. "That looks like a mighty fine idea."

She flashed him a rare smile.

Numerous others chimed in. "I'll try it."

"Can you make me one?"

Before long, all Joseph could hear was the scrape of fork and knife on the plate and some satisfied grunts.

Joseph looked up from the delicious meal to find her staring at him. He winked, and she turned away. "Don't forget to eat the salad, boys, or there won't be any dessert."

Groans filled the room.

CHAPTER 18

LATE SEPTEMBER 1875

*J*oseph dug his spade into the last row of beets. He could get this stretch done before it was too dark if he pushed through. The rich Shenandoah soil did not disappoint. He pulled large beets free of the earth and shook the soil off. Harvesting the fruit and vegetables took up long hours, and often Joseph worked through the evening meal like he was tonight, taking advantage of every hour of daylight. He missed seeing Lucinda at mealtime, but she mostly ignored him, so it was not a big loss.

Had he heard God wrong? Shouldn't he have seen some progress by now? Even a glimmer of hope would be nice, but she was steadfast in her quest to ignore him, treating him like a distant stranger. How would he win her when she didn't even talk to him?

"Lord, what are you doing? Nothing is happening, and the patience I came with is wearing thin."

Be still and know that I am God.

That verse rankled. He hated to be told to be still when all he wanted was to act. If nothing was going to happen, he could be back home building his own farm, his own business, his own life, instead of working another man's field.

Jeb called to him from the edge of the field. "Call it a day, son. It's almost dark."

Joseph squinted into the gathering darkness. He straightened his aching back and pulled the shovel from the earth. Digging up carrots, potatoes, and turnips was backbreaking work, but they had a bumper crop for the market. Joseph walked across the field feeling the grit of dust on his skin. Jeb waited for Joseph to join him.

"I talked to Lucinda today," Jeb said, a sparkle in his eyes. "I asked her to keep you a plate of food warm for the next few weeks until the harvest is done. She said she would be staying late to do the dishes and wouldn't mind. Why don't you hurry on over to the cook hall?" Jeb winked as if there was some kind of special about what he set up. Little did he know she would just ignore him, and he'd eat alone at a great big table.

"I'm grubbier than a hog in a mud puddle. Won't be heading anywhere until I get this grime off my body and into some clean clothes."

"Suit yourself," Jeb said as they walked toward his house. "But enough is enough for one day. Tell you the truth, Doris has lots of leftovers from supper, but I thought you'd have a hankering for whatever Lucinda made." He winked again and slapped him on the back. The dust billowed from Joseph's clothing. "You really did get covered today."

"That's what a day of digging does. How about I clean up under the pump out here, and if you don't mind asking Doris if she's got some grub for me, I'll eat out on your porch and then hit the hay."

"You don't have to work such long hours, son. You can quit when the rest of the workers do."

"It's what I would've done at home."

"You're a good man, Joseph. I'm sorry Lucinda's not warming up to you."

"Not your fault. I guess it's the way it's always been, only before at least we were friends. Now she won't even talk to me."

"For what it's worth. I think you should quit work when the others do, go spruce yourself up, and arrive well after everyone else is gone. Think of some clever conversation once you have her all to yourself and resurrect that friendship."

On the porch, Joseph sank into a wooden rocker. He was far too tired to even eat, but his stomach growled.

"It'll take a few minutes to heat something." Jeb stood with his hand on the door.

"Not a worry. I have to clean up anyway."

"Think about what I said. I appreciate all the work you're doing. Surely, I do. But that's not why you're here. You, me, and the Good Lord know this." Jeb slammed the screen door on his way in.

At the well, Joseph striped off his shirt. He pumped cold water over his head, shook his hair, and washed his upper body with his handkerchief. He hated to put back on his dusty shirt, so he left it off. No one would see him on the porch in the dim light.

He sat back down and closed his eyes. The crickets' evening song relaxed his body as he rocked. Hadn't the good Lord said it was not good for man to be alone? And here he was having given up his birthright, and for what? Loneliness ached straight through to his bones. When Lucinda had married and moved away, he had hoped he would forget her and find another. But having her so close, within reach, and her not wanting him—that took lonely to a whole new level. He had contemplated taking it slow, renewing the friendship, waiting a year or even longer. But not this. It was as if they had no history, no connection.

A squeak on the step alerted him. His eyes popped open to

see Lucinda with baby Samuel. She didn't see him. He held his breath, not wanting her to find him sitting in the dark, shirtless, and dejected. Part of him longed to speak, but he remembered how he had startled her before. She paused as she reached the screen door and dropped a kiss on the sleeping child's brow before entering the house.

As much as he hated the grime, he slipped his dirty shirt over his shoulders. Before he could do up the buttons, the screen door reopened. Lucinda walked toward him with a plate of food.

"Pa said you just got in from the field. Looks like we both worked late." She handed him the tin plate.

"Can you sit a moment?"

She rocked on her feet and stalled, her body pointed toward the door.

"For old times' sake. We used to be the best of friends." It sounded like he was begging, but he didn't care.

"I have to get Sammy to bed."

"What happened to us? To our easy friendship."

"I...I don't know what you mean."

"Yes, you do."

"Give me a few minutes to get the baby down, and I'll come back out." She turned and disappeared into the house.

A smile broke free. Joseph whispered into the heavens, "Thank you." He dug into his food with gusto.

The squeak of the screen door announced her return a half hour later. Though his body ached for sleep, his mind whirled in chaotic cacophony.

She carried a lone candle in a copper candlestick holder and placed it on a small table between them. Flickering shadows danced across her beautiful face as she sat down. He had to breathe in slowly to steady the empty plate and slide it onto the table.

"New look?" She flashed a smile and pointed to his open shirt as she slid into the chair beside him.

He looked down, mortified at the open shirt. "Sorry." He hurriedly tried to do the buttons. "Shirt was so dirty I didn't want to put it back on after washing."

Her glance traveled up his wide chest and returned to his face. "I'm sure a few of the ladies at church would be impressed with a peek at that physique."

His heart bucked. That was the kind of remark the old sassy Lucinda would have made without thinking. "There's only one girl I'm interested in impressing."

She looked at the floorboards and rocked her chair back and forth. "If you mean me, those days are long since gone." She would not meet his gaze.

He stood looking down at her. He wanted to haul her up into his arms and show her just how much those days were far from gone. "How about we start with going back to being friends rather than you are ignoring me?"

She rose in one swift movement. "There's no going back. Don't you get it?"

"Then let's move forward."

He inched toward her. His pulse thumped in rhythm with his crazy heartbeat, and his senses ran sharp. He was so close, her sweet breath fanned his face. "There's nothing but the future ahead, Lucinda, if you'd only give living a second chance." He grazed his knuckles down her upturned face.

"See, this is why I ignore you." Her words came out jilted and breathy.

"Why, because I make you feel?"

"No, because you don't know what the word friend means." She gasped as his thumb brushed over her lips. She grabbed his hand, and their fingers interlocked. His breathing roughened, and her body swayed toward him.

Her other hand found its way to his chest and caressed an

unnerving path to his throat, to his chin, to his lips. It was his turn to breathe in sharply.

He lowered his head slowly, giving her every opportunity to pull away, but she leaned in. His lips brushed her forehead, each closed eye, and the tip of her nose. With only inches separating their lips, he asked. "May I kiss you?"

She answered by circling her arms around his neck and pulling his lips to hers.

He brushed her mouth with aching gentleness. Fire met flame. His lips crushed against her in a tender agony, speaking words he was not yet ready to voice. She pressed into him with responsive lips and a bolt of desire ripped through him. He did not want to scare her off.

With tearing slowness his mouth left hers, and he dragged his screaming body away. He took her hand and led her to the porch rail to gaze at the first twinkle of stars against the inky sky. It took numerous deep cleansing breaths to calm his racing heart.

She leaned against him. The wispy swirl of her scent beckoned him back into her arms, but he removed his hand from hers and hung onto the rail.

Her words were drenched in longing. "That was the most beautiful kiss…"

He clung so tightly to the wood rail that it bit into his palms.

"Why do you think I'm here, LucyBug?"

"I…I—"

"I'm here for you. I'll give you as much time as you need, just please don't shut me out." Joseph ventured a look at her beautiful profile.

"But that's just it. You think time will make a difference." A tear ran down her cheek. "I'm used up. No man will ever want me nor should ever want me."

"I want you."

"It's because you have no idea… You think I'm still that

happy-go-lucky girl you grew up with instead of the wicked woman that God knows I am."

She turned and raced for the door.

"Lucinda."

She stopped, one hand on the screen door handle.

"I'll help your pa finish bringing in the harvest and preparing the fields for spring, but after that, I'll respect your wishes and return home if you want me to." He held his breath. She stood silently without turning. "Do you want me to go?"

A long moment passed. "Yes. Please go." She pulled at the handle and rushed in.

His heart plummeted into the soles of his boots. How could she tell him she had received the most beautiful kiss in one breath and then ask him to leave in the next? He must've heard the good Lord wrong.

~

*L*ucinda flew up the stairs and rushed into her room. She flung her body across her bed and wept into her pillow. The last thing she wanted to do was alert her parents or wake Samuel. She let the tears come in their fullness. Drenching. Despairing. Desperate. She cried for every dead dream, for every lost hope. She wept for a beautiful life that could've been hers had she made different choices.

She hadn't thought in years of when he first called her Lucy-Bug. It had been her thirteenth birthday, and he'd brought her a bouquet of bluebells from his ma's garden.

"Are you sweet on me, Joseph? If a boy brings a girl flowers, it means only one thing." She'd teased him mercilessly. His face turned beet red.

"No. Ma told me that's what I should bring, now that you're considered a lady."

"Oh, so you think I'm a lady."

"A Ladybug with the emphasis on the bug part. Nope, even better, a LucyBug. Yup, that's your new nickname. That's what I'm going to call you from now on, LucyBug because you bug me so much."

"Why, Joseph Daniel Manning, that's no way to treat a lady on her birthday." She had stomped her foot and he had laughed all the more.

For years he had called her LucyBug. When had it stopped? And why had she not noticed?

Now, what could she offer Joseph? Faithful, trusting, protective Joseph. Another man's child? A damaged body that most likely could never bear him a son or a daughter. No. If she let him in, he would get to know the inner person, the one who couldn't get her husband to like her, much less love her. She'd only disappoint him and ruin his reputation. He was far better off going home and choosing a marriage partner with one of the many untainted girls clamoring after him, those with a purity she'd lost that day when she rebelliously snuck off to the forest.

If only she could turn back time and be the spirited, happy girl she once was for Joseph. When he kissed her, she forgot herself. For a moment, she felt like she mattered, like she was precious, desired, and worthy. It was why she had to stay clear of him. He would never understand, but the greatest gift she had to offer him was her distance. He deserved far more.

Even God had no use for her. He didn't answer her prayers. How often had she begged that Nat would love her, begged that he would turn his life around, that God would protect her from his dark side, all to no avail?

I heard every prayer. I sent your aunt, your uncle, your sister, your best friend to rescue you.

Lucinda sat up in bed. She rubbed her eyes with shaking hands. It was as if God had spoken directly into her spirit. Come to think of it, it was odd how many times her aunt or uncle had shown up after Nat arrived home from town, and how often they would stay until he'd passed out in the bedroom.

Then Jeanette arrived with her loving care. And Joseph—always Joseph. How did one balance both strength and tenderness so naturally? Then there was the miracle of Nat messing with the wrong woman and being run out of town. And Ma and Pa taking her back home as if she were a lost treasure, not the disobedient disappointment she surely was.

All of them had kept loving her despite her failure.

Grace.

She flung her body back down on her bed and covered her head with her pillow. Why had the word Jeanette made her promise to discover come to mind? Was that what grace meant? She was too exhausted to think straight. The tears fell in earnest, slowly subsiding to the point she almost slept.

She rose from the bed and slipped out of her day dress and into her nightwear. She should be grateful she had a roof over her head and supportive parents, not crying like a spoiled child. She had made her bed, and now she had to lie in it.

But why did Joseph have to be so beautiful, inside and out? And why had she been blind, so very, very, blind?

CHAPTER 19

*L*ucinda gathered up Samuel's necessities for the day as she worked her way around the kitchen. She placed her hands on her hips. "Do I have everything? Diapers, favorite blanket, extra set of clothes, toy?"

"Have you thought about how you're going to manage the trek over to Katherine's every day all winter with Samuel in tow?" Ma asked.

"Funny you should ask. I was just talking to Katherine yesterday, and it makes sense for me to move over there. She has so many rooms, and it would be one less thing I have to manage in a day."

Ma's face fell, and she turned away.

Lucinda moved to her side and slid an arm around her shoulders. "Ma, you and Pa have been amazing and so helpful, but I have to work—"

"No, you don't. We have more than enough."

"Yes, I do. You have no idea what I went through. Working keeps my mind off it." She shook her head. "I have to work."

Ma turned toward her. "I'm sorry I ever agreed to that marriage. I was so worried about what people would say that I put my daughter in danger. All for what?" She lifted tear-filled eyes to Lucinda.

"It's not your fault, it's mine. That day I snuck off to the woods, I sealed my own fate. Then when Nat wouldn't stop when I begged—"

"What?" Ma's hand flew to her mouth, and her voice rose a few octaves. "You asked him to stop?"

Lucinda turned away. "Never mind. It's too shameful to talk about."

Ma moved closer. "Did you ask him to stop, and he just took what he wanted?"

Lucinda looked at the knots on the floorboards.

"Lucinda, tell me." Ma's voice held that note of authority that Lucinda, even in her most rebellious days, didn't dare ignore.

She raised her head to meet the fiery flash of anger in her ma's eyes. "He said there comes a point of no return for a man."

"And at what point did this happen?"

"I don't want to discuss this."

"You need to. It's true that it would be difficult for a man to turn away in the last moment if you changed your mind—difficult, but not impossible—and any gentleman would do so. Though if he were truly respectable, he'd never put himself in that position in the first place."

Lucinda gulped back the sob sticking in her throat. It was hard to go back there in her mind. "It...it wasn't the last moment. I said no the minute he started to rip at my dress."

Ma's eyes widened. "Rip at your dress? Oh, dear Lord, why didn't you tell me?"

"Because it was my fault. I snuck off. I brought it on myself."

Ma paced the kitchen floor. "He raped you. He used your naivety, lured you away, and took advantage of you. A man that age knew exactly what he was doing inviting you into the forest. He took your innocence against your will. This is not your fault."

"But, Ma—"

"But nothing." Her hand dropped. "Any man who won't stop when told to is an animal. Oh, if I could get my hands on him now." She fisted her fingers and paced the kitchen floor.

Could it really be that Nat should have stopped? Was it possible he had the whole thing planned from the beginning? Based on his behavior—threatening to tell the town she was tarnished goods, and then how he treated her in the marriage— it was not a far reach to believe his cruelty went back to that day.

"I thought he loved me. I thought it was my fault, that I was the one who—"

"No, my darling daughter. No, it wasn't your fault."

"I shouldn't have been there."

Ma marched over and put her hands on Lucinda's cheeks. "Do I wish you had listened and stayed away from that man? Absolutely. But no girl deserves what happened to you that day. Please. Believe me on this."

Tears fell down her cheeks. A spike of hatred stabbed fresh. If Nat had not taken what he did that day, she would not have been forced to marry him.

Ma gathered her close and hugged her into her shoulder. She smoothed her hands down Lucinda's hair. "There, there. Think of Joseph. Can you imagine him or any other man you know not stopping when you ask them?"

She could not. Especially Joseph. He was the epitome of respect. Nat had so brilliantly twisted the narrative to be her fault, her sin, her wickedness.

Ma pulled out of the hug. "If anyone is to blame, it's me. To think I gave my daughter to such a beast." She wrung her hands. "Pa didn't want you to marry him. He said God had told him—"

"I know. I heard that conversation. I was standing outside your bedroom door."

"It's all my fault...mine." She slumped into a chair. Her head dropped into her hands. "How will you ever forgive me?"

Lucinda slid to her knees beside her chair. She pulled Ma's hands away from her face and forced her to look at her. "The marriage was not your fault. I was ashamed by my pregnancy and taken in by Nat's good looks and charm. I believed he loved me when all he loved was the chase. I chose to marry him even after a good man like Joseph told me he loved me." She rested her head upon her ma's lap.

Ma gently stroked her hair. "Do whatever you need to, my dear. Move to Katherine's. Whatever makes your life easier. I was being selfish because I love having you and Samuel here, but I'll visit."

Lucinda raised tear-stained cheeks to her ma. "Thanks for understanding."

~

A dusting of light hinted at dawn. Lucinda fed Samuel and put him back down before dressing. Lucinda loved her new rooms, one for her and one for Samuel. Moving here had been the right choice. Not only had Katherine given her a choice of rooms in her too lavish home, she supplied a nanny for the hours Lucinda worked. Now that Ma knew more of the truth, her regret at having pushed the marriage would add to her guilt, and Ma didn't know the half. Distance would help Lucinda not to make that mistake again and let the truth leak out.

She twisted her auburn curls into a tight bun at the nape of her neck, gave one last glance into the mirror, and curled her nose at the freckles sprinkled there. She picked up her candle holder, checked on Samuel, who had drifted off and then crept down the stairs. As others slept, she had bread to make and much to prove. Delilah had put her in charge of the meals for the working men, saying it was time she stepped back and did less. But Lucinda knew Delilah was watching, and she aimed to please.

Outside, the cool of an October morning invigorated her. She pulled her shawl a little tighter around her body and scurried across the yard toward the summer kitchen. Sun rays nibbled the eastern ridge.

She would have to light the free-standing oven. It would take some time to get the bricks thoroughly heated and the ashes removed and ready for her bread. Soon, she would be doing all the cooking inside, but as long as the weather held, she cooked here. She loved this oven, and everyone loved her bread. In fact, everyone loved whatever she made. Other than Sammy, cooking was the only thing that gave her solace and filled her days with purpose.

Lucinda walked to the cook hall to start on the bread dough and breakfast. With each passing moment, dawn's pearl-gray glow mustered strength in the light of the gathering sunrise. She hoped the two ladies Katherine had hired to help her would arrive on time. They had much to do. Libbie and Helen were hard workers but had little concept of punctuality.

"Good morning."

She jumped at the sound of a cowboy's voice and whirled around. "My goodness, Craig. You've got to stop doing that." She took a few hurried steps backwards. "You just about scared the skin right off my body. What are you doing up at this hour?" Lucinda's heart kicked against the walls of her chest.

He stepped back and put his hands in the air. "Whoa. Sorry that I scared you, Miss Lucinda. I was just on my way to the privy and saw you beelining across the yard. Wanted to tell you for a while now how much I love your cookin'. Reminds me of home."

Lucinda took a deep breath and worked hard to still the jagged racing of her heart. She had no reason to fear this mild tempered cowboy. "Thank you." He looked young and home-sick, but then she was not a good judge of character, was she?

"That's a right fine compliment for sure because my ma is a mighty good cook." He threw her a grin that widened to a full smile, revealing two crooked front teeth. His eyes glowed a bit too warmly.

"I best be getting at your breakfast or I'll have some unhappy men on my hands."

He laughed. "We do get a bit grouchy when our grub is late, don't we?"

"Yes, you do."

He lifted his cowboy hat in her direction and turned his matchstick frame to leave. She shuddered as she continued toward the cook hall. What a mess she was. She couldn't even manage a simple one-on-one conversation with a harmless fellow.

Lucinda breathed easier once the workers arrived and she was no longer alone.

"Helen, you're on the flapjacks, and Libbie the bacon." She tried to say it without a tremble in her voice.

"Is something wrong?" Helen said. Both women moved in and stared her down.

"I'm fine. Even better now that you're here and we can get on with all the work—"

"You don't sound fine," Libbie said. "Did something happen?"

Lucinda waved her hand away. "No time for sweet pleas-antries. Come on we're behind schedule."

"That's what you say every day." Somehow Helen's perma-rosy cheeks and grin brought calm. Her chubby arms encircled Lucinda, and she squeezed tight. She waved Libbie into the circle. "We're not doing any work until we have a group hug and a smile from our boss lady."

Lucinda could not hold back the lift of her lips. "All right, now on with the day." She stepped out of the circle and snapped her fingers.

"The way you boss us around, you'd think we were the children and you the mother," said Helen, "but truth be told we're both double your age."

Libbie patted her on the head. "What are you now, Lucinda? All of seventeen?" Her snapping brown eyes continually twinkled as if she were up to no good.

Lucinda drew her head up to her full height, but both women still towered over her. "I'm eighteen, and don't you forget it." She was not going to tell them she'd just had her birthday a month ago.

They laughed. "Eighteen going on fifty by the sounds of it," said Libbie.

"Whatever works to get you gals moving in the morning."

Libbie cut large slabs of bacon and laid them in the frypan. "So, what has you in such a dither on a bright sunny day? I know when something's a-bothering you."

Lucinda felt the heat creep up her neck into her cheeks.

Helen poured fresh milk into the flour and began whipping up the batter. "Yup, that red is a telltale sign of some good gossip. Out with it."

"Nothing really."

"Nothing, my eye. You're wound up tighter than a runt rooster." Libbie laughed at her own words.

"It's just that one of the cowboys keeps popping up everywhere I go and hangs around after mealtime. It makes me uneasy."

"Which one? Mama Helen will be all over the boy with a switch if I have to."

"It's Craig. Scared me have to death this morning when I was walking here in the near dark. And I feel his eyes following me whenever I'm serving the food."

"You best come to terms with the fact you're a pretty little thing that attracts attention most everywhere you go," Libbie said.

"I'm a divorced woman with a child."

"Like I said, a pretty little divorced woman."

"I'm not interested in starting anything with anyone."

"What about Joseph? We both done seen you watching him when he's not looking."

Helen nodded in agreement.

Lucinda peeked at the rising bread. Couldn't be a better time to punch it down. She grabbed the bowl and dumped the dough on the floured counter with a smack. "Get to work." She waved one hand and began punching with the other.

"Ha. Redder than a maple leaf in autumn," Libbie said.

"Yup, her lips aren't talking but her face is sure telling a story." They both laughed.

Though hard at work, their tongues took no rest. Lucinda loved them but wanted to stuff a dough ball into their flapping gums.

"I'll keep an eye on that Craig boy at breakfast. How about I help you serve this morning?" Helen added a squirt of vanilla into her batter.

"What, and leave me out of the fun?" Libbie turned from flipping the bacon. "No way, we'll all be serving this morning. Yes'um we will." She pointed her fork and waved it up and down.

"That's a perfect solution. Two sets of eyes to scope out the problem. And I have just the idea if that boy is interested and Lucinda is not."

"I assure you, I'm not interested." Lucinda gave a good punch to the dough.

"What's your idea?" said Libbie. "Don't keep us dangling."

"First let's see if we have a problem. And give me some quiet so I can ruminate about my plan."

"Quiet works real fine for me." Lucinda said. "You two are like squawking magpies."

Libbie harrumphed. "And that's the thanks we get for our loving concern."

Helen laughed. "She doesn't know it yet, but she loves us."

Lucinda smiled down at the breadboard as she cut the large dough ball and shaped them into pieces that would rise into perfect loaves.

When breakfast came, Lucinda grabbed the bowl of scrambled eggs and warm bread, Helen held a steaming plate of flapjacks and maple syrup, Libbie brought the bacon and jam. Together, they headed out of the kitchen.

"I've had my breakfast, but just the smell of this bacon makes extra room right here." Libbie jiggled her generous belly. "Sure hope those boys leave some leftovers."

Helen looked over. "Libbie concentrate. We have more than bacon to worry about here."

Libbie nodded. "I can watch and talk at the same time."

"All right, Lucinda. You go in first." Helen waved her on.

"Now look who's bossy." Lucinda threw back the remark as she entered the cook hall. She was used to every eye turning her way. After all, she did hold their food. It was the eyes that lingered that caused angst, and one set in particular—Joseph's. He was the hardest to ignore, and obviously if Libbie and Helen had picked up on her interest she was not hiding her affection all that well.

Back and forth they went with second and third helpings of food, then they began to clean up the plates as one by one the cowboys trickled out. Joseph and Craig lingered to the last moment before each made the effort to wish Lucinda a wonderful day and thank her for the meal.

Lucinda entered the kitchen with a stack of dirty plates to find Libbie and Helen had their eyes pinned on her.

"You're right about the young lad Craig. He most definitely is fixated on you," said Helen.

Libbie added a "Mmm-hmm."

"Now what am I going to do? I thought with all the gossip of me being a failure at marriage and having a ready-made family, I'd be left alone like I want to be."

"Are you sure?" Helen asked.

"More than sure."

"Then my plan will work splendidly." A look passed between the two ladies.

"I can see we're not going to get any work done until you've spilled the beans." Lucinda placed her hands on her hips. "What is it?"

"You've told us a hundred times, if not more, that Joseph is just a friend. Right?"

Lucinda's throat tightened, but she choked out a "yes."

"So, you can ask a friend for a favor."

Lucinda gulped back the knot closing up her airway. They wouldn't know she did everything in her power to stay away from her best friend.

Helen launched in. "The way to thwart attention is to make the others think you're taken."

"And not only taken, but under the protective wing of another man," Libbie added.

"Craig is certainly all eyes," said Helen. "I suggest you go to Joseph, who is *just* a friend, after all, and ask him to pretend he's your boyfriend. It'll give a clear message to young Craig to get over his infatuation and stem the leering looks of the others."

"Others?" Lucinda's voice cracked as she croaked out the word.

Their heads bobbed in unison. "Sorry to say, but when a woman is divorced, men tend to look at her differently. As if somehow, she invites a more forward approach," Helen said.

Lucinda's heart picked up speed. She couldn't deny their

observations. That old familiar anxiety threaded its way up her spine and stitched pockets of fear into her mind. No. She didn't want to go back to that insecure place. "What do you mean by that?"

"You have a number of them way too interested, and not in a respectful way. The best thing would be to get the only man in the room who is truly your friend to help you out."

Lucinda could barely breathe. These women couldn't begin to understand the panic their words were evoking. Would it be fair to lean on Joseph once again? To ask him to be her protector. He had promised to always be there for her, but this…this was asking too much. Yet he hadn't tried to change her mind when she made it clear they could be no more than friends. Surely, he had accepted the way things were. Plus, he was heading home soon, which would allow just enough time to make this believable without complicating things between them. And it would give her a chance to end their relationship with true friendship.

"Hmm, your plan may work."

Helen shoulders went back and her chin lifted. "Of course, it will."

"I agree. I'll ask Joseph tonight."

Helen's blue eyes, and Libbie's jet black eyes, popped to twice their size and they looked at each other with triumph.

"He's due to head home for the winter soon, but there should be enough time to pull off the ruse you're talking about. Then all winter, I can play up how much I miss him to the rest of the cowboys, and I'll be left alone."

She gave the women a quick hug. "What would I do without you?" She forced a smile. "Now, back to work we go. We have work to do." As she dug into the dishes, she wondered. Could their crazy plan work? Or did she just want any excuse to be near Joseph before he disappeared out of her life forever?

CHAPTER 20

*J*oseph surveyed the field in the inky evening light. He had a couple more weeks of work before he would head home. He believed in keeping his word, even if it meant the agony of seeing Lucinda every day. When he was done helping Jeb prepare the fields for spring planting, he would be gone forever. His heart had never felt heavier. A dull ache permeated every moment of every day. He was still as much in love with Lucinda as he had ever been, yet obviously he had heard God wrong, for nothing was happening. His yearning for her had overruled common sense. Now, not only did he not have Lucinda, but he'd also lost the land he loved.

Joseph worked long days on purpose. It kept him from having to see her at supper, right before he went to bed. Didn't matter how dog tired he was he still struggled to sleep as thoughts of her consumed him. When he finally drifted off, he would dream of them together, only to awaken tormented by his lonely reality.

He grabbed his tools and headed in from the field. He needed a shower, some fresh clothing, and a way to get her off his mind. How had he become so infatuated that he thought

God wanted him to give up his birthright and come to this farm? For what? Maybe if he went back now, his father would agree to his brother and him sharing the farm. There was more than enough for both of them. He prayed it would be so.

He slipped into the outdoor shower, lathered his body with soap, and pulled the chain above for a cold bucket of water to rinse away the grime. He toweled dry and dressed. It would be another cold meal. He worked through supper most days, and arrived at the cook hall after everyone, including Lucinda, was long gone. At Jeb's request, Lucinda kept a meal on top of the cooling wood stove in the kitchen attached to the cook hall. Sometimes it was lukewarm, but today it would be cold. It was pitch dark as he opened the door to the cook hall. Normally, he felt around for the candle in the candlestick holder on the table by the door and lit it. Today, however, a faint light flickered in the kitchen. He made his way from the long hall to the warmth of the glow.

Lucinda was rocking her baby in the old chair he used every night to eat his supper. Her auburn curls hung loosely around her shoulders and flowed freely down her back. He took in a deep breath. He had not seen her hair down often, and his heart responded with a gallop.

"What are you doing here?" His voice sounded clipped and unfriendly, but it was the only way he could get the words choked out through his tight throat.

"Hello, Joseph." The sound of his name so softly spoken on her lips made him want to pull her into his arms and yet run at the same time.

He moved to the chair and gazed at the baby. His cherub cheeks and bright green eyes looked just like his mama's. Sammy gazed up at him as the thumb in his mouth rhythmically back and forth. An overwhelming flood of emotion hit Joseph, and he held out his arms. "May I hold him?"

He didn't know what in the world possessed him to ask, but an urge so strong replaced all common sense.

Lucinda stood, a smile forming that brightened her beautiful eyes. "If you'd like to."

He took the baby and nuzzled him close. Samuel's thumb popped out of his mouth, and he grinned. Joseph made a funny face close to his and pulled back quickly. The child gurgled and cooed.

Joseph looked up at Lucinda, whose eyes were wide with shock. "He typically doesn't go to men, not having a daddy in his life... Pa gets right put out when Samuel cries when he tries to hold him."

"How old is he now? He's as solid as a rock."

"Almost nine months."

"Well then, he's old enough for this." Joseph lifted him above his head and swooped him back down.

Samuel laughed and kicked his legs free of the blanket around him.

Lucinda caught it.

Joseph lifted him up again, and the game was on. He finally brought him close, and the child nestled into the crook of his neck. The thumb went back in his mouth.

"You must be starving," Lucinda said. "I kept your food warm tonight. How about I get it on a plate for you?"

He nodded. "But wait a few minutes. I'd like to hold him a little longer." He took the blanket from her hand and slipped into the rocker. With the child snuggled into his shoulder, he felt more at home than he had since coming to work here. In that moment, the Spirit spoke into his soul.

You are home. The three of you are family.

His hands tingled, and his heart raced. He couldn't look up at Lucinda for fear everything he felt would be written on his face. As he rocked, he could hear her moving about, but he closed his eyes and let the love he felt for the child well up inside him. He prayed for the baby, for the baby's mama, and for himself. His hand smoothed up and down the child's back until he felt him grow limp. Little Sammy had fallen asleep in his arms.

When Joseph opened his eyes, Lucinda was standing close. Her eyes shimmered with tears.

"He never held our baby."

Joseph was speechless. *Oh, dear God. What do I say?* "Then he missed out on one of the most beautiful gifts of life."

"He did, didn't he?"

Joseph stood carefully with the sleeping child peaceful in his arms. "Thank you. This was the best part of my day. Heck, the best part of my week. No make that the month. Nope, I take that back. I kissed you within the last month. That tops all." He dropped a light kiss on her forehead and transferred the child into her arms. "My stomach hurts, I'm so hungry. Will you stay and visit while I eat?"

She slid back into the rocker. "I'd love to."

He smiled, because she'd said it like she meant it.

"I actually have a favor to ask. But you have to be honest if I'm overstepping the boundaries."

"Ahh, that's why you're gracing me with your presence. You want to use and abuse me, like the good old days when you'd show me attention and then run away."

Her face fell.

"Hey, I'm only joking. I loved any attention I got from you. Still do." He picked up his tin plate and sat at the small table in the kitchen. "Shoot. What do you need?" He worked hard to keep his voice cheerful and upbeat.

"You know what. It's wrong. Forget it."

"What? No. Tell me."

"I feel bad because I actually do want to use our friendship. It all seems so cold and calculating now."

169

He waved a fork at her between bites. "Don't go and pique my interest and then not tell me what you're thinking."

"Uhh, well…one of the cowboys is becoming bothersome. He keeps showing up, and this morning it was in the dark when I was heading in. I felt a little uncomfortable. I'm sure he's fine, but after Nat, I get scared easily."

"I bet it's Craig. I'll talk to him."

"No. I don't want to stir up trouble. And both Helen and Libbie seem to think there are others looking at me in less than a respectful way. Apparently, that comes with the joy of being a divorcee."

"I know. I've heard things I haven't liked it, but I thought you'd be angry with me if I interfered."

"The ladies I work with had an idea. They suggested, since we're just friends…"

Those two words sent a jolt of pain.

"…maybe you could pretend to be my boyfriend until you leave."

He almost choked on the food now stuck in his throat.

"That would send a message that I have a protector. Then, all winter I can make them believe I'm pining away for you, and they'll leave me alone."

He gripped the fork so hard his knuckles turned white. How could he pretend something he wanted more than life itself, then leave and never return?

"Please, Joseph."

He would do almost anything for her, but to pretend to be her man when he was not? That was asking the impossible.

"It would give me the winter to heal a bit more, work through some of my irrational fears. I'm sure they're harmless, but I just can't deal with men right now."

"So is it Craig?" He stalled for time. He couldn't think straight. In one moment, he thought God assured him that the three of them would be family, and in the next he was reminded that he was only a friend, one she didn't seem to care would disappear shortly.

"I'll tell you if you promise not to say anything to him."

"All right." He puffed out at breath in exasperation.

"Yes, it's Craig."

"I knew it." He clenched his hand into a fist beneath the table where she could not see it.

Again, the Spirit spoke into his mind.

She needs this time to heal, and she needs your protection.

But how could he possibly manage this?

With Me, all things are possible.

He barely held in a groan. He needed details. He needed promises. He needed to know how soon he could put a ring on her finger. Instead, he was instructed to help.

He forced his voice to sound normal when he asked, "So, what exactly would this look like? We'd have to spend some time together in order to make this look real." The thought both thrilled and terrified him.

"I'm aware of that," she said.

"I'll do it on one condition."

"What's that?" She looked up from her sleeping child, her eyebrows arched over widened eyes.

"You really are my friend. We meet here each evening while I eat supper, and we act like the friends we once were. And please bring Sammy. I know you work all day, so time with him is important."

"You'd really do this for me?"

"I'll do this for my long-time friend. The girl with the pigtails I used to pull and the snapping green eyes that lit up like fire whenever I would threaten a kiss."

"The kiss that never came until…"

He finished the thought she didn't. "Until it was too late. I've often wondered what would've happened if I hadn't been so scared back then." He scraped his plate clean without looking at her.

"Those kinds of regrets, I dare not entertain." Her voice was so soft that he almost couldn't hear her.

A shadow passed across her face. He fought the ache that clawed at his heart. He had to get out of there. With a burst, he rose to his feet, went to the basin, and cleaned his tin plate and utensils, as he did each night. He whirled around to tell her good-night and almost bumped into her. The baby had been placed on a makeshift bed in the corner he hadn't noticed before, and she stood close. Really close.

"I appreciate you doing this for me." She stood on her tippy toes and kissed his cheek.

Everything in him screamed for more, but he pulled quickly away and patted her shoulder. "It's best we behave like friends unless we're in public and need to perform."

Her hazel eyes shadowed with what looked like sadness, but she nodded.

"Get the little man, and I'll walk you back to the house. I don't want you alone at this hour."

"I do it all the time."

"Not anymore. I'll meet you at whatever hour you get up in the morning and walk you here, and in the evening, I'll escort you back. We have to make this relationship look authentic, now, don't we?" And he needed to make sure Craig didn't show up again when she was alone and vulnerable.

She picked up her sleeping child, turned to Joseph, and smiled. "Shall we, my friend?"

"We shall." He was fairly certain he had failed to hide his smile—and his heart.

~

*H*ow stupid could she be? Lucinda paced her bedroom floor. On one hand, she had asked Joseph to be her friend, and on the other, she'd practically begged for a good-night kiss. Everything within her had wanted his protective arms around her and his lips firmly planted on hers. And, if truth be told, her body ached for a whole lot more. Was she ever going to learn?

Why had she agreed to his condition, which would only bring him closer after she had promised to keep her distance. Her senses sang at the thought of what lay ahead. Her hands tingled. Shivers of delight ran up her spine at the thought of his presence. And to see how he had enjoyed and doted on her child, well, that erased every bit of resolve she had left. Oh, how she wanted the man she should've never given up in the first place.

She stood in the dark, looking out at the moonlit landscape. She should be dog tired after working all day, but after her encounter with Joseph, there would be no sleep. She went back to pacing. A wash of moonbeams splashed through the open drapes, lighting up the room. Perfect for her midnight vigil.

When she was a child, she'd delighted in the influence she had over Joseph. Now, though he didn't know it, he held far more power over her than he realized. She wished with everything within her that she could erase time and offer him the pure, clean, whole Lucinda.

If only what she had left could somehow be enough. Every broken piece. Every wounded corner. Every sorrow-filled pocket. But all she had to offer was another man's child, a damaged womb, and the specter of divorce that haunted her. Being reminded today how disrespectful a divorced woman is viewed, she thought of the shame she could bring to his family.

Best she put away her longing and remember he was doing her a favor. She really did need his help. The thought of advances from any man filled her with dread and fear. Memories she worked hard to stem flooded in. A forest. Nat's strength against her tiny writhing body. The times he had stood over her with a bottle and a fist. Hatred raged. All available men terrified her—except Joseph.

～

*J*oseph had gotten up early and walked Lucinda to the cook hall. He sat at the breakfast table, every nerve in his body aware.

She came out carrying a platter of food. He barely noticed it. She caught his eye, and a rare smile broke free—a smile just for him. She came around the table and leaned in. The smell of sweet lavender assailed his senses as she placed the plate directly in front of where he sat. Always careful never to touch the men, she purposefully placed a hand on his shoulder. Fire shot through his bones.

Joseph glanced around the table. Most every eye in the room was on them. She looked at no one but him. She served platter after platter, bringing them out and placing them directly in front of Joseph. He took some food and passed it along. By about the third run, Joseph noticed wide grins on the men's faces—all except Craig. His scowl spoke a thousand cranky words.

The oldest cowboy broke the spell after Lucinda dropped off another platter of bacon in front of Joseph and walked out. "All right, farmer. Did you finally manage to move from friendship to something more?"

Joseph picked up a piece of crispy bacon and took a bite. "Wouldn't you like to know."

Lucinda walked back in and stood beside him. The girl who rarely said a word looked straight at him and asked, "Do you have everything you need?"

He rewarded her with a nod and a warm smile. She turned to go, but he reached out to touch her hand. "See you after work?"

"I surely hope so." She squeezed his hand, and a jolt of awareness shot up his arm.

The men started to hoot and clap.

She whirled around and scurried into the kitchen. He could hear Helen and Libbie laughing above the din of the cheering cowboys.

"I guess I got my answer," the old cowboy said. "Now pass me that pot of grits."

Joseph lifted the warm pot and sent it down the table. Was he stark raving mad? What made him think he could play at the game of love and not be consumed? Joseph's insides flipped and flopped. How would he put up with weeks of this? From one look at Craig's dejected face, the plan was working well. But could Joseph's heart really take such close proximity without the urge for a whole lot more?

Joseph stood. He had lost his appetite, there was only one thing he wanted. He best get to work. The sooner he was done helping Jeb, the better. Going home was looking mighty fine. He wouldn't be able to handle this bittersweet agony for long.

"So much in love you can't eat?" His friend Paul looked at his half-eaten plate and laughed.

"That sums it up." He flipped his cowboy hat on his head.

The table of men guffawed as he walked out, a purposeful gait to his step. Even if he didn't feel confident, any fool could look the part.

CHAPTER 21

The past two weeks had been both the best and worst weeks of Lucinda's life. Her heart looked forward to evenings with Joseph more than her mind was willing to acknowledge. She stood over the stove in the cook hall, cooking Joseph fresh vittles rather than have him eat leftovers. Sammy played on the floor.

"How's my little man?"

At the rich timber of Joseph's voice, the pulse in Lucinda's throat thrashed like the wings of a hummingbird. She turned to see him swing Samuel up in his arms and tickle his belly with a kiss. What would it feel like to have his lips on her stomach? She squelched the wayward thought.

"You worked late."

He went into a lengthy explanation about what had been accomplished that day and then asked about hers. Their conversation sounded like one that might be had by a husband and wife catching up after a long workday. The only part missing was the best part, the kiss as he entered, the tenderness in his eyes as he came close and said how much he'd missed her and how beautiful she was, the sinking of two bodies onto a bed. All the things she had imagined marriage to be but had never experienced with Nat.

"Come back to us." He waved his hand in front of her face and laughingly swung baby Sammy close. "Sammy wants a kiss, Mama."

She leaned forward and kissed Samuel's chubby cheeks, and then Joseph pulled him away. The baby gurgled and laughed.

"Coming in for another one." Joseph stepped closer and swung Sammy in. As she leaned in with puckered lips, he pulled the baby to his chest, and his mouth landed on hers.

Everything within her burst into flame, and she opened her mouth in invitation. He drank of the nectar she offered like a parched man in a desert. It wasn't until Sammy started squirming in protest at being locked between them that he dragged his lips away. But not without coming back, one, two, three times for quick kisses. He lifted and whirled Sammy in the air. "Sorry, young man, but your Mama is just too divine to ignore."

She turned her attention back to the meal bubbling on the cooktop. A wash of feverish heat that had little to do with the wood stove spread from tip to toe. Her hands shook as she tried to fill his plate with food. What happened to them keeping things on the friendship level?

After that first day and a little teasing about Joseph's special treatment and private meals, all advances and inappropriate remarks had stopped. Even Craig barely looked her way, and he was no longer lurking in the shadows. Their plan had worked splendidly, except for one detail. She could no longer deny that she was desperately, hopelessly, fiercely in love with Joseph.

His deep voice reverberated behind her as hands landed on her shoulders. "I know you'd like me to apologize for that kiss, but I'm not sorry."

She stiffened, wanting to turn into his arms and beg him never to leave, to marry her, spend forever with her. But nothing had changed. She was not worthy of his love. She would only complicate his life and bring him more sorrow than he could imagine.

His hands moved down her arms. She shivered in delight. He pulled her back against his solid chest and held her. She couldn't stand the agony any longer and turned into his arms. Gazing up, she begged. "Kiss me, Joseph."

His lips crushed against hers, hot and needy. Her hand found its way to his chest, where the strong beat of his heart pounded beneath her fingertips. There was no mistaking the effect she was having on him. For the first time in her life, she wanted to give a man everything he wanted and more. There was no fear. There was no taking on one part and submission on the other. There was only a desire that ran equally hot between them.

He groaned as she moved her fingers across his chest. He stayed her hand when it went lower.

She pulled from his lips. "Joseph, I want you. I want to please you. Let me—" She pressed her body unashamedly against him, moving with the experience she had.

He tore himself away. "I want you more that life itself." His breathing grew ragged. "But I dare not sin against both you and God by taking what is not mine to take. I'd marry you on the spot if you'd have me."

She squeezed her eyes closed to stem her rising tears. A few squeezed out and dripped down her cheeks. For a moment she had forgotten all reason. She had tried to drag down a godly man. What must he think of her? She was no better than the scoundrel she'd married. A loose woman, impure in thought and deed. A dangerous temptress that not even God could redeem.

And what kind of man had the strength to pull gallantly away? What must he think of her brazen offer? Would he still propose marriage if he knew half of the things she had been driven to do just to please Nat? No. He was far too good a man for the likes of her.

"Have you ever been with a woman, Joseph?"

"There's no woman for me but you."

"Then run. I have no more to give than what I just offered. I shall never marry again nor trust my son's life into the hands of any man."

"I'm not, Nat." His voice hardened. "I would never hurt you or Sammy."

"I know. I know because, had I kissed Nat with half that, he would've taken everything I offered and more."

"Is that what he did when you got pregnant? Took more than you offered?"

She couldn't meet his eyes, couldn't utter the truth, yet refused to lie.

Her silence caused a low growl from Joseph's throat. He moved across the room, his fists clenched. "God knows I want to hurt that man so much the thought of it burns my blood." He slammed his fist on the table so hard that the dishes rattled.

Sammy, who was sitting on a blanket on the floor, whimpered.

Shaking, heart racing, words tumbled free. "See! There's violence in every man, simmering just below the surface." She crossed the room and swooped up Samuel, then lifted her eyes to Joseph.

Her words hit their mark. His face looked like a herd of wild buffalo had trampled in.

She shouldn't have said it. There was a big difference between a man going toe to toe with another man and a man using his strength against a defenseless woman. And her father had never laid a hand on any of them, ever. Nor had Joseph. In all their years of friendship, he had been nothing but kind.

But she needed him to go and never look back. Her cruelty was her kindness.

He walked toward her. "If you honestly think I could ever hurt you or baby Sammy, we have nothing, not even friendship. Is that where you want to leave this conversation?"

Everything within her longed to smooth the creases of worry her words had etched into his furrowed brow. She wanted to gather him close and never let go. Instead, she said nothing. Did nothing.

He leaned forward and kissed Sammy's brow. "You be a good boy for your mama, you hear?" The baby cooed and smiled up at him.

Lucinda almost capitulated and begged him to stay.

"I've finished up my commitment to your pa. I was only staying to help you. But I think we've accomplished what we set out to do. The men have left you alone. Correct?"

She couldn't speak for the lump in her throat, so she nodded.

"You can tell them I'll be back in the spring, but we both know that's not going to happen. I'm sorry beyond words for the way Nat hurt you. If I could take every wound upon myself, I would." His words were gentle and calming, soaked in compassion. He thumbed away a tear that rolled down her cheek. "Part of me will always love you, but I need to get on with my own life. I'll pursue you no more. It's like chasing the wind. If you ever decide you want me, you know where to find me."

A gasp slipped from her lips.

"Good-bye, my little LucyBug." He placed a featherlight kiss on her forehead and walked out of the room.

She clapped a hand over her mouth so she would not call him back and beg his forgiveness.

Sinking into the chair with Samuel, she rocked back and forth.

Not once had Nat said he loved her with half as much feeling. And Joseph had used that sweet nickname he had given her many moons ago. Oh, the agony.

~

That night Joseph tossed on his bed like a canoe in stormy gales.

"Oh God, I'm sorry. I heard wrong. Obviously, my own desire for her overruled what You were trying to say."

No, you have followed Me.

"Then why this?"

This is not about you. Now she is assured of your love.

"So she can throw it back at me."

Pain precedes the blessing.

"Please rid me of this love she clearly doesn't want."

She wants you, but she needs Me more. My healing. My forgiveness. My love.

"Am I to go home?"

Until I send her to you. Now pray for her. For Samuel. For Nat.

"I will not pray for that monster."

You are mine. And I am yours. You will pray even for your enemy. It is My way.

Joseph drew in a deep breath. It took all he had to lift his voice. He started with the hardest—Nat. The minute he opened his mouth in obedience, peace filled his soul. The anger and disappointment fizzled. Power flooded in, and with it, sorrow for Nat's lost soul.

~

Lucinda cried herself to sleep. She woke at dawn determined to find Joseph before he left. She had to apologize for her cruel words. There was no way he deserved to leave thinking she was actually scared of him. The only thing she was scared of were her deep feelings for him.

She fumbled with her day dress, tied her hair in a quick knot at the nape of her neck, and sped down the stairs. The house was still quiet.

She raced across the yard in the near dark to the bunk house Joseph shared with Paul and hammered on the door. She didn't care who she woke. She hammered again.

"I'm coming. I'm coming." A muffled voice came from within, but it didn't sound like Joseph.

The door swung wide. Paul stood with his pants riding his hips and his belt unbuckled. His shirt was haphazardly buttoned, and his hair stood in every direction.

"I need to talk to Joseph."

"Oh, for cryin' out loud. Did you two have a spat? He came storming in and woke me last evening and now you're on my doorstep waking me up before the sun has even thought about rising."

"Please can you get him?"

"He's gone."

"He's what?" Had he gone to the fields early? No he had said he was done working with Pa.

"He's gone for good. He shook me awake about an hour ago and said good-bye."

Lucinda wheeled around and ran as fast as her legs would carry her to the barn. Maybe she could still catch him.

She burst through the double doors and ran to the end where he kept his horse. Both horse and saddle were gone.

If only she could ride like Katherine, because she'd saddle up and light out after him, but she couldn't. She didn't even know how to saddle her own horse.

She hung her head. Shame spilled out like the poison from a lanced boil. She had been so cruel. She should've just been honest, told him why she would never be good enough for him, the horrible things she'd done when she was married to Nat. She touched her abdomen, which would never hold another child because she'd trusted that snake of a husband. If Joseph knew it all, he wouldn't want her, and he deserved to know. Instead, she had wounded the only man who truly loved her because she could not own her part in her disastrous marriage. What a coward she was. What a fool. He was far better off without her cruel tongue and wanton ways.

~

"*J* won't go back on my word," Joseph's Pa said. "You waltz in here in the middle of the night, slip into your old bed, and think things are just going to be as they've always been?" He slammed his spoon beside his bowl of porridge.

Joseph kept his voice cool and detached. He looked around the kitchen. More clutter than ever filled the room, shrinking it in size. Come winter, he'd have to get serious about some organization inside—if he was around come winter. "I merely want to talk to Nigel. I'll respect—"

"Can you assure me you're here to stay?"

"If the Lord wills," Joseph said.

Pa snorted. "Then why are we having this conversation if you're not even sure you'll stay? I have no intention of upsetting the apple cart just to have you run off again. If you want to make this your home and your future, then you make a commitment. And invite that purty little Esther to be your wife alongside you. She would ensure you finally get over that shameful woman—"

"No."

"What do you mean, no?"

"I follow God's lead first, then yours."

Pa slammed his hands on the table and rose. His glare was hot enough to turn ice into steam.

"Pa, there's nothing I would like more than to feel zero for

Lucinda. After all that's happened, my heart feels like it's been tilled under a couple times over, and yet I love her."

"You're obsessed with her." A muscle in his jawline clenched.

"Call it what you will, but I can't drum up feelings for Esther when I love Lucinda any easier than you could accept that the love of your life was gone when Ma died. Why haven't you remarried? Lord knows we could've used a tender touch around this place, and you had women who were interested."

"That's different." Pa's shoulders sagged. "I could never. I still love your ma."

"I know you do. Maybe we're more alike than you think." Joseph laid a hand on his father's shoulder. "You and me, we love for life."

Pa scratched at his head. "What am I supposed to do with that?"

"Believe that I pray and listen to God on this matter."

Pa settled back in his seat and lifted his spoon. "What happened back there at the Richardson spread? Does that divorcee think she's too good for the best farmer in the valley? You'd think she'd be grateful any man wants her after—"

"She needs time. Her marriage was… She needs time to heal." Joseph wouldn't tell his pa what she'd been through or how his visit had ended. He was still reeling from her accusing words.

"You think time will make a difference? You've been hanging around that girl like a lovesick puppy for as long as I can remember. If she didn't pick you back then, she sure as shootin' ain't gonna pick you now."

His words sliced deep. "Thanks for your support."

Pa set his spoon down again. "I shoot with a straight arrow, son. Some things are just not meant to be. And I heard she couldn't keep her husband happy—"

"The rumor mill spews all kinds of stories and lies."

"Why, when it concerns her, do you assume everything a lie?

Was she not pregnant before she was married? Doesn't that say it all?"

Joseph thought of that moment in the kitchen when she'd all but begged him to take her to his bed. If Lucinda had done to Nat what she had done to him, it would be tough for most men to resist. Without the help of God, he would never have been able to step away.

He couldn't think about that. "Pa, I just want to talk to Nigel. If he doesn't agree, I won't push the idea. But it's got to make sense to you first."

"Having you here has always made sense. Your brother is a hard worker, but he's not a smart one."

"He's smart, Pa."

"His head is always on his latest tinkering. Can't get that boy in the dirt where a farmer needs to be. He's more interested in finding a way to short cut the work with some fandangle contraption he invents."

"One day it's going to work, and we'll all be better for it."

He lifted his spoon again. "Fine. Go talk to your brother. Whatever the two of you decide is all right with me. Every day you're here is better than a day you're not." He waved Joseph off and dug into his porridge.

Joseph headed to the barn, where he knew he would find his brother. The cow was bawling to be milked, the horses needed water and feed, but Nigel was bent over his latest invention. He didn't even glance up as Joseph approached.

"Can I talk to you?"

"Seeing that I'm the boss," Nigel said, "how about you look after the animals before Pa starts barking? Then we'll talk."

"Looks like you haven't moved since the middle of the night when I brought you some grub."

"I haven't. This thing is so close to working I can taste it. And when I'm done, there'll be no more pile of hay that reaches to the rafters. It'll be pressed into nice square blocks and tied with twine. Every barn will have two to three times the capacity for storage." Excitement resonated from his voice even after a night with no sleep.

Joseph marveled at his brother's tenacity and the way his brain would hone in on an idea and not let it go.

Much like Joseph's poor heart did with Lucinda.

Maybe they were all more alike than any of them cared to admit.

"Can you concentrate if I talk while I milk Buttercup?" Joseph asked.

"Yeah, shoot."

"I have no idea if Lucinda will ever come calling, but I have hope. And when she does, I'd like to marry her on the spot."

"Still sweet on her, eh?"

"It's complicated."

Nigel laughed. "Women. That's why I stay clear. Don't have the time nor energy to figure them out. And I'm glad you're back. I don't have the patience to do this farming thing full time. I need a spell to myself each day or I'll go stark raving mad."

"So, if you and I share the farm, that's all right with you?"

"For sure."

Joseph wasn't sure Nigel was paying full attention, and he didn't want to take advantage. With a pail and stool in hand he moved to Buttercup. He smoothed his hand over her full udder and whispered soothing words. She stomped one hoof and swished her tail, then settled into the rhythm of his hands on her teats.

"You know how, when I left, Pa was upset and gave you the farm?"

"I never wanted it, nor do I need it. Give me time in a day to work on my inventions, and I'll be happier than a hog in a mud puddle. Just don't leave again. I can't handle the pressure Pa puts on. And all those workers coming at me all day, wanting this, wanting that. They're never happy. I like the way it used to be, me working alone in the fields and then coming home and working on my inventions alone, the emphasis on *alone*."

Joseph laughed.

"I'm serious. Promise me you're here to stay, and you can have whatever you want."

Joseph paused before speaking. "I had time to think and pray on the way back here. I left by telling Lucinda if she wants me, she knows where to find me. I feel confident that is the final word on the matter."

"Good then. Plant away. Build away. Just get me some porridge, will you? My stomach is distracting me."

Joseph got up from his stool with a warm bucket of milk and brought it over. "Here, have a drink, and I'll go get you some of Pa's lumpy porridge. After Lucinda's fine cooking, it turns my stomach."

"We sure do need a woman around this place, but I'm far too busy to take the time to court Esther. And you, a guy who could have his pick, are stuck on the one girl who doesn't want him." He laughed. "Don't we make a pair? If Ma were still alive, she'd be some disappointed."

"That she would."

Nigel lowered his head and resumed tinkering, once again lost to the world around him.

"$\mathcal{C}$oming to church today?" Katherine offered like she did each Sunday.

Lucinda looked down at her breakfast and shook her head. She picked up her fork and stabbed into the flapjack. God wouldn't have much use for the kind of woman she was. After what she had done to entice Joseph and the way she'd sent him away with her cruel words still ringing in his ears, she wouldn't be able to face him at church.

"Come on, sis. Colby is busy with the calving, and I need someone to keep the kids in line. With Jillian in her terrible twos, and Seth so active, it's hard to keep them happy for long. And I'm more tired these days with this little one on the way."

She rubbed her large abdomen making Lucinda feel bad for not being helpful. "Pa and Gracie will be there."

"Maybe not. Seems Ma hasn't been feeling so good lately, so one of them stays home with her."

"What's going on with her anyway?"

"She brushes it off, refusing to see the doctor, so who knows. I don't think it's anything serious. Seems to hit her only on Sundays, if you know what I mean."

They both laughed.

"Yes indeed, like hay fever, Ma and I share the same allergic reaction to church," Lucinda admitted.

"It's time to get over that." Katherine's amusement faded, and she gave Lucinda a long look. "God has been good to you, Lucinda, bringing you out of that dark time in your life and surrounding you with people who love you and Sammy."

"I can't argue with that." She wanted to find a way to be mad at God, but it was herself she was mad at.

"Then come."

"No…no. I can't."

"Why?"

"Joseph may be there, and it's awkward between us."

"Pff." Katherine set her teacup on the table and waved her hand. "Lately, he's had the girls buzzing around at church, and for the first time, he's actually engaging them. You must have made it clear you weren't interested."

"I did."

"Then there's nothing to worry about."

Lucinda had walked right into that one, pretending things were over between them. But they would never be over for her. Joseph had her heart pumping in the palm of his hand. He just didn't know it.

"Please come." Katherine reached across the kitchen table and touched Lucinda's arm. "With all our work, we have so little sister time together."

"All right." Lucinda forced a weak smile as her insides began to leapfrog. She wanted to see if Joseph was happy—if he had moved on, even if it would be torture.

"Oh, that's wonderful. And I have just the dress. I got one back from Clarisse that is far too short. It will be perfect for you."

Lucinda hit Katherine's arm. "As if the seamstress would

make a mistake like that, not to mention you're pregnant. You've been trying to buy me a new dress for weeks now."

Katherine stood and held out her hand. "I'll never tell. But it's a lovely shade of green that'll make your eyes pop."

Lucinda put her hand into Katherine's and let herself be led up the winding staircase to the bedroom.

∼

*L*ucinda climbed the steps into the church holding up the folds of the warm muslin fabric of her new dress in one hand and Sammy in the other. She had balked at the extravagance and unnecessary detail given to the day dress. The tiny rosebud print, the high respectable neckline trimmed in a white lace collar, the puffy sleeves, and the lacy ruffle around the bottom—it all seemed too much. When she slipped on the matching bonnet, Katherine had been so pleased. Meanwhile, Lucinda had worked really hard not to show her dismay. The whole ensemble seemed to shout for attention, the last thing she wanted.

In years past, she would have flounced in and walked slowly down the center aisle turning this way and that, pretending to be looking for someone so nobody would miss her. Today, she hurried to a back row and slipped in.

"We normally sit up there." Katherine pointed to the front.

"Go ahead." Lucinda was not going to budge. She shifted her sleeping child to a comfortable position in her arms.

Katherine slid in beside her, with Seth and Jillian between them. "This spot is just fine."

Lucinda was anything but fine. She could see the back of Joseph's head. His pa and brother sat to one side of him and a blonde sat on the other side beside an older couple. Esther Dwyer. No one could mistake those beautiful golden locks. She leaned in, and Joseph dipped his head to hear something she said. They laughed.

The service began, and the congregation rose to sing a hymn. Lucinda couldn't force herself to join in. The words of *Amazing Grace* stuck in her throat. Grace…there was that word again. She had promised Jeanette she would delve into what it meant, but she hadn't done it. For the first time, the words of the song popped off the page.

Amazing Grace, how sweet the sound,
That saved a wretch like me…

Yes, every part of Lucinda felt the wretch, the failure, the problem.

I once was lost, but now am found, was blind but now I see…

She knew she was lost, but what was she supposed to see?

Through many dangers, toils and snares we have already come…

Yes, many dangers to be sure.

T'was grace that brought us safe thus far, and grace will lead us home…

She was home, wasn't she? In the haven of her family. But why did she feel so lost, so empty, so incapable of being the woman she wanted to be?

Was grace that taught my heart to fear, and grace, my fears relieved.

That made no sense to her at all. Lucinda had so much fear. Fear that she would never be good enough—as a daughter, a woman, a mother. Fear that she deserved more punishment. But oh, how she would love her fears to be relieved.

How precious did that grace appear the hour I first believed.

Did she believe? Everything was so complicated. God had let her down. No, she had let God down.

Those simple words of the song restricted her ability to breathe. The meaning of each line called to her, haunted her, taunted her. In her confusion, her need, even Joseph was forgotten. It was as if she were all alone and God was speaking. But so was the enemy of her soul, and he was telling her she was not worthy.

The congregation sat.

Seth kept kicking the pew in front of him. Jillian wanted to run, and baby Samuel woke up with a cry. "I'll take the kids out into the cloak room where they can run and play," she whispered to Katherine.

"I'll take them." Katherine started to rise, but Lucinda pulled her down. "This whole church thing means more to you than me. I'll take them." She whispered to the kids. "Come with auntie." They were up and hurrying with her to the door.

When she turned to make sure they were with her, Joseph turned in his pew. His head snapped up, his eyebrows arched. Their eyes locked, and he smiled.

She turned away.

One look into his beautiful face, and she was fighting back tears. Why had she come?

The small cloak room had two other moms and a few children. Lucinda had gone to school with both the women. They turned their back to her without a word and talked to each other as if she did not exist. It was the same response she'd received in town.

She would never subject Joseph to this kind of shunning. She knew who she was. A loose woman. A divorcee. A failure. There was no such thing as grace for her.

～

" *L* and sakes, girl, what has gotten into you?" Delilah waved her hand in front of Lucinda's face. "Here I am trying to teach you my secret pecan pie recipe, and you not paying me any mind."

"Sorry. My concentration is a tad scattered lately." She shook her head, coming back to the kitchen around her. There was no way Lucinda was going to be talked into going to church ever again. It was not the snubbing she received or even seeing Joseph talking to a pretty girl, it was that song that still had not left her mind. That word, grace, which called her name in the middle of the night, in her still moments with Sammy, and even in the thick of day with work pressing in.

"You best get that mind back on task. We have a lot of work if'n we're to pull off this Christmas ball. Katherine and Colby have invited the whole community, and we have to do them proud."

"I know. I know."

"It's only two weeks away, and we don't have time for your head to be somewhere up in them there clouds."

Lucinda watched Delilah roll out the pie crust dough. But her mind was still on that tiresome word.

She had to ask or she would never be able to focus.

"Do you believe God's grace is for all people?"

Delilah stilled her rolling pin and turned toward Lucinda. "No question in my mind."

"Even for the likes of Nat who...who...?"

Delilah put the rolling pin down. "We is gonna take a break and have some tea." She dusted the flour off her hands and waddled to the stove. "Sit." She waved at Lucinda.

"But we have so much to do."

"Nothing is more important than the Lord's work." She took the kettle and poured the steaming water into the teapot.

Lucinda could not figure out how a simple conversation was the Lord's work, but she sat down. When Delilah had a bee in her bonnet, there was no point in arguing.

"Tell me what you think grace means?" Delilah asked as she set a teacup before Lucinda.

"I...I think it means forgiveness."

"Kind of, but that's closer to mercy. Mercy is undeserved pardon for all the things we done fall short on. I know I've had plenty need for mercy."

Lucinda was confused. "Then what does grace mean?"

"Grace is undeserved favor. God gives us the gift of His love and guidance here on earth and the promise of heaven when we die. None of which we deserve."

"Much like the love my family has given me."

"Yes. That's true. But you is easy to love, girl." Delilah squeezed Lucinda's hand.

"Tell that to the ladies at church, or the town folks." Lucinda could not get the way she had been rejected by even the ladies at church out of her head.

"You pay them no mind. If'n they do not treat you like the lady you are, they have the problem." She pointed her finger at Lucinda. "Too be sure, God is going to deal with them."

"But how can grace be for someone like Nat?" She was thinking of herself but could not bear to ask. Her teacup trembled in her hands.

"If a heart is truly repentant before the Lord and sorry for the harm they done, then grace and mercy are there for the asking." Delilah scooted her chair closer and reached out both hands, palm up. "For you too."

Lucinda put her teacup on the table and placed her hands in Delilah's.

"Can I pray for you?" Delilah asked.

Lucinda nodded.

"Lord Jesus, speak to Lucinda now. Tell her how precious she is to You. Tell her how loved she is. Amen." Delilah let go of her hands and clapped hers together. "There. Now we let the Spirit of God do the rest."

Lucinda had no idea what Delilah meant, but that short

prayer stuck like honey. Sweet to her soul. Was she really precious? Did God truly love her?

Hope struck a note in her heart long since played. She rose from the chair feeling lighter. Lots to think about, but she best pay attention to that pecan pie.

CHAPTER 23

*J*oseph whistled his way into the kitchen. "Are you two ready?" he yelled at his pa and Nigel, who had not yet emerged from their bedrooms. "Time's a-wastin'. We have to go." He couldn't help but feel excited. Katherine and Colby were hosting the annual Christmas ball, and Lucinda would be there. He hadn't seen her since that brief moment at church. When he had looked for her after, she was gone, and so was Katherine.

"You seem mighty perky." Nigel came out of his room and clapped him on the back. "Someone special you're fixin' to see?"

"Shut it, or I'll box your ears and ruffle up that perfect head of hair."

Nigel smoothed his hands over his head. "It is perfection, is it not?" He laughed. "But seriously." His smile evaporated. "Haven't seen you this happy in months. Hope the evening goes well for you."

Joseph nodded. "It'll do my soul good just to see her." He shouldn't feel that way after the way they'd parted, but there was nothing rational about his love for her.

Pa entered the room. "See who?"

Joseph had no intention of riling his pa with a straight answer, but before he could shake his head at Nigel, the dunderhead spoke.

"Who do you think besides one cute little redhead?"

Pa's jaw clenched. "Don't be ridiculous. Your brother has finally got some sense in that head of his. Don't you, son?"

Drat that Nigel.

"Come on, Pa," Joseph said. "Let's go. You know I have nothing but common sense." There was nothing common nor sensible when it came to his sorry heart concerning Lucinda, but he was not going to ruin a perfectly good day by getting into it with Pa.

Pa relaxed and slipped into his overcoat, placing his Sunday top hat on his head.

Joseph lifted both eyebrows at Nigel behind Pa's back.

Nigel shrugged and mouthed, "I'm sorry."

The ride felt like it took forever, the cart bumping over ruts and frozen ground. It had not snowed enough for the sleigh, and the frozen ground was far from smooth. But every jar and jostle brought him one step closer to seeing Lucinda. Nothing could burst the bubble of happiness he had inside.

When they arrived, Joseph took the steps two at time up to the white colonnaded portico. The doors of the stately home opened without him knocking. His coat and hat were taken, and he and Nigel and Pa were ushered into the ballroom.

Joseph's insides leap frogged. He scoured the room, hungry for the sight of one lady in particular. She was nowhere to be seen. He had three women beelining his way, but no Lucinda.

"Rescue me," he whispered to Nigel.

"I can't exactly take on all three, and I know they're not gunning for me."

"Do your best." Joseph felt badly turning away, but he wouldn't fill up his dance card before securing at least one from the woman he'd come to see. He weaved throughout the room, refusing to make eye contact or slow long enough to be accosted. Where was she?

Finally, he caught sight of her standing in the alcove at the end of the hall, gazing out a window into the dark. A bolt of fire ripped through. Every cell in his body responded to the sight of her.

He walked her way. "Hello, pretty lady." He couldn't help his mouth from saying what his mind thought.

A vision of loveliness turned to greet him. "Before you say anything. I need to apologize. I've felt so terrible for the way we last parted. I didn't mean what I said. I came to your bunk house the next morning to beg your forgiveness, but you were gone." Her words tumbled out fast and feverish. "Then I tried to write...at least a dozen letters, and the words wouldn't come."

"It's all right."

"No, Joseph, it's not all right. I use words as weapons, and it's inexcusable. I'm so sorry."

He could barely concentrate on what was coming out of her mouth. She looked amazing. He was trying not to stare, but the light green velvet dress with layers of dark green ruffle was cinched in at the waist, accenting every curve. The off-the-shoulder bodice with only a necklace to adorn the creamy white flesh drew his eyes and flamed his desire. He tried to refocus on her hair. Swirls of copper silk framed her petite face with a long thick curl draped down one side. He could think only of running his hands through it. Wide autumn eyes beckoned he gather her in his arms and never let go.

"I know. It's too much, isn't it?" She looked down, smoothing her hands nervously over the folds in the skirt. "Katherine insisted that Clarisse make an original for me. Between the two of them, I didn't have much say."

"You look stunning."

"I just wanted to stay in the background and serve, but Katherine would have nothing to do with that. She said no sister of hers was going to serve at the ball. So here I stand, in the shadows. Afraid to make an appearance."

"You've never been shy…" The minute the words were out of his mouth he wanted to pull them back.

Her eyes cast down, and she turned back to stare into the darkness. "I'm not that person anymore. You have no idea how the other women treat me."

He didn't know what to say. How could he comfort her?

"May I be the first to add my name to your dance card?" He held out his hand. "And I will not take no for an answer."

She handed him her card. "I won't mind if you're the only one. I…I mean, you know, the cowboys still think we're a couple. It keeps them at bay, and I'm eternally grateful."

Joseph couldn't contain his elation. He would use that ruse to his advantage. "I'll just have to sign for at least three dances. That way we'll keep the rumor alive." He hurried to scrawl his name

"No, Joseph. That will only hurt your chances—"

"Too late. It's done." He handed her back the card and held out the crook of his arm. "I shall start and end the evening with you and enjoy a dance in between."

She slid her hand into his arm. "I can't tell you how much I was dreading this."

As the music began, he led her onto the dance floor. The feel of her in his arms sent his pulse thumping in crazy rhythm to his erratic heartbeat.

"Smile," he whispered. "Let's give them something to talk about."

She gazed up at him with a look he could not decipher. Half sad and half… Was that longing? If only he could read her mind. This much he knew—they were far from over.

He led her in a fast waltz around the room, hoping that at least one of the dances with Lucinda would be much slower. He caught the scowl on his pa's face as they whirled by. He'd face that tomorrow. Tonight, love joined the dance of emotions on the floor of his heart, and he could not deny the hypnotic pull.

Nigel whizzed by with Esther in his arms. She was smiling up at him, and he was spellbound. Maybe there was something there after all. Joseph could hope.

"Thank you for getting me out here. I don't think I could have done it without you." Lucinda curtsied at the end of the dance. "I shall look forward to our next one."

"The pleasure will be all mine." He sounded like a lovesick fool. He had better fill his card with dances, and fast. She was an elixir he could not handle.

It was not hard to fill up the evening with willing partners. And Lucinda didn't seem to be having any trouble either. The other women may look down their noses at Lucinda, but the men sure didn't. She had more than enough attention.

His eyes scanned the room as he whirled in the arms of Esther.

"You're looking for her, aren't you?

"Always," he said.

She laughed. "I'll help you."

"You're a good sport."

"Anything for love. And in turn, I'll ask you to put a good word in to Nigel for me."

Joseph grinned. "Deal."

They scoured the room together. "There she is. Talking to your pa, who doesn't look happy at all."

Joseph could not see Lucinda's face, but he could see Pa pointing their way. What was he up to?

When it was his turn to dance with Lucinda again, he could not find her anywhere. He continued to fulfill his dance obligations but grew increasingly worried as the night wore on and she didn't resurface. He had to find her before it was time to leave. Who knew when he would see her again, and he couldn't leave without a good-bye regardless of their past. Guests were already thinning. The last of the evening snacks had long since been put out. Pa and Nigel would soon be on him to go.

Joseph wandered the halls of the mansion feeling somewhat obtrusive taking such liberties. After poking around too many rooms, he peeked into an area that looked like a library. And there she was, sitting in a chair in the light of a lone candle with her head cradled in her hands. He heard the sound of soft weeping.

"Lucinda?"

Her head snapped up. Tears flowed down her alabaster cheeks. "What are you doing here?" Her voice sounded resentful and harsh.

"I came to say good-bye."

"Why. I'm a nobody to you."

He slowed his steps across the room. "I think you know me better than that."

She stood in a flash of fury and marched over. "Stop with the platitudes."

"Stop what?"

"Stop encouraging this"—she waved her hand back and forth between them—"whatever this is between us when you know your pa hates me, and you're engaged to be married."

"I'm engaged to no one."

"Your pa told me. He said you and Esther are—"

"It's not true." He stepped closer to her. "It's what Pa wants, but it's not true." He gathered Lucinda in his arms and pulled her close. She sobbed into his shoulder. If the thought that he was engaged to another had her crying, it could mean only one thing.

She had feelings for him. He'd believed it and hoped it, but to have it confirmed… His heart soared.

He kissed the top of her head and leaned back slightly. Thumbing a tear from her bottom lashes, he bent to kiss the watery flow. She stood still as if she dared not move. His kiss slid across to the tip of her nose. He heard an intake of her breath. Still, she did not move.

With one hand, he lifted her chin, their eyes met. The flickering of the candlelight brought out golden flecks that sparkled in the tear-washed green. It was like he could penetrate the hidden constellations of her heart…a pulling, a reaching, a need. A whisper of perfume touched him. His throat went tight and parched. He lowered his mouth slowly, giving her ample time to decide. Her breath so sweet and intoxicating. Her lips enticing. She didn't press in or move toward him, but neither did she pull away.

His lips touched hers, and the floodgates of desire opened. A need so fierce, so strong, so potent ignited between them. The heady power went straight for his spine and spread like a bolt of lightning through his body. Mouth to mouth, kiss for kiss. Their hands grew frantic, their bodies meshed, clothing felt restrictive and unnatural. He was losing all will to control the fire that raged.

He was shocked when she ripped out of his arms, leaving him heaving for air.

"No, Joseph. I will not bring you down. I will not." She ran. The slamming of the door brought him back to earth.

He slid into the nearby chair, his legs too weak to stand. *Oh God, what just happened? What have I done? What would I have done had she not stopped me?*

~

*L*ucinda flew down the hall and up the stairs to her bedroom. She flung her body onto the bed, angry she couldn't get out of the ridiculous evening gown without help. She'd have to wait for Katherines' maid at the appointed time. Thank heavens this was a once-a-year occurrence.

She thought back to the girl she'd once been, the girl who

had wanted all this...fancy dresses, a big mansion to call her own, maids to help her dress and undress. All so pretentious and shallow. Today, if she could have her heart's desire, she wanted nothing more than to be a good mama and earn respect enough to be with the man she loved. But only being a good mama to Sammy was within the realm of possibility.

She pounded her fists against the pillows and sobbed into the cushions. All evening, the women had snubbed her at every turn, refusing to speak to her even when she'd spoken to them. She deserved that. If there had been any question about the rumors swirling around her when she married and left town, they were answered when she arrived back in town with a child months too old.

That was bad enough, but the way the men had flocked around her, all too friendly and overt, had sickened her.

Joseph was the only man she trusted.

"Oh God, if you're up there, You know how I tried this evening to be so careful. I didn't push myself on Joseph nor even encourage him until he..." But oh, how that interlude had been a temptation.

Somehow, realizing that her wanton ways could bring even Joseph down had given her the strength to break free. But was that good enough? Was God pleased? Strange how the more she considered what grace meant and the possibility God would extend a fresh start, the more she wanted to be worthy. But how could she possibly earn so big a pardon?

As for Joseph, as much as she wanted him in every way, after what had been confirmed tonight by the townsfolk, it didn't matter whose sister she was or if she looked like a lady. There was no grace. Joseph's pa was right. If she cared about Joseph at all, she'd stay clear. Just remembering the spite in his eyes made her shudder.

Why had Joseph made those advances? Didn't he understand the hatred his pa had for her?

~

*I*t was dark and cold outside as they rumbled home, but Joseph was hotter than an overstuffed pot-bellied stove. "What were you thinking, Pa, telling Lucinda that Esther and I were engaged?"

"If you didn't have rocks in your head, you would be engaged."

"So now my own father, who has preached honesty and biblical principles all his life, is going to stoop so low."

"I have good reason. If you won't protect your good reputation from the likes of that woman, I will."

"You have no right meddling in my life." Joseph's voice thundered into the darkness. The buggy wheel dipped into a rut and slammed them together before righting itself. Joseph held the mare steady.

"I have every right. I'm your father."

"Stop. Both of you, stop." Nigel who sat between put a hand on each of them.

"Don't you talk to me that way," Pa said.

"Your plan is flawed. You're pushing one son on Esther, who does not love her, when you got another sitting right beside you who does."

Joseph's anger melted. God was so good, Joseph laughed out loud. "You love Esther?"

"I do. I've loved her for as long as I can remember. But Pa wanting you to have her has always gotten in my way."

Pa slapped his knee. "By Jupiter. If that don't beat all."

Silence filled the crisp winter air. They huddled in the cold with breath frosting between them as the buggy lurched up a hill, its springs groaning in protest.

"Tonight," Nigel said, "I got the chance to dazzle her with my charm, and we had time alone to talk. Esther has no feelings for Joseph. She told me he'd been honest with her months ago, and there's nothing between them but friendship."

"'Tis true," Joseph said.

Pa leaned forward and looked past Nigel at Joseph. "If Esther can get over you, why can't you be done with that woman?"

"I love Lucinda, and Esther only loved the idea of me. Big difference."

"You truly love her?" Pa spat out the words like they were bitter to the taste.

"I do."

"She's no better than the likes of my ma, who ran out on us."

Joseph heaved a heavy sigh. How many times had they gone around and around this same mulberry bush with no resolution? If only he could tell his pa about the abuse Lucinda had suffered, but he'd promised never to tell a soul.

"What happened with your ma?" Nigel voiced the question Joseph had asked numerous times.

"I don't want to talk about it. She's dead to me."

Nigel got the same answer Joseph always got.

⁓

*I*t had been a month since Joseph last saw Lucinda. He tossed on his bed as he'd done most every night since the Christmas ball. There wasn't enough work in the dead of winter to make him drop into bed exhausted and forget the feel and taste of her lips, her body melted into his...

He threw off his covers. The memory was too vivid. He let the cold chill of the winter air cool the heat.

"Where do I go from here, God?" he whispered into the heavens. "I know she's attracted to me. And You know what she does to me. I'm a man who loves You more than life itself, but I almost lost control. Had it not been for her... I hate to think what would've happened in the dark of that library.

Flee temptation.

"I didn't, she did."

Your failure was her success.

That made Joseph pause.

What had she said? She had told him that she would not bring him down. He flung himself out of bed, rubbing the back of his neck as he paced. She had thought of him and his reputation. What a selfless act.

She's changing.

That was true. Back in the fall, she'd thrown herself at him. But when he'd nearly lost control, she'd been the one to pull away. "Thank you, God, for that way out."

She loves you, but she has a lot of healing to do.

"But when, Lord? When? I've waited so long." He went to his bedroom window and pulled back the curtains. A thin crescent moon winked down on him as if God were smiling.

Be still and know that I am God.

He whispered those words over and over until his eyes grew drowsy. He slipped back into bed feeling a peace he had not felt in a long while.

CHAPTER 24

Spring 1876

"So, did you find your knight in shining armor in the big city?" Lucinda asked.

"Hardly." Jeanette sat cross-legged on the end of her bed. "There was someone I was falling for who actually showed me interest, until I found out he was married. Seems he was only interested in one thing." She pointed at her well-endowed bosom. Tears spilled from beneath her glasses.

"Why that cruel… Oh, you don't even want to hear what I think." Lucinda bit her tongue to swallow back the words. "Men. You just gave me another reason to be done with them." To belie her words, Joseph and Pa came to mind. She knew that not all men were the same, but it was easier to shut herself down then to face the feelings she had for Joseph.

Jeanette wiped her tears. "I have to believe there are good ones out there."

"It's the bad ones who damage a person for good," Lucinda said. "Men like Nat and the likes of whoever that guy was."

"I should've known something was up. I'm plain and homely—"

"That's not true—"

"Ahh, you can't change your story now that we've become close. In the past you've made fun of the way I looked."

"In the past, I've been a selfish, prideful brat who didn't want to hear the truth from my older and wiser sister."

"That may be part of it, but we both know, in this family I got the ugly stick while the rest of you got the beautiful. Even Gracie gets far more male attention than I ever have, and she's only fourteen. Do you realize that when that jerk kissed me, it was my first kiss?" She lowered her head, and her cheeks flamed red.

"That's because men look on the outside rather than seeing that you're the most beautiful of us all on the inside."

Jeanette swirled her fingers over the rose crocheted bed cover. "I made this when I was thirteen and gave it to Katherine and Josiah for their wedding present. Never thought she would keep it all these years, especially with all the money she now has."

"When I moved in here," Lucinda said, "she told me I was fortunate to get this, as it's her all-time favorite. You're smart and talented. There are so many reasons for a man to fall in love with you. I hope this bad experience will not turn you off men for good."

"Like you?"

Lucinda nodded. "That's different."

"Why? Are you going to let Nat have control for the rest of your life?"

"He doesn't have control." Lucinda popped off the bed, her words came out in a burst of anger.

"If what he did keeps you scared and alone, then he still has control. And what about poor Joseph? Where is he, anyway?"

"He returned to his father's farm last fall. I keep hoping he finds someone to marry."

"You know he's far too honorable to marry someone he doesn't love. And he's only ever loved you."

Lucinda's insides fluttered at the thought and she sank back on the edge of the bed. She couldn't forget their last meeting and how easily that could've gotten out of control. She best stay clear.

"Don't you see him at church?"

"I don't go that often."

"You're coming with me tomorrow. I need you by my side. I don't want people asking me about school when all it does is make me cry. When you're around, I become invisible, just the way I like it."

"But I—"

"It's the least you can do for me." Jeanette hopped off the bed and headed for the door. "Have Sammy ready." The door clicked behind her.

Lucinda paced the room. What if Joseph was there? The only way she could manage life was to stay far away from the temptation he was. She took a deep breath in. Then again, it was church and springtime. Farmers were busy. She expelled the air and dropped on her bed. He would not be there.

❧

*C*hurch had not yet begun when Lucinda walked in. She perused the sanctuary. There was both a flood of relief and a stab of loneliness when she realized she'd been right. Joseph was not there. Jeanette pulled her up to the front, and she slid into the familiar family pew beside Gracie and Pa. This was way too close.

Jeanette turned toward the back before she touched Lucinda's arm. "I want to say hello to Joseph."

Lucinda's eyes snapped up and her head swiveled. There he was, leaning against the far wall with his cowboy hat in hand. He must've just arrived because his pa and brother were heading to their usual spot beside the Dwyers.

Jeanette headed his way.

Lucinda locked eyes with him, and everyone else in the room faded. He held her gaze, not faltering even as he gave Jeanette a quick hug. Jeanette whispered something, looked her way, and he laughed, all the while not breaking his stare. His lopsided smile pulled at her heart strings. She wanted to run into his arms and run out the door at the same time.

He winked and her hands tingled. She snapped her gaze back toward the front, hanging onto Sammy when all he wanted to do was squirm his way down. He started to howl, not at all impressed at being restricted. Everyone turned in her direction, and heat rushed into her cheeks.

"How about I take him outside and let him run until the service starts?" Joseph's deep voice reverberated in her ear. He was standing in the aisle, hardly noticing that the whole congregation was watching. "If he still remembers me." A blend of musk soap, freshly mown hay, and leather invited her head closer to his.

Jeanette stood behind him, nodding. "Good idea."

"He won't go to just anyone, and it has been a while…" She closed her mouth when Samuel went willingly into Joseph's arms. Before she could think, the two of them were gone.

Jeanette slid in beside her and nudged her with an elbow. "See, I told you he has eyes for no one but you."

"Shush," Lucinda hissed.

Jeanette smiled and stood for the first song with the hymnal in her hand. Lucinda reluctantly joined her. Pa and Gracie were oblivious to the tension, singing their hearts out.

She snuck out on the third song to check on Samuel. Her heart twisted at what she found. Joseph was running around the yard chasing her toddler while Sammy squealed at the top of his lungs, his chubby legs teetering as he ran as fast as a fifteen-month-old could. Joseph grabbed him and swung him high.

Sammy giggled, kicking his legs and waving his arms for more.

Tears slipped down her cheeks, and she pressed back the sob trying to push free. She could not watch them. They were so beautiful together. She turned back inside and slid into the pew.

Preacher Mark started his message, and for the first time ever, she had difficulty tuning him out.

"I had a completely different message planned for today, but this morning when I got up early to spend time with God, I opened my Bible to Luke chapter fifteen, and He told me to speak on the first parable. I haven't had as much time to prepare as I usually do, so bear with me.

"I'm going to retell a story, a parable told over two thousand years ago. One Jesus told the Pharisees and the teachers of the law who looked down on him for making friends with the hated tax collectors and sinners. Jesus said, 'suppose one of you have a hundred sheep but one goes missing, will you not leave the ninety-nine who are doing well and go out after that lost sheep? And when you find it, will you not be overjoyed?'"

The pastor looked up from the Bible. "Let me put this into relatable context for today, since not many of us are shepherds."

The congregation chuckled.

The pastor focused on Katherine's husband. "Hey Colby. You run a horse ranch, correct."

"You know it," Colby said.

"Suppose one of your fine broodmares gets out of the pasture or barn and is roaming free. Would you go out and find it?"

"No question about it."

"And Joe. You raise cattle?"

"Sure do."

"If some of your herd go missing, do you just throw up your hands, and say oh well?"

"No, sir. I get on my horse and look for 'em."

"In this parable, that's exactly what the shepherd does. He goes out looking, and when he finds the lost lamb, he doesn't rant or rave or get angry at the lamb for wandering away. No. He's full of joy. He puts the lamb on his shoulders and carries it home. In other words, God is not looking down with a scowl on His face if you've wandered from the fold. He has lovingly come in search of you. But He's a gentleman. He will not force you to join Him. He holds out His arms and whispers, 'come, let me carry you. Let me heal you. Let me take you home to where it's warm and safe.'"

Lucinda's heart raced. Heat fingered its way from the pit of her stomach to the nape of her neck. Why did she feel like that lost lamb?

"The shepherd in this parable calls his friends and family in, and He throws a party, a celebration. Gentlemen, what do you feel like when you find the lost mare or the wandering cattle?"

"Relieved and thankful," Colby said.

"Mighty fine." Joe let out a whoop that caused everyone to laugh.

Everyone but Lucinda. She twisted her fingers in her lap until her knuckles turned white. This silly story was reaching into her soul and pulling at her heart strings.

"That's how Jesus feels when one of us who have wandered from Him willingly returns. He looks for us. He cares every moment we're gone. He waits with His arms wide open for us to come running so He can lift us up and carry us through the muck and mire to safety. Our sins are forgiven. Our burdens are made light. Our healing can begin."

The presence of something unseen filled the room. Goosebumps prickled Lucinda's skin, and her heart pounded. It was as if the preacher was talking straight to her. She kept her eyes riveted on her lap.

"Jesus says in Luke 15:7 that there is more rejoicing in heaven over that one sinner who repents than over the ninety-nine righteous people who do not need to repent. Is there anyone here who wants to bring that kind of rejoicing in heaven today? Is there anyone who wants to cause a celebration both down here on earth and in the heavenlies? Come talk to me after the service, and I'll pray with you."

Organ music filled the room. Lucinda had no idea how, but the next thing she knew, she was up at the altar. She dropped to her knees, tears streaming down her face. Sorrow filled her heart for her past willful disobedience, selfishness, and for her hatred for Nat. Tears fell as she repented of having wanted a man she knew all along was not the man God wanted her to have. She wept knowing how that decision led to a baby being ripped from her womb. For the first time, she understood the full weight of her sin, but she understood God's love for her more. Peace like nothing she had ever experienced filled her soul as she prayed with Preacher Mark.

With a tear-stained face, she rose from her knees full of unexplainable joy. She turned to see her family gathered around, Joseph holding Sammy, who was fast asleep on his shoulder. She hugged each family member.

"I knew there was a reason you should be here today," Jeanette said.

"Thank you for always loving me so well." Lucinda smiled and moved on.

"Welcome into the family of God," Katherine said. Colby stood by her side smiling at her.

Gracie and Pa piled around her with hugs so tight she could barely breathe. Pa couldn't speak for the tears running down his weathered face.

"I feel so good. Like never before."

Pa pulled back. "Ain't it wonderful? Now there's only your mama left."

Lastly, Lucinda walked up to Joseph. She held her arms out, and he stepped in carrying her sleeping child. She kissed Sammy's flushed brow and hugged Joseph tight. She dare not kiss him or she would never stop.

"I'm so sorry, Joseph. For every way in which I've brought you down."

"Shh. You've already apologized."

But she hadn't apologized properly. There were so many things she wanted to say.

He kissed the top of her head. "We'll talk later. Right now, all heaven is rejoicing, and I've never been happier for you." He pulled out of her embrace when all she wanted to do was hang on tight. He passed the sleeping child into her arms. "I think I tired him out good."

"Thank you."

Jeanette clapped her hands together. "Come on, family, we can't have a celebration without food."

Lucinda turned to Joseph. "Will you join us for lunch?"

The smile lines around his eyes crinkled, and warmth filled his voice. "I'd love to, but I came with Pa and Nigel, and we've already accepted an invite to the Dwyers' for lunch."

"I understand."

"Joseph, we have to go." His pa stood a few feet back and barked out the order.

Lucinda looked beyond Joseph to his father, who jutted his chin, his lips curled down. He gave her a steely-eyed scowl before turning away.

She breathed in slowly. The peace was still there. God had forgiven her, even if Joseph's Pa never would.

CHAPTER 25

"What is with the continual humming?" asked Libbie.

"'Tis true. It's like someone gave you a happy elixir," added Helen. "Come on, spill the beans. Do you have a man in your life?"

Lucinda graced them with a smile but did not say a word, just went back to her work.

"Well, I do declare. The insolence of the young today." Libbie harrumphed.

"I think we call it quits until she gives us some information." Helen threw an arm around Libbie's shoulder in a double stance.

"Yes indeed, she's going have to finish the meal for all dem cowboys without us unless she fesses up."

"I have two men, actually." Lucinda smiled sweetly.

"What?" they screeched in tandem.

"Jesus and my little Sammy."

"Jesus?" Libby said, turning back to chop the vegetables. "Why, He ain't no man. Last I heard, he's the Son of God."

"And you've been a mama for over a year now, and I've never

seen you this happy," Helen added, still with her hands on her hips.

"Jesus and I are finally at peace. I became a Christian on Sunday. Can't that be enough reason for the joy?"

"Mmm-hmm, that it can. But I'm a thinking it's something more." She turned from the sideboard and pointed with her knife. "You have hope in them there eyes," Libbie said.

"Seriously ladies, there is no man." Heat rushed to her cheeks as her mind went to Joseph. She would love there to be more, but she had a lot of healing to do, and he was not chasing her. He obviously still felt something for her, kissing her the way he had at the Christmas ball. But then nothing, and that was months ago. Sunday had been the first time he ventured anywhere close. He knew where she lived. She believed he had really meant what he said when he told her that she would know where to find him. It would be up to her to make the first move.

"Ha. I see that flush." Libbie waved her hand. "There's more to this story than she's telling." She turned back toward the wood stove and the meat she was browning.

"Truthfully, it's not that I wouldn't love there to be a certain man," Lucinda said.

Their heads spun around like two owls on a perch.

"I love Joseph." The words were out of her mouth before she could think. Honesty came so easily now. "And I don't want to lie to two of my very best friends."

Helen clapped and Libbie's toothy grin widened.

"We done knew that months ago," Libbie said. "It's just taken you a long time to admit it."

"But there's nothing yet—"

"She says there's nothing." Helen's cheeks burned bright with excitement. The women looked at each other and laughed.

"What I mean is, I have so much damage from my first marriage, and now that I'm no longer mad at God, I can embrace His healing. Before I enter into any relationship, I have a lot of work to do. I need to trust, first God, then my own decisions, because I've made so many bad ones."

"Sounds reasonable," Helen said.

"I know this is not very spiritual, but we want you to hurry up and get to the happily-ever-after part," Libbie admitted.

"That's assuming Joseph still wants me after all this."

"Oh, he'll want you," said Helen. Their heads bobbed up and down.

"I pray so. Because he deserves more than the broken soul I've been."

"If he still doesn't have a woman in his life after all this time, he's a lifer," said Libbie.

"A lifer?" Lucinda asked.

"The best kind of man to have. My George is a lifer. That means they love for life."

"And my Elliot too." Helen nodded. "Look at me. I'm about seventy pounds heavier than when we married, and he still calls me beautiful every day."

Joy bubbled up and out at the thought. Joseph was a lifer. He had loved Lucinda since they were kids. She could not contain her smile.

"By that look on your shining face, I think you know Joseph is the man for you. Yes'um you do." Libbie smiled, and Helen looked her way with her head bobbing up and down.

She would seek God and His healing. She'd allow Joseph in if he still wanted her. She would pray for the courage to reveal the truth. Oh yes, she and this newfound God of hers had big plans.

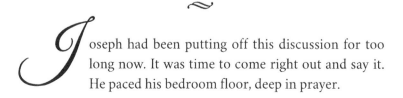

Joseph had been putting off this discussion for too long now. It was time to come right out and say it. He paced his bedroom floor, deep in prayer.

"Oh God, give me the strength to face this problem head on."

The prayer brought a steady peace. He squared his shoulders and headed to the kitchen. There was no point in wasting any more time.

"Pa, I'd like Ma's wedding band." It annoyed him that his voice hitched. He wanted to sound confident, for this conversation was about a lot more than a ring.

Both Nigel and Pa's heads shot up from the breakfast table.

"What for?" Pa's eyes narrowed.

"You know what for."

"I'm saving that ring for Nigel, for when he gets around to popping the question to Esther."

Nigel took a bite of his burnt toast and shook his head. "Not necessary. Esther already showed me her grandmother's ring. It's a beauty. It's got a rock the size of an acorn."

"Good that's settled then." Joseph's twisted gut uncoiled.

"Not so fast," Pa said. "I know your ma would've loved it going to the Dwyer family, but not to that woman—"

"Don't say it, Pa. If you do, you're negating the cross and everything Jesus did there. Do you think that He died only for your sins?"

"Don't you talk to your father that way," Pa spat. "The Bible says to respect your elders."

"It also says that without love we have nothing."

"Whoa, you two." Nigel held up his hands. "This is going nowhere good."

Pa clenched his jaw, but he held his peace.

Joseph couldn't let it end with no decision. He hated conflict and it had taken everything he had to broach the subject, but he had to press on.

"You know we've been seeing each other after church as friends, but someday soon I'm hoping it will be more."

"Just because I didn't say anything doesn't mean I approve."

"I've seen your looks, and so has Lucinda. She knows you don't like her."

"Yet you're so dang set on having the one woman in the valley I don't approve of. Why?" He pushed his chair from the table and crossed his arms with a jerk.

"I've told you many times. I love her. I've loved her since we were kids. Nothing has changed."

"And just how is that going to work if you do get married. You're not bringing her and some other man's kid into my home. I have my principles."

Joseph's heart dropped. He had never been more disappointed in his father. "I sure didn't think you'd pour out your dislike so vehemently that it would include an innocent child. That makes up my mind. After all that Lucinda's been through, I'm not about to subject her to mistreatment from you."

Pa slammed the table with his hands and stood. "And what exactly is it that she's been through? Seems to me she got what she asked for."

Joseph clenched his jaw. He wanted to scream out the atrocities, but he had vowed never to repeat the information. "It's not my story to tell."

"Oh, that's convenient." Pa moved closer, the glare in his eyes clearer.

Joseph straightened his back. "As much as it will break my heart to leave here, I know that Jeb will always have work for me on the Richardson spread. And I'm welcome in their home."

Pa's eyes grew large.

"They'd gladly give us a room until I can build my own place. For that matter, so would Colby and Katherine in that big old rambling mansion where they have a dozen empty rooms."

"But…" Pa sputtered. "I'm not telling you to go."

Joseph spoke in a gentle tone. "When Nigel leaves to marry Esther, because, let's face it, Pa. Esther is not coming here after the way she's been pampered her whole life. Look at this place."

He gestured to the cluttered mess. "You'll be an old soul who has no one to take over the farm, a man who can no longer manage the workload. Your farm will go to seed, and you'll have nothing but silence to rock on that porch out there. But you'll have your principles and your unforgivness to keep you company."

Nigel whistled between his teeth. His gaze flicked from Pa to Joseph and back.

They both knew that Pa was about to explode, but Joseph was not backing down.

"I love you, Pa, but I'm in love with Lucinda. I aim to spend the rest of my life with her. If you shun her, you shun me." Joseph had never stared down his father, but he wouldn't back down this time.

A troubled light crept into Pa's eyes. Tears gathered. Suddenly, he looked years older than he had moments before.

Joseph wanted to hug him and give him whatever he wanted, but this was too important.

"Fine. Have your mother's ring, if it means that much to you."

"It's not the ring as much as your blessing I was looking for."

Pa turned away. "Let's start with the ring. I wouldn't give it unless I knew you were right. I need to forgive. I'm just not there yet."

"She's never done you any harm."

"I wasn't referring to Lucinda. I was thinking of who she reminds me of."

Joseph drew him into a hug. "Thanks." His heart swelled in gratitude to God because not only had Pa used Lucinda's name, but he had identified the source of his pain.

Pa slapped him on the back and stepped away.

Behind Pa's back, Nigel gave a big smile and a nod of his head.

Joseph went to the barn and let out a hoot of joy.

～

*S*pring turned into the first blush of summer, and Lucinda openly flirted with Joseph. She hummed as she put the finishing touches on the picnic basket. They'd made a habit of picnicking on Sunday afternoons. Each time, little by little, she opened up, revealing the horror of her marriage. She acknowledged her rebellious spirit and what had taken her down the Nat Weitzel road. She revealed what she now understood was rape and her unplanned pregnancy, the beatings, the abuse, the control Nat had over her, the fear and hatred she felt for Nat that she still struggled with. She disclosed almost all of it.

One thing remained to tell, the story of her lost child. Now that she was strong enough to face the truth, she had visited Doc Philips and had explained how she rarely had her cycle and what had happened. His examination revealed her deepest fear. She had so much internal scarring and damage, it was unlikely she'd be able to conceive again. If Joseph still stayed after revealing this truth, she would beg him to marry her.

There was a peace in preparing to tell the last and most difficult piece of her story to Joseph—the part that would directly impact his life. Whatever God brought into her future, either marriage to her childhood sweetheart or remaining single, she had an assurance God would give her strength. Today was the day.

The creak of the cook hall screen door brought a smile to her face. Joseph must be there. He had taken Sammy over to her parents' house after church because Pa was lamenting how he rarely got to see the boy with his work schedule. Her parents were going to keep him for the afternoon. Lucinda was thrilled to have her one visit a week with Joseph all to herself.

"I'll be right there. Just finishing up our lunch." She hummed a hymn from the service that morning, settled a piece of

Joseph's favorite chocolate cake in the basket, and put a towel over the top. With the basket in hand, she was ready.

"Lucinda."

She whirled at the sound of a voice she would never forget. The basket crashed to the floor. A scream got stuck in her throat. The only word that came out was strangled and hoarse. "Nat."

$\mathcal{N}$at lifted his hands, palms out, an expression of surrender that looked so alien on him, she didn't know what to make of it. "I'm not here to hurt you. I just want to see if you're all right and visit my son."

Lucinda clutched at the chair in front of her, her knuckles turning white.

A jagged scar disfigured one side of his face. Folds of gnarly, twisted flesh ran a line from his forehead to his jaw. The other side was as handsome as ever. His left eye drooped into a jagged mutilation of skin with a second scar that ran down his cheek to the edge of his lip, which hung in a permanent downward twist. He tried to smile, but only one side of his face responded.

Instinct told Lucinda to run, but experience told her to stand still. There was nothing Nat loved better than to chase her down before he doled out his cruelty. Any show of fear fueled his rage.

She did something new. Her lips moved silently in prayer. *Jesus protect me. Send Joseph.*

"What did you say?" Nat moved closer.

"Not one step closer or I'll yell to high heaven. On a Sunday afternoon, that'll bring every cowboy my way. They all take Sundays off and are lounging around within hearing range."

"Give me just a moment, Lucinda. Just one. I promise. I'm not here to hurt you."

"What do you want?"

"I've found the Lord and I'm a changed man. I'm so sorry for the way I treated you."

Lucinda blinked at his words. Was he making fun? Joking? Mocking? Or… were those tears in his eyes?

"I messed up big. I don't expect you to forgive me, but can I please see my son? That's all I ask."

"To what end? It will only confuse him, and then you'll be gone again."

"I remember when he was born, and I knelt at your side. I wished he would grow up to be a far better man than I am. I didn't know how to be that man back then. Now I've found Jesus, and I know what the missing link is. I can finally be the father I want to be." His gaze flicked to her left hand, and his eyes brightened. "I see you're not remarried."

"No, but she's engaged, soon to be married." Joseph walked past Nat and put his arm around her shoulders.

Lucinda collapsed against him. Relief flooded over her. She wanted to sink into the nearest chair, but Joseph held her steady. *Thank you, God.*

"Why no ring?"

"Not that it's any of your business but just so that you know she's out of your life for good, I'm getting my Ma's ring resized to fit." Joseph lifted her trembling hand to his lips and gently kissed it. "I'm here now, darling."

"I want to see my son," Nat said.

"You don't have a son." Lucinda squared her shoulders, feeling a whole lot more confident with Joseph at her side. "You forfeited that right when you called him a squawking brat and left us for another woman. Now go, and don't ever come back."

Joseph stepped forward. "You heard the lady. You ever step foot on this property or anywhere near Lucinda again, and you'll answer to me. You hear? We'll see how good you do against a real man instead of a woman half your size." Joseph was a good six inches shorter than Nat, but his stocky build and bulging muscles would be a force to be reckoned with against Nat's thin, lanky frame. She looked at the two men staring each other down and wondered what she had ever seen in Nat. His white, pasty skin and skinny arms looked wimpy next to Joseph's suntanned, sinewy strength.

Nat turned and walked out.

"I'll be right back." Joseph kissed her forehead. "I want to be sure he leaves. I'll get a couple of the cowboys to escort him off the property and beyond."

Lucinda collapsed to her knees and wept. She picked up the picnic basket and the food that had scattered in every direction. *Why God? Why did he have to return when I'm trying so hard to forgive him?* One look at the man, and the emotions had come flooding back in. She shivered as a chill ran up her spine. The memories bubbled to the surface and choked the joy out of her soul. Her hands fisted and her legs trembled. She wanted justice. By the look of the scar on Nat's face, someone had given him a taste of the medicine he had given her, and she was glad.

How could a Christian love the cruelty of revenge? And yet she did. No point in hiding the truth. She thought she had given all to Jesus, but the yearning she had to see him dead returned after one moment in his presence. Maybe she was not changed after all.

Joseph returned. "He's gone." He gathered Lucinda in his arms and held her tight.

She tucked her trembling body into the warmth of his arms. His tender voice talked her off the ledge of fear, but what was she to do with the surge of hatred that pumped through her veins?

"You're all right, my LucyBug. You're safe now." He smoothed his hand gently through her curls. She wanted to stay there forever.

$\sim$

*J*oseph took the church steps two at time. He loved Sundays in every way. Time with God and time with the love of his life. Lucinda turned as he walked in and waved him over. He slid into the pew beside her, and she slipped her hand into his. Adrenaline shot through his veins. There was nothing church-like about the distraction she caused.

If she didn't tell him that she wanted him soon, he was going to implode. Did God really want him to wait for her to make the first move? How much more overt could he have been than to tell Nat they were engaged? She hadn't balked at the statement because she'd needed the protection, but why had that not triggered the obvious? He hadn't lied about ma's ring being resized. It was now ready for her beautiful finger.

Sammy lunged from Lucinda's arms straight to Joseph. His tiny arms tightened around Joseph's neck.

"How you doing, little man?" Joseph was rewarded with a big smile. He'd had no idea that love for a child who was not his flesh and blood could run so deep. The child had won his heart, and there was nothing he wanted more than to make it legal and be Sammy's father. They would become a family and give Sammy a bunch of brothers and sisters. The thought tugged at his lips, turning up the smile he could not contain.

Between Colby's men, Lucinda's Pa, and whatever time he had, they worked out a plan so that Lucinda was never alone. But he wanted to be her husband, her defender, not living in a different place where he only got to see her once a week. Especially with the possibility that Nat was still creeping around.

And where had Nat gone? Was he gone for good? Joseph struggled to decide if he should call on Marcellus Latchum and take him up on his promise. But that would result in the good side of Nat's face matching the other, or worse. It would serve him right...wouldn't it.

The battle within raged as he farmed his fields, lay in his bed at night, or even sat in church. There was a side of him that wanted revenge for all the damage Nat had done to Lucinda. But God kept whispering forgiveness into his soul. He'd extend mercy as long as the man stayed far away. But dare he come back...

Lucinda's hand grabbed Joseph's knee, and he looked up from Sammy. She nodded to the right, her eyes wide with fear. Joseph saw the man just as Nat made his way past them to the front of the church. He slipped into a pew on the opposite side of the aisle, where he could glance back at Lucinda easily.

"What's he doing here?" she whispered.

Fury filled Joseph's body and rippled down his spine. "Not sure. But don't worry. I'll be dealing with him directly after the service."

They stood to sing, but Joseph couldn't choke out a word. He looked down at Lucinda. She was nibbling on her baby fingernail, a sure sign of tension. Why, the nerve of that scoundrel to use a place of worship to manipulate and cause fear.

He held Sammy and slipped a protective arm around her shoulder. Nat turned to stare at them. The bad side of his face was exposed.

"He looks as dark as he is," she whispered. "Maybe now the women will think twice about believing that bold-faced liar."

Her agitation showed by the clip in her voice and the ice in her fingers as she grabbed Joseph's arm. "I just want him gone."

"I know, my darling. So do I."

Nat kept glancing at them throughout the service. When

Preacher Mark gave the invitation to come for prayer, Nat sent them one more look and walked forward.

Joseph wanted to scream at the theatrics. His thoughts were brewing into a storm.

There were no tears, no falling on his knees, no show of expression at all, but who was Joseph to judge the soul? What if Nat truly was repenting?

"He told me he already found Jesus, so why the going forward? I have to get out of here." Lucinda pushed past Joseph and ran down the aisle and out the door. Joseph followed with Sammy in his arms.

She was out by the oak tree, bent over and gasping for air.

He hurried to her side. "You're all right. He can't hurt you anymore."

She wheezed in and out. "Just when I think I'm healed enough to marry you, he returns to show me how far I have to go. Ever since he showed up, I'm having nightmares again."

Joseph's free hand fisted. He wanted to punch that man into next week for the damage he had done. How did Nat have the gall to show up again? He pulled her close and held on tight. Sammy played with the rim of his cowboy hat as she sobbed into his shirt.

"I want you and Sammy to go home with Colby and Katherine. Colby will keep you safe. I'll join you later. I have some business to take care of." He pulled out of the hug and handed Sammy to her.

Her eyes bulged. "No, Joseph. You can't trust the man. He'll pull out a gun, a knife—"

"Shh. You need to trust me and God." He could feel the bitter acid of anger in the back of his throat. Could he really say what he needed without his anger talking through his fists?

God help me.

People began to filter out the door, many of their eyes

watching Joseph, who stood at the bottom of the steps waiting. He ignored them all until he caught sight of Nat.

"A word with you." Joseph pointed to the tree at the side of the yard.

Nat led the way and, once out of ear shot, turned to face him.

"What I have to say I'm only going to say once." Joseph's voice held a steely grit. "You'd better understand and heed my warning."

One of Nat's brows raised. The other didn't move.

"You may start a new life anywhere but in this valley. And if you've really found Jesus and changed, you'll leave the woman you brutalized alone."

"What, no forgiveness in your heart? That's my kid and my wife you're trying to steal."

"This is not up for discussion. Do you remember Marcellus Latchum?"

"How do you know him?"

Nat tried to sound tough, but Joseph could hear the quiver in his voice. "The only reason you're alive today is because I told Marcellus I would not be an accomplice to murder. But you have to know he was none too pleased about what you did to his daughter, the same thing I have since learned you did to Lucinda. Just so there's no mistake, it's called rape when a woman doesn't consent."

Nat's jaw gaped.

"One word to Marcellus that you're back in this valley, or even this state, and he and his boys will hunt you down. I suggest you go and never look back. If you return, there'll be no more talking. Understood?"

Nat's eyes furtively moved back and forth behind Joseph. "I understand." He turned and hurried off.

Joseph spun to see Colby, Jeb, Nigel, and a couple of the

ranch hands standing behind him in a semi-circle. Even his Pa was there.

He smiled his thank-You up into the heavens. Without saying a word, God had arranged a small army for reinforcement.

~

"*I*'m still so angry." Lucinda walked beside Jeanette in the orchard. Small green apples were forming on the branches. A summer breeze kissed their cheeks. "What Nat did to me…will I ever be able to truly forgive?"

"That's a biggie, but God wouldn't ask us to forgive if it were impossible." Jeanette dipped her head under a low hanging branch.

"It's like I surrender it to God one day, and then pick it up the next. Some days I have zero anger, and then a single memory can bring it all crashing in, making me feel like I haven't made any progress at all."

"I've never had anything as big as you have to forgive, but I've had some hurtful circumstances. It's kind of like giving your thoughts to God one at time, as they come."

"Easy to say, but how does that work in real life?"

"Take the way that married man acted interested in me, for instance. The more I thought about what he did, the more my anger grew, making forgiveness impossible."

"I know what that feels like. So, what do you do?"

"I ran across a verse in 2 Corinthians 10:5 that helped me a lot. It says to bring every thought into captivity to the obedience of Christ. That means to not let my negative thoughts run wild but bring each one to God. I started doing this when I was struggling to forgive him and the terrible thoughts and memories lost their power. God removed the pain associated with them so I could see the situation through the eyes of forgiveness."

"Are you saying the minute a terrible memory comes to mind, I should give it to God?"

"Yes. That's it."

"Just like that?" Lucinda snapped her fingers. "It's gone?"

"No. We still have our memory, and it's hard at first. You'll feel like you're praying constantly, but little by little that hurt no longer has power over you and forgiveness becomes natural."

"And that works."

"I swear it does." Jeanette turned toward her with a hand to her heart. "It changes this."

"What if Nat's for real and he has changed? Don't I owe him the right to see his child?"

"You owe him nothing." Jeanette resumed her walk.

"But I'm supposed to forgive."

"Forgive, yes. Let him back into your life or your son's life? No. That's not a requirement of forgiveness."

"But Nat said being a father is the only reason he has left to live."

"If he's really changed, then Jesus will be enough reason to live. Forgiveness does not equal trust." Jeanette snagged a green apple from a branch. "Take a bite." She thrust the apple in Lucinda's face.

"From that bitter thing? It's not ready."

She threw the apple on the ground. "Exactly my point. Nat is not ready. If he truly had a conversion, then time will tell that story, and you can deal with this down the road with Joseph by your side. And what's the hold up with you two, anyway? Obviously, you love each other like crazy."

A stab of guilt pierced Lucinda's heart. She knew why she stalled with Joseph. It wasn't because she didn't love him but because she still hadn't revealed the worst of her secrets. She could not give him his own child. With the stress of Nat's return, their few moments together had been consumed with talk of her safety and Nat's whereabouts, and she didn't have the reserves to bring up another tough subject. Also, Nat's return had fueled her anger, and she didn't want to go into marriage angry. "Things are complicated."

"Only as complicated as you make them. Can I be frank?"

"When aren't you?"

"You need to start thinking more about Joseph than yourself. He's been so patient. The guy's a near saint. He works his own farm, and when Pa gets overwhelmed, he comes running. He's out there right now, helping Pa sort out what to do about some bug in the corn field. Where do I find a man like that? And let me tell you, if I did, I wouldn't keep him waiting."

Lucinda smiled at Jeanette. "I know. He's the best, and you're right."

"When are you going to get that I'm always right?" She laughed and hugged Lucinda's shoulders. "I'm heading back to the house now." Jeanette turned. "Are you coming?"

"I need some time to myself."

"You're not to be left alone."

"We've always been safe in this orchard." Nat would never know I'm here.

"You still need protection. No one is sure if Nat left or not."

"Colby has people scouting the property. How could Nat come so far without being noticed?"

Jeanette shook her head. "I don't like it."

"I just need some time in the outdoors alone with God."

She paused a long moment, clearly considering. Finally, she said, "All right, but don't be long."

Lucinda breathed in the late afternoon air. Warm waves of sunlight carried on a steamy gust of the wind kissed her cheeks. Dried grass crackled beneath each step. She stopped walking at the edge of the orchard and lifted her face to the canted rays. Wispy clouds scribbled into the blue, and a hawk dipped and rose. *Oh, to be that free.* With her eyes closed, she stood in the tranquillity, enjoying the sound of silence. Her heart opened to God. "Speak to me," she whispered.

Trust Me.

She knew exactly what God was saying. The one piece of information she held back from Joseph needed to be spoken. *Oh God, what if he doesn't want me when he finds out he'll never have a child of his own?*

Trust Me.

Lucinda breathed deeply. She had trusted Joseph with all the other atrocities. Why was this one so hard? Guilt jabbed. She knew why...something she had not even admitted to herself. She had wanted that weekend away with Nat so much—to make her marriage work, to please him. She hadn't heeded the warnings God had given her. The girl in the store whom Nat obviously had a past with, the way he was all too accommodating, the new dress material and comments about how she could wear it right away, the chill she'd felt when she'd met Madame Dovel. And the biggest—the tea that didn't taste like tea. Though Nat had schemed to make it happen, Lucinda was responsible for the loss of her child too. How would she tell sweet, pure Joseph? Could God forgive even that?

Trust me.

And why shouldn't she trust God? He had saved her from a terrible life made by the choices of willful rebellion. She experienced the peace of forgiveness and grace deep in her soul. She turned back toward the farmhouse with a smile on her face. Sammy would be waking from his nap soon. She needed to get back.

"You're more beautiful than I remember."

Her eyes popped wide, and she wheeled around. Nat was close. Too close.

Dear God, help me. Panic edged up her throat.

"Do you know how long I've waited to find you alone?"

Why had she not listened to Jeanette? She was such a fool.

"And I see you still have no ring. You're waiting for me too, aren't you?" A mirthless smile crawled across Nat's lips. One side of his mouth drooped, enhancing the twisted mess. "We had some good times together, didn't we, baby?" His lustful stare undressed her as it slithered over her from head to toe.

Nat grabbed her shoulders, pulling her in. She was close enough to see every ridge on his jagged scar and smell the alcohol on his breath. A glazed look flashed in his eyes. She knew that look well. Craving. Hunger. Power. If she struggled, she would only feed the beast. She stood completely still, a mouse in the presence of a cobra. The look in Nat's eyes spoke murder.

Joseph, gentle Joseph, flashed through her mind. She would never be able to tell him just how much she loved him. Why had she wasted so much time? Her mouth opened, but only a squeak came out.

One arm crushed her against his body, and the other pulled her hair back. He slammed his crooked mouth against hers, silencing her scream.

No. This was not going to happen again. She jerked back in a rage, catching him by surprise, and dropped low. A good size rock lay at her feet. She snatched it up as he yanked her body up by her hair. She almost got the side of his head before he grabbed her wrist and twisted. The rock fell from her hand as she yelled out in pain.

CHAPTER 27

"You what?" Joseph's heart kicked against the walls of his chest.

"She's walking in the orchard," Jeanette said. "She needed some time alone."

"Which direction? Some of the men thought they saw Nat creeping up the fence line."

"Oh, dear Jesus, no." Jeanette's hand went to her throat.

Joseph shouted, "Where is she?"

She pointed. "But she could be anywhere by now."

He took off running. Fists pumping, he tore between the rows, begging God for guidance. Frantically running one way and then another, he looked up and saw them at the edge of the orchard. She was not fighting him. Her head was tilted back, and she was kissing him.

No.

He stopped dead, then noticed that her hands were flailing, her hair was yanked into his fist.

Fury filled his body and rippled down his spine. He flew at Nat and wrenched him backwards by his shirt. Nat staggered, and Joseph punched him squarely in the jaw.

Nat howled as he fell to the ground.

Joseph jumped on top and hammered Nat's face with his fists. Nat twisted his lanky body and they rolled in the grass until Nat was on top. He stood with a snap and whipped out a pistol from his coat pocket.

Lucinda flew at him from behind smashing the side of his head with a rock. He dropped his gun, stumbled back and then ran.

Joseph scrambled for the gun in the tall grass, but by the time he found it, Nat was a good distance away. "Run, you coward," Joseph yelled after him. "Cause Latchum and his boys are going to hear you're back in Virginia. And if I ever see you again, I'll put a bullet in your skull myself." He lifted his hand to the blood dripping from his knuckles and wiped it onto his pants, then hurried to Lucinda's side. She collapsed onto her knees, her dress billowing around her.

"I'm so sorry. All I wanted was a few minutes to myself." Tears pooled in her eyes and poured down her ashen cheeks. "Thank God you came." The quiver in her voice turned into an uncontrollable whole-body shake.

He gathered her close. "You're going to be all right. I'm here now." He smoothed his hand over her hair. What kind of animal does that to a woman? He held her until she quieted and relaxed against his chest.

"I tried to fight...to scream..." She gulped back a sob.

"Shh, my darling. It's not your fault. Let's get you back to the house." He helped her stand.

She gazed up at him. "I don't want to go anywhere without you. I don't want to live one more day without you by my side. When Nat came at me, all I could think about was that I'd never told you the words I've longed to say for so long now. I love you, Joseph. I love you with all my heart. Will you marry me?"

As a jolt of heat shot through him, he wanted to shout a hallelujah, but she was not thinking straight. "Lucinda, there is nothing I want more than to marry you, but you've just been attacked. Your thinking is—"

"My thoughts have never been clearer." She stood on tippy toes with her lips raised to his. "I love you. You're my soul mate, my best friend, the man I love more than life itself."

He lowered his mouth slowly to hers, and she held nothing back. He crushed her closer, his body surging with awareness. The gentle kiss blazed with passion and ignited like a spark to fuel. Dancing in flames of sensation, he caught her hand in his to stop the insanity.

She tore away. "Let's get married soon?"

"Yes." He kissed her lips once. "Yes." Twice. "And yes." His lips landed on hers where words were no longer necessary.

~

*L*ucinda tossed from one side of her bed to the other. No matter how she moved she could not get comfortable. She ripped the covers off her body and padded to the window. The dark of night closed in as a billowing cloud scuttled across the moon's path. Nat was out there somewhere, lurking in the shadows. He had an obsession for getting what he could not have. Would she ever be safe?

She whispered against the glass. "Oh, God, I want him dead. I want this nightmare to be over once and for all, not him popping up here and there. Next time he won't waste his time. Is this wrong?"

Until you forgive, it will never be over.

How could she marry Joseph with such hatred in her heart? Nat's attack had opened up wounds that were obviously not healed. She was bleeding again. Hemorrhaging hatred. That man had stolen her virginity. He had shattered her confidence. He had crushed her self-worth. He had destroyed the chance of future children. No other emotion made sense other than hate.

Forgiveness sets you free.

Her heart felt the squeeze of God's Spirit, but she needed justice.

Vengeance is Mine.

Why then did the desire for vengeance feel so right?

Trust Me.

Didn't You tell me to trust You just before Nat attacked me?

I did.

To have that monster come out of nowhere. How was that a reward for trust? Lucinda flung the curtain shut and paced the floor. She was a mess. Fighting with God. Fighting with the urge to hate, which felt a whole lot more natural than forgiveness. Fighting with her own lack of self-worth and the truth she needed to tell Joseph. How could she have asked Joseph to marry such a wreck?

Jeanette had told her to take every thought captive.

She lifted her gaze to the ceiling. *God, I give You the chaos. I give You my hatred. I give You my fear. I give You dear sweet Joseph, and if I'm not the best for him, then please, please help me have the strength to let him go.*

Tears gathered and rolled down her cheeks. She twisted the ring Joseph had put on her finger. Could she truly be selfless enough to let him go? And what about Sammy? Didn't he deserve a daddy? She flung her body back onto the bed and let the tears fall.

A peace washed into the room...to her, over her, and through her. She did not have any answers, but the One who did was with her. That much she knew. She burrowed into the covers with a sense that God was pleased with her surrender, and the weight of her troubles lifted.

*J*oseph looked over the swaying field of wheat. The afternoon breeze ruffled the tips dressed in vibrant hues of gold and yellow. The landscape popped against the brilliant blue sky. He took a deep breath in. Life was finally coming together. He had slipped his Ma's ring on Lucinda's finger, and he was going to be an instant daddy. And the thought of a whole passel of children playing in the yard made his heart sing. And she would be near—where he could protect her. He could not help smiling.

A bumper crop covered every inch of their farmland. The improvements he'd made on the farm had been successful. People often patted him on the back and told him he was a gifted man, but he knew God was blessing everything he touched.

The only thing left was to tell Pa that he and Lucinda were officially engaged and that the marriage would take place soon. He prayed every day for his pa, hoping that he was working through his childhood pain.

Joseph turned from the field toward the barn and saw Pa headed his way. No time like the present.

"Great looking crop." Pa slapped him on the back. "Thanks to my boy here."

Would he feel the same by the time their conversation was done? "We're blessed."

"Blessed." He nodded. "But all this doesn't just magically happen." He waved toward the fields. "You put in a lot of hard work, and I'm proud of you."

Pa was pleased with him. No better opportunity would present itself. "I have some exciting news. Lucinda and I are engaged."

The smile vanished from Pa's face, and deep-set wrinkles furrowed his brow. "I had hoped things were simmering down between you two, what with the boy's father coming back in the picture and all."

A ripple of concern ran up Joseph's spine. "He has never *fathered* the child. And you know how he attacked Lucinda. I want to marry her immediately and keep her safe."

"And bring the problem to our home."

"If that's the way you feel then no, I will not. As I told you before, I have other places to live and a job anytime I want at the Richardson ranch. I don't want to leave you or this farm. I always thought I'd be the one to look out for you as you get older. But if that's what you choose—"

"What choice do I have?"

"Pa, I want to be here for harvest, you know I do. I've invested my life into working the land, our land. It's what I was born to do. But I love Lucinda, and I'm going to spend the rest of my life with her. If you can't assure me you'll be kind, then I won't bring her here."

"Can't you wait until next year, give yourself time to build a cabin?"

Joseph stepped back at the surprising question. "The plan was always to build onto our house when I get married. Remember?"

"That was before." Pa looked at the ground and kicked at a rock in the dust.

"Does this mean you don't want her in your home?"

He did not answer.

"I thought you wanted grandchildren. Lucinda is a wonderful mother. She's not like your—"

"I don't want to talk about my ma." He looked back up. "I suppose you gave the fact she's a divorced woman considerable thought?"

"I did and I don't care."

"Tongues will wag."

"Until they find the next new thing to go on about."

"Well, if you're sure, who am I to stand in your way?"

"I've never been surer about anything in my life."

"All right then. Do as you wish." Pa walked away with his head down mumbling to himself.

Joseph's gut twisted and knotted. Would Pa accept Lucinda and Sammy? He looked back over the fields. He really didn't want to give up all he had worked so hard to achieve.

CHAPTER 28

*L*ucinda stood in the farmhouse kitchen awaiting Joseph's arrival. She had to tell him. The wedding was only three days away. Today was the day. If Joseph still wanted to marry her after he learned the truth, she would walk down that aisle with her head held high.

Day by day, growing in her relationship with God, her confidence was increasing. And the way Joseph lavished love on her, her self-worth was climbing out of the pit it had been in for too long. Just as Jeanette had suggested, following biblical principles really did work. Each negative thought she had of Nat, she immediately gave to God, praying for his soul. The feelings of hatred were easing one good decision at a time. She was learning to trust God with her bad memories of Nat. She could trust him with this too.

Nervousness nibbled at her confidence. Her future depended on the outcome of this conversation. She'd given her cooking job away and had already trained the new girl taking over her position.

"Hello, beautiful."

Lucinda turned to see Joseph holding out a bouquet of bluebells.

"For my LucyBug." His slow, easy smile melted the trepidation in her heart. He loved her.

She took the flowers and inhaled their scent. "Ahh, my favorites. Do you have any idea how much I love you?" She planted a quick kiss on his lips.

He grabbed her close. "All I get is a little peck?"

"It's all I dare, if you know what I mean?" She nuzzled his neck, and he groaned and let her go.

"Do I ever. Saturday can't come soon enough."

"I'll put these in water, and then we're going for a picnic." She fiddled with the flowers in the mason jar until she got them just perfect.

"What about Sammy?"

"Jeanette has him for the afternoon. And I've made all your favorites." She held up the basket. "Let's go."

He held out his hand, and she interlocked her fingers in his. Awareness tingled up her arm.

Always the gentleman, he helped her into his buggy and hopped up beside her. "Where to, my lady?"

"Down to the creek for sure. I love that spot."

"Our spot?" The buggy lurched forward.

"Yes. I love the memories there of us fishing as kids, and me hoping you would kiss me—"

"Oh, I wanted to, but I was shaking in my boots. How about I make up for that today?"

She smiled at him, hoping he would still feel that way after she told him everything. Her feelings tumbled one over the other...pleasure, panic, pain.

It was a picture-perfect Shenandoah summer afternoon. A soft breeze feathered her face, lifting the edges of her sun bonnet. Overhead, birds darted and dipped. A nearby thicket teemed with families of rabbits. A cottontail loped out across the trail in front of them. She squeezed Joseph's hand, and he pulled her closer, navigating the wagon with one hand, his arm around her. She laid her head against his shoulder, and he kissed the top of her head. Life could not get more perfect.

Why mess with perfect?

Where had that thought come from?

He loves you. Leave it there.

The old Lucinda had hidden many a truth, but she was a new creation. No, she had to tell Joseph. Give him a choice. This was his life too.

Maybe you can have children. You can't be sure.

Why hadn't she thought of that? Maybe she could give Joseph a son or daughter. Why should she create trouble before she knew for certain?

Yes, that's right. Why look for trouble?

Oh, she liked the thought of waiting. Her God was big enough to give her a miracle, wasn't He?

"Here we are." Joseph hopped from the buggy and held out his arms. She dropped down, and he swung her around, kissing her soundly before touching her feet to the ground. She breathed in the wonderful scent of musk and leather.

"I think you'd better get that picnic basket before I get completely sidetracked."

She lifted her hand to the side of his face. "How did I ever get so blessed?" Her thumb slid to brush over his lips, and he grabbed her hand, kissing every finger slowly.

"It is I who has been blessed. I not only get my beautiful, spunky, LucyBug, but I get little Sammy too. I can't wait to give him a sister or a brother to play with." His lips brushed hers with aching gentleness. "Let's start with a little girl, just like her mama. Now, that would melt my heart." His lips found hers again. She could barely kiss him back.

Trust Me. Tell him the truth.

That was the inner voice she recognized. It was the same message she had heard for days.

He pulled back, still holding her in his arms. "What is it? Is something wrong?"

She twisted free. "No. No. Nothing's wrong. I just love you so much. I'm afraid of getting carried away." The lies came out fast. One after another. "I want to do this right." She was still way too good at them.

"You're right. Let's eat. That'll keep me busy." Joseph laughed as if he was the happiest man alive. She didn't have the strength to steal that from him. Not today. Not in their special spot.

She needed him. Sammy needed him. Surely God would understand.

Yes, God, would understand.

❧

LATE JULY 1876

On a bright sunny Saturday morning, Lucinda and Joseph stood with a small group down by the creek. Only immediate family and a few close friends had been invited to their wedding.

Lucinda wore Katherine's wedding dress. Jeanette had shortened the length and personalized the fit to perfection. Lucinda's auburn hair was swept up into an elegant coil at the back of her head, and Ma's lace-trimmed veil drifted in the breeze as she strolled toward Joseph, standing proudly next to Preacher Mark.

She gazed up at the man she loved. Oh, how long she had made him wait for this day, and yet his smile was wider than the Shenandoah River was long. He took her hand in his. How had she been so blessed to get a second chance? True love this time.

Only one thing nagged at her conscience, and she prayed for

a miracle. Surely, God could give them a child. He would have mercy, for she would've never consented to what Nat organized behind her back. She brushed the ugly thought aside. It was a day for happiness.

The ceremony was quick and perfect, and her heart soared when she heard those final words. "You may kiss the bride."

Joseph's lips descended upon hers with warmth and fire. Chuckles filled the air before he finally pulled away.

"It is a wedding," he said. "Surely there are no restrictions to the length of time a man can kiss his beloved."

Everyone laughed.

"I invite you to join us for lunch." His arm swept out toward the tables set up under the oak tree. "By the tantalizing smells coming our way, I'd say we're in for a feast. Thanks to all the ladies for their wonderful contributions." He raised his hands to clap, and everyone joined in. The small crowd gravitated toward the food. "Let's make this fast," he whispered in Lucinda's ear. "I want plenty of time to get my beautiful bride to our surprise destination before nightfall."

Butterflies danced in her tummy at the thought of them finally being together. Her family was going to look after Sammy while they had a week to themselves. She'd been given no more details. She couldn't remember ever having had a whole week off of work and responsibilities, and she didn't count the trip to Dayton, which had turned into a week of horror. She pushed those black thoughts away. Today was a day of celebration and love, not darkness. She squeezed Joseph's arm as he finished his last bite of food.

"Come, my LucyBug." Joseph stood held out his hand. "It's time to leave the family behind and start our life together."

She placed her palm into his strong, work-toughened hand that she loved so much. Nat's had always been soft, yet harsh. Joseph's were calloused from his hard labour, yet ever so gentle.

"Let's say good-bye to Sammy and sneak away," he said. "I've waited a lifetime for you. I don't want to wait one moment longer."

"What? Are you going to stop the wagon on the way and make love to me in the tall summer grass?"

"Nope," he said. "You deserve far more effort than that." He kissed her cheek and threw an arm around her shoulder.

Her heart skipped and bubbled like a turbulent creek. She was both nervous and excited. Would she measure up to his life-long dream?

"Give me a few minutes to change, and we'll be on our way."

He nodded. "I'll do the same."

Joseph's Pa stood off to the side. She smiled at him, but he looked away, pretending not to see her. Apprehension nipped at her mind. Was Joseph wrong? He had told her his pa had given his blessing to marry. She could not think about that now.

She scanned the crowd, catching her sister's eye. "Jeanette." She nodded in the direction of the house.

"Coming."

Lucinda ran into the farmhouse with Jeanette at her side. With Jeanette's help, she slipped out of her wedding dress and pulled on her traveling outfit. The sharp tailored skirt and matching green jacket accented her tiny waist and auburn hair.

After removing her veil, Jeanette fixed her hair.

"I'll miss you," Jeanette said. "With you moving to his farm, we'll be lucky to see each other on Sundays." Her voice cracked.

Lucinda hugged her tight. "This is your fault. You kept throwing us together."

"I know. I couldn't bear to see you so unhappy. Both of you. I'm a romantic at heart." She gave a quick hug. "Now, go. Joseph has waited long enough." She picked up Lucinda's carpetbag, put it in her hand, and shooed her out the bedroom door.

Lucinda raced down the stairs and out to the yard, where the guests gathered.

Everyone was smiling at them as they climbed into the

wagon, except Joseph's Pa. He stood at the back of the group with his arms crossed and a dark look on his face. It was hard to miss. She shivered in the bright sunshine, remembering another man she could never please. Where was Nat? She scoured the area, as she found herself doing a lot lately.

The wagon lurched forward, and they waved good-bye and headed off.

CHAPTER 29

*L*ucinda laid her head against Joseph's shoulder. The Mighty Alleghenies bordered the valley to her right, and the craggy Massanutten to her left. The buggy rolled along the valley bottom. Fertile fields of vegetables, hay, and fruit trees resembled a patchwork quilt over rolling hills. Sunlight played hide-and-seek with the clouds, shadows and light dancing across the open fields. The silence between them was comfortable.

"I'm so happy," she whispered, "and thankful to God that you didn't give up on me. I know I don't deserve a man like you who had a lineup of would-be wives—"

"Shh," he said. "Nothing but good thoughts and words today. You deserve as much happiness as I do, and I couldn't be more filled with joy than I am in this moment." He kissed the top of her head. "But I do have to admit, I'm looking forward to what this evening will bring."

She could feel heat flood her cheeks.

He laughed. "I like the fact that you still blush, sweet LucyBug."

"And I like that you still remember that nickname."

"How could I forget the girl who followed me around like a hungry mosquito?"

She batted his arm. "I did not. You followed me around, pulling my braids, calling me names, anything you could do to get my attention."

"Can't argue with that. I fell in love the first moment I caught sight of a sassy redhead standing at the edge of the school playground, looking so lost and forlorn. I instantly wanted to protect you, as fiercely as I still do today."

"You know how to make a girl cry in the sweetest way." Lucinda swiped at the tears that dropped free of her lashes.

"Happy tears, I hope?"

"Only happy. All you've ever brought me, Joseph, is happiness."

"I'll remind you of that someday soon when you're spitfire mad at something I've done, like track in mud on your clean floor or…"

She raised an eyebrow. "You think I'm going to clean your floors?"

A smile played at the corner of his mouth. "Not only mine, but Pa and Nigel will be tracking through as well. That is, until I get our own section of the house built. I'm sure you'll find more than a few reasons to get that sassy temper of yours fired up."

"I've lived in a house with four sisters stealing my clothes, intruding in my private space, and making a mess of my area. I think I'll be able to handle the three of you."

He chuckled. "I have no doubt."

"Do you think they'll be all right with me there? Your Pa—"

"Will be just fine," he finished.

"I can't blame him for being less than thrilled with you marrying a divorced woman with a ready-made family. How are they going to take to a noisy child?"

"They'll love him—and you. Your cooking alone is going to reel them in. Besides, I like that you'll be surrounded by three men who all know how to use a gun if need be. Pretty sure that coward is long gone, but…"

He said no more. Just the mention of Nat sent a chill up her spine. News traveled that he'd skipped town after word got out that the sheriff, Joseph, Colby's men, and the Latchum boys were all looking for him. Lucinda shivered at the thought of Nat's capacity for hatred and hoped he was gone for good. She pressed him out of her mind. He had no right to invade her wedding day.

"We're almost there, darling."

The afternoon's slanted rays splashed against the eastern ridge, and the landscape was dotted with homes closer together. Golden threads of fading light spread a lemony warmth across the fields. There could not have been a more perfect July day. Her insides fluttered with the thrill of anticipation. Would she make her husband as happy as he had already made her? Nat had drummed in how useless she was in every way, so much so that, even on a perfect day like today, anxiety bit at her mind. Would she be good enough?

Joseph's smile seemed etched on his face as they turned up the gravel drive to a stone mansion with a large veranda and sweeping green lawns. His lopsided grin highlighted the delight tugging at his cheeks. He looked like a man with purpose as he leapt from the wagon.

He held out his strong arms and swung her down. "You may not have had much of a wedding with such quick preparations, but you shall have a honeymoon to remember. When you're old and gray with your granddaughters gathered all around, you shall tell of this day."

"You're awfully sure of yourself, Mr. Manning."

"I am, Mrs. Manning." A twinkle of merriment danced in his gentle blue eyes, the kind a girl could swim in, much like the swirl of the Shenandoah.

She beamed up at him.

"Well, you have to put one foot in front of the other darling, instead of mesmerizing me with that inviting look, or we'll stand here forever."

She shook the fog out of her head and giggled. "It's what you do to me. I look into your face, and kindness is all I see. I never want to leave."

"You shall never have to." He hitched the horses to the post and guided her up the few steps onto the sprawling veranda.

A man dressed in a dapper suit with coattails and a top hat opened the heavy wood door and motioned them in. "Welcome to Rosewood Inn, Mr. and Mrs. Manning. My name is Thomas Gibson, and I shall be at your service." He removed his hat and bowed his head. Dark eyes shone beneath silver and black curly hair. With a sweep of his hand, he beckoned them in. "Your room is ready, and supper will be served shortly in the dining room just off this entry." He pointed, and Lucinda peeked in to see four tables, each privately situated in a different alcove.

"Follow me. I'll give you a quick tour of the shared spaces and a bit of the history." He walked down the hall. "The proprietor, Mrs. Rose Jackson, started this business after her husband passed because she couldn't bear the thought of living alone in this grand old home. She has her own wing and is fiercely private, but her hope is that each patron will find their love deepened by their stay." He chuckled, his black cheeks shining. "Mrs. Jackson believes in all things romantic. Indeed, she does."

He stopped at one door and pointed in. "The library. Feel free to read anything you like. However, we do ask that, if you stumble upon another couple, you find a different spot in this lovely home or surrounding grounds to enjoy. We want each couple to experience privacy. It's why we only book four couples at any time."

Lucinda looked up at Joseph and smiled. He squeezed her waist with the arm he had fastened around her.

Mr. Gibson rambled on, pointing out a few more rooms all

beautifully appointed and decorated to exude warmth and welcome. The drawing room was graced with a floor-to-ceiling stone fireplace, the parlor perfect for a high afternoon tea, and there was even a private balcony off a second-story solarium. Lucinda made a mental note to return.

"On Saturday evening, a band will play right here." Mr. Gibson led them into a ballroom. "Plan on a delectable meal and an evening of dancing. Favorite tunes played upon request. Now, let's head outdoors for a quick tour." His wide toothy smile invited them onward.

Lucinda pulled Joseph back behind Mr. Gibson and whispered, "How can we afford such luxury?"

"Nothing is too extravagant for my girl."

She tried to push away thoughts of Nat's overspending and reminded herself that Joseph was Nat's polar opposite, but how was it possible a mere farmer could provide such lavishness? Why did the exercise of trust feel like a mountain she was not sure she could climb? No, she would not start her marriage this way. Joseph was not Nat. She squeezed Joseph's hand and planted a quick kiss on his cheek.

They did a short tour of the wraparound veranda and gardens, seeing numerous spots for lovers to stroll and sit in privacy along the way. In the stables, they saw an elaborate Phaeton carriage waiting for a lover's ride, or for the more adventurous couple, horses that could be taken out for a private gallop in the acres of rolling hills, wooded pastures, and flowering meadows. "You'll never get lost. Mrs. Rose has her vast acreage fenced so that when you come to a fence you can follow it back. It circles the property and will always lead home."

"Lastly"—he handed Joseph an envelope—"this is your invitation to the secret garden." "Come with me." An arched doorway clustered with blossoming vines beckoned them in, but Thomas Gibson did not open the door. "Your time in the garden will be scheduled at your convenience, so I suggest you discuss it and let me know as soon as possible what time frame suits you. No one will enter that secret garden at the time you are booked. You may lock the entrance behind you once you enter. If the weather permits, you may schedule one of your meals out there.

"If you're not completely satisfied with your stay, Mrs. Jackson has a full refund policy. Her only wish is that you leave this place more in love with each other than when you arrived."

Lucinda had no words. Was this place for real? Life could not possibly be this good. Her heart bubbled with joy. Thank you, God, for your goodness and grace.

Trust Me.

There it was again, every time she talked to God, she heard that same reminder. She knew what God wanted her to trust Him with. She pressed the message down.

"And finally, let me show you to your room." They returned to the house and wound up the wide carpeted staircase. "Our guest suites are in four opposite quadrants of the house. Two up and two down with many empty rooms in between for maximum privacy. Yours are to the left." He pointed in that direction. "Follow the hall to the last door, and you shall find your room. Your carpet bags have already been delivered." He handed a key to Joseph.

"Thank you, Mr. Gibson."

He winked at Joseph as if they had worked out a plan. "I shall leave you now but will be at your service anytime during your stay." With a slight nod of his head, he turned and disappeared down the staircase.

Lucinda turned to Joseph clutching both arms and looked up at him. "A whole week of this. Have I died and gone to heaven?"

"I hope you think that by the end of the evening." He swept her up into his strong arms as if she weighed nothing and carried her down the hall.

She giggled as he swept open the bedroom door. "Joseph, are you suggesting the best is yet to come?"

"I surely am." His lips came down on hers as he slowly lowered her feet to the floor. Their kiss grew hot and needy. He groaned as he pulled away. "I would suggest missing the evening meal, but I saw how little you ate at lunch and I can put my need aside for at least another hour. But Lordy be, what you do to me."

"We have time." She ran her fingers down his chest.

He caught her wandering hand in his. "I want the first time to be special…to be savored."

"Savored?" That was a new idea.

"But I'll need a moment when you are not touching me." His deep laugh resonated through the room as he stepped back and rubbed the back of his neck.

She marveled at how selfless he was. There was no doubt to his obvious need. She remembered a man, a forest meadow, and his need. Nat had said there was no way for a man to stop, but Joseph had proved Nat a liar once again. Oh, how she loved the man in front of her with all her heart.

"Did you want to freshen up before we head down? The sooner I get us out of this bedroom, the better." His lopsided grin and sparkling eyes made him irresistible. She had to look away to gain control.

Everything in the room was perfect from the rich ornately carved furniture to the navy paisley wallpaper, which was complemented with light blue paint on the rest of the walls. The room had feminine and masculine decor. Lacey curtains hung between heavy navy drapes. A light blue crocheted rose coverlet topped a navy quilt. The throw rug on the gleaming hardwood floors was as soft as clouds.

She crossed to the washstand, to a beautiful matching bowl and pitcher filled with water. She fingered the soft towels and washcloths. "It's almost too beautiful to touch."

He came up behind her and put his arms around her, gently pulling her against his strength. He drew her hair back on one side and kissed her neck. "That's how I feel about you."

"Oh, Joseph, you say the most endearing things." She tried to twist in his arms to give him a kiss.

"No distractions. Freshen up." He poured some water from the pitcher and dug his hands in.

"No fair. You're distracting me." She bumped him sideways and dipped her hand in and flicked water in his face.

He grabbed her around the waist. "Oh, I intend to do a whole lot more, Mrs. Manning, but not until you eat." They shared an end of the same towel to dry off, and as he dried his face, she moved in. The minute he lowered the towel, she pulled his head down to hers.

"It isn't food I need right now. You're all I want," she whispered.

Her lips moved slowly across his strong jaw before meeting his. His mouth opened to hers. Warm. Pliant. Needy. A ripple of delight ran a tremor from tip to toe.

Her hands struggled with his buttons, but he pulled his lips from hers and grabbed each one. "Slow it down, my LucyBug. We're in no hurry." He gently lifted each hand and kissed the inside of her wrist, then up her arm until he was at her neck.

She had no idea something so simple could feel so delicious. A warm knot settled in her stomach.

He kissed the racing pulse in her throat that fluttered like a butterfly and lingered there. She took in a sharp breath. She was completely clothed, and he had done no more than kiss her, but she had never been more aware of a man. Every nerve-ending tingled.

He lifted her into his arms and slowly lowered her onto the bed. He removed her shoes and massaged out the tired knots in her muscles, moving slowly up her legs to her knees. All the while looking deep into her eyes. She held his gaze with all the need she felt blazing through.

"That feels so wonderful. No one has ever massaged my feet or legs before."

He smiled. "Now to get rid of the tension in your back from all that bumping along in the wagon." He pulled her to a seated position and worked the buttons on the front of her jacket with his eyes rapt on her face.

"That's the front not the back," she teased.

"I'm well aware. That's why I'm focused elsewhere for the time being." When the buttons were undone, he slipped the jacket from her body. She had not kept her corset on for the traveling and had only a thin cotton chemise beneath the jacket.

One glance down, and he took a sharp breath in. "Turn around." His voice sounded raspy and breathy.

He kneaded the knots from her shoulder blades and down her back until her body felt like liquid heat. His hands stopped moving, and she could feel the warmth of his breath fan the back of her neck. With her chemise still on, he kissed a trail from the top of her spine to the small of her back. She had never felt anything so exquisitely beautiful in her life. He lay beside her and pulled her back into the curve of his body.

"I could die a happy man just sleeping with you like this."

"And I, a happy woman." She rolled to face him. "I want to slip into something special." She kissed the tip of his nose and slid from the bed. Picking up her carpetbag she went behind the privacy screen.

When she returned in her graceful gown, his eyes drank her in with a stare that crackled with heat.

"You are beyond beautiful."

She stood at the edge of the bed, suddenly unsure of herself. Everything about this man was different, from his words of tenderness to his ability to think of her more than his obvious need, to the way love poured from his eyes.

He held out his hand and lifted the covers. She slid in beside him and laid her head on his chest. She could feel the pounding of his heart and knew he was as affected as she was. His sweet breath tickled her nose as she breathed in the spicy hint of cologne.

His mouth reached for hers. She tasted her name upon his lips. In between each kiss he offered a different endearment.

"Darling."

"Sweetness."

"Beautiful."

"The woman of my dreams."

"My little LucyBug."

The flame inside her spread like wildfire through her body. He slowed the dance, caring about her every desire. In a song as old as time, they came together. Everything but pleasure faded.

Spent in his arms, she snuggled against him, her head on his chest.

He played with the locks of her hair.

"Joseph."

"Hmm."

"Where did you learn…? I mean, I thought you said you never—"

"You are my first. But I was not too proud to ask a few questions, knowing you would be more experienced than I."

"But I'm not, he never…" Her voice cracked. "He just jumped on me, and I never—I felt like such a failure because I felt nothing." The sting of tears pressed behind her eyelids.

"Shh, it's all right." He smoothed his hand over her hair. "You were never the problem, he was."

"With you, I finally understand what it feels like, the passion between a man and a woman in love. Instead of dreading the closeness, I will most definitely want to do that again." She giggled.

"Me too." He kissed the top of her head and turned on his

side with her back pulled into the curve of his body. "I love you more than life itself, LucyBug."

She smiled in the darkness and lay awake thinking about how blessed she was to have him.

Trust Me.

There it was again. *I do trust you, God. I trust you to give us a baby.* Maybe even now the miracle had begun. She rubbed her abdomen.

"Are you asleep yet?" she asked.

"I'm trying to, but someone keeps talking." He tempered the amused words with a kiss on the back of her head.

"I'm hungry."

He tickled her ribs, and she squealed. "Go to sleep. There's nowhere to get food at this hour."

"Yes, we did take our time." She giggled. She lay still for a few minutes, and then her stomach let out a loud growl.

He slid from the bed, and she heard some rustling of clothes.

"What are you doing?" She spoke into the darkness.

"I'll be right back." He lit the candle in the holder by the bed, and she heard the bedroom door open and close.

A moment later, it opened back up. Joseph moved into the room carrying a tray laden with fruit, bread, cheese, meats, and some sweets.

"They left this right outside our door with a note. It says, *Because you missed the evening meal...*"

Lucinda laughed, pulled herself out of bed, and slipped into her wrapper. She straightened the bedcovers and waved him over. His eyes were all over her. "You'll have to wait," she said. "Because this time I really do need to eat."

"I bet I could make you forget all about food, even when you're starving." His eyebrows danced up and down, and confidence oozed from his voice.

She was no fool. "I bet you could too."

His laughter shook the room.

CHAPTER 30

"*A* secret garden. How enchanting," Lucinda whispered. "Who would think to create such a thing?"

"My friend, Rose Jackson." Joseph didn't want to say more.

"What? You know her personally?"

"I do." Joseph smiled down at Lucinda, trying to think of something brilliant to distract her. He had said too much.

"We've been here almost a week, and you're only telling me that now? Why haven't we met the illusive Rose Jackson? I was beginning to think Thomas Gibson owns this place. Every one of the staff report to him."

Joseph worked hard to keep his expression flat. He said nothing, only kissed her lips.

"Come on. We don't want to miss one moment we have in the secret garden. I'm told this is the highlight." They walked hand in hand across the veranda, through the common gardens and toward the far corner, where the secret garden entrance shrouded in blooming foliage and the arms of the mighty Oak and Sugar maples kept it hidden from the world.

"Joseph, how are we paying for all of this?" Lucinda asked

the question with a tremble in her voice. "This week and all these amenities must cost a fortune."

He stopped walking. "That's the second time you've asked about this."

A slight frown furrowed her brow. "It's just that...well—"

"Out with it. I know when something is bothering you." Joseph put a tease into his voice and smiled to ease her obvious angst.

"I don't even like to mention his name and spoil a perfect week, but Nat would spend money we didn't have."

"All right. Let's get one thing out on the table. Nat was part of your life, your history, your experience. As much as I would love that not to be, I came to terms with it a long time ago. I don't want you to be afraid to speak of anything in your past, ask me anything about our future, or bring up any subject. You hear?"

She nodded, and he kissed the tip of her adorable, freckled nose.

"I have the money because I believed God would someday bring you to my door. Every crop, every season, every year since I was sixteen, I've been saving. Thought we'd have a big wedding, but this is better. And, as I've said, I know the owner. I'm sure he—she's given me a deal."

She leaned her head onto his shoulder, and they continued walking. "Have I told you yet today how much I love you, Joseph Manning?"

His heart pounded inside his chest at how happy she sounded. "You can tell me again." He slipped the key into the garden door, and it swung wide. They stepped into an oasis of trickling fountains, blooming flora, and twittering birds. Joseph latched the door behind them so that no one else could enter.

They moved down the path toward the center of the garden. Huge trees canopied the perimeter of the garden shrouding the area in privacy and mystery. Everywhere he looked, color burst from raised flower beds, hanging pots, and blooming trellises.

Lucinda twirled around, her arms spread wide. "This is absolutely gorgeous." She laughed.

He gazed into her wide hazel eyes, a combination of green and gold depending on the light. Today, golden flecks sparkled in rain-washed green. Swirls of copper silk burnished in the afternoon sunlight framed her beautiful face. Cinnamon-toned freckles caressed her nose, and her little bow mouth begged to be kissed. His blood ran hot as he took in her slim frame, full in all the right places.

"So are you." His voice broke like it had when he was a teenager. His love for her nearly dropped him to his knees.

She came toward him and wound her arms around his neck. "How did I ever get so blessed?" Her sweet breath mingled with his. "I don't know what I want more, to explore the garden or to explore you in the garden?" Her voice was soft and silky.

"Let's do both." He reigned in his need and twirled her in his arms until she was leaning back against him. "Look to the left." Her head turned in that direction, and then she ran toward the large swing hanging from the branches of a sturdy oak.

"I've always loved to swing," she said, as if he didn't know.

"Yes, I'm quite aware of all the times you made me push you on the school ground. I have a feeling nothing has changed."

She sat on the swing and kicked out her legs to get it started. He could barely drag his eyes away to walk around her and give her a big push. Higher and higher she went, giggling all the way. He came around to the front and just watched the princess he had married. Her soft pastel pink dress lifted in the breeze, and he caught a glimpse of her shapely legs. At this rate he would not be letting her swing for long.

"I'm so happy." She laughed out loud and scuffed her cute little matching pink shoes just to stop and fling herself into his arms. "Pinch me if I'm dreaming." Her smile was intoxicating.

He pinched her lightly and took off running—mostly to rid himself of the need to take her right there on the cool summer grass.

"Hey, that hurt." She chased him.

He knew where he was going, as Thomas had explained the outlay of the garden. He ran down a cobblestone path straight into a small cabin in the far-right corner of the garden. She piled in after him, and he swung her up into his arms. "You have a choice," he said, holding her tight. "One pinch or one kiss."

She wrapped her arms around his neck and pulled his mouth to hers. He walked across the room while she showered him with kisses—his forehead, his eyes, his nose, his cheeks. Together, they fell onto the bed. "That's a whole lot more than one." He inhaled the misty swirls of her perfume.

"And I've only started," she said, with a sassy grin. "Today, I call the shots, and you listen."

He was more than willing to surrender.

～

*S*he lay spent in his arms. The secret garden and this incredible man that God had somehow saved for her—exceeded her wildest dreams. How was she worthy of such extravagance? Such grace?

She wasn't, not when she was keeping something from Joseph that he had every right to know.

He lifted up on one elbow. "I can't help but notice, but sometimes, like right now, your facial expression changes, like you're thinking of something difficult. Is it him?"

She gulped back a knot that formed in her throat. This was the perfect opportunity to tell him, but she remained silent refusing to meet his gaze.

Trust Me.

Why that same message, again and again, until she wanted to

scream stop into the heavens? Sometimes the Spirit of God was so inconvenient.

He traced a finger down her arm. "You trust me, don't you, my darling? You can share anything. I don't want you to suffer alone."

Her heart picked up speed, pounding within the walls of her chest. Surely God wouldn't mind if she waited a bit. She had conceived quickly in the past. She rolled out of Joseph's arms, stood, and slipped on her chemise. "It's our honeymoon. Not the time...for any of that." She hurried behind the screen to dress for the dinner that would be served on the patio.

When she came out from behind the screen, he was dressed and waiting. An expression she had never seen before on him, much like disappointment, had stolen his smile. "Do you forget we've been friends for years? I know when something is bothering you, and I don't care if it's our honeymoon." He took her hand and led her outside to the table set for two. He pulled out her chair, and she sat down.

A needle of worry threaded its way from her stomach to the lump in her throat. What could she say? She certainly was not going to ruin their honeymoon with the truth.

He sat across from her and held out his hand. She placed hers into it, and he squeezed.

"You're the best man God has ever made, Joseph Manning. How did I ever get so blessed to call you my husband?"

"I feel the same in return. Now let me be your husband. Let me help you through the pain."

She looked into his eyes but could not get words past the knot in her throat.

"Did I do something wrong? Something that reminds you—"

"No. Never. You're the opposite of everything that man did to me."

He studied her face. "Can't you tell me, LucyBug? You're my

best friend, and I'm yours. You should be able to tell me anything."

The lump in her throat grew larger, and she pressed back tears.

Trust Me.

She knew what God wanted her to do. And she would never be free until she spoke the truth. Her body broke out in a cold sweat. If she told him, everything would be turned inside out. Her world would never be the same. He would have no reason to ever trust her again.

Ache and longing filled his voice. "The best way to start a marriage is together. That means sharing the easy and the hard, the good and the bad."

His words burned a hole in her heart. She had to speak up. "I should've told you. I meant to tell you, but there never seemed a right time."

CHAPTER 31

"**W**hat?" Like jackrabbit thumpers, Joseph's heart raced in his chest.

"I should've told you *before* we married, but I loved you so much and couldn't bear the thought of losing you. I was so selfish." Her voice trembled.

He had never seen her so distraught. A sinking feeling hollowed out his gut. "But you know you can tell me anything."

She stood quickly and paced.

"What is it—?"

"I need to get this out before I lose my nerve again." She plopped back in the chair. The story about the loss of her second baby came out stilted, filled with sorrow, and punctuated with a stab of anger. "I'm trying to forgive that monster for what he did to me, to us, to our future."

Joseph had his own pocket full of rage aimed at Nat that he still worked on emptying, so he understood how she felt. But why hadn't she trusted him enough to tell him sooner? Did she really think that he would love or want her less? How shallow she must believe his love for her was. His elbows hit the table, and he dropped his head in his hands.

266

"Say something, Joseph."

He didn't have the strength to look up.

"Please. I'm so sorry. I would do anything to back up the train wreck that marrying Nat created, but I can't." She was sobbing now. "Please. I beg you. Forgive me for not being able to give you the children you want—"

"You don't get it." He snapped to his feet. "You have no idea why I'm upset?"

"You...you want to be a father. I should've given you a choice before we were married."

Joseph took a deep breath to control his anger. "I need to think."

"But Joseph—"

"I'll meet you up at our room later."

He hurried out of the garden into the twilight. Fine pickle he was in now, being on his honeymoon and hearing the worst news of his life. The soft approach of evening light brushed over the valley, the perfect time for a lover's walk, not a lover's quarrel.

Joseph hands fisted, and his feet picked up the pace. He marched past the barn and down the trail into a wooded copse. He pressed both hands to his temples to slow the pounding of blood screamed through. "God, my God. What are you doing?"

The truth shall set you free.

Yeah, I feel so free right now. The woman I love more than life itself doesn't trust me with the most horrific experience in her life, and I want to do damage to that rapist, wife beating, child-killing beast. How can I begin to help her with hatred in my heart?

The truth shall set you free.

What truth? The truth that Nat raped her, and You gave them a child? The truth that Nat beat her into the battered waif I rescued, while You did what? The truth that I will never hold my own flesh and blood in my arms because my wife's body has been damaged beyond repair? That truth? That's the truth that will set me free?

The truth shall set you free.

"I don't like Your truth. I don't want Your truth." Joseph spoke the words into the gathering darkness with a bite to his voice.

"Joseph, my friend. May I join you?"

Joseph jumped at the sound of a voice and spun. How embarrassing for Thomas to find him in this state.

"I saw you race out of the garden. I was going to leave you to your privacy, but you know how it works when the Spirit urges. I resisted until I noticed Lucinda wandering around. She's crying."

"I just needed to clear my head."

"I told her I'd find you. She's gone to rest in your room."

"Thank you, Thomas."

"Do you want to talk about it?"

"I wouldn't know where to begin."

"Come on, brother, let's sit." He pointed to a nearby log in the waning light. They sat in silence for a few minutes.

"Do you remember the first time you found me hiding in your barn, wounded from a rebel bullet and as scared as they come?"

Joseph nodded.

"You didn't scream and bring the adults running. No, you showed compassion. You hid me and snuck me food. You were my friend—me, a grown man, and you what, maybe eight or nine?

"I was eight."

"I'd never had a white friend before. Then your Ma found out where her leftovers were going, and I could see by her kindness where you learned what it means to serve the Lord in love. Without your parents nursing me back to health and their connections to the underground railway, I would've never survived the war."

"She was a good mother," Joseph said. "Hard times when she passed away." He didn't feel like idle chitchat with Thomas but didn't want to be rude. But what did any of this have to do with his problem?

"I want to return the favor," Thomas said. "You two looked so happy, but with all newlyweds, there tend to be things to work out. This is common."

Bands of pain tightened across Joseph's chest. He couldn't sit. Once he started talking, the story flooded out as he paced back and forth.

"The way I see it, you have to start with forgiveness," Thomas said. "And you can't forgive that which is hidden in the dark. That's what God meant when He told you that the truth will set you free."

A hot breath escaped. "I don't want or need this kind of truth." Joseph folded his arms across his chest.

"You sure do. Without truth, Lucinda carries the weight of that horrific assault all alone and the guilt that she somehow deserved it by marrying the man. Hidden in the dark, her secret would grow big enough to rip you two apart."

"I suppose you're right."

"I know I am. You need to be thankful for this truth because now you can go to the Lord and ask Him how best to love her through this. She needs you like she's never needed you before. And I bet she thinks you left because she can't give you a child."

"That's not why I walked away."

"Are you sure?"

"Absolutely, I was angry because she didn't trust me enough to tell me the truth before we were married. Now, she'll second guess forever, wondering if I would've still married her."

"Pretty hard truth to confess."

"I guess she'll never understand the depth of my love for her." He rubbed his hand at the back of his neck.

"Never is a very long time. And you have the rest of your life to show her what love really means. How about we pray together, and then you return and make sure she knows how much you love her, with or without more children?"

Joseph sat beside him and bent his head.

Thomas began. "Our Father, who art in heaven...

Joseph wrestled. The words "forgive us our debts, as we forgive our debtors" hit hard. The obedience of forgiveness seemed next thing to impossible. While Thomas continued his prayer, Joseph lifted one of his own. *God, I know I need to but...*

Joseph, my child, just say yes, and I'll give you the strength.

"Please help me."

Joseph lifted his head. At some point, Thomas had stopped praying out loud, but his head was bent and his lips were moving.

"Thanks, Thomas. God knew I needed you."

"Don't mention it."

"I know my anger at Nat will ebb and flow in the months to come, but I've taken that first crucial step of saying yes to God."

"That's all it takes. God sees the heart." Thomas clapped him on the shoulder. "Let's get back before it's as dark as pitch out here. Your beautiful bride needs you."

They stood and started down the path.

"So, do I tell Lucinda that I ran into Mrs. Jackson or Thomas Gibson?" Joseph teased.

"Your wife is extremely intuitive. She gave me a thank-you card addressed to Rose Jackson, but the message was pointed at me. She thanked Rose for all the little things I personally did for her. Like the extra feather pillow she requested for you and the band that played her favorite song during the dance. She even mentioned the chicken dumplings she so loves but finds too fussy to make. She sees right through me."

"She's a smart one," said Joseph.

"You never told her?"

"I promised I would not."

"Feel free. I believe the Rosewood Inn's secret is safe with her."

CHAPTER 32

*L*ucinda lay on the bed alone. Dusk turned to darkness. Mr. Gibson must not have found Joseph. Was her husband gone for good? She would deserve that. How had she been so selfish, so wrong, not to share the whole truth? The doctor who'd attended her had not been wrong in his assessment. Her cycles were few and far between, and to heal internally from whatever that woman did to her had taken a long time. Lucinda was damaged goods, and Joseph, of all people, deserved a family. The way he loved Sammy with such a loving father's heart before they were even married... How cruel of her to take that from him.

Maybe an annulment could take place. No one need know the details. She wouldn't want the stigma of divorce for Joseph. This was not his doing.

No more deception.

"See, God, how wicked I am. My first thoughts are to deceive. How can I call myself Your child?"

You are my child, but you must learn to do things My way.

"I want to, Father. I truly do. Even if Joseph leaves, as he has every right to do, I want to go forward with You in my life. I made a big mess of things on my own. Please don't give up on me God."

"I am right here. I will never leave you nor forsake you."

The door creaked open, and Joseph's head poked in.

Her eyes popped open.

"Do you want the rest of me?" His lips curved into a winsome smile. "I'm sorry I ran off in a huff."

Lucinda could not believe her ears. He was saying he was sorry when it was all her fault. "Get in here." Lucinda waved her hand, and he entered.

"I was so worried you wouldn't want to see me tonight or any other night." She slipped off the bed and tentatively walked toward him, too unsure of herself to throw her arms around him like she wanted.

He stopped a few feet from her. His smile had faded. "That's what bothered me the most."

"What do you mean?" She was confused.

"Did you really believe I would love you less because we can't have another child?"

"I...I thought I could pray for a miracle and we'd never have to have this discussion. But God was not pleased with that."

"You didn't answer my question."

"I want to give you our baby so much, and I thought you'd be as disappointed as I am."

"I am disappointed. I'd be lying to say otherwise. But do you really think that would've changed my love for you? Would've kept me from marrying you?"

"Doesn't it? You were angry at me."

"Yes. For the first time in a very long time, I was truly angry with you."

Her thoughts circled and scattered. Nothing fit. Her brain refused to fit the puzzle together.

"Do you understand why?"

Could her battered heart take the honesty? He had every

right to be angry. To turn and walk away and never look back. "I'm sorry. I don't."

"You didn't trust me with the truth, and you carried this horrific act of violence not only against your baby, but also against you, all alone. It breaks my heart to think what you've been through, but you didn't give me the opportunity to walk alongside you. I'm not only your husband and lover, but I'm also supposed to be your soulmate, your best friend, your defender."

Heat swept over her. "The other day at the creek, when you said how much you wanted a little girl, I was too ashamed to tell you. But I was also selfish. I love you more than life itself, and I couldn't bear the thought of losing you, and of Sammy not having the wonderful loving daddy you are. I felt so inadequate."

He pulled her into his arms and crushed his mouth to hers. He kissed her into silence and then pulled back. "I don't want those words to come out of your mouth again. You're not inadequate. Don't you realize how much I love you?"

"I'm so sorry…so sorry. Will you forgive me?"

He swung her up in his arms and lowered her gently onto the bed. "No more secrets?"

"No more secrets." She pulled him down beside her. Her hands cupped his cheeks, and she caressed his skin with her thumbs. "As long as I live, I shall never understand why God loved me enough to keep you for me. Jeanette told me how many other women were interested."

"Because we complete each other, LucyBug. Only a big God could know that."

"Hmm, I love your faith. Wish mine were half as strong. I still feel my old ways rear up—"

"Shh." He placed a finger on her lips. "Whatever mistakes you've made, you did not deserve the abuse you suffered."

"I'm trying to believe I'm forgiven, but the consequences live on. And although I thought I was giving my hatred of Nat to

God, in moments like these, with all he took... I literally hate that man."

Joseph's brows knit together. "I feel it too, but as hard as it will be, the only path to freedom is to forgive him."

Her whole insides twisted in protest. "To be honest, most days that feels like a big task."

"I know. It won't be easy, and it sure as shootin' won't be an overnight victory, but Thomas reminded me earlier—"

"Thomas found you?"

"We had a good talk, and he reminded me that I'm forgiven in the same way I forgive others. If I don't forgive Nat, I'll hurt myself and allow him to have continual power over my thoughts."

"But I want to give you your own baby, your own flesh and blood, and he stole—"

"I have Sammy."

"But he's not...I mean you've been amazing with him, but—"

"He is my son."

"And he's enough?"

"My life has never been more complete."

"You may be just saying that, but it's one of the kindest things you've ever said."

Joseph rolled her beneath him and leaned so close that his breath fanned her cheek. "I shall never lie to you. Never." His declaration was fierce and steadfast. "You and Sammy are more than enough."

She looked into his soft blue eyes, sleepy, dreamy, and kind. "I believe you."

"Good." He gave her a quick kiss.

Her stomach growled, and he laughed. "All right, I know what I have to do, though I could stay here all night just looking at you." He smoothed his fingers across the side of her face and through her long hair. "Get comfortable, and I'll go in search of food." He rolled off the bed, and she followed him. "A repeat of last week when we missed our first meal."

"Last week was a lot more fun," she said sassily.

He laughed. "I so agree."

Again, the door opened and closed and immediately opened again. "You won't believe the loaded tray of scrumptious goodies waiting for us."

"I love this place," Lucinda said, flopping down on the bed. "Rose Jackson sure knows how to run a high-class establishment. Still can't believe we can afford it. The ladies I see walking around here are wearing dresses that would cost a farmer a whole year's worth of wages."

Joseph's eyes lit up, and he threw her a lop-sided grin. "It's my connections."

"Out with it, Joseph Manning. What are you not telling me?"

"What will I get for this classified information?" His eyebrows danced up and down as he joined her on the bed. They sat cross-legged across from each other for their midnight picnic.

She lowered the tone of her voice. "What do you want?"

"Oh, I could think of a very good trade. A very good trade indeed."

"I'll give you a sample if you come a little closer." Her breathing shallowed as he leaned across the tray for a slow, sweet kiss.

He pulled back. "Let's eat while I tell you a wonderful bedtime story—before we get to dessert." He looked down at the cleavage peeking from her wrapper. "Even if we never have children, we're sure going to have fun trying."

She giggled, and her heart burst with joy. He was treating her with the same richness of love he always had. "You're distracting me." Lucinda popped a grape in her mouth. "And I want to hear the story."

"Well, it started years ago when I first met Thomas Gibson.

Our family saved his life during the war. He never forgot that favor. He's the reason we can afford to be here today."

"I can't believe he would want to come back here, having been a slave in this household. Wouldn't that conjure a whole lot of bad memories?"

"I said he grew up here, but I never mentioned the word slave."

Oh, this story was getting good, and the man telling it was beyond beautiful on the inside and out. "Do tell."

"Rose Jackson's very rich but very cruel husband died young, leaving Rose a wealthy widow. She married again and had a son, but the world never knew."

"Thomas?"

"Yes."

Lucinda clapped her hands together. "I knew it. He has an air of ownership and confidence about him."

"He said you were most intuitive."

"Tell me the rest." She rubbed her hands together.

"Patience, my love."

He took a few bites of his bread and cheese and chewed slowly just to tease her.

"Come on…"

"Thomas grew up in the protection and love of his white mother and black father, but as far as anyone else knew, Terrance Gibson, Thomas's father, was merely Rose's butler. And because the color of Thomas's skin was very dark, folks believed he was Terrance's son. Then the war broke out, and as time went on the South demanded black slaves join the Confederacy to serve in some capacity—usually as cooks or to perform manual labor. Rose held off as long as she could until pressure demanded that both Terrance and Thomas go. Terrance assigned the job of helping the medics retrieve bodies on the battlefield. He did not last long. Thomas waited for the opportune time to make his escape, unwilling to help an army fight the North, who were fighting for the freedom of his people. He got shot trying to escape and made it as far as our farm."

"So, your family helped him make it North safely, and after the war he came back to Rosewood Inn because of his mother?"

"You're such a smart girl." Joseph leaned forward and gave her a quick peck between bites. "See if you can guess the rest of the story. You get only three questions. Make them count."

Lucinda pursed her mouth and put a finger to her lips. His smile said he was enjoying this too much.

"All right, my first question…Can I meet Rose Jackson, and if not, why?"

"That's two questions. But I'll count it as one because I can answer it with one sentence. You'll have to wait until heaven."

"So, Rose has passed away, and the inn now belongs to Thomas. That makes sense."

"Is that a question?"

"No that's an observation. But why doesn't he just say so?"

"His mother and he established this inn after the war, but since the South still doesn't abide a wealthy black man in authority, he humbly plays the role of a butler, and the visitors keep coming. He loves his work and wants to carry on with the legacy and the promise he made to his mother."

"What's that?"

"That, my dear, is number three, your last and final question before I partake of my dessert." Joseph removed the tray from the bed and lay down beside her. A warm sensation curled in the pit of her stomach as he opened her wrapper. His thumbs caressed an unnerving path from her throat to her chin to her lips.

"Well, are you going to tell me?"

"Patience is a virtue, LucyBug, and I'm quite enjoying bugging you."

"You're incorrigible, Joseph Manning." She smacked away his wandering hands. "Not until you finish."

"Rose Jackson's legacy was as Thomas said the day we first arrived, that she wants couples to leave this place more in love than when they arrived."

"And Thomas's promise to his mother?"

"You are over your quota of questions, my lovely."

"I'll make it up to you." Two could play at that game. She began moving her hands over his body.

"Thomas promised to work, love, and pass this place down to his children until the day comes when a black man or woman can freely own and operate a business where white folk won't deem the proprietor's color of skin a deterrent."

"Is Thomas married, then? Does he have kids?"

"Ahh, girl, you're killing me." He grabbed her wandering hand. "Your hands say you're finished with your questions, but they haven't told your mouth."

She giggled. "Just answer the question."

"Yes, he's married. Yes, his wife works as the head chef. Yes, all five of his kids can be found in positions around the place, and yes, I want you."

Her body tingled with awareness, and what began as a gentle kiss erupted with passion. His touch made her soar and melt. A riptide of emotion pulled them both under as they came together and then came up for air. For the first time there was nothing between them but love. No dark secret to haunt the shallows of her mind. No guilt at what she could not give him. Only love, sweet love. They were going to be all right.

She collapsed on his chest with the beat of his heart tugging, reaching, speaking out his love. "I love you so much, Joseph Daniel Manning."

Joseph lifted her hand to his lips. "I feel the same about you, my LucyBug. I feel the same about you."

He shifted onto his side and pulled her into the curve of his body. Nat had never held her after. He had always turned away. Drat. Why did she have to think of that man? Where was he anyway? A chill of concern crawled up her spine. She nuzzled in closer, and Joseph kissed the nape of her neck.

"Go to sleep, or I'll have to change that name from LucyBug to Jitterbug."

He chuckled at his own humor and she joined in, but she could not quite erase the uneasiness. Joseph could not be with her twenty-four hours a day.

Trust Me.

Dear God, I claim what Your word says. You will never leave me nor forsake me.

CHAPTER 33

*L*ucinda entered the kitchen at dawn with a tremor in her hands. It was her first morning in her new home, and with Sammy still sleeping she intended to impress Joseph, Nigel, and his pa with a wonderful breakfast. She hoped Joseph was right that his pa would get comfortable with her there. She remembered how he had turned away when she'd smiled at him at the wedding and stood with grump on his face when they left. Hopefully she was wrong about what she thought she saw. Thankfully Nigel was happy for them.

She looked around the messy kitchen. Clearly it had been a long time since these three men had a woman in this house. Would they resent the intrusion?

She hummed a hymn softly and prayed for guidance as she familiarized herself with the kitchen and the supplies she could find on hand. Every nook and cranny was filled to overflowing with paraphernalia from tools that belonged in the barn to broken dishes no longer usable. Opening a food bin was her complete undoing. Weevils swarmed in the rancid flour. She rushed the container out to the front porch. There would be no fresh bread today. The only thing she could find that looked remotely fresh was a container of oatmeal. Why was she surprised with a bunch of bachelors?

The first meal she prepared was going to consist of oatmeal, some scrambled eggs she hoped to find in the hen house, and fresh milk from the cow. Her heart sank. She wouldn't be impressing anyone today.

With her hands on her hips she surveyed the space, calculating the hours of scrubbing and sorting she would have to do before this kitchen would be fit to work in. Right now, she didn't even want Sammy playing on the floors. Where were Libbie and Helen when she needed them? She would miss those girls something fierce.

Joseph's frame filled the doorway as he rubbed the sleep out of his eyes. "I turned over to give you a morning hug and you were gone."

"Why didn't you warn me that the kitchen looked like a pigsty? How am I supposed to make a decent breakfast?"

He moved into the room with a smile on his lips. "Good morning to you too, sunshine." He grabbed her around the waist and kissed her full on the mouth. She wanted to stay angry, but his kiss sweetened the bitter.

She pulled back. "There are no supplies, and look at this place, Joseph. Really look at this." Her hands swept around the room. "Grime and filth, not to mention tools that belong in the barn."

"Yeah, sorry about that. Mama would turn in her grave if she could see her kitchen now. We men tend to keep our eyes on the livestock and crops, and over time, whatever we had in our hand found a place in the kitchen."

"I can't live like this."

"I don't expect you to." He regarded the room. "I don't know where to begin." He thrust his hand through his hair.

"Can you fetch me some eggs and milk? After breakfast, I plan to scrub this place spotless. Anything I put out on the porch, you'll have to find room for in the barn. And we'll need to make a trip to town. There are weevils in the flour, no spices, and don't even get me started about the layers of burnt-on food clinging to the pots and pans."

He caught her around the waist. "See, LucyBug, I knew there'd be things to get your dander up."

Her shoulders dropped. "I'm not angry. I'm disappointed. I know your pa doesn't care for me and I wanted to make a good first impression. And now I can't." She fought hard to hold back the tears.

"How about I get some bacon from the smokehouse, too, and I'll forgo the fields and help you in any way I can today. Between the two of us, we'll bring a fresh new look to this kitchen by tomorrow." He smiled that winsome grin.

"Yes, please."

"I'll fetch the milk, eggs, and bacon first, and then I'll be back as soon as I feed the cow and chickens." He gave her a quick peck on the cheek and hurried out the door.

She drew a basin of water from the pump and scrubbed the few pots and pans she would need to cook their meager breakfast.

Soon, bacon was sizzling, and her nerves settled. The savory smell wafted from the kitchen and beyond. She hoped it would welcome the hungry men to the table. Bacon, eggs, and thinly sliced fried potatoes Joseph had brought in from the root cellar browned in the pan. A hot steaming pot of creamy oatmeal awaited the crew. It was by no means a breakfast to her standards, but it was the best she could do without flour to make bread or pancakes. She set the table, hoping Sammy would not awaken until she was done serving.

Nigel wandered into the kitchen. He raked a hand through his hair, which stood on end in every direction. The gesture didn't help. She stifled a smile.

"Haven't smelled something this good in long time. Hope you made some for me."

"Of course. Have a seat. Everything is hot and ready."

He slid into a chair. "I wasn't going to assume you'd cook for the lot of us, but am sure obliged."

"It's my pleasure. But I'll have to create some order to this kitchen so I can do a better job tomorrow." She set a plate of bacon and a bowl of scrambled eggs on the table.

"Your cookin' looks mighty fine to me." He popped a piece of bacon into his mouth. He leaned back on his chair, closed his eyes, and chewed. "Not burnt to a crisp. Mighty fine indeed. None of us could get the bacon cookin' right." His eyes popped open as he grabbed another piece and held it up. "This is perfection."

Joseph's pa wandered into the kitchen. What should she call him? Pa felt too familiar, Mr. Manning too formal, and Daniel too disrespectful. She would call him Pa, as it would be the courteous thing to do.

"Good morning...uh...Pa." How awkward.

He didn't acknowledge her. "Where's my oatmeal pot?"

The pot was sparkling clean in clear view, warming on the wood stove. "The oatmeal is ready."

"I make the oatmeal just the way I like it. Don't need anyone meddling with my routine."

Lucinda clenched her fists in her apron pockets. Nat's words of constant disapproval came to mind.

Nigel laughed. "Lumpy and so thick it could be used for glue. That I won't miss. Have a seat, Pa. Lucinda has worked hard, and you're going to enjoy the feast."

"Humph." He slid into his chair at the head of the table and looked at her with disapproving eyes...the way some of the townsfolk looked at her. Like she was worthless. Her spirits sagged.

Oh God, help me. I don't want to go back to feeling that way. Let me believe what You've said about me. I'm a new creation.

Lucinda scooped out hearty portions of oatmeal for the men, hoping Joseph would return soon. His pa just plum near scared her. She set the bowls before them.

"Thank you." Pa's voice held a begrudging tone.

Nigel dug into his oatmeal with relish. "Wow wee, that's good. What did you do to make it so fine?"

Lucinda couldn't help the smile that split across her face. "A little fresh cream and a generous amount of brown sugar is the secret."

Pa grunted. "Hmmm, tastes the same to me."

"Doggonnit, Pa, admit that it's the best oatmeal you've had in years."

"Best oatmeal in years?" Joseph entered the kitchen and crossed to the stove. "Give me an extra dollop." He held out his bowl and kissed Lucinda's cheek as she leaned in with a scoop of oatmeal.

She could feel the heat race up her neckline into her cheeks. She would have to tell him that some things were not meant to be done in public, and kissing her in front of his grumpy pa was one of them. She was glad to hear Sammy's soft cries and have a reason to escape.

"You men help yourselves. I have a baby to attend to. I'll get my breakfast later." She rushed from the room. Would she ever feel at home under the scrutiny of her father-in-law's obvious contempt for her? Could she really live in a place where she was not wanted?

~

*J*oseph looked at his beautiful wife as she readied for bed. He had to pinch himself to know it was real. He had dreamed about living with her for far too

285

long. But why did she have that worried look on her face? Wasn't she as happy as he was?

She slid into bed beside him.

"What is it, my darling?"

"What, do you read me like a book?"

"Always have."

"Your pa doesn't like me. Doesn't matter what I cook, he complains. Doesn't matter how hard I work, he has something negative to say."

There was no doubt her observations were accurate. He'd been hoping his pa would warm up, but it was not happening. "I'm sorry, I'll talk to him." He wrapped his arms tightly around her, praying for wisdom.

She sighed. "Don't say anything. That'll only make things worse. It's because I'm divorced, right?"

"You're a married woman now, and you're all mine." Maybe he could distract her thinking. He nuzzled the back of her neck, but she pushed him away flopping onto her back on her side of the bed.

"I'm not what he wanted for you."

"How about we pray together about this? After all, Pa is a Christian and God has been known to soften grumpy old hearts."

She turned toward him. "So, you agree there's a problem?"

Gosh, he couldn't win. To admit his pa was being unreasonable would make her feel she's living in another hostile situation, but to ignore his pa's rudeness wouldn't validate her legitimate concern. He shot up a prayer for wisdom.

"He has childhood trauma which he will not talk about. Don't know much more than his mother ran off and divorced his father."

"He thinks we're the same?"

"Can we pray together and then talk about this, LucyBug? I just feel we really need God's wisdom."

She nodded and he gathered her close. As they each prayed, a solution came to him.

After saying amen, he kissed her. "I think I know what the solution to our problem is, but first let me talk to Pa. Then I'll reveal the surprise."

"I like the way you said *our problem,* and I love surprises. I'm most curious."

"I'll give you a hint…it includes a home for the love of my life. Can you trust me with the details?"

"I trust you with my life." She nestled in close.

He breathed in the sweet fragrance of lavender, content to hold her in his arms.

～

The next morning Joseph followed his pa to the barn. He would not put this conversation off. She was too important. "Pa, wait up. We need to talk."

Pa turned and grunted. "Out with it, boy. I could tell by the way you were eyeing me at breakfast when I merely commented on Lucinda's burnt flapjacks that you had a cud that needed chewing."

There was no point in arguing, but Pa was responsible for the burnt flapjacks. Lucinda brought a fresh one hot out of the pan, and he complained it wasn't done enough, so she put it back on and he complained it was burnt. "Breakfast is merely an indication of a much bigger issue."

"Spit it out. I don't have time to stand around yakking like an old woman. The fields are awaiting."

Joseph whispered a quick prayer. *Dear God, give me strength to stand firm.* "Just want to tell you that you're going to have a lot more work come harvest than you bargained for, because I'll be unavailable."

Pa's eyes squinted. "And what exactly does that mean?"

He had Pa's attention now. "Since you've chosen to make Lucinda feel unwelcome in our home, we have only two options left, leave the farm which I'm not going to do because believe it or not, you need me as much as I need you. Or build us a cabin before the snow flies, which is what I plan. I won't have time for farming."

"What do you mean? We have more than enough room for your family."

"I agree, and we'd gladly stay and add on for a bit more privacy as discussed, but Lucinda has already suffered enough. I won't subject her to any more abuse."

"Abuse!" His voice rose like the squawk of an angry crow. "I mention her burnt flapjacks, and now I'm an abuser?"

"Have you been loving or even fair to her? Have you welcomed her and treated her like a daughter?"

Pa flipped off his cap and scratched his head before crushing the cap back down.

"No disrespect, but the way I see it, my first responsibility is to my family—Lucinda and Sammy—and you're making it difficult for her to feel at home."

"I need you in the fields. It was horrible last year when you weren't here. Nigel can't manage the workers, and it's too much for me."

Joseph softened his voice and stepped closer. "I can't make you like her. I had so hoped you'd see the beautiful giving person she is, cleaning that hovel we lived in, making those amazing meals, scrubbing your dirty long johns, for heaven's sakes, all without a word of complaint. Mama would be proud to see her house today, not like it was a few weeks ago."

Pa looked at his feet and then across the wheat field, which was going to need harvesting soon. "She does cook up the finest vittles I've ever tasted."

"She deserves a home free of tension, and I aim to give her that."

"You're right, son. Can you give me another chance? If she's still not comfortable by month's end, then you do what you need to do."

Joseph relaxed his shoulders. It would have killed him to not take control of the harvest, but he had been prepared to follow through.

Thank you, God, that Pa is willing to try.

Pa threw an arm around his shoulder and gave a quick squeeze. "I could tell her that I appreciate her fine cookin', and that little boy is really growing on me."

Joseph hugged his thin wiry shoulders. "She would love to hear that." It was about as much of an apology as he was going to get. It was enough.

CHAPTER 34

*L*ucinda stoked the fire in the wood stove for breakfast. Her bread was already rising, and she had breakfast prepped. Cooking for three farmers was far easier than cooking for a ranch full of hungry cowboys. Nigel was always appreciative and pleasant. She just wished there were some way to win over Joseph's Pa. He was always the last one to any meal and the first to leave. It was like her presence put him on edge. Yet yesterday the lunch and supper meal had been decidedly different. Pa seemed more cordial, and thankful. Maybe there was hope.

"Good morning, Lucinda."

She jumped. That had been Pa's voice, but he had never used her name. She spun. "Good morning." She worked hard not to show her surprise.

"I was praying...and well...I got up early to talk to you. Alone."

Her heart rate picked up speed. Would he beg her to leave and take her son with her?

"Seems the Lord is nudging me, rather strongly I might add,

to apologize to you for the way I've treated you this past month since you arrived."

Had she just heard right? An apology? What had Joseph said? Before she could process his last remark, he said, "I'm sorry."

Words stuck in her throat. Her chin quivered, but she held herself together. Was this really happening?

He wandered to the stove, pulled his tin cup from the shelf, and poured himself some coffee. "Look at this. A cup I can find, and it's clean, not to mention hot fresh coffee, and is that bread dough in that bowl? You sure make the best bread I've ever tasted."

Lucinda could not believe what she was hearing. Was he complimenting her? She plunked down at the table.

He brought his coffee and sat across from her. "I've never told anyone this story." He looked above her head as if he were no longer seeing the room.

She remained silent.

"I was no more than seven when she left, but I remember my ma. She was petite and beautiful, like you. I didn't understand much back then, but she had strange men coming and going when Pa was away. He was a railroad builder, gone for weeks at a time."

Lucinda didn't want to breathe for fear of interrupting. Why was he confiding in her of all people?

"She just up and left one day with one of those men. All I remember is his fancy clothes and top hat. She patted me on the head and told me to be good until Pa came home. I started crying. Begging her not to leave me."

Lucinda swallowed the knot in her throat.

"I still remember watching that fancy buggy roll away. I ran and ran trying to catch up, screaming and crying. I finally stopped when I could no longer see it."

Tears rolled unchecked down Lucinda's cheeks.

"I never saw her again, and Pa didn't get home for days."

Lucinda put her hand to her mouth. "How did you manage?"

"I lived on raw eggs, potatoes, and carrots. Thankfully, I knew how to get water from the pump and feed the chickens. I didn't know how to build a fire, and it was early spring, so nights were cold."

"How terrifying." Without thinking, Lucinda reached across the table and took his weathered hand in hers. She squeezed and then pulled her hand back.

"After all these years of burying my past, God is finally getting through. I need to forgive her or I'll go on hurting others, like you. You don't deserve my anger."

"Do I remind you of her?" Lucinda held her breath.

"Because it got around that you were pregnant…"

"Out of wedlock. It's true."

"I judged you as a loose woman like her, and then when you abandoned your marriage, I thought you were the same kind of cold woman my Ma was. But…but I see how you love your son. I see how you love *my* son, and I'm sorry. You're not the same." Tears glistened in his eyes. "Not the same at all."

Should she tell him her story? He had confided in her. Would he even believe her?

"Joseph has alluded to your suffering," Pa said, "but has kept things private. I reckon there has to be more to your story than what I, and all those like me who judge you unfairly, understand. I don't need to know the details. I just need to ask you to give me a second chance at welcoming you into our family."

Lucinda let out a hiccuped sob. "Give me a moment." She pulled her handkerchief from her pocket and dabbed at her eyes and nose. "I'm not sure who would believe me, so I don't talk about my time with Nat. Joseph is the only one who knows everything." To be able to say that truthfully felt so wonderful. God's ways were the most liberating.

"You don't have to tell me."

"I want to. You trusted me with your story, so I'll trust you with mine. It's true, I was willful and stubborn. I didn't listen to my parents and snuck off to the forest with Nat. I thought he was going to propose. But what happened there... It was not what I wanted." She couldn't believe the words that poured out, more than she'd intended to tell.

He was crying, she was crying.

He rose and held out his arms, and she walked in.

"Can you ever forgive me, Lucinda, for adding to your pain?"

"Already done," she whispered into his shoulder. "All I want is to make Joseph happy and be a good wife and mother. And I'd like nothing more than to have us live together in harmony."

He pulled back. "We can do that. Can't we?"

"Yes, we can." She smiled through what were now good tears.

"And you can tell Joseph my story," Pa said. "It's time for some healing to take place, and judging from what just happened, it starts with being honest instead of keeping secrets."

LATE OCTOBER 1876

"Can't help but love the girl. Thought she'd never be good enough for my son, but how wrong was I?" Pa gave a hearty slap on Joseph's back as he slid into his chair at the breakfast table. "Look at this feast. Hate to say it, but she's even a better cook than your ma was."

"Makes me rethink making more time for Esther," said Nigel.

Joseph pointed his fork at his brother across the table. "If that's the case, you're going to have to learn how to talk without your mouth full, as well."

Nigel stuffed a whole piece of crisp bacon into his mouth. "Who me? Why would I miss an opportunity to speak just because my mouth is full?" He made a funny face at Sammy, who sat in his highchair pushed up to the table beside him. Sammy giggled. Nigel did it again.

Joseph couldn't believe the change in his pa and how much Nigel and Pa had taken to Sammy and Lucinda in just a few months. God had indeed blessed him, and Lucinda was happier than he ever remembered seeing.

"Where is that bride of yours this morning? Obviously, this spread didn't magically appear." Pa threw out his hand to the scrambled eggs, bacon, fruit, and flapjacks that graced the table.

"She was tired. I told her to go get another couple hours of sleep, and I'd look after Sammy and do the breakfast clean-up."

Pa winked. "Why is she so tired, son? Have you been keeping her awake at night?"

Joseph could feel the heat spread from his neck to his brow.

"Like I said"—Nigel smirked—"he's making me rethink this whole wife thing for a variety of reasons." Both Pa and Nigel burst into laughter. Sammy joined in, which made them laugh all the louder.

"Very funny." Joseph punched his brother playfully. "The sooner I get my own wing built the better."

"Come on, we're just having a little fun," Pa said. "I like things just the way they are. This rambling farmhouse is big enough for us all without you being off in your own wing. I could die a well-fed old man with my grandkids gathered around."

Lucinda had shared that she'd opened up about the abuse to Pa, but apparently she hadn't told him about her inability to have more children. Understandably so.

"Sounds like he's already working mighty hard on more grandkids for you, Pa," Nigel teased. His eyes twinkled with merriment.

Joseph attempted a smile, but his heart squeezed tight. He had all but forgiven Nat, but he still wrestling with that one.

The food disappeared faster than the time Lucinda had toiled to make it.

"I'll trade you the dish cleanup and looking after Sammy here for the chores in the barn," Nigel said. "I'm working on a drawing that would be much more comfortable doing indoors than in that drafty old barn. And thanks to your wife, I can now find the table."

Pa rolled his eyes, and Joseph jumped at the plan. He didn't mind hard physical labor one bit. "You're on."

Joseph kissed Sammy on the head and headed outdoors.

The sunny late October morning held a crispness in the air. The maples and oaks on the property were turning brilliant shades of scarlet, copper, and gold. He lifted his eyes to the north, where a copse of elms protected the farmhouse against the bitter winter winds. The peaceful scene of colorful trees swaying in the breeze and the golden rolling pastures lifted his soul with thankfulness. Life could not be better.

He milked the cow, mucked out the stalls, fed the chickens, watered and let the horses out to pasture. He headed out to the fields to meet Pa. They were going to discuss the spring planting.

A scream that sent a chill up his spine came from the house. "Jooo-seph." Lucinda's frantic cry split the morning air.

He lit out running for the house, Pa on his heels.

CHAPTER 35

*L*ucinda was sobbing. Her words made no sense. "He's gone. He's gone."

Joseph tried to console her by taking her in his arms, but she spun free.

Nigel came running from the backyard. "He's not back there, either."

"What's happened?" Joseph directed his question at Nigel because Lucinda was crying hysterically.

"Sammy. I left him playing on the kitchen floor. I ran out to the outhouse for only a minute. When I came back, he was gone. I thought Lucinda had woken up and taken him into her bedroom, so I sat and worked for a bit. But when she came out about an hour later and didn't have him...We've looked everywhere."

"He's been gone for an hour?" Pa asked. "Oh, dear Jesus, help us."

"Nat's taken him. I just know it." Lucinda clutched the front of her dress, bunching it into a ball in her hands. "In the past he's threatened to kill Sammy, just so I wouldn't have him." Her knees buckled and she dropped to the floor.

"Pa, get the horses ready. You stay here with your gun in case he returns."

Pa hurried out the door.

"Nigel, grab your rifle and take Lucinda to Katherine's. Round up the gang at the ranch and get back here as fast as you can. Start the search around the farm and fan out. Let's pray to God Sammy's just wandered into a field somewhere close. I'm going to ride into town to Sheriff Holden and round up the posse. I'll be back to join the search as soon as possible."

Lucinda shot up. "I'm not going to Katherine's. I need to look for my son." Fire flashed in her eyes, and her words were stilted and angry.

Joseph grabbed both her shoulders. "Do you trust me?"

She looked down at her feet.

"Do you trust me?"

"Yes."

"Look at me, Lucinda. I need you to promise you'll do exactly as I ask. You're in as much danger as Sammy, if you think this has anything to do with Nat—"

"I know it does."

"Then a man this desperate will stop at nothing to get what he wants, and he wants you."

"Come on, we're wasting valuable time." Nigel's voice was elevated with a sense of urgency.

"I'm not moving until Lucinda promises me."

"I promise." The words came out strangled, followed by a wail.

Joseph crushed her close for a quick hug and ran out the door.

~

*T*he day turned into darkness at Katherine's house, and still Lucinda heard nothing from the men. Ma, Katherine, Jeanette, and Gracie huddled together in prayer, Delilah, Abe, Libbie, and Helen joined in, too.

Lucinda couldn't take another moment of prayer. She wanted to scream. She wanted to shout. She wanted to rail at God. She knew she'd been too happy for it to be true. She jumped up from the chair and hurried from the room up to her old bedroom.

Jeanette ran after her and entered the room directly behind her. Lucinda turned to Jeanette's arms open wide. She fell into the warmth.

"If anything happens to Sammy, I think I'll die." Her words hiccoughed through the sobs. "Oh, dear Jesus, he's not even two, and it's cold out there at night. It wouldn't take much… a fall from Nat's horse, exposure from the cold, Nat's temper if he cries too much." Lucinda trembled as panic wrapped its paralyzing tentacles around her chest and squeezed. Here, she'd thought she had forgiven Nat, but if he took Sammy too…

"That's it," Jeanette said, soothingly. "Let it out. Scream if you need to."

Lucinda pulled free of the hug. "You're not going to tell me to get down on my knees and pray?"

"You've already done that. God heard your prayers the first time. He has this in His control."

"Control. That monster snuck into our house in broad daylight and snatched my baby. How does God have this under control?"

"I don't know, but He does."

Lucinda wanted to both bop Jeanette in the nose and hug her all at the same time. But somehow her words of faith brought comfort.

"So, you believe everything is going to be fine?" Lucinda asked.

"I believe God has this in His control."

"What's that supposed to mean?" Lucinda stepped out of the hug and paced.

"Bad things can happen to good people, because there is evil in this world. Look at what happened in your first marriage."

"But I wasn't good. I—"

"Made some mistakes, yes. But you didn't deserve what happened to you."

"I know. I know. I'm just so confused. I need someone to tell me my baby is going to be all right." She fell into a chair sobbing, her head in her hands. "I want my Sammy back."

"I know you do. We all do. And this may have nothing to do with Nat."

She looked up, a spark of hope flickered in her heart, but Jeanette looked anything but convincing. "You don't believe that. Don't lie to me."

"Maybe not, but I do believe our God is bigger than the likes of Nat."

Lucinda rocked back and forth sitting on the side of the bed while Jeanette's arm tightly hugged her shoulders. Her body trembled. Night was falling. Evil stirred in the dark. Nat was always the worst amid the shadows, his drinking fueled deeper wickedness. One night in a drunken stupor, and her baby could be dead from the elements. They had no proof Nat had taken Sammy. Not one of them had seen him. If Nat buried Sammy's body somewhere out in the black, no one would ever know what truly happened.

"If Nat does anything to Sammy... No, I don't want that hatred back in my soul. I thought I finally surrendered it all to God. Why would He let this happen?"

A freight train of fear was gathering strength and speeding

down the rails of her mind. If she didn't get back to praying, she would derail.

"Pray with me, Jeanette. I'm so afraid. I thought I couldn't pray anymore, but the opposite is true. If I don't pray, I'm going to go crazy."

"Into bed with you. You're freezing cold. I'll sing to you like I did when we were kids, and I'm going to pray that when you wake in the morning, you'll open your eyes to Sammy and Joseph."

Jeanette took Lucinda's cold and shaking hand, and they climbed into the bed together. Jeanette sang *Amazing Grace,* and the message of grace washed over Lucinda's soul. She never wanted that hatred for Nat back. She closed her eyes and prayed for his soul, for her baby's protection, and for Joseph, who would be as frantic as she was. Surrender and peace flooded in. Sleep had its way.

~

*N*ever before had Joseph felt raw fear claw its way from his gut to his throat. He swallowed hard against the constriction of air. Night had pressed in, and they were no closer to finding Nat or Sammy than when they'd started. The search party had reconvened at the farmhouse, where a number of the neighboring women had come to make food for the group. They crowded into the kitchen as Sheriff Holden recapped the day.

"Not sure this is a kidnapping," Sheriff Holden said, scratching his head. "We can't find any footprints or tracks. You're assuming Nat came in, but no one actually saw him, correct?"

"That's correct," Nigel said.

"So, Sammy could've wandered off into the fields. You did say there was a missing hour?"

"We've combed the area," Joseph said, collapsing into a chair. "That's the first thing we did—every square inch within a mile of the house. A lot further than any toddler can venture." He dug both hands through his hair.

"We'll start again at daybreak. Not much can be done in the dark. And I'm going to bring Tom the tracker in on this one. He's an old native to the area, and he has a dog. I swear they talk to each other."

A muscle in Joseph's jaw tightened. He jumped to his feet. "Why didn't we call him today?"

"Whoa there, Joseph. I stopped by his house, but his wife said he wouldn't be back for the day. He had gone fishing, and she didn't have a clue where. She said she'll be sure and tell him, and he'll be here first thing with the dog. In the meantime, I suggest we all hunker down and get a good night's sleep so we have fresh energy and eyes come daybreak. Between this house, the barn, and the neighbors who've offered their homes, I'm asking everyone to find a place to rest and be ready to go at first light."

Joseph's nerves were on edge. How could anyone sleep when his boy was out there somewhere? How would he face Lucinda if he could not return Sammy to her? The mere thought sent a chill of terror that climbed each bone of his spine, piercing straight into his skull.

Joseph nodded in Nigel's direction as the crowd dispersed. "Outside," he mouthed. Nigel followed Joseph out. When they were clear of the others, Joseph turned. "I'll go crazy if I can't do something."

"Me too."

Joseph looked up at the few scattered clouds and full moon. "If Nat is out there, we should be able to see a fire. It's a long shot, but I'm not going to sleep a wink anyway."

Colby and two of his ranch hands joined them. "We're not about to sleep anytime soon, so whatever you're cooking up, we're in." Colby pointed to his lead hand. "Hank here has an idea. Tell them, Hank."

"I've lived in this valley my whole life," Hank said. "I know the mountain trails and the main roads like the back of my hand. I know most every rundown deserted shack someone could hole up in, because I've used them when I'm caught in the rain or can't get home before dark. There's a log cabin about an hour ride north, tucked into the foothills away from all eyes but close enough to come and go if he was bent on spying on your place."

"That sounds like good logic, Hank," Joseph said. "If he's been sneaking around staking out our farm, he's been back and forth for days now, waiting for the opportune time."

"Yeah, I bet he was close, maybe even listening in on our breakfast conversation," said Nigel. "We had the kitchen window cracked open. I double checked that one. For him to know that you and Pa were in the field and that I had run out to the outhouse—he had to have been watching and waiting for the perfect moment."

"We questioned everyone in the area," Joseph said. "Old man Jordan said he thought he saw a man on a horse on the outskirts of his property around about the time Sammy went missing, but he can't be sure if there was a child. His eyesight is not too good these days. My hunch is that it was Nat with Sammy."

"Yeah, my mind has been racing all day," Colby said, "first hoping we'd find the boy, of course. But as time went by, the kidnapping scenario began to make more sense. Especially with him having the nerve to show up at the ranch and accost Lucinda. This guy will stop at nothing."

Joseph's insides somersaulted.

"Whatever you're up to, I'm not being left behind," said Pa, elbowing into their small circle. "I'm a crack shot." He held up his rifle. "And I love that kid." His voice wavered with emotion.

Joseph nodded. "We very well may need your skill."

Pa grunted. "Good." He swiped a tear from his weathered cheek.

"Let's pray before we head out." Colby launched into a quick prayer. "God, we need You. We need Your wisdom. We need Your protection. We need to find Sammy. May Your hand of guidance be upon us now. May You hold Sammy in Your protective arms. Amen."

"All right, let's saddle up," Joseph said. The horses have had a break, some food and water, and we have God and the moonlight on our side."

"You boys up to something?" Sheriff Holden came out of the shadows.

Joseph squared his shoulders. There was no way he was going to be dissuaded. "We have an idea, and we're going to check it out. I won't be sleeping tonight anyway."

"If it were my son, I'd be doing the same. I want the rest of the troops refreshed for tomorrow, but I'm coming with you boys."

Joseph looked up to the star-studded sky as he swung up into the saddle. Every cloud had vanished with the moon glaring down. *Thank you, Jesus.* He bundled up against the cool October air with a pair of leather gloves, an extra layer of clothing, and his heavier cowboy hat. The thought that Sammy could be out in these elements with no proper clothing chilled him to the bone. He slid a blanket into his saddlebag.

The seven men slipped into the night, silently following Hank's lead. The darkness blurred the hollows and folds of the land, but Hank seemed to know exactly where he was going. The light of the moon silvered the vast sweep of rolling farmland, and shadows increased as they entered the tree line.

Fear lapped the edges of Joseph's anxious mind, but God's presence held back the urge to scream. *Dear God, let this be Your wisdom, let this be Your guidance.* The prayers flowed incessantly. They were his calm. His center. His composure.

Hank stopped and slid down from his horse. "We're close, but we want to leave the horses here. We want nothing to alert him when we get there. How do you want to proceed?" Hank nodded to Sheriff Holden.

"On a night this cool, he'll probably have lit a fire, and the smoke will give us a clue if someone is inside. Either way, we proceed with caution. When we come to the cabin we'll fan out around the place and assess. Now who's most experienced with a gun?"

Pa and Hank raised their hands.

"All right, boys, the three of us will enter through the door," Sheriff Holden said. "And how many windows in this place?"

"Just one," Hank said.

"Nigel, you'll watch the window in case he tries that escape," Sheriff Holden said. "And Joseph, you'll be right behind us ready to snatch up Sammy. Colby, you and Eli will be backup outside. If something goes horribly wrong inside and Nat escapes out the door, you're on. I don't anticipate this, but I'm always ready. Seen a lot of weird things in my day. He could have a friend. There could be a band of them. We just don't know."

Joseph hadn't considered that thought. His hands went clammy, and his lungs felt hollowed of air. He took a deep breath in.

"We'll communicate with hand signals only," Sheriff Holden continued. "No talking whatsoever until we get inside. And watch where you're stepping. We don't want the snap of a twig to alert. Understood?"

They all nodded.

"Any questions?"

"I have one," Joseph said. "What if it's someone else in there?"

"Then they're going to get a rude awakening. Not the first time I've had that happen either. But we'll only use our weapons on my command." He looked at Pa and Hank, and they both nodded. "All right, we're ready. Hank, lead the way."

CHAPTER 36

They walked deeper into the forest until they reached a small clearing and a dilapidated log cabin. The railing was busted, and the steps leading to the porch sank into the ground on one side. One glass pane in the window was broken. The moon drenched an eerie frosted glow over the moss-covered roof. Hank held up his hand and put his finger to his mouth, pointing to the smoke rising from the chimney.

A child's cry split the air. "Mama."

Joseph almost jumped out of his skin. He would know Sammy's voice anywhere. He turned to the group and nodded frantically. Smiles split across every face. Sammy was alive. Sheriff Holden pointed, and they moved into the positions they'd discussed.

"Shut up, kid," Nat said. "I want your mama too, but it looks like neither of us are going to get what we want."

Sammy wailed.

Something crashed against the wall. It sounded like a broken bottle. "Shut up. Shut up. Shut up."

Sammy quieted, and Joseph's heart broke for the boy, frightened into silence.

Shuffling sounds on the inside made it easier for the men to get into position without being heard. Candlelight flickered from the window and from the cracks around the door in the one room shack.

"Farmer boy thinks he can steal my woman," Nat muttered. "If I can't have her, ain't nobody gonna have her." He let out a loud belch.

Sammy whimpered.

"Thought maybe I'd feel something for you kid. Never have and never will. Got a nice little hole dug deep in the thickets."

The pound of blood thrummed in Joseph's ears. Nat's words were slurred, but his intentions were clear.

"Your mamas next." He burped. "But I'll wait a couple months. Let her suffer real good." A mirthless laugh came from inside the walls.

Joseph had his pistol on his hip at the ready, keeping both hands free to grab Sammy. They balled into fists. Terror sliced through his mind. What if Sammy started howling before they could get in there and Nat finished him off? What if, when they burst in, Nat got to Sammy before they could? Was he standing over him at the moment? *God, help us.*

The four of them stood on the steps, ready to burst through the door, but Sheriff Holden held up his hand and mouthed the word "wait." He crept back down the steps and motioned to Colby and Nigel to join him at the edge of the clearing.

Joseph's anger overpowered his fear. He wanted to bust through that door and do some real damage. His fingers itched above his gun.

Be still and know that I am God.

What an inopportune time to be given a Bible verse. Joseph turned toward the three men, huddled close. What was Sheriff Holden doing? Joseph couldn't hear, but Colby and Nigel were nodding at his instructions.

Nigel went back to the side of the house to guard the

window, but this time Colby was back far enough to see both the window and the front door. Sheriff Holden resumed his position on the front porch but with his eyes on Colby. When Colby nodded, Sheriff Holden slammed his body through the front door with the other three following.

Everything happened fast, but it seemed to unfold in slow motion for Joseph. Nat reached for his gun, but Sheriff Holden shot him in the chest.

Hank and Pa fired a few more bullets and Nat crumbled to the floor.

Joseph raced across the room to Sammy, whose eyes were wide and bloodshot from all his crying. Joseph swept him up and ran outside, where Pa and Nigel joined him. They huddled in one big hug.

Nigel lot out a loud whoop of joy.

Pa wept, repeating over and over, "Thank you, Jesus, my grandson's safe."

Sammy's chubby little arms crept around Joseph's neck. "Daddy."

A muscle jerked in Joseph's jaw as tears let loose and coursed down his cheeks. "Yes, Daddy's here. Daddy's here."

Sammy laid his head against Joseph's shoulder. His trembling subsided, and his thumb went into his mouth.

Joseph's heart squeezed so tight, he thought it would implode. He looked up to where half the full moon winked from behind a drifting cloud. *Thank you.* He knew from where his help had come.

~

*I*t was four in the morning when Joseph, Sammy, and Colby got back to the ranch. Sammy was fast asleep in his arms as he handed him down to Colby before he dismounted. "Can't even tell you how thankful I am to be able to give this boy back to his mama." Joseph's voice cracked. He fought back tears as he took the boy back into his arms.

Colby nodded. "God is good."

"He sure is." They walked toward the house, their lantern swinging in the dark. The front door swung open, and Lucinda's family poured out.

"We've kept an all-night prayer vigil," Katherine said. "Jeanette finally got Lucinda to fall asleep. It took a lot of prayer and some real finagling. She made us promise we'd take her home at daybreak for an update."

"Even I prayed," Lucinda's ma said.

"Thank you." Joseph beamed at the group. "God has answered your prayers."

"Come." Jeanette waved him up the steps of Katherine's home. "You look exhausted. I'll take you to her."

Joseph slipped quietly into the bedroom. He lowered his body next to her, Sammy between them. "My darling, look who's here."

Her eyes blinked open in surprise. Lucinda looked down at her sleeping child and began to weep. "Am I dreaming?"

"Sammy is right here beside you, and so am I."

She layered kisses all over his face and Sammy's, murmuring "Thank you, Jesus, thank you." Tears poured down her cheeks. "Joseph, how can I ever thank you?"

"We had an army of helpers, and so many people praying. God has been faithful to our cries."

"Yes, so faithful."

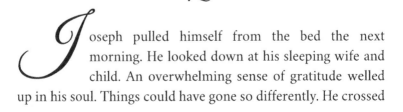

*J*oseph pulled himself from the bed the next morning. He looked down at his sleeping wife and child. An overwhelming sense of gratitude welled up in his soul. Things could have gone so differently. He crossed the room to the washstand and poured fresh water into the bowl. He washed his face and splashed water over his bare torso.

"You're so handsome," Lucinda whispered.

Joseph thought she was talking to Sammy, but when he turned her way, her eyes were on him.

"Everything about you is beautiful...your soul, your body, your mind...your spirit...How I ever thought Nat..."

He slid back into bed beside her. "Nat's dead."

Her eyes widened. A moment passed before she said, "Tell me everything, but I have to be honest. I'm relieved, but also sad for his soul. Does that make sense?"

Joseph nodded. "I've battled all kinds of emotions, and some I'm not proud of, but relief...Yes, absolutely. He was a dark man."

Lucinda looked down at Sammy. "God gave him plenty of chances to change, but he chose otherwise, and now it's too late. I'm just so grateful that I didn't continue on the path I was going for the sake of this little guy."

"And for the sake of this big guy." Joseph threw his arm around her, and she nuzzled in close.

"Tell me what happened."

"Are you sure you want to know?"

"I need to know."

"When I think how God worked out every detail, I'm in awe." Joseph relived the evening. "In the last minute, when we were about to bust down the door, Sheriff Holden suddenly halted everything. He conferred with Nigel and Colby again. At that point I had just heard what Nat intended to do to Sammy, and I wanted to burst in and kill him myself. Had God not given me that Bible verse to be still, I could have jeopardized Sammy's life." He shuddered, and she wrapped her arms around him tighter.

"What was the sheriff doing?"

"He wanted Nigel to peek in the window and signal Colby, who signaled the sheriff as to when it was safe to enter. He didn't want Nat too close to Sammy in case bullets flew, and he was so right. God knew we needed the sheriff's expertise and experience."

Lucinda squeezed his hand. "God is so good."

"Yes, He is." Joseph dropped a kiss on both of them. "We can both rest now."

CHAPTER 37

November 1876

*J*oseph looked up as Sammy came screaming into the kitchen with Nigel chasing him. "The big bad wolf is going to get you. Going to get you, Sammy."

"Daddy. Daddy."

Lucinda stepped into Nigel's way, and Joseph swept up Sammy into his arms and threw him on his shoulders. They danced around the kitchen in playful laughter with Nigel roaring behind them, his arms flailing in the air like a madman.

Joseph's eyes gravitated to his wife. She laughed. She played. She acted like she was happy, but something wasn't right. He pulled her into a whirl with Sammy, but she wouldn't meet his gaze.

"Are you all right?"

She stepped out of his arms. "I'm fine. Just feeling a little punky today."

"What's all the ruckus?" Pa asked as he came into the room.

"Sorry about that," Lucinda quickly said. "We forgot you were trying to have an afternoon nap."

"No problem. I was just wondering what kind of fun I was missing out on, sleeping the day away."

"Papa. Papa." Sammy stretched out his chubby arms to Pa. Joseph passed the child, and Pa snuggled him close. "Ahh if that doesn't melt an old man's heart, I don't know what will." He lifted up Sammy's shirt and tickled him with his whiskers.

Sammy's giggle filled the room.

Pa lifted his head and turned to Lucinda. "You can have ten more of these, and you'll never hear me complain. The noisier the better."

She gave a brave smile, but Joseph didn't miss the way she turned away and crossed the room to the stove as if she were busy.

His heart lurched. He could feel her pain.

∾

*L*ucinda stood before the mirror in her bedroom and smoothed a hand over her body. There was a decided pouch. Could she be pregnant? There was no way of knowing with her cycles so irregular. But no. The last two pregnancies she had been sick from the get-go. The desires of her heart were playing havoc with her emotions. She began pulling on her nightwear. The chemise fell in soft folds down her shapely figure. Where once she had been so afraid to become pregnant with Nat and lose her shape for fear of his anger, there was nothing she longed for more than to see that decided bump of growth—a baby who would be a part of her and Joseph. It would never happen, and somehow, she had to give up the smidgeon of hope that lingered and quit imagining the possibility. At least she was past the stage of begging God for a miracle every day.

She felt guilty every time Pa mentioned a growing family.

She should've told him that portion of her story, but it was the part that hurt the most. The pain that lived on.

The bedroom door opened, and Joseph slipped in. "Hello, beautiful."

She turned toward him. There would be no better time than right now, in a moment of privacy, to share that they needed to break it to Pa that there would never be more grandchildren, but even saying the words aloud made it more final.

"Joseph, I've been meaning to speak to you—"

"You sound much too serious for someone who looks as delicious as you do." He wrapped his arms around her and lowered his lips to hers.

Everything within her wanted to escape into an evening of passion, because voicing the reality felt like she was giving up faith on the possibility of a miracle.

She pulled away. "You're distracting me."

"Give me a moment to get out of these work clothes, my dear, and I'm all yours." He removed his shirt and turned to the wash basin, splashing water on his face and neck. She loved his nightly routine—the muscles on his arms and back rippling beneath the movement of washing and drying.

She slid beneath the covers, and he turned toward her.

"You keep looking at me that way, LucyBug, and there'll be no room for words until morning."

"Good idea," she said with a seductive whisper to her voice. "I have energy for only one more activity tonight, and it doesn't include talking."

It was all the invitation Joseph needed.

Dawn came all too early.

"Good morning, sleepyhead." Joseph bent over and kissed her lips as he always did. He was dressed and ready for another workday. She would rise with him and begin breakfast while he looked after the animals.

"I guess I'd better get at it." With a mighty yawn she sat and stretched her arms.

"Why don't you let us boys fare for ourselves for a change, and you get some more sleep? I did kinda keep you awake last night." He winked.

"No. No. It's my pleasure."

"What, me keeping you awake?"

She tried to sound serious. "I meant cooking. I enjoy that far more than cleaning up after you messy men."

"You don't have to cater to us every day. We did manage by ourselves a lot of years."

"Ha, you call the chaos I came into managing?"

He chuckled. "Which makes me think I know what you wanted to talk to me about last night."

She slid out of bed and secured her wrapper around her. "What?"

"You want your own home rather than adding on our own wing but don't know how to tell me, right? I know Pa and Nigel are putting on the pressure to be one happy family, but they have a lot to lose if you choose to leave."

"No. No. It's not that. I think it's time to tell your Pa that I can't have more children. I hate for him to keep his hopes up when…"

He wrapped his arms around her. "I didn't want to speak out of turn and tell him something you weren't ready to discuss, but I agree with you."

"I hope this won't change the way he feels about me. Things have been so good."

"Do you want me to tell him?"

"I think you should."

"And you're sure that you can put up with all of us? That you don't want your own space?"

"I love your pa and Nigel, and so does Sammy. It wouldn't feel right without them."

"And they love you." He kissed her lips thoroughly. "But then, what's not to love?" He lifted his finger and tapped the end of her nose. "The finest freckle-faced female to grace the earth."

"Now, you know how much I hate my freckles."

"Well, I love them." She lifted her hand to swat him, but he danced out of her reach, his laugher echoing out the door and down the hall as he disappeared.

She didn't think it was possible to be more in love with Joseph than she had been on her wedding day, but her love for him kept deepening. There seemed to be no boundary, no border, no limit to what her heart was capable of holding.

Joseph had fulfilled her deepest desires and most delightful dreams. They were not only lovers, but also each other's best friend.

She would probably always feel a pang at not being able to give Joseph more children, and some days were harder than others, but she would never regret the one good thing that came out of her first marriage—sweet Sammy. He was such a joy.

And the rest of it...every day she embraced forgiveness, and every day her freedom in Christ grew. She refused to live her life in shame and regret, no matter what people thought of her. Life was for living, and she was going to live it to the fullest, with the man and little boy she loved with all her heart. Praise filled her soul for the blessings she'd been given, and she lifted her hands to the heavens. It was time to accept all God had given her and let that be enough. "Thank you, Jesus," she whispered. "Thank you for my amazing life."

Christmas 1876

*L*ucinda could wait no longer. She had barely slept a wink all night. She slipped from the bed and lit a candle before joining her sleeping husband in the bed once again. She leaned forward and brushed a whisper of a kiss on his lips, and then another, and another. Slowly, Joseph awakened. "Hmm."

He tried to pull her closer and deepen the kiss, but she resisted. "Wake up, Joseph. Wake up." She kissed his mouth between each word. Her arms circled the muscled column of his neck, where her fingers played in his hair.

"What a lovely awakening." His voice was throaty and inviting, and she almost lost her concentration.

She kissed the pulse in his throat. "Merry Christmas, my handsome prince. Open your eyes."

"Hmm... it can't be morning already."

"Come on, sleepyhead."

He forced one eye open and then another.

She grinned down at him in the flickering light of a lone candle.

"Why is there a candle burning in the wee hours of the morning? What time is it anyway?" He leaned toward the table at the side of the bed for his pocket watch, but she caught his hand and pulled it away.

"It's Christmas morning. That's all you need to know."

"It was Christmas at 12:01, and you didn't wake me then."

"Trust me. I wanted to. Numerous times in the night. You're lucky I waited as long as I did." She bounced out of bed. "You have to be fully awake for this. Sit up."

"This better be worth it, Mrs. Manning, or you'll owe me some sweet payback."

"Oh, this will be worth it."

"Your eyes are sparkling like when we were teens and you

were up to mischief." He sat up, shifting a few pillows behind his back for comfort. "I haven't seen you this excited in…forever."

"Are you ready?" She could barely contain herself.

He nodded his head. "I'm fully awake and very ready."

"All right, close your eyes, and no peeking until I say so."

"You just told me to open my eyes, now you want them closed?" he teased.

"Joseph Manning, I've been waiting for days to give you this Christmas surprise. Now, cooperate."

"All right. All right, my fiery lady." His hands covered his eyes. "They're tightly closed."

She hurried to get herself ready. "All right. You may open your eyes."

She stood sideways to him, her chemise gathered up exposing a bare belly—a protruding belly. Truth slowly dawned in his eyes as she held her gown up with one hand and rolled her hand around her belly with another. Heat built in her cheeks. "A little Manning junior lives in here."

In the flickering light, his expression went from shock to wonder, like fitting a last piece of a jigsaw puzzle together. He jumped from the bed and let out whoop. She was in his arms in an instant, and he whirled her around before gently setting her back on her feet.

"Sorry. I got carried away. I need to be more careful."

Her laughter filled the room. "I'm not going to break. Whirl me around all you like."

He dropped to his knees in front of her and kissed the mound. "This is your first kiss from your daddy. Expect a life-time more." He rested his head against her. "I had prayed. I had hoped. Then I had accepted whatever God decided."

"Me too." A bubble of laughter slipped free from her lips. "I'm so happy, I could cry. The desire of my heart…to give you our baby is right here." She placed her hands on her stomach.

He stood and cupped her face in his hands. Then kissed her lips with aching tenderness. "I can't believe it's true."

"Me neither, that's why it took me so long to clue in. I had been feeling so emotional and tired, but no morning sickness like with Sammy and..." She shrugged. "I brushed it off. Even though I knew my dresses felt tighter, I thought it was all that homemade bread and finally feeling relaxed and loved enough to gain a few pounds."

"So when did you know?"

She pulled him to the edge of the bed, and they sat. "A few weeks ago, when we visited Ma and Pa, I felt that first flutter... when the baby moves. I was shocked. There was no mistaking that wonderful feeling of life inside my body, but I wanted it confirmed."

"How did you do that?"

"Remember how I wanted to stay that extra day and go into town for supplies with the girls?"

"Yes."

"I also went to see the doctor. He said I was about four months along."

"Why didn't you tell me?"

"I hope you don't mind, but all I could think of is what a great Christmas gift this would be. And trust me, it has been so hard to keep this secret the past few weeks. I almost told you a hundred times." She giggled.

He pulled her back on the bed and kissed her soundly before gazing deeply into her eyes. "I'm beyond surprised, and this is the best Christmas gift ever." He moved one hand to gently lay on her stomach. "Our very own Christmas miracle."

Did you enjoy this book? We hope so!
Would you take a quick minute to leave a review where you purchased the book?
It doesn't have to be long. Just a sentence or two telling what you liked about the story!

Receive a FREE ebook and get updates when new Wild Heart books release: https://wildheartbooks.org/newsletter

Don't miss the next book in Shenandoah Brides Series!

Gracie's Surrender

March, 1879
Shenandoah Valley

"You're turning down *another* marriage proposal?" Ma put her hands to her temples and rubbed. "But, Gracie, he's such a fine young man."

The walls of the parlor room closed in on Gracie. Why did men continually misread the situation when she gave them no encouragement at all? It was so frustrating.

"You're eighteen now and quite old enough to become a wife. And George is an upstanding—"

"I never meant to encourage George. And I certainly didn't think he was about to propose. We barely know each other."

"What do you mean you barely know him? Our families go way back," Pa said.

"But I've never looked at George that way." It was time to tell them a truth they may never understand. Especially Ma. Gracie lifted her head high knotting her trembling hands together. "I have no intention of ever marrying." She added a firmness to her voice she did not feel.

"Why ever not?" Pa's bushy brows knit together. "Thought most every girl looked forward to that day."

That familiar memory came flooding in. Would Rosina's outstretched bony fingers forever haunt her? "Well, not this one. I like George, but I don't love him. I want to devote my life to Jesus and—"

Ma's hands flew into the air. "For heaven's sakes, there's that Jesus talk again." She turned to Pa and wagged her finger in his face. "This is your fault. One-by-one, every one of our daughters have followed in your footsteps, but this is taking it way too far. Set her right." She pointed at Gracie.

Rather than prolong the agony, Gracie took a deep breath. She might as well get it all out. If they weren't happy with her now, they sure wouldn't be after she told them the rest of her plans.

Pa moved across the room to stand in front of her and gently placed his hands on her upper arms. "Tell us what you're thinking, girl, neither Ma, nor I understand. A woman can love Jesus and be married, too."

"I know that, Pa, but I feel God is calling me to move to Richmond and work in the orphanage."

"Richmond?" Ma's voice rose a few octaves. "It's not bad enough you don't want to marry George, but you want to move to Richmond as well?"

"Please give me a moment to explain." Gracie pointed to the parlor chairs. *Dear God, please help Ma understand. I don't want to hurt her.* "Can we sit?"

Pa put his arm around Ma and guided her to a chair. "She is an adult, Doris. We should at least bend an ear." Ma slumped down into the chair and turned her head to look out the window. Pa chose the chair beside her and gave Gracie his full attention.

"Ma, remember when we visited Grandmother and Grandfather when I was twelve and I met that street urchin named Rosina?"

Ma nodded her head. "I'll forever regret letting you and Bryon go back and try to find that child the next day. You've never been the same."

"I'm not the same…that experience and then revisiting the orphanage with Amelia and Bryon again last year, has deeply impacted my life. The need is so great and there's not enough hands to—"

Ma's head snapped toward Pa. "See. Every time I let one of my children go to Richmond for a visit, they come back with the fandangled idea of moving there." Her eyes blazed as she turned back to Gracie. "And what about a family of your own? How are you going to do that without a husband?"

Pa reached out to take Ma's hand. She pulled it free and turned her head back toward the window. He nodded at Gracie to continue.

"I don't want to be distracted by men when there are so many children in need."

Ma let out a loud harrumph.

"Besides, weren't you just talking about how Grandmother is grieving Grandfather so terribly? I could cheer up her lonely days."

"Doris, you did say you were worried about your mother. Amelia confirmed she hasn't been doing very well since your father passed. We could let Gracie give the orphanage a trial run and give your mother some much-needed company at the same time."

"Well, I never!" Ma got up from her chair and pointed a finger. "You're siding with her. Was all this cooked up ahead of time—you two and that God of yours?"

"No." They both answered in unison as she marched from the room. The stomp of her feet could be heard on every step up to her bedroom before her door slammed shut.

Gracie's hands scrunched her dress tightly. She relaxed and smoothed out the wrinkles. "Pa, you understand, don't you?" She stared at the floor planks. Would he be disappointed in her as well?

"I'm not sure I do."

Gracie looked up into his kind brown eyes.

"But far be it from me to get in the way of what God is telling you to do. Your ma on the other hand…" He rubbed his work worn hands back and forth on his brow. "…she's going to need some time. When were you hoping to go?"

"As soon as possible. Thought it would be easier for George if I'm not around. And I've already secured an invitation from Grandmother to stay as long as I like."

"Must you cut the tie so abruptly? Your ma's heart is going to take a beating to let her baby girl go."

"She still has Jeanette and weren't you both just willing to marry me off to George?"

"But George is a ten-minute buggy ride away. Richmond is another story."

"I'll promise to return home more often."

"Well, I'll be holding you to that, girlie. And don't worry about your ma, I'll talk to her." He stood. "She may not be tickled pink, but she'll come around. Just be sure this is something you really feel you need to do."

"Thanks, Pa." Gracie flew across the room into his arms and planted a big kiss on the top of his brow.

The sky was as blue as forget-me-nots with the morning sunshine teasing the buds on the trees to respond to its glory. A beautiful spring day to travel. Gracie settled in her seat anxious for the train to leave. A thrill pulsed through.

A lurch and a chug and they were off, her new adventure unfolding. Each mile the train rumbled down the track away from the Shenandoah Valley, Gracie's excitement grew. Why did she feel as if her life was finally about to begin?

"May I sit here?"

Gracie turned from the window to see a strapping young man with a wheedling smile. Instinct told her to keep her distance, but politeness forced a response. "I haven't paid for two seats." She laughed to hide her nervousness. The last thing she needed was attention from any man.

A distinguished gentleman from across the aisle looked their way and raised his eyebrows. What had she done that was inappropriate? Should she have told the stranger to sit elsewhere? Having been raised on the farm, she had little knowledge of worldly etiquette.

"John Deleware." The stranger tipped his cowboy hat in her direction and slid into the seat. His smile widened and he moved a tad too close.

Gracie turned toward the window and gazed out. She didn't want to be rude, but nor did she want to encourage him.

"May I have the pleasure of your name?"

Gracie sighed heavily. She hated to be discourteous. "Gracie...I mean Grace Williams."

"I like Gracie a far cry better than the formal Grace. I would wager a bet, that your personality most likely suits Gracie?" He pulled out a small can of chewing tobacco and popped some in his mouth.

"I suppose it does." She answered timidly, not comfortable with the stranger's overt interest. Why did her looks always have to be a magnet? She had prayed she would make it to Richmond without undue attention.

"So where are you coming from and where are you headed?" he asked between chews. He turned momentarily toward the aisle and spat. A rivulet of spittle hit the back of the seat in front of him. He did nothing to remove it. Gracie took the opportunity to look back out the window, hoping to ignore him.

"Well?" he said, not taking the hint.

She turned his way. "Mr. Deleware, please don't take this personally, but I have a lot on my mind. And I would prefer to be left alone."

"Oh, too hoity-toity for the likes of the working cowboy, hey? I know a brush off when I hear one."

"It's not that. I've chosen to give my life in service to God and—"

A loud mocking laugh filled the air. "Your life in service to God?" His voice doubled in volume. "What, a nun?"

Gracie's cheeks bloomed hot. "No, not a nun—"

"What a waste of God-given beauty. You're meant to make some man very happy, not be closeted away in some monastery somewhere."

"I do believe the lady was politely asking you to leave her alone," the man from across the aisle said.

Gracie nodded.

Mr. Delaware swiveled in his seat. "What's it to you?"

The man slid across the seat and stood. He removed his top hat and still stood a head above Mr. Delaware, who had also popped up.

"What? Are you her guardian?"

"As a matter of fact, I'm her brother. Now, move along, cowboy." His deep voice resonated authority.

Mr. Delaware looked back and forth between the two. "A nun is not worth my time anyway." He spat out a large gob of chewing tobacco and sauntered down the aisle to his original seat.

"Thank you, brother." Gracie smiled up at him.

He leaned close. His sweet breath fanned her face. "I over-heard you saying you were giving your life in service to God. I'm a Christian too, so that makes you my sister in Christ." He straightened and looked down at her. "Best not give that smile so freely away to strangers. Offers the wrong impression."

Gracie could feel the smile melt from her face and her ire rise like steam from the train engine. A girl couldn't even be friendly in this world without men taking it the wrong way.

He slid back into his seat without a sideways glance in her direction. Much to her chagrin his strong jawline and formidable countenance drew Gracie's interest the rest of the way to Richmond. She found herself peeking his way one too many times. A man without a wedding ring who was not bent on making her acquaintance was a rare find indeed. They could be friends. Too bad their paths would never meet again.

Matthew kept his eyes riveted to the landscape out the train window. He could see nothing but a blur. Who would let their young and beautiful daughter travel unchaperoned? Was she really that naïve she thought she could smile that infectiousness smile and not draw the men in like the bell chime of a Sunday morning steeple?

Women who looked like her were not the kind that gave their life in service to God. They were the kind that got snatched up and married off in record time. If she was not going to be a nun, who was she and what was her plan? And why didn't she have a guardian with her?

It bothered him that he wanted to turn and stare at her like most of the men had done when she entered the train—married and unmarried alike. She had smiled at everyone and stopped long enough to chat with a little girl sitting beside her mama. That was when her big doe-like eyes came alive and sparkled with joy. Though he had wanted to be immune to the attraction he felt, he was not. Her dark wavy hair was plaited in a braid that swung around to the front and hung long down her torso. Her hair style and clothing were not the latest fashion, but all was eclipsed by the petite vision of loveliness she made. Slim, delicate bones, with curves in all the right places.

He shook his head against the pull and closed his eyes. When was the last time a woman had consumed his thoughts? He was prepared to wait for the one God had for him, not get side-tracked by mere physical attraction. He knew better than that. How shallow of him. He ventured a sideways glance hoping to dispel the odd sensation causing the erratic beat of his heart. Her profile was turned toward the window, so he took a moment to do what almost every man on the train had already done...enjoy God's creation of perfection. Round, bright cheeks that looked petal soft, delicate earlobes, and a button mouth that was smiling at something through the window. Did she smile all the time?

Before he could avert his eyes, she glanced his way. He quickly turned his head back to the window. Richmond could not come fast enough.

He did not look again. The train jostled and screeched to a stop. He wasted no time in gathering his few belongings and stood to leave, as did she. The gentleman in him bid he allow her to go first. "After you," he said.

"Thank you, brother," she said, with some definite sass on her lips.

For the first time in a long time he felt an uncontrollable urge to kiss that smile right off that generous mouth. Instead, he watched a coachman hail her over and the two of them disappear into the crowd. Good thing. What was happening to him, this sudden attraction to a perfect stranger? She was perfect and it irritated him to the core. Any longer in her presence and he would've done something completely out of character—like ask her to dinner.

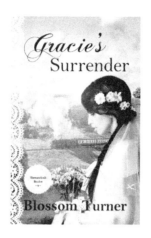

Get GRACIE'S SURRENDER at your favorite retailer!

ABOUT THE AUTHOR

*I write because I can't **not** write. Stories have danced in my imagination since childhood. Having done the responsible thing—a former businesswoman, personal trainer, and mother of two grown children—I am finally pursuing my lifelong dream of writing full-time. Who knew work could be so fun?*

A hopeless romantic at heart, I believe all stories should give the reader significant entertainment value but also infuse relatable life struggle with hope sprinkled throughout. My desire is to leave the reader with a yearning to live for Christ on a deeper level, or at the very least, create a hunger to seek for more.

Blossom Turner is a freelance writer published in Chicken Soup and Kernels of Hope anthologies, former newspaper columnist on health and fitness, avid blogger, and novelist. She lives in a four-season playground in beautiful British Columbia, Canada, with gardening at the top of her enjoyment list.

She has a passion for women's ministry teaching Bible studies and public speaking, but having coffee and sharing God's hope with a hurting soul trumps all. She lives with her husband, David, of thirty-nine years and their dog, Lacey. Blossom loves to hear from her readers. Visit her at blossom-turner.com and subscribe to her quarterly newsletter.

Don't miss Blossom's other book, *Anna's Secret*, a contemporary romance and Word Guild semi-finalist.

BOOKS IN THE

SHENANDOAH BRIDES SERIES

Katherine's Arrangement (Shenandoah Brides, book 1)

Amelia's Heartsong (Shenandoah Brides, book 2)

Lucinda's Defender (Shenandoah Brides, book 3)

Gracie's Surrender (Shenandoah Brides, book 4)

WANT TO JOIN BLOSSOM'S SUPPORT TEAM?

If you enjoyed this book and love reading and would like to be a part of my Support Team as the next book launches, contact me through my web page at https://blossomturner.com, under the "Contact" heading.

A Support Team member will receive a free advance copy of the next book *before* it is released and promises to support in the following ways:

• Read the book in advance and have it completed by release date.

• If you enjoy the book, leave a review on Bookbub and Goodreads before release date as soon as you are done reading. Right after the release date, copy that review onto the other retailers, Amazon.ca, Amazon.com, Kobo, Barnes and Noble, and Apple Books. I will send you all the links so it is super easy.

• Promote ahead of time on social media, FB, Twitter, Instagram, or where ever. (I will send you memes to post before release date so everything will be easy. I will not inundate you with too many.)

I will have numerous prize draws for the support team members, in which your name will be entered to win a free signed copy of multiple books in the series, a gift card for Amazon. I will try and make the process as fun and painless as possible, and hopefully you will enjoy the read. Those of you who have joined my team before and left such wonderful reviews, I thank God for you and consider you a part of my writing family.

I thank you in advance for joining me on this journey!

(Sorry, open to residents of Canada and the USA only.)

ACKNOWLEDGMENTS

To put in words my thank you to the amazing team at Wild Heart Books seems somehow inadequate, but I will try. To publisher/final editor Misty M. Beller and edit team Erin Taylor Young and Robin Patchen, you have my sincerest thanks for elevating my work way beyond its original first draft. Wild Heart Books is a pleasure to write for, the company is well-run and the professionalism second to none.

To my critique partner Laura Thomas who spends hours fine-tuning my story, thank you from my heart. And to my amazing support team who read the book before it hits the market and then encourage others to read, as a new author your gift of time is invaluable. I thank you.

And as always, but by the grace of God go I. Without His outstretched hands of help each day when I sit down at the keyboard, I could not accomplish half of what I do. Thank you, Jesus, for being a living, breathing, wonderful part of my every day.

If you love historical romance, check out the other Wild Heart books!

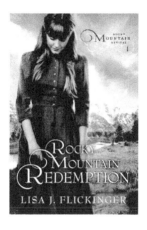

Rocky Mountain Redemption by Lisa J. Flickinger

A Rocky Mountain logging camp may be just the place to find herself.

To escape the devastation caused by the breaking of her wedding engagement, Isabelle Franklin joins her aunt in the Rocky Mountains to feed a camp of lumberjacks cutting on the slopes of Cougar Ridge. If only she could out run the lingering nightmares.

Charles Bailey, camp foreman and Stony Creek's itinerant pastor, develops a reputation to match his new nickname — Preach. However, an inner battle ensues when the details of his rough history threaten to overcome the beliefs of his young faith.

Amid the hazards of camp life, the unlikely friendship growing between the two surprises Isabelle. She's drawn to Preach's brute strength and gentle nature as he leads the ragtag crew toiling for Pollitt's Lumber. But when the ghosts from her past return to haunt her, the choices she will make change the course of her life forever—and that of the man she's come to love.

~

Marisol ~ Spanish Rose by Elva Cobb Martin

Escaping to the New World is her only option...Rescuing her will wrap the chains of the Inquisition around his neck.

Marisol Valentin flees Spain after murdering the nobleman who molested her. She ends up for sale on the indentured servants' block at Charles Town harbor—dirty, angry, and with child. Her hopes are shattered, but she must find a refuge for herself and the child she carries. Can this new land offer her the grace, love, and security she craves? Or must she escape again to her only living relative in Cartagena?

Captain Ethan Becket, once a Charles Town minister, now sails the seas as a privateer, grieving his deceased wife. But when he takes captive a ship full of indentured servants, he's intrigued by the woman whose manners seem much more refined than the average Spanish serving girl. Perfect to become governess for his young son. But when he sets out on a quest to find his captured sister, said to be in Cartagena, little does he expect his new Spanish governess to stow away on his ship with her six-month-old son. Yet her offer of help to free his sister is too tempting to pass up. And her beauty, both inside and out, is too attractive for his heart to protect itself against—until he learns she is a wanted murderess.

As their paths intertwine on a journey filled with danger, intrigue, and romance, only love and the grace of God can overcome the past and ignite a new beginning for Marisol and Ethan.

~

Lone Star Ranger by Renae Brumbaugh Green

Elizabeth Covington will get her man.

And she has just a week to prove her brother isn't the murderer Texas Ranger Rett Smith accuses him of being. She'll show the good-looking lawman he's wrong, even if it means setting out on a risky race across Texas to catch the real killer.

Rett doesn't want to convict an innocent man. But he can't let the Boston beauty sway his senses to set a guilty man free. When Elizabeth follows him on a dangerous trek, the Ranger vows to keep her safe. But who will protect him from the woman whose conviction and courage leave him doubting everything—even his heart?